Praise for the Novels of Eric Jerome Dickey

Waking with Enemies

"There's a lot of fun to be had . . . and the high-octane narrative will have readers burning through page after page."
—*Publishers Weekly*

"Raunchy and violent, featuring classic Dickey scenes of sex and mayhem. A necessary follow-up for those who were enthralled by Gideon and crew in *Sleeping*." —*Library Journal*

Sleeping with Strangers

"A wild ride. This fast-paced thriller . . . [will] keep readers on edge . . . taut, fast, and bold. Total blockbuster entertainment."
—*Publishers Weekly* (starred review)

"An action-packed classic noir thriller that draws you in from the first page." —*Ebony*

"Suspenseful right up to the cliff-hanger ending, gritty, graphic . . . amazing." —*Booklist* (starred review)

"A fast-paced cliff-hanger . . . one of Dickey's most satisfying novels yet." —*Essence*

Chasing Destiny

"[A] strong sexy heroine." —*Kirkus Reviews*

"Sul——————————" —*Publishers Weekly*

continued . . .

"No one does it like Eric Jerome Dickey."
—*The Black Expressions*™ Book Club

Between Lovers

"Provocative and complex."   —*Ebony*

Liar's Game

"Steamy romance, betrayal, and redemption. Dickey at his best."
—*USA Today*

Cheaters

"Wonderfully written . . . smooth, unique, and genuine."
—*The Washington Post Book World*

Friends and Lovers

"Crackles with wit and all the rhythm of an intoxicatingly funky rap."   —*The Cincinnati Enquirer*

Milk in My Coffee

"Heartwarming and hilarious."   —*The Cincinnati Enquirer*

Sister, Sister

"Bold and sassy . . . brims with humor, outrageousness, and the generosity of affection."   —*Publishers Weekly*

ERIC JEROME DICKEY

PLEASURE

DUTTON
— est. 1852 —

DUTTON

— est. 1852 —

An imprint of Penguin Random House LLC
375 Hudson Street
New York, New York 10014

Previously published as a Dutton hardcover and NAL paperback.

First Dutton paperback printing 2016
11   13   15   17   19   18   16   14   12

Dutton Trade Paperback ISBN: 978-0-451-22598-6

THE LIBRARY OF CONGRESS HAS CATALOGUED THE HARDCOVER EDITION OF THIS BOOK AS FOLLOWS:

Dickey, Eric Jerome.
Pleasure / Eric Jerome Dickey.
p. cm.
ISBN 978-0-525-95045-5 (hardcover)
I. Title.
PS3554.I319P57 2008
813.54—dc22
2007050534

Set in Janson Text
Designed by Leonard Telesca

Printed in the United States of America

for Dominique

Be careful, Anaïs, abnormal pleasures kill the taste for normal ones.

—Eduardo, Anaïs Nin's cousin in the movie *Henry & June*

O N E

I touched myself as I sat in my office chair, computer on, its glow illuminating my trembling body, a body dressed in a Radical Designs wife-beater, nothing else. My left arm was behind my head, legs spread apart, feet on my desk, head leaning back on the chair, eyes closed tight, moaning, pulling my hair as my fingers played a brilliant song on my sex. I needed orgasm. I jerked, shifted, kicked pages of erotica to the floor, let my work fall like leaves as I panted. My breathing was so ragged, close to dying a thousand tiny little deaths. A mirror was on my wall and I adjusted so I could witness my self-pleasuring, wanted to see me pleasing me, wanted to become a voyeur, obsessed with my own taste.

The fire grew. The wetness grew. But I could not come.

I shifted and moved like I suffered from severe jactitation, continuously tossing and twitching.

I wanted to come so badly.

I stopped, trying to take control, patting my sex, murmuring incoherently.

I murmured as my sense of sound returned, murmured until I heard their voices.

Above my head, mounted on the wall, the early morning news was coming on the airwaves, already talking about the nonstop crime in the Atlanta area, robbers shooting and injuring three people at Greenbriar Mall. Was hard to come with talk of brazen holdups and double killings as the background noise. Was hard to achieve nirvana when your sense of sound was being flooded with negative images.

My sense of sight returned in degrees, this world gradually becoming clearer.

Outside my window there was the morning's glow, the sun was rising like an impending orgasm.

On the wall facing me was a framed poster of Anaïs Nin, the writer I adored. Hair black and pulled back. Her dress dark and modest. The phosphorescent hue that defined her complexion, her features the combination of three lineages: Spanish, Cuban, and Danish. Her skin powdered. Lips the color of my heart. It looked as if she was staring at me. It looked like she was watching me.

I closed my eyes, orgasm evaded me as if this were a game of hide-and-seek.

I was wet. I was on fire. I needed to come.

I left my office, tugging my wife-beater over my head, the talk of crimes in Adair Park and Fairburn fading behind me, breathing uneven, dropping my shirt on the floor, legs wobbly and weak.

I was as I was when I was born: naked, vulnerable. Flames rising, I staggered up carpeted stairs, looking up as if I were trying to climb to heaven, taking one stair at a time, moving through the dimness of the main floor of my townhome, neck moist, breathing becoming thicker. I stumbled by pictures. So many images from Carnival decorated my walls, my mother and I wearing dramatic outfits made of feathers and tails, many pictures of us in many outfits over the years, from when I was a child up until last year, some of them when I was posing with a group of Moko Jumbies. There were photographs I'd taken with mud all over my body, as an art form, a teenager with braces looking like Mudder Earth, mud all over my skin just like I was one of the masqueraders from the launch at San Fernando Hill.

The ache was spreading as I went up a second flight of stairs to my master bedroom, body tingling. I stumbled inside my walk-in closet, anxious to get to my black file cabinet, breathing harder as I unlocked my storage unit, pulled out toys, tossing vibrators and Ben Wa balls to the floor until I found the right stimulator, hurried to my bed, knocked books off my bed, sent *The Witch of Portobello*, *The Zahir*, and *Veronika Decides to Die* flying to the carpet, put my literary reading in flight, that desperate act being akin to blasphemy. I spied at my erotic madness, saw myself suffering in the ceiling-to-floor mirror on the right side of the room, watched my pained expression as I rushed to turn on the stimulator, that humming tingling my hand, saying it missed me, its love song telling me it wanted to please me, a song of desire that sent its sweet chorus, its harsh and stimulating vibrations moving up my arm. I moaned. Swallowed as I crawled on top of the bed, not bothering to pull the covers back. My throbbing was intense, my fire rising. I closed my eyes and spread my legs, I took the vibration to my swollen clit.

Electricity coursed through my body, made me tense as I called out to the heavens.

The absence of a lover did not move my hormones into a state of hibernation.

The absence of a lover did not keep this body from needing to experience a sweet release.

I squeezed my breasts with my free hand, pinched my nipples, tried to suck my nipple, but the sensations were too strong. Surges attacked me. But tragedy happened. When I was close to orgasm, the vibrations decreased. The vibrations stuttered. The song stopped. I took the stimulator and slapped it in my hand, beat it against my palm, trying to revive my over-the-counter lover. It whined. The batteries were old, and as if it had a bad heart, my lover was dying. I wanted to scream. I dropped the stimulator, heard it humming a farewell hum as it fell on the bed. This was frustrating. This was so damn frustrating.

I took my tingles to the bathtub, sat on the edge as I filled it with water, added jasmine scents, turned the jets on, eased inside the water and let the eight jets send intense streams of water against my body, each stream a liquid phallus, put my feet on both sides of the tub, allowed those bursts to flow across my clitoris, eased closer, adjusting until I found the right spot, my spot.

Something behind me rattled. I jumped, opened my eyes in terror, ready to scream.

Someone was here with me. Someone was inside my home.

The abrupt sound had come from my bedroom. No more than five feet away from my bathtub. It had been a clatter. A brief jangle. I sat frozen where I was, covered in water, this bathtub the womb, and I was as helpless as a child in embryonic state. Waiting. Listening.

Home invasions. Burglaries. The news of all the crimes in the Atlanta area rushed into my mind. *Murder. Rape.* My breathing ceased. Steamed-over mirrors surrounded me. The shutters in my bedroom were closed, that part of my home filled with shadows my eyes couldn't penetrate.

My cellular hummed. I jerked again, still startled but relieved.

That was the clatter. That was the noise that had delivered me into the mouth of terror.

Nervous laughter escaped me as I shook my head, as I felt my heart beating in my throat.

The terrifying rattle had been the hum of my cellular against my mahogany nightstand.

My fingers eased across my navel, breathing thickening as I squeezed my stomach, as I began massaging my inner thighs, again sliding my fingers between my legs, spreading apart my yoni lips. I was floating, disconnected from my corporeal self. And inside that altered state of consciousness I wasn't traveling alone. Her spirit was with me.

I heard her whispering, her voice serious, her tone warm, *"There were always in me, two women at least, one woman desperate and bewildered, who felt she was drowning . . ."*

She was here. Her Spanish, Cuban, and Danish features so clear, clearer than they were on the image I had of her in my office. Anaïs Nin smiled at me. Her teeth even and beautiful, that evenness so appealing, gave her perfection and beauty, any imperfections she owned were irrelevant, overshadowed by her petite stature and humanness, a humanness that made her glow as if she were my beacon.

I reached for her, my eyes telling her that I desperately desired a conversation with her, my pleading face encased in rapture, telling her that I needed to ask her things I knew she'd understand.

Anaïs's specter faded like a fata morgana, her soft words remaining, resonating, bringing tears to my eyes as I came, as water splashed, as I writhed, as I experienced an amazing rush of sensations.

Breathing labored, I remained where I was, suffering, unable to mollify this desire.

Tears trickled down my face because this body would not yield to satisfaction.

My home phone began ringing.

My sex throbbed, again calling out to my hand, demanding the comfort of my fingers.

As the telephone announced that the call was from New York, my fingers took me toward another orgasm. It came so damn fast. My orgasm arrived like a determined storm. I held on, afraid it might sweep me out to sea. As soon as that one finished, another voluptuous orgasm covered me, consumed me, devastated me; back-to-back orgasms had left me tingling from my forehead to my toes.

My cellular hummed again.

Again, without warning, a thousand little deaths approached me. Orgasm overwhelmed me, maddened me as I came, came hard, came praying for this to end. Phone ringing. Cellular humming. My moans loud enough to drown all sounds.

I came praying I was done, not knowing this was only the beginning.

Self-pleasuring was popcorn.

My body was telling me it needed steak.

Maybe it wasn't normal to need orgasm, to seek orgasm several times a day. Maybe I needed to talk to a professional. Maybe I needed to find a new lover. I didn't have sex a lot but I had a respectable sex drive. The need to be touched, the need to feel stimulation, the need to exist in a state of arousal, the need to have all desires quenched, allow the tension to build up and start all over again, all of that lived in me.

I cleansed my clit stimulator, took it back inside my closet, picked up vibrators and Ben Wa balls, returned all the toys to their hiding place—the file cabinet drawer at the back of the walk-in closet.

I needed to find an unselfish lover whose strength and desire matched my own.

A lover with an open mind. A lover who understood me and allowed me to be me.

I was erotic. I was beautiful. I was powerful.

I deserved to find pleasure that surpassed my imagination, better than any I had experienced.

I needed a lover who could enhance and embolden my sexual cravings.

I didn't want to be with anyone right now, but at the same time I didn't want to be without passion. I needed to be touched by a man's hands, feel his weight on me, feel him sinking inside me.

Tingles remained, disturbing me. My vagina was swollen. It seemed as if I was always wet.

If I was a man, I would exist in a constant state of erection.

Water dripping from my flesh, a fluffy towel wrapped around my breasts, I crossed into my bedroom, damp feet on soft carpet, and went toward the nightstand, the morning air now cool on my breasts and thighs as I picked up my cellular. I expected to see an early morning text message from my mother, her being up and in the gym at this hour—even with the three-hour time difference—wouldn't surprise me. But it wasn't my mother who had disturbed my personal moment.

What did I do wrong? Irregardless of what you think, I'm worried about you. Irregardless of what you think, your the only woman I love. Your the only one. Please call me back. FROM: Logan.

The interruption of orgasm had been caused by the man I was trying to forget, the man I wanted to forget about me. Part of my brain began firing like crazy, my frontopolar gyrus, the part of my mind that dealt with irritation. I cursed Logan. Months had gone by and Logan still rankled me. He continued to pursue me. Seeing his name always gave me instant regret and overwhelming pain.

I went to my home phone, a private number that had been given to only a handful of people, checked my caller ID, saw my Overworked and Underpaid New York Editor had called. He was in his office early this morning. He was a workaholic, like me.

I sat down on the carpet, the ends of my hair wet, moved the towel from my waist and put it under my butt. I put in *82, the code to unblock my number, followed by his office number, knowing he wanted to talk about the issues with the novel I was rewriting. I shifted gears, closed my eyes on my tingles. On my aching. Thought about work. Tried to shift to that frame of mind. Focused on rewriting. With the amount of work I was doing it was closer to ghostwriting. Notes from Mr. Overworked and Underpaid New York Editor said to keep the language from being too deep, keep my vocabulary unchallenging, and do whatever I could to replace sensuality with vulgarity and crassness. I had issues with dumbing down work, for it was through the dumbing down that the writer disrespected herself, disrespected the craft.

I did not want to cater to those who were afraid of words, those who embraced ignorance as if it was their favorite religion, as if they had forgotten about those who marched for their physical and intellectual freedoms. All of that was on my mind, but not voiced, in the name of professionalism.

In his wonderful British accent he said, "It's not supposed to be Dostoevsky."

"Dostoevsky? This is below *Beetle Bailey*."

"You're brilliant. Work your magic."

"I should bowdlerize this mess."

"Let the vulgarities stand, lest the book be reduced to the size of a pamphlet."

"This prose is handicapped. Painful to read these crippled metaphors without cringing."

"I told him to strengthen his bloody metaphors."

"And he said?"

"He asked me what a metaphor was."

We laughed.

I said, "And the way he shifts tense. Damn. Has he heard of *Elements of Style*?"

"He probably thinks *Elements of Style* is a bloody rap group."

We laughed harder.

We agreed that true erotica, at its best, was more than sex. It was a study in human behavior. In the complications of existing. It focused on human desire. Desires that were being acted upon.

He said, "Miss Bijou, you are far from being simple, but keep the changes simple."

"I know, I know. Leave out the depth. Get to the sex, skip the philosophizing, and get it over."

"And it needs a better ending. See what you can suggest."

"Would be great if he could come up with a sudden or unexpected reversal of circumstances."

"He's not capable of manufacturing a moving peripeteia."

"If all else fails, for this audience, just have the characters miraculously end up in the same church at the same time singing a negro spiritual, then call it a wrap. The end. Amen."

"I don't need to read another horrible deus ex machina ending. Anything but deus ex machina. I'd rather all the characters died in a plane crash before I read another one of those bloody endings."

We laughed.

On a serious note, my tone now somber, I said, "You ever notice that all the books with women seeking pleasure end in tragedy? Same for the movies. As if it were punishment."

He said, simply, "I noticed. And you're right, it is punishment for a woman to obtain pleasure."

"Why?"

He answered my complicated question by saying one word, "Control."

Control.

Logan wanted to control me. He wanted to bowdlerize my desires and sanctify me.

I deleted his message. Needed to get him out of my head.

My cellular hummed again. It was a duplicate message from Logan. He had re-sent the same messages, typographical errors and all. *Your* instead of *you're*. *Irregardless* instead of *regardless*.

His text messages bothered me as much as his misused words,

both were fingernails across my mental chalkboard. He had driven me to clichés. In my world clichés were the doorway to madness. When words that were sent electronically upset you, a man had too much fucking power.

And giving away that power gave me frustration. And that frustration fostered guilt.

I thought that maybe something was wrong with me. If a man who had Logan's credentials, his looks, his unwavering desire for me, if a man like that couldn't please me, something had to be wrong with me. But it wasn't just me. The physical attraction was present, but the chemistry was nonexistent. There was more to humanness, more to the inner makings of a person than a fabulous résumé.

Physical attraction was about aesthetics, not sexual performance, not mental stimulation. Without a mental connection, a remarkable sexual performance yielded no lifelong guarantees.

It was only lust. And lust was not love.

His sexual performance had been appreciated, but far from awe-inspiring. Hardly memorable.

His lingam did not fit my yoni the way a key should fit inside a lock.

It was just another erection. Another hardness made of flesh and blood, a piece of meat that gained girth and length, the part of a man that became engorged when aroused. He could tear down a brick wall with his bare hands but he could not let loose my heart. His key had rattled inside me, but my heart had not opened for him. He had rattled me then as he was rattling me now.

I didn't question my heart, it would be foolish to do so. I only accepted its choices. I had exercised my freedom, acknowledged my needs, and taken on other lovers. Inspired by curiosity and the needs of a woman, I had engaged in zipless affairs. I'd had one-night stands. Without regret. I had been pleased by strangers. And I had found that invigorating.

I had found that powerful.

To be able to have a man, then walk away before emotions took root, that was power.

I turned the television on, in search of a much-needed distraction. I tuned to the local news.

Jewell Stewark was reporting. *A pastor was shot and killed while selling watermelons out of his pickup truck.* Her voice was so strong, so professional. On gigantic billboards placed all over Atlanta she was promoted as "The Jewell of the South." She owned the complexion that the powers that be in Hollywood—and men of color—seemed to cherish more than the darkness of the motherland. Some said she had a backside that rivaled both Kim Kardashian's and Beyoncé's physical assets. Those were the comments that had been posted in *AJC*'s "Vent" section, not my words, because I couldn't care less. Some had written in she had the blended complexion that made the good old boys in the South and middle America feel safe. Others had said she was simply beautiful, so stop hating.

I agreed with the last group, the ones beyond complexion and racism, another minority group.

After reporting that an Atlanta city councilman was proposing a law to ban sagging, a law that would also fine women who went jogging in sports bras or let a little thong show, The Jewell of the South moved on to the next matter and said, "And I'm looking for all of my fellow Jamaicans in the ATL."

Hearing her mention the largest island in the West Indies borrowed my attention.

She said there were so many Jamaicans in Atlanta she was doing a special report called *Atlanta, Georgia: Jamaica's 15th Parish*. I didn't know she was an island girl. I had read that she had roots in Portland, but I thought that meant Oregon, not Portland Parish in Jamaica. She didn't have any hint of a Jamaican accent, no hint of Jamaican Creole or Jamaican English or Rastafarian in her Southern accent.

In the West Indies the islanders said the rowdy and violent

rebels were kicked off the slave ships in Jamaica and the nonviolent captives remained, were sold as the slave ships moved south, Christian slavers making stops at many of the islands and keys that spread toward South America, selling Africans like they were animals, the last of the human cargo being sold at the last stop down in Trinidad.

Jamaica was said to be populated with the spirit of the Carib Indians; those Indians violent and war-loving, their cannibalistic history hardly discussed. My mother said we were more like the Arawaks, the peaceful and nonviolent Indians who had been conquered and slaughtered by the Caribs.

With the growing violence in Trinidad, I'd often told her that was debatable.

But my mother knew our history better than I did.

My mother had worked the sugar fields in Trinidad, had worked sugar fields the same way the people in the Southern states had picked cotton. My mother had killed chickens with her bare hands and cooked those chickens, had milked cows, had done all of that as a little girl and a teenager. My mother came out of the womb working and would probably go into the ground doing the same.

My life had been so different from my mother's, and she had wanted it that way.

Those were my thoughts as I stood in my bedroom window, pulling my hair back into a ponytail.

I smiled at the television, smiled at her lovely face, a woman with roots in the islands.

Atlanta's Jewell of the South was Jamaican, her history rooted in Carib Indians.

Once again my cellular rang, again I cursed, this time the ring tone from *Sex and the City.*

I answered, "Cut to the chase. I'm writing."

"I don't see how you live in the South. Young black men being incarcerated for dating white women. Nooses hanging from trees at schools. It's like going back toward slavery days."

It was the forever-ambitious and hardworking Hazel Tamana Bijou-Wilson. The power-hungry woman who used to work at Denzel's Mundy Lane Entertainment, then worked with Debra Martin Chase at Whitney Houston's Brown House Productions before going over to Will Smith's Overbrook Entertainment. She's moved on since then. Moved on and was just as famous as any talking head on the lot. She was an NAACP Image Award winner who was spotlighted in *Essence* and *Ebony* magazines.

She was my mother.

I said, "Did I not just tell you I was writing?"

"But you move from Southern city to Southern city. Help me understand that, could you please?"

"You want me to come back home that bad, don't you?"

"And dammit, I'll say whatever I have to. Need you here. You're my best friend."

"Look what you did. Now I'm crying."

"Are you really crying?"

"Hell no."

She laughed.

I said, "I have an idea to run by you."

"What kind of an idea?"

"Will tell you later. Let me get some work done."

"Spill it. What's the idea?"

I told her, "After I finish my next ghostwriting project, I'm going to start writing my first sci-fi story."

"Why sci-fi?"

"This project I'm working on . . . it's . . ."

I couldn't tell her what was on my mind. Couldn't tell her that I thought that my work had been affecting me, stirring me, couldn't say that even though the words were not well-written the images were strong enough to rouse my own imagination, potent enough to make me touch myself, powerful enough to create the need to orgasm, powerful enough to have me stripping away my clothing, touching my longing sex as I hurried upstairs to my bathtub, powerful enough to have me masturbating at sunrise.

I looked at the walls in my office. Beyond my images of Anaïs Nin were framed posters of Hazel Dorothy Scott, the first African American woman to have her own television show, *The Hazel Scott Show*, a show they pulled because she publicly opposed McCarthyism and segregation. We shared a common history and the same birthday, so I felt connected, if only by the arrangement of the stars. This powerful need that lived within me, I wondered how much of my angst was driven by my birth sign.

In the end I cleared my throat, ran my fingers over my hair, that sensual twinge remaining.

I became the modest daughter, the woman who preferred to remain as close to virginity as she could in her mother's eyes, the offspring of those raised with strong Christian values, religious ideologies forced upon us as a result of slavery and colonialism, and told my mother, "I just need to refocus, work on something different for a while."

"It's always good to mix it up. Good. Dare to be different. Don't become a one-trick pony."

We blew each other kisses and hung up at the same time.

I wiped my eyes, tears clouding my vision. When she told me I was her best friend, I'd started crying. Not much. Just a little emotion seeping out of my soul. She told me she missed me *and* I was her best friend. That really got to me. Made me laugh a bit. My mother missed me so much she called to cause drama. I missed her too. I couldn't ever live with her again, but I missed her too.

If I moved back to L.A., I'd go back to living in my mother's shadow. This was the woman who had Hollywood on speed dial, the woman who chatted with A-list and B-list celebrities most of the day.

I loved her, would die for her, but I needed my own life, my own successes, my own failures.

I remember when I told my mother I wanted to be a writer and she looked at me as if I was losing my mind. She wanted me to be an actress. A talking head that dramatically regurgitated the words of someone brilliant. But Hollywood has never been kind to brown-skinned women, not the way they have embraced those of mixed heritage. Even before I had that realization, I had no desire to be an actress. I was too stubborn to be forced into someone else's image of me, never owned the need to live up to someone else's idea of who I should be. I was a writer. I was the type of writer I wanted to be. Not a Hollywood writer whose words were taken into that television and movie factory, cut and modified until the original idea resembled the final product as much as the Michael Jackson in the Jackson 5 resembled the Michael Jackson of today. All that to say I was what I was destined to be at this moment in my life.

I looked around me, looked at all of my friends, friends who were in hardback, some in paperback. There were hundreds of books in my office, more books than most people had in their entire homes, the momentary highlight of my bookshelf being my Erica Jong collection, Hillary Rodham Clinton, and more than a few by Anne Rice. Anaïs Nin's works were forever on my desk, those being the only novels I read and studied over and over, pages dog-eared; words, phrases, so much highlighted in each one. She was honest. She had been daring. Her words made me want to live the opposite of afraid.

She had become my obsession, the spirit I saw as if she was alive, knowing she was deceased.

Germaine Greer. Sartre's *Being and Nothingness. The Mandarins. Women: Myth and Reality. The Woman Destroyed. Memoirs of a Dutiful Daughter. A Vindication of the Rights of Women.*

I was surrounded by literature that reminded me I wasn't a deviation from the norm.

I had work to do, but my mother's lovely singsong voice remained in my ear, had put Trinidad on my mind. I went online and read the news from *The Trinidad Guardian. Gang leader gunned down, shot twenty times over deal gone sour. Cops bracing for reprisals.* That slaying was in the Morvant/Laventille area, where my father was born, where my mother grew up in a shantytown, lived in a shack made of bricks and garbage on the side of a hill in an area that was controlled by gangs, the kind of life she had to get away from, the kind of life that put my father in his grave while my mother was pregnant, his existence ending two months before I was born. My mother still had a home in Port of Spain. A mansion really. She called it our Roots Home. On Lady Chancellor Road. A hill so high that when I climbed to the top it seemed like I could tiptoe and touch the sun.

Ambition born in my blood, I wrote as long as I could, my mind not cooperating this morning. It was like that sometimes. So I remained productive. Used work to distract me from other feelings. From life itself. Part of me still tingled. Part of me still craved. The time had come to feed another addiction.

Another craving rooted in pain and pleasure.

Another addiction had me fidgety, caused me to shut down and leave my home in a hurry.

Top up on my car, air conditioner on high, an hour later I exited US Highway 78 at exit 8.

Every car and truck on the road had a severe yellow tint. Pollen season. Atlanta's fifth season had arrived and pollen had spread like snow.

I was making my way toward Stone Mountain Park. The elderly blue-haired lady in the booth saw the yearly sticker in my window and waved me through. She knew I was a regular. I headed to the right, to the main parking lot. That was the starting point of the legendary trail that circled the granite mountain.

I rushed and pulled my hair back into a ponytail, didn't do a great job, really didn't care. The heat from my mane would rest on my neck regardless. Would irritate me as I ran, its weight becoming unbearable as I perspired and it held my sweat. This kind of heat made me want to get it cut boy short. At least cut off six inches or more, have it cut back to shoulder-length. I gave up on that idea, stretched my hamstrings and calf muscles, went to the mile marker at the edge of the lot, and started my timer.

I started jogging slow and easy, my iPod on my arm tuned to the Queen of Soca, Alison Hinds, the first song in my most played, followed by Tessanne Chin's brilliant and powerful reggae, and then one of my favorite songs, Tanya Stephens singing about the streets, the anthem of so many island women.

Mile one was a sub-nine. A decent warm-up. The shade was wonderful, acres of trees to my left and right, not many bikers and bladers were whizzing by in their dedicated part of the lane.

Old fears came alive, my heart raced, and I slowed down when I saw a loose dog over in the trees. I hated dogs. I was not an animal person. Was bitten by a German shepherd when I was a kid, maybe seven years old. So whenever I saw a dog it triggered that unwanted memory.

Other joggers were looking that way; walkers had stopped and were staring out into the woods.

In the woods a huge white mutt was engaged in copulation with a smaller black dog. The huge white dog had its paws around the smaller dog's waist, holding her, pulling her into his humps.

Tail wagging, a third dog—that one many shades of brown—stood in line, his pink penis erect, his tongue wagging, shifting in his impatience, barking for the other to finish so he could seek his orgasm.

It was a season of insatiability.

I checked my watch and ran on. Picked up my pace to make up for lost time.

I tackled another hill, the sounds of insects and bugs all around me, sweat dripping down my back. I ached. Arms low, back straight, I maintained my smooth heel-toe roll.

Mile three. Twenty-six minutes into my workout. Speeding up. Sweat pouring like a waterfall.

I was running downhill, coming out of the shade, Stone Mountain Lake to my right.

That was when I saw him.

He was shirtless, most of his body exposed, his physique beyond pedestrian, beyond ignorable. Sweat dripping from his skin like rain. Like a Mandingo warrior god who'd risen out of the ocean.

He was speeding toward me, running uphill as if the battle with gravity was meaningless.

Black running shorts, black socks, black running shoes.

That was all he had on, so in my eyes, he was almost naked, only his crucial body parts hidden.

He was running at an amazing clip, somewhere between six- and seven-minute miles.

I wiped sweat from my eyes and he came into focus, one that did not negate the first impression. Tight eyes, bronze skin with a brown sugar glow. He was lean, had done so many sit-ups his six-pack had evolved into an eight-pack.

We made eye contact, time slowed down, and the cruelest of all throbbing began.

THREE

Time elongated. Sounds ceased. The world fell away.

In my mind, in that moment, we were in a relationship.

His muscles. How they flexed and released with each stride. He was focused. I was impressed. His speed. His strength. Wondered how that energy translated into other venues. Small waist, broad shoulders, top of his body a perfect V shape. His chest strong, arms slightly bent, everything so toned.

Both of us barely clothed, both of us sweating, both of us living in pain.

In that moment, in my mind, we had become lovers.

I saw his features. The rise and fall of his chest as he breathed in through his nose, out through his mouth. My breathing pattern was the same, the breathing of true runners. Felt like we were one.

Time sped up again. Became as intense as the zenith of an orgasm.

We passed each other, now a blur. Both of us enveloped in heat. Dripping sweat. Like lovers at the end of erotic violence. The kind I hadn't had in so long.

I ran on, ran faster, became fire moving away from gasoline.

Our eye contact had lasted no more than two seconds.

But it felt like forever. It was powerful.

That moment was over. That powerful moment had passed.

I glanced back at him. Wanted to get that final view as our

moment ended, as energies faded. Wanted to catch a parting glimpse of his back, see how it flowed into his backside from this angle.

Much to my surprise he was already looking back at me. He caught me glancing back at him. For a moment I felt exposed. But I'd caught him looking back at me too. And he had looked back first.

He checked his watch and ran on.

I checked my watch and picked up my pace, remembering what I had seen, my mind photographic in moments like this. He was stimulating, sensual. Wondered if he would be in the parking lot when I made it back around. Wondered if he was with someone. Had someone. Or just needed someone to kick it with tonight. I wasn't beyond being with someone who had someone.

I wasn't proud of that fact, but it was true. Not many were above operating in that mode. Needs brought out the selfishness in us all. What had been done to me had been done to others in the name of my own selfish needs. At times carnal needs were too strong, undeniable. It was harder between sundown and sunrise. I missed lying next to a man at night, being spooned, his hands caressing my curves, him nuzzling and kissing the nape of my neck, cupping my breasts, pulling my nipples while I moved my ass into him, feeling him harden as he eased his hand from my breast to my thighs to begin touching my yoni.

I whispered one of my favorite quotes, "Be careful Anaïs, be careful."

I hit the section of the course that was next to a park area. No trees over the trail. The sun burned down on me as I took the challenging incline that rose up at a heartbreaking angle and became rolling hills between miles three and four. That section had signs telling runners and walkers to remain on the pavement, two-way traffic was allowed in that section of the five-mile loop.

I thought I saw him again, running the section that forced us to run on sidewalks. Saw him in the distance. No more than an eighth of a mile away. He was racing toward me again.

The same shirtless, tight-eyed runner I'd passed not too long ago.
He was still running hard. Harder than before, his pace now
probably in the low sixes.

I slowed down, ready for him to flirt with me, maybe turn
around and run with me, ready for him to chat me up, was hoping I
didn't look too bad, hoped nothing was in my nose, my hair pulled
back in an awful ponytail, skin so dank, not the best me I could be,
but still looking good enough—at least I hoped.

We did that brief wave and the thumbs-up signal that runners
do. That motion of solidarity.

Then he ran right by me.

I glanced back at him, did to him what men had done to me so
often.

He didn't look back that time. I had become pedestrian. Rejection humbled my ego.

But this was Atlanta, after all. Where most of the educated, good-
looking, and upwardly mobile men were gay. The ones who looked
like LL Cool J were more interested in the ones who acted like
Little Richard than a heterosexual woman like me. A woman had to
entertain lesbians to get a date down here.

I heard lesbians treated women better than the men did. Too bad
I wasn't in that club.

Life goes on.

I passed the enormous bas-relief on the north face of the mountain, the largest bas-relief in the world. Three figures of the Confederate States of America were carved there: Stonewall Jackson,
Robert E. Lee, and Jefferson Davis. Lots of minorities were out here
now, but not back in the day of segregated public facilities. This
mountain was the site of the founding of the second Ku Klux Klan
back in the early 1900s, and the Klan was involved in the design,
financing, and early construction of the monument.

I ran by that history, held my pace, and sped by that reminder as
fast as I could, began taking the hill that paralleled the picnic area,

that steep hill was the last hill, kept a decent pace as I pushed myself up that long and steep rise, embraced the pain from mile four until the end of the run.

My fantasies and I had run the five-mile course that circled that ball of granite, had made the hilly loop in less than forty minutes. The humidity made the air so thick it felt like I was inhaling and exhaling through a wet blanket, breathing hard, sweating like I was living in a sauna.

I stopped in the main parking lot long enough to get hydrated. I changed the music on my iPod, put on music by Carina Ayiesha, would let her reggae and Spanish songs lead me the next five miles, restarted my watch and started back jogging, ran the course in the opposite direction, all of the downhill becoming uphill, just kept my pace steady as I ran by the images of former slave owners engraved in the side of the mountain, that last mile being a grueling incline that had me in the kind of pain I loved.

At the end of the second five-mile loop I stopped my watch. Looked at the time on the stopwatch portion. I cursed. Angry at myself for not breaking forty minutes. Shaking my head, took my iPod off as I went to my car, grabbed a bottled water, hydrated, and headed toward the trail leading up the mountain.

I saw the dogs again. Running from the woods. The girl dog was running at a decent pace. Two dogs were behind her, harassing her, pink dicks sticking out of their furry bodies.

She looked back, saw they were still chasing, and ran fast, vanished on the other side of the lot. The male dogs never stopped pursuing. She was in heat, her scent leading them wherever she went.

I headed across the railroad tracks, followed people that were walking uphill, over fallen trees, broken ground, headed up the side of this bitch of a mountain. Once across the railroad tracks there was a pathway, a hiking trail that led up the side of that ball of granite, that path being about a mile and a half from bottom to top. Worked the hell out of my calf and butt muscles. The mountain's lower slopes were wooded. A sign said the rare Georgia oak was first discovered at the summit, and several specimens were along the walk-up trail and in the woods around the base of the mountain. The extremely rare Confederate daisy flowered on the mountain, growing in rock crevices and in the wooded areas.

My sentiments were obvious, expressed in the way I shook my head.

Seemed like everything in this area was called *Confederate* this or *Confederate* that, all the streets and stores were named after segregationists and slave owners or called *plantation* this or *plantation* that. With that history everywhere, I was surprised so many minorities had flocked to this part of the country.

Bottled water in hand, I kept a steady pace, fought the mountain like I was doing battle with age and time, fought the humidity, heat, and elevation, fought until I made it to the top, not until then did I bend over, hands on my thighs, breathing so tight, sweat dripping in my eyes.

I stood up and looked out at miles of trees, saw so much beauty, the city of Atlanta far off in the distance. It felt like I was Queen of the Hill as I panted and drank water, my sweat dripping on the same spot where the young and virile college-educated men stood shirtless in the movie *Stomp the Yard*.

I was 1,683 feet above sea level, 825 feet above the surrounding plateau.

The top of the mountain was a surreal landscape of bare rock and rock pools. I stood off to the side and stared out at all the real estate and forests covering Lady Georgia, the place that had once barred Ray Charles from earning a living within her boundaries.

I was alone, staring out at the most heavily forested urban area in the country.

Just me and my personal issues, concerns spiraling, worming deeper inside my head.

I'd never envisioned living in Smyrna, but Logan had *inspired* me to leave Memphis.

Bad relationships had the power of inspiration. Bad relationships made the world claustrophobic.

While I watched people struggle up the mountain, I stared out at the trees, gazed toward downtown ATL, and wondered how realistic it was for a woman to expect one man to fulfill every need that she had. Pleasing a woman was a Herculean task. And so was pleasing a man. Wondered if it was wrong for a man to feel the same way, that no one woman could please him in all ways.

Sweat dripped down my face into my eyes.

I saw him again.

I saw the shirtless golden-skinned man who had been running like a track star. His eight-pack glistening. Muscles flexing on his Mandingo frame. He looked like sex. Pure unadulterated sex.

He was hiking up the hill, taking the steepest part like he was a warrior in training.

Staring at him intoxicated me. That dark, uncontrollable side of me wanted to take over.

Had been so long since I had passion. Maybe that was why these thoughts consumed my soul. A starving woman always thought of food, at least until she was fed. But once I started, I had a tendency to overeat. Had a propensity toward carnal gluttony. And gluttony always created guilt and shame.

I almost ran away from that golden-skinned Adonis. *But.* There was always a *but.* There was always an exception. The sexy way he frowned. The way he was breathing, so smooth. In control. I licked my lips like I was lapping the perspiration away from his beautiful skin.

The tight-eyed Mandingo stopped to stretch his back, jumped up and down like he was shaking the pain off, and started back hiking. His trek was bringing him closer and closer to me.

I lowered my head, hoped the lust drained out of my eyes before I went blind.

I prayed for him to walk by me. But he paused in front of me.

I looked in his face, his expression a blend of ecstasy and pain.

I didn't say anything, stared at him, waited to see if he was going to continue his journey.

But he didn't move. He gazed in my eyes, wiped sweat from his face, from his tanned skin.

He disturbed me the way I had disturbed other men.

Once, maybe three years ago, I was in the aristocratic bowels of London, late at night, coming out of the Mansion House tube. I was alone in the financial district, close to the midnight hour, heading down a narrow alley that led to 30 Queen Street, the air chilly as I hurried toward the flat I was letting for that month. I'd come into the alley and a European man in a black suit, a man who had the look of a powerful diplomat, was walking toward me, his shoes clip-clopping on the narrow pathway. Clip-clopping until he raised his head, his breath steaming from his mouth, clip-clopping until he raised his eyes and saw me. My hair was down, my dress black and fitted, covered by a coat, but that coat was open enough to reveal my mild cleavage. He stopped walking when he saw me. In the softest voice he cursed and called his god's name in the same vulgar expression. He scared me. His expression, the way his mouth opened wide and his eyes opened wider, the way he stared, his body language told me he was stunned by what he saw, and then, right then, he unzipped his pants, took out his sex, and as he gazed into my eyes, eyes that were terrified, his lust overwhelmed him. He masturbated, became rough with himself, his penis pink and substantial, that ruddiness a contrast to his dark clothing, to the dark skies, to the dark pavement, to the dark moment. His pleasure was desperate and hurried, his voice muffled, his face in a violent rapture, his eyes locked on mine the entire time. Like a snake. Prepared to strike or spew venom.

I wanted to run away from that pervert, but I couldn't move, frozen by fear.

He grunted. He erupted. He staggered. He moaned.

When he was done, he stood there, winded, drool seeping from his mouth, his face becoming slackened, his desire leaking from his thick hand to his black suit pants to his shiny black shoes.

He lowered his head in shame and began blubbering uncontrollably.

He apologized to me, begged for my forgiveness, told me he had never done anything that sordid before. He said he didn't know what had happened, just cried that I was so bloody beautiful.

He pled temporary insanity.

I closed my coat, my heels moving at a hurried pace as I made a wide arch around him, avoiding his river of come, rushed toward Queen Street, horrified and disgusted.

On that night, I didn't understand that perverted man, why he would do something like that.

In this moment, I understood.

At this moment, on this mountain, I wanted to stare in the eyes of this Mandingo warrior god and please myself to his image, wanted to stare in his beautiful eyes and come with a quickness.

He said, "Nice view, huh?"

His baritone voice was smooth, articulate, educated. I licked my lips, cleared my throat, purged my thoughts, sent them to the land of the impure as I turned my frown upside down, forced a smile, my smile feeling tentative, hopefully unreadable. It took a moment of searching, but I found my voice.

My voice cracked, throat dehydrated as I said, "Depends on what you're looking at."

"Looking at what's beautiful, taking in God's creations."

I nodded. Awkwardness invaded me. "What's that over there?"

He pointed. "Downtown Atlanta."

"Thought downtown was in that direction."

"Kennesaw Mountain is over that way."

My feet kept moving, shifting my body. Kept touching my hair. He had me rattled, nervous.

In that moment I saw things I hadn't seen before. The tattoos on his arms and stomach. On his right arm he had a tattoo of a female angel with her wings wrapped around herself, the angel extremely beautiful. There was a cross on his left shoulder. The word KENYA tattooed on his left forearm. I assumed he was Kenyan. He had run with the grace and speed of a Kenyan. The tattoos didn't pull me in like the nice nipples on his chest. Erect nipples that looked like seeds had been planted and penises were in bloom. Saw the way veins rose out of his muscular arms. Sweat raining from his skin like tears, he held up a hand, blocked the sun from his eyes, and gazed at me. Looked right in my eyes. I had to look up to make that eye contact happen. He smiled. Showed hints of his straight, white teeth.

I wanted to find something wrong with him. Needed to find some fault. There was none I could see. He was astounding. Created visual molestation.

The heat, the humidity, running, the thunderstorm in the distance. I wasn't prettied up. I was gritty. Animal urges blending with the sensuality of working out, living in the zone of pain and pleasure.

Before I could readjust, before I could deal with this awkwardness, something else happened. It was as if I had imagined our conversation, as if I had daydreamed his presence.

I saw him *again*.

I saw him coming up the mountain *again*. I blinked a hundred times. Blinked away from what had to be a dream. A hallucination. A fantasy. Once again the golden Mandingo was hiking up the mountain, coming toward me like a déjà vu. Same smile. Same black running shorts. Same physique.

He was just now coming up the mountain.

And inside this magical moment he was standing next to me at the same time.

The second Mandingo came over and stopped in front of me.

He looked at his doppelganger, panted, and said, "You found the roadrunner."

"Told you I was going to find her."

Mouth wide open, I stared at them. My world shifted. It was like I had fallen into a Philip K. Dick sci-fi movie. One dealing with clones. Was surreal. Was unreal. Same baritone voice. The only real difference was the first one I'd met had body art. The one without the tats looked more reserved, more businesslike. The other had the bad-boy thing going on. And the one without the tats wore a wedding ring.

The heat had me delirious. The altitude and dehydration had me seeing a split screen.

I said, "Am I having a heat stroke? Am I seeing double?"

The one who came up last panted and said, "You're in a Doublemint chewing gum commercial."

There was an abrupt crackling in the sky. Loud enough to make everyone on the summit stop and look out into the distance. People scaling the face of the mountain did the same.

All around us the heavens were growling, skies becoming restless and dark, filled with electrical surges. Like my body and soul. The noise arrived and its grumble became endless. A warning that soon rain would be falling. Soon lightning would be striking down the damned.

Despite the rumbling skies, my eyes wouldn't move from them, couldn't cease staring, evaluating.

I said, "Identical twins."

The one with the tats said, "Saw you running."

The other with the wedding ring said, "I passed you first. You ran at a good clip."

Again I touched my arm and realized I was sticky. No makeup on. Lips dry. So unpretty.

I should've run away from them. Should've run down the mountain as fast as I could.

Nervousness rising, thoughts impure, I said, "Went around the mountain twice."

The one without the tats said, "We did three loops."

I said, "Fifteen miles. Nice."

"We were on the last loop when we passed you."

The one with the tats nodded. "What's your name?"

"Nia Simone."

"Nina Simone?"

"No, Nia Simone. Nia as in purpose."

The one with the tats said, "Nia, as in the fifth day of Kwanzaa."

I smiled a little. "Right."

"And Simone like . . ."

"Like the writer Simone de Beauvoir."

"Gotcha."

The one wearing the wedding ring repeated, "Nia Simone."

"Yeah."

"Named after the existentialist feminist Simone Lucie-Ernestine-Marie Bertrand de Beauvoir."

I paused, amazement rising in my expression. "No, wasn't named in her honor."

"Was joking."

I asked, "Are you familiar with her work?"

"*The Second Sex*. Existence precedes essence."

"You're aware of her theories?"

"She took a lot from Jean-Paul Sartre."

"And Mary Wollstonecraft."

"I'm not familiar with Wollstonecraft."

I was impressed. Literature and those who took time to read different points of view, I always found them more fascinating. Just like that, I found the married man more interesting, if only for a moment.

Sweat dripping from their bare chests, they maintained their identical smiles.

I asked, "You guys always hike up here?"

The one with the tats smiled, motioned at his brother. "Mark hikes up here at the end of the run."

That let me know the one *without* the tats was Mark. The *unmarked* one was Mark.

"Karl, the storm is about to hit. The wind is picking up. Getting cooler." Mark pointed at the dark clouds that were moving our way. And that let me know the one with the tats was Karl. The one with KENYA tattooed on his body was Karl. My mind created word associations, a memory exercise.

Unmarked, Mark. KENYA etched in his skin, that was Karl.

Mark wore a wedding ring that had both disappointed me and captured my attention.

Mark went on, "Karl's a photographer."

His brother chuckled. "I have an eye for beauty."

"He was determined to find you before we left this mountain."

I said, "You're photographers?"

"I'm a developer." That was Mark. "My brother is a photographer."

Karl asked, "You model?"

"Not at all."

"What do you do?"

"Writer."

"Really? What do you write?"

"Ghostwriting. Trashy novels. The kind that are populated by louche characters wasting their days in brothels, strip clubs, and seedy bars. Nothing comparable to Simone de Beauvoir."

Mark said, "What a coincidence."

I asked, "What do you mean?"

"Karl does trashy photos. Probably the same louche characters you write about."

"Erotic." Karl flipped his brother the bird. "I do erotic photos from time to time."

Karl rubbed his sweaty tat, then wiped the sweat away from his nipples, that simple move, that sexy move made sweat drain down across his glorious and godlike eight-pack.

"I just came back from the UK."

I said, "I love the UK. Which part did you visit?"

"Was in Brixton and Central London."

"On holiday?"

"Work."

"Really?"

"Did a project for a book I'm putting together."

"Louche characters, I take it?"

"Classy and erotic."

"Like I said, louche characters."

"It's classy." The tattooed twin laughed, his laughter full and hearty, making his solid frame echo a joyous sensuality. "I did an American project two years ago, now doing an international thing. Mostly when I'm in town I do weddings, funerals, special events, headshots, stuff like that."

I swallowed. "Always . . . uh . . . always wanted to learn photography."

Karl asked, "You ever been to the W?"

"Once or twice. Nice bar."

Mark said, "There's a little function going on over there later."

Karl stretched, his abs looking like balls were implanted under his skin. "*Rolling Out* magazine. Photographer I know is having a little get-together."

"I see."

"If you're free, swing through." Karl gave that invite. "Starts around nine."

I said, "I have some writing to do. But I'll keep that in mind."

He was staring at my breasts, focused on my nipples. They ached, they were erect, pushing against my sports bra, little stone mountains. He moved his eyes from my chest.

I stared at his nipples too, then I looked down, in a glance saw his sex was hanging to the right.

Then I quickly put my eyes back on his.

I swallowed. Then I ignored the fact that the one with the tats had just asked me out.

I turned to Mark. "And you're a developer? As in developing photos?"

"Homes. Planned communities."

We started walking back down the ball of granite at the same time.

The twin with the tats led the way, some spots rugged, all uneven. The kind of trail that was better to hike up than climb down because hiking down a mountain this steep was bad on the knees. Every time I looked up I saw his tight backside and muscular back in front of me. The twin sporting the wedding ring walked down behind me. Whenever I looked back, I saw his package hanging to the right.

I evaluated them again, evaluated them as if they were the same person, as if they were one man. Beautiful complexions. Teeth like Hollywood movie stars. Seductive smiles.

They had me in the middle, like they were protecting me, surrounding me with their sex.

On the steep sections they helped me down. Not that I needed help, but I didn't refuse their unneeded assistance. Each time they touched me, a new wetness grew between my legs.

The sense of touch, so powerful, regardless of how simple the touch.

Rain started falling before we made it halfway down the mountain.

On the way down I saw the making of clear freshwater pools being formed by rainwater gathering in eroded depressions. Heard those depressions were home to unusual clam shrimp and fairy shrimp. The tiny shrimp appeared only during the rainy season, and I heard that the adult shrimp died when the pools dried up, leaving behind eggs to survive until the next rains.

They waited while I got down on my haunches and stared at nature.

Another electrical boom in the distance.

The married twin said, "We'd better hurry."

We moved on, made it to the bottom, crossed the train tracks, headed to the parking lot.

The air was getting thicker. Felt a telling breeze coming on, the herald to a storm.

The one with the tats said, "We're going to Five Points and hit the Flying Biscuit."

"Come on. Let us feed you."

"Nah. I'm going to shower and stay in. Get some writing done."

The married one backed off, then the one with the tats stepped up. "Well, hold up for a minute."

The rain had slowed, almost stopped, but the sky boomed again.

I motioned at the sky. "I have to go."

"We'll be right back."

Part of me wanted to bark and run into the woods, race across the red dirt and hide among the trees. They went to their vehicle and drove back to my car. The twin with the tats was driving a four-door Jeep Wrangler, a burgundy color with a black hardtop. By then I was still standing next to my car, towel in hand. They pulled up and stopped on the side of me. They had T-shirts and Atlanta Braves baseball caps on. They gave me their business cards.

The tatted twin held up a camera, an expensive Nikon.

He asked, "Do you mind?"

I dabbed my arms. "Knock yourself out."

From the inside of his ride he started snapping photos of me, his Nikon clicking over and over, his flash like lightning. The rain started again. A cool rain that made me tingle. I set free a soft moan. Rain fell on my skin. The rain felt good. I imagined steam rising from every pore as I cooled down.

I asked, "You finished?"

"Be natural. Don't look at the camera. Pretend I'm not here."

"Is that how you do it? When you're taking your erotic pictures."

"Just be natural. Pretend you're one of the louche characters in your trashy novels."

I didn't feel sexy, but he made me feel sexy. Made me feel sexy as hell.

The skies boomed again, the warning not to be misinterpreted.

I said, "You done, or do you want me to keep posing until I get struck by lightning?"

He laughed, then put his Nikon away.

I glanced inside his Jeep, saw a plastic batsman hanging from his rearview mirror.

I wiped rain from my face and said, "Cool batsman souvenir."

The one with the wedding ring leaned forward. "What do you know about cricket?"

"I love cricket. Mom played. I played some. Back home everyone plays cricket."

"Where are you from?"

"Trinidad. I'm a Trini."

They looked at each other and laughed hard.

The one with the tats said, "We were born in Barbados."

I yielded a smile. "Why do you have KENYA tattooed on your arm if you're from Little London?"

The photographer's smile lessened. Edges of pain surfaced, then went away, his true emotions veiled by a quick yet gentle expression, one that made him look vulnerable, human, and wounded.

He said, "We're Bajan."

"You guys don't sound Bajan."

The photographer smiled. "We moved around a lot but we grew up out here."

The married one laughed, then he mocked me. "You no Trini. No singsong in your voice."

"Some. Not like my mother. She took me to California when I was still a baby."

"Which part?"

"Grew up in L.A."

"You know Barbados?"

"I know about Crop Over. Cave Shepherd. St. Lawrence Gap."

"And we know about eating doubles. Carib beer. The borough of Chaguanas."

They laughed and smiled identical smiles. Those smiles as delicious as doubles.

The one with the tats motioned at his souvenir batsman. "Bought it in Antigua."

I nodded. "Wonderful island. Three hundred and sixty-five beaches."

"We were there in March. Went for the Stanford 20/20."

"So you saw Barbados lose to Trinidad."

"Just when you seemed to be so likable. No need to open old wounds."

"You were there for the Stanford 20/20? So was I."

"You and your boyfriend? Your husband?"

I smiled at his flirty question, his way of checking my status. I answered, "Me and my mother."

"Really?"

I asked, "Where did you guys stay?"

"Dickenson Bay. You?"

"Leased a condo at Jolly Harbour."

"Other side of the island."

"Yeah. Outside of cricket, we did a lot of snorkeling. Jet-skiing.

Windsurfing. Devil's Bridge. Pigeon Point Beach. Got massages at Touch Therapies. Spent a lot of time in the countryside."

"We were at Sandals."

Sandals was a couples-only resort. I knew he didn't stay there with his brother.

I swallowed, uneasy yet fascinated, introduced reality when I asked, "Was your wife with you?"

He paused. "She came down for a weekend."

"Your wife, did she enjoy 20/20?"

"She's not a cricket fan. Couldn't care less about the sport. Or any sport, for that matter."

"Too bad. What did she do on the island?"

"Same as everyone else. She sat on the beach. Took her to that rainforest one day."

"I took my mother to the rainforest. We did the suspension bridge. The cat walk. The wobbly bridge. Did all of the challenge courses."

"Small world."

"She left and you were probably liming with the diligent women at Wendy's or The Blue Diamond."

They laughed, had the expressions of men exposed, those naughty laughs telling me they were surprised I knew the names of the places men went to buy nude dances and lease working women.

The married one said, "You must've been following my brother all over the island."

The way he said that was exposing, competitive, and at the same time awkward and strange.

The skies boomed again. Driven by the sound, we all looked to the darkening skies.

The photographer said, "Swing by the W. We can talk about the islands. And soca."

His brother added, "And cricket."

"If it's not storming. If I'm not writing. If not, it was nice meeting both of you."

We waved and they drove away.

Identical twins.

Dual desires.

I stayed where I was, accepted the rain until I was wet all over. Wetter in some places than should be allowed. I eased inside my Z4, headed out of the park, took to I-78, then found my way to I-285. Rain came down hard. Changed from mild to treacherous in the blink of an eye.

The temptation was too great. The look in the photographer's eyes, his intentions were clear. He'd hiked up a mountain to find me. As if he knew what I was thinking. As if he knew my feelings.

Both had given me business cards. As if it was up to me to choose the flavor of my sin.

Or tuck my tail between my legs and run into the woods.

There was nothing more exciting than the possibility of a new lover.

Nothing more stimulating. Nothing as frightening.

But.

Yes. There was always a *but*.

The men who were easy on the eyes were never painless on the heart. I had learned that when I was attending Hampton, my senior year devastating and life-changing. Innocence destroyed forever, idealist views of love murdered, who I was before never attainable.

Life moved forward.

Rain. The bringer of floods. The diluter of fires.

I took the business cards in my hand, looked at each as if I was still staring at Karl and Mark, impure thoughts so strong as I whispered, "Be careful, Anaïs. Be careful of abnormal pleasures."

I let my window down, stuck my hand out into the rain, allowed my fantasies to slip through my fingers, gave their cards to the elements, to thunder and lightning, rainwater baptizing my strong desires.

FOUR

Soon I was passing Spaghetti Junction, where 285 and 85 crossed, a zillion lanes of traffic and off-ramps and overpasses. The rain was hard and steady, the drive slow and cautious.

I was on the phone, once again, with my mother, the Bajan twins on my mind, but those wicked thoughts were fading. Our conversation had picked up where we'd left off, talking about my new project. She was always interested in and supportive of my work, no matter what I did. Loved her for that.

My mother asked, "What got you thinking in the sci-fi direction?"

"I saw this article on dating, about how it had changed since women outnumbered men on the planet, and I thought, what if that wasn't by accident? What if there were more women for a *reason*?"

"Okay, O ye creative daughter. The sci-fi part?"

"Okay, so what if some super-advanced alien race was making it happen that way, making it so all of the men were gradually becoming extinct? What if they had found a way to manipulate the XY sex-determination system, knowing females have two of the same kind of sex chromosome?"

My mother said, "The homogametic sex."

"Right. And they know males have two distinct sex chromosomes."

"The heterogametic sex."

"Yeah. Somehow they make the Y in the male XY invalid. But the X is still good."

My mother laughed. "Who saves the day?"

"Angela Bassett."

"I love Angela."

"But?"

"Has to be a man. Preferably a young, white man *under* forty."

"Kill my dreams. Why can't it be a woman?"

I changed lanes, an accident up ahead.

She said, "You'd have to go Jodie Foster or Charlize Theron."

"And you call the South racist."

"Hollywood has an institutional racism the South has yet to realize."

"So Jodie or Charlize."

My mother made a contemplative sound, the soft grunt of a powerful woman who had been in more than a few meetings in Hollywood and understood the bottom line of that business better than most. In her mind, when it came to serious films, ethnic thinking had led many to the back of the unemployment line. She'd acted when she was a teenager in Trinidad, produced her first play when she was in her twenties, and had written some of everything over the years. I was only a shadow of her achievements.

She said, "Nia, why not rock it the other way?"

"What do you mean?"

"Why not make it so the *men* outnumbered women? Why not have the aliens control the XY thing the other way? Earth could become like a prison, all that testosterone in a massive war for survival. The few women left are cherished because they will be the Eves of the planet. Men killing each other to get to the last women alive, maybe having a lottery to pick a winner. Let the men be desperate for a change."

"Or even better, the men could start having battles in arenas like gladiators."

"You could have *young* yoni and *old* yoni, but they all kill for a night with the young yoni."

"Damn, mom. That's messed up. Brilliant, but messed up."

"It's a statement about our society. And how Hollywood puts mature women out to pasture. The mature women would be the sage characters, the more sensual beings, let that message shine through."

"Gotcha."

"Show how men go through a midlife crisis, get stupid, and leave their wives for younger women."

I laughed. "I'll add that to my notes."

"And if you use any of my input, I want my ten percent."

"Whatever."

"By the way . . ."

I asked, "What?"

"You said it's raining?"

"Cats and dogs."

"The weather is perfect here. And I'm going to Roscoe's for lunch and Crustacean's for dinner."

"I hope you get fat and sunburned."

"Don't hate, just pack and come back home, dammit. I'll get the mayor to give you a key to the city if you come back. I'll make them give you your own lane on the 405. Come home. I miss you."

"Miss you too."

We laughed. After the laughter died down we blew kisses and hung up.

My windshield wipers were working overtime as I changed from 285 to 75.

My music was, once again, inspired by the islands, Destra Garcia giving me her soca rhythms, my mind on my hunger, planning to go home and cook callaloo soup with fresh spinach and crab meat.

I sped down the off-ramp and it hit me that I hadn't checked my postal box in a few days, so instead of going right up Cobb Parkway toward Spring Road, my journey was modified.

I went left, up Cobb Parkway past Barnes & Noble and Cumberland Mall, then pulled into the strip mall that housed Circuit City, Toys "Я" Us, L.A. Fitness, and the Smyrna branch of the U.S. post office. I wanted to check my post office box before going home and shutting down, knowing I would be in for the night.

I wish I hadn't gone to the post office.

There was junk mail. And a really heavy letter, one that had the size and weight of a subpoena.

For a second I felt anger, wondered what the hell was going on now.

The envelope with the weight of a court order, it was a letter from the man I had left behind.

First a text message. Now this bullshit.

I stood in a trance, rain falling outside, holding a weighty message from Logan.

Every extremity went numb. His aroma was on the letter. He had invaded my senses. I moved my ponytail out of the way, rubbed the back of my neck, then put the letter down on the counter, rubbed my temples, felt an intense headache coming on, the damp floor squeaking underneath my damp running shoes as I paced, squeaking as I shook my head, squeaking as I tried to keep my blood pressure down.

I'd abandoned him on Beale Street, had left Memphis in May and put distance between us, using that distance and lack of communication to dilute whatever had happened between us. Seeing his name on the envelope, his address up in Memphis, inhaling his scent, all of that put me in a state of panic.

In a world filled with text messages, e-mails, faxes, he had broken down and sent me a letter.

I counted the pages. Six. There were six pages, filled top to bottom. Each word written on his personalized Strathmore envelopes and paper, crisp and conservative linen in the whitest of whites.

It started with a classic poem.

> *How do I love thee? Let me count the ways.*
> *I love thee to the depth and breadth and height*
> *My soul can reach . . .*

Then his words followed, his struggling to articulate what he felt for me inked on paper.

It was only romantic when that was what you wanted.

I did not want this. This was the opposite of romantic.

Your beauty is like an eclipse. Can't look at it directly without going blind.

I shook my head, aggravation swirling inside me.

The L-word was written on every page, as if the more he wrote the L-word down, the more it would make me feel as he felt. There was no such thing as love by osmosis. It was manipulative, criminal the way he abused the L-word. If that was how he felt, it was unsettling, because I didn't want him to feel this way. He knew I didn't want him to feel that way, not returning his calls was a clue, and he knew that I'd rather he felt the opposite of this way. Six pages. Six pages handwritten top to bottom.

Nauseous feelings rose up inside me.

I bent over until they went away.

I stared at the rain, frowning, shaking my head. I was in a trance. Across the parking lot was a billboard for the local news featuring The Jewell of the South. I focused on her, stared at her femme fatale eyes—eyes that looked strong, eyes that made me feel stronger than I was at the moment.

Damn, Logan. Let it go.

I had hoped that his desire for me had been cremated and scattered to the winds, set on fire by my negligence. I had let go. I didn't want to be brutal. I only wanted to be honest. But when it wasn't what the other person longed to hear, honesty tended to be brutal. Honesty sounded cruel. Honesty was evil.

The only other option was to lie. But a lie would not open the doors to my freedom. A lie would enslave me to what I was trying to escape. A lie did not benefit me in any positive way.

Sometimes trying to be honest without being brutal was like trying to swim and not get wet.

Thunder boomed as I ran through the downpour and raced to my car.

As soon as I closed the door, I picked up my cellular and called Logan. Chalk that up to irresistible impulse driven by a mixture of angst and rage.

Logan answered on the first ring. "Is this my Trini girl finally calling me back?"

I swallowed. He knew I had been born at Port of Spain. He knew my father had been killed before I was born, knew that a year later my mother had ended up meeting a hardworking and financially prudent man from Los Angeles, then my Trini days were over and my West Coast life began. Not many people knew that. Not many people knew much about me. I liked it that way.

I said, "Logan."

"I miss you."

His desperate and sincere tone halted me, made me, in that moment, feel massive guilt.

"Was worried about you, Nia. Been sick worrying about you."

"Just got your . . . your . . . the . . . that . . . the letter you sent, I just got it."

"What do you think?"

Guilt gave way to anger. Anger that wanted to make my peaceful spirit turn evil. But that was my frustration. A caged emotion that wanted to lash out like a riled tiger.

So many errors were in his letter. It killed me how educated people still didn't get that *your* was a possessive and *you're* meant *you are*. And the phrase wasn't *could care less*, it was *couldn't care less*. *Could care less* meant you still care. Right now I *couldn't care less* about Logan.

I wanted to tell that college graduate and successful business-man to learn the difference between *their* and *there*, that there was no letter *D* in congratulate, wanted to tell him to relearn the *I* before *E* rule, really wanted to point out *irregardless* wasn't a word, wanted to drive home, take a red pen and mark corrections all over his bloated six-page manifesto and mail it back to him, FedEx, over-night.

I took a breath. "I'm . . . we . . . look . . . we really should talk, to clear the air between us."

"Good. I'm in Atlanta."

I paused. "*What?*"

"I'm in the ATL."

"What are you doing in Atlanta?"

"Drove down in the rain."

"You drove four hundred miles in the rain? Why would you do that?"

"I need to see you. This has to be handled face-to-face."

I closed my eyes, rubbed my neck. "Are you really in Atlanta?"

"It's raining hard. Skies are black. Lots of thunder and light-ning."

"When did you get here?"

"Not too long ago."

"What are you doing here?"

"Was waiting to hear from you, left you a few messages, said I was coming down."

"Well, we hadn't agreed . . . even if you left a message . . . we hadn't talked about you coming down here. There is more to an agreement than you leaving a message, then doing what you want to do."

"Why haven't you answered my calls?"

Pressure mounted and I rubbed my temples, the answer to that question seemingly obvious.

What I felt was the opposite of pleasure. I had left him. I had sensed there was going to be an emotional earthquake, knew in advance, and had left without warning. Now that earthquake was here.

He asked, "Can I come over?"

"No."

"I've been driving close to seven hours on bad roads. Will you at least meet me?"

"Where are you?"

"Midtown."

I said, "You're in *Midtown*? Where in Midtown?"

"Atlantic Station."

"Okay. Then take 75 up to Howell Mill Road. That's about halfway."

This was my area. I didn't want him near my home, didn't want him to try and pull the I-need-a-place-to-crash-tonight routine. He had my mind all messed up. Had my thoughts all over the place.

He said, "Okay. Howell Mill Road. Then what?"

I paused, thought about it. "You know where Wal-Mart is?"

"I can find Howell Mill Road with my GPS. Where is Wal-Mart?"

"When you get off, go left. You'll see a brand-new plaza on the left. A Verizon and a Starbucks and a Ross are up top. Wal-Mart is down on the lower level, underground. Meet me down there."

"When?"

"Now."

I hung up.

My heart beat like I had just finished a grueling run.

I was afraid.

I had left his number programmed in my cellular so whenever he called, DNA LOGAN popped up on my screen. *Do Not Answer,*

Logan. I hadn't responded to Logan's calls, text messages, faxes, hadn't responded to any form of communication for almost a season. When I was done, I was done. Cold turkey if I had to. Up until the text message he had sent this morning, he'd stopped reaching out at least a month ago. Never expected to hear from him again. At least not this soon. Not like this. In my mind he had finally cut bait and moved on. Maybe because I had moved on a long time ago. I cursed. Here I go with this madness. I didn't want to deal with this insanity. I thought this part of my life was over. I thought I was free. But I was wrong. I had to go get my freedom. I had to fight for what I already owned.

As I drove through the storm I practiced what I was going to say, a preacher preparing her sermon. But I trembled as if I was a runaway, caught and imprisoned, going before the parole board.

My vocabulary was sufficient, my education superlative, but still I looked for the words that would make him understand that this was over. I wanted to tell him that if we continued, this relationship would become a caricature of a real relationship, and in the end he would hate me as I would hate him.

I wasn't a woman to him. I was something else to conquer. And once he conquered me I'd become ordinary in his eyes. And like the rest of the women he'd been involved with, I'd become superfluous.

As he had become superfluous to me.

I tried to understand me, why I did the things I did. I'd rushed into too many relationships, had promised loyalty because loyalty was expected, knowing that loyalty was not what I was capable of giving, not forever. Not since Hampton.

As far as I was concerned, man was the most disloyal creature on the planet.

I made it through the storm and went to that underground parking structure at Wal-Mart.

Logan's Range Rover pulled in right behind me, parked next to

me on my driver's side. My heartbeat was in my throat. He was on
his cellular; he motioned at his phone, then smiled at me. Veins rising in my neck, I smiled too, my smile being a frown turned upside
down.

Again I took a deep breath.

I eased out of my car. I didn't check myself in the mirror, didn't
arrange my hair, didn't wipe oil from my face, left myself the way
I wanted to look for him, the opposite of pretty.

Two women passed by, women who were pushing overloaded
Wal-Mart baskets, both were smoking and looked like creatures
who loathed the sun and lived on caffeine, nicotine, and Krispy
Kreme. They looked at me in my sweaty clothing, my ashen face, my
wild hair, and gave me a frown that said they despised people who
tanned well and looked like they lived on tofu and organic food.

Those women might outlive me. But in the end, my coffin will
be easier to carry.

Logan got out of his Range Rover, hanging up his cellular as he
came toward me.

The women in the Tri-State area looked at him and lost control.
Women who were financially strained, women who needed supple-
mental income to make ends meet, they did their best to get next to
him. He never had that power over me. I wasn't one of the women
in the world who was desperate to be taken care of. I only needed
pleasure. In the end, his sex had released liquid boredom inside the
latex barrier between my thighs, his best stroke had made yoni
yawn, close her dry lips, and fall into a deep slumber.

Logan could not please me the way I desired to be pleased. Logan could not fuck.

How do you tell a man he is sexually incompetent without making it seem as if you are attacking his ego? He claimed he could buy
and sell the better parts of Memphis's Shelby County whenever he
felt like it. He had a large home, expensive cars, tailored clothing,
was more popular than Jerry Lawler. None of that impressed me. I

grew up around oceans and Hollywood celebrities—the real celebrities—saw them walking through my home with their shoes off, saw them sipping beers and watching games in my den. I had my own money, so I had my own economic power, lacked desperation and need, and with financial independence came a new kind of clarity. I didn't have to settle for less than I deserved. I didn't need to tether myself to any man for financial reasons.

He came too close, touched my arm right above the elbow, and I felt the opposite of moist.

He touched me on my arm and I yanked away.

His smile lessened as his eyes widened.

I shook my head.

He thought that touch would reawaken some desire inside me, some desire for him that had never taken root. He didn't understand me. When I was no longer attracted to a man, when he was no longer fulfilling me, I couldn't imagine him in a sexual way. He saw that in my eyes. He saw that in my body language. I felt sorry that he was hurting, but there was no attraction, the thrill was gone.

He took a deep breath, nodded, his lips tight, vulgarities dancing in his eyes.

"Logan . . . look . . ."

"What did I do wrong?"

"Why are you here?"

"Are you seeing somebody else?"

"That's not the issue."

"Are you?"

"I'm not answering that."

"I drove down in this storm to see you."

"I didn't ask you to."

"Nia . . . I'm here."

"What do you want, Logan?"

"What did I do wrong?"

I took a hard breath. "Nothing. You didn't do anything wrong."

"I love you."

"Maybe that's the problem. I don't love you, Logan."

"Maybe not now. But do you think, maybe if we gave it some more time, do you think you could?"

"Waiting for me to love you would be like waiting on Santa Claus."

It looked like he was about to fall apart.

I felt the same way. This was mentally exhausting, took more energy than running a marathon.

A white teenager passed by, leaning to the side like he wanted to be pimp of the year, his car packed with his white friends, windows up, but his music so strong we could hear his black idols peppering the air with foul language, a duet that gave equal time to misogynistic and misandrist lyrics.

The genocidal music faded like some relationships never would.

I asked Logan, "Are we done?"

He rubbed his neck for a moment, then cleared his throat, said, "I left some stuff at your place back in Memphis."

"I know. They're at my townhouse."

"When can I come get my things?"

"We'll arrange something."

"Can I come now?"

"Not now. We'll . . . I have your address."

"So I'm here and I can't come by to pick it up?"

"No."

"You shacking up or something?"

Again I rubbed my temples. "Look, Logan, I can FedEx it all to you first thing in the morning."

"FedEx."

"Let's not make this any more painful than it needs to be. No need to drag this out."

He chuckled. "No need to drag this out. Is that right?"

"No more than it's already been dragged out."

He nodded. I did the same.

The things he had left at my place in Memphis, I had already put them in a ragged box. His name was written on that box in bold letters: LOGAN. I had already unmarked my territory. I had dragged that box with me when I moved, kept it in the garage, left the things he had left behind amongst things unwanted.

The rain eased up. It didn't stop. Just eased up.

Logan shifted. "You make it sound like I didn't mean a damned thing to you."

"We've come this far . . . we met by chance . . . had *wonderful* experiences together . . . for what it's worth, I would really like it if we could end this in a kind way . . . in a way that allowed us to be friends."

"Friends?"

"Yeah. Friends. Platonic friends. Without benefits." I took a sharp breath. "Let some time go by, when you're not so intense, and maybe we'll reconnect as platonic friends."

Wonderful experience. Losing benefits. I had to sound like an executive from a Fortune 500 company firing an incompetent employee in the mailroom.

He frowned at me like he wanted to fill me up with his ardent craving, the craving that had made him drive almost four hundred miles of two-lane highway from Memphis through Birmingham to Atlanta.

He said, "You've always been different."

"You say that like it's a bad thing."

"Always been sarcastic and difficult."

A long stretch of silence assaulted me. I wasn't being honest. I wasn't telling the truth. Not the truth that lived inside me. It remained veiled in sarcasm, was given indirectly by lack of phone calls and absence. I had avoided this moment, its cruelty. The truth was an ugly pimple on the face of a beautiful lie. I was tired of avoiding him, tired of mind-wrestling on a level that was beneath me, beneath all I strived to become, exhausted by this beautiful lie, now it was time to acknowledge the truth.

With a sigh preceding my words, I said, simply, "We're not equally yoked."

"Equally yoked?"

"We're not . . . you don't do it for me."

"Bullshit."

"I have submitted to my desires and had new experiences while I was with you."

"Submitted to your desires? What the hell does that mean?"

"To you it would mean that I was unfaithful to you."

That paused him.

He said, "You're telling me you cheated."

"I'm telling you that I followed my desires, let them lead me toward new experiences."

"How many times?"

"Twice."

"Twice . . . with the same guy?"

"No."

He gritted his teeth. "Two men."

"Yes."

"Two goddamn men."

"Yes."

"In my city."

"You don't own Memphis."

"I was born there."

"And I was a taxpaying citizen at the time."

People passed by us pushing baskets filled with provisions from Wal-Mart.

He asked, "Who?"

"None of your business."

He shook his head, sucked his lips. "Is that all you need? To be screwed?"

"I was unhappy and I needed to feel good."

He shook his head.

I said, "We aren't equally yoked. Let's just leave it at that and move on."

"What does equally yoked have to do with you having sex with other men?"

"In bed. We're not equally yoked. What I want you can't give me. Out of bed, we have had fun. But it was the kind of fun where other things entertained us. The games, the concerts. But the more I think about it, if you can't understand me on a mental level, we're not equally yoked there either."

"The way you scream and holler in bed, and I don't satisfy you?"

"Just because I allow myself to have an orgasm doesn't mean I am happy."

"What do you need in order to be satisfied?"

"I don't know what I need."

My hands were shaking. Sweat dampened the back of my neck, my heart beating fast.

He was frustrated. "What about real intimacy, companionship, being with somebody you trust?"

"Tell me this, am I the only woman you've slept with since you've been with me? Am I? Can you answer that? I'm not trying to chastise you, all I'm saying is that I understand, and I'm asking, can you understand me? Can you understand what it feels like to feel human, to have desires you wish to explore? Because the other women you were with, that was a desire you chose to explore."

"What other women?"

"I've never been faithful to any man I've been with. Not since college."

"Why are you telling me this?"

"Because I know they weren't one hundred percent faithful to me either. You betray. I betray. We betray each other. I knew I couldn't give them everything they needed, not all the time, not when what they needed was beyond me. Don't look at me like that. Don't look at me like I'm crazy."

There was a hard pause between us. People passed by, rushing out of Wal-Mart, the smell of rain and asphalt mixing in the air, every inhale harder than the one before, the air so thick and damp.

Logan spoke with a calmness that made a mountain of goose bumps raise on my arms. He said, "You were with two men. In my city. While you were my woman."

"I might share myself with others, but I will always belong to me."

"You *shared* yourself with two motherfuckers while you were with me."

Logan made a harsh step toward me. Then he looked around. People were staring.

Logan went to his Range Rover, head down, his steps slow, heavy, shaking his head as he got inside. I interpreted that as the white flag of surrender. His engine started and I took a deep breath.

His reverse lights came on and he backed out, headed toward the ramp, left without looking back.

He sped away, his Range Rover slashing through rain, his tires splashing fallen water.

My inhales were difficult, as if I was being strangled.

I sat in my car, shaking, letting Logan go to wherever he was going. My head ached. My nerves were too bad to drive. Tears formed in my eyes. My lips trembled. I clenched my teeth and screamed. Then I leaned over the steering wheel. Salty tears fell. I created my own thunder and rain.

I didn't want to be alone. I didn't want to die alone, somewhere in a bed with some incurable illness and no lover at my side, or living alone and dying abruptly only to be found dead days, maybe weeks after I had made that unexpected transition to whatever destination we had after this existence.

No, I didn't want to be alone, not in the end, not when it was time. But I didn't want to be with him. Not with Logan. I didn't want to end this existence with him staring in my eyes at the dimming of my day. And I didn't want him to die holding my hand when he experienced the same eventual moment.

If I was being selfish, then that selfishness was my right. I had no husband. I had no children. Right now selfishness meant I was loving myself first, taking care of my needs the way I felt they should be taken care of. I didn't want to sacrifice myself for anyone who wouldn't sacrifice themselves for me.

Then why in the fuck did I feel so goddamn guilty?

Confusion angered me. Made me feel inept. Made me lash out in defense. Made me primal. Confusion meant there was no control. My mind was floundering, each thought collapsing.

I jumped when there was a tap on my window.

Logan was back.

I opened my mouth, prepared to start screaming obscenities.

But it wasn't Logan. It was two of the members of Wal-Mart security.

What they saw in my face scared them, made them back away from my window.

I told them I was fine, waved them away, told them to leave me alone.

They did.

I started my car, drove away, rain falling hard as I passed the line of stores leading to Howell Mill Road, my eyes spying through my fast-moving windshield wipers for Logan, searching for the man who felt that loving me made me owe him a debt, my eyes not finding him in the storm.

He was gone.

This had become the cycle of my life, collecting wonderful experiences, having my freedom threatened, fleeing like a war criminal, leaving body bags everywhere I went.

I never wanted to hurt anybody. It just seemed to end up that way. We damaged each other. People. We always damaged each other.

I just wanted to be free.

It was my right to be free.

My right to explore my sensuality and sexuality unrestricted by any man.

Tears fell from my eyes like rain. My head ached. I needed a fucking drink.

I needed to escape this pain and find pleasure.

FIVE

Nighttime was when the primal urges struggled to take control.

Nighttime was the time when the unhappy became restless.

It was nighttime.

I was stressed. I was unhappy. I was restless.

By ten P.M. Georgia state troopers had the interstates lit up with their flashing lights, a ton of speeders had been busted by radar and pulled over on I-285 between I-75 and Georgia 400, the 400 also being known as the Alpharetta Autobahn. I kept my speed right at the limit until I exited at Ashwood/Dunwoody, headed toward the scent of apple martinis.

The W Hotel was across from the far end of the Perimeter Mall, just shy of California Pizza Kitchen. I eased around the roundabout, saw the arm was up on the visitor lot, decided to save the valet money and went into that lot, sat in the car, Alexander O'Neal singing "If You Were Here Tonight" on Sirius, checked my makeup, reapplied lip gloss, thanked God for MAC and how it made my skin look.

Every W was so sexy and sophisticated, attracted beautiful people. It was a great place for hanging out on my laptop or lounging. Loved the way the lobby was laid out like an airy living room with free-form seating. The low tables were sexy as hell. Everyone was already here, the crew from *Rolling Out* magazine and their followers sashaying and peacocking around with drinks in hand, flirting hard, relaxing on the sofas, laughing, and schmoozing. Hundreds of votive candles had the first floor lit up.

I searched for familiar faces and didn't see the twins. Maybe they didn't come. If they did, I doubted if they would flirt with me. They might not remember me, or recognize me since I was in decent clothing. My hair was done. Face made up. And I was three inches taller. There were a lot of women here. Attractive women of all sizes and complexions. Too much competition in a city where the women outnumbered the men about twenty to one. Women with bodies like strippers and ass measurements that equaled their waists plus twenty inches. Even if they didn't swing from a pole, they owned the physiques that the churchgoing men, rappers, and politicians loved to decorate with dollar bills.

I looked around. Loved that Miami feeling of the place, the colorful and artsy furniture. Loved the way they had couches on the patio, loved the large cushions on the furniture.

Loved the sexual energy. Orgasmic desires crackled like an electrical storm.

I felt good. Loved to get dressed up. The MAC makeup, the perfume, the sexy clothes, it was fun to walk into a room, hips moving with the confidence of Natalie Portman in the final moments of the movie *Closer*, hair down as if to say I was uninhibited, and see the effect I had on men.

A nice-looking man walked over to me. Wavy hair. Freckles.

He said, "Would you like to go to room 521?"

"Excuse me?"

"Would you like to come up to my suite with me?"

"I'm not your type."

"And what is my type?"

"Women who look hip and chic but in reality are pathetically lonely and desperate. And broke. Smiling women sitting on their low self-esteem, women who never had attention given to them in a healthy way. Women who confuse emotional abuse with affection. That's your type."

"I'd love to drink your bathwater."

"I piss in my bathwater."

He walked away, headed toward a group of women, ready to continue his hunt.

Alcohol diluted shyness and made fools of once-noble men.

I smiled at a few people, found an open spot at the bar. Ordered an apple martini. Men would come over now. Men were smart. Smart enough to let a woman order a drink first before making a move. If I were a man I'd do the same. Wouldn't waste a dime, let alone ten dollars on a stranger.

Sexual predators disguised as perfect gentlemen. Gold diggers disguised as respectable ladies.

I looked around the room, witnessed all the sexual arousal. Human beings were capable of sexual arousal and it had nothing to do with the urge to procreate. That made every day mating season.

Sometimes I wondered if primal needs, if sex was the only thing that united men and women. The need to seek pleasure. The urge to procreate. Take away those needs and each sex would render the other useless, pointless. Without desire one sex would have destroyed the other a billion years ago. Men would've tossed all of us women to the dinosaurs—if we hadn't poisoned and castrated them first.

I laughed at myself. Laughed hard and shook my head.

When I started thinking like that it was time for me to head back home.

Before I could get up, a brother sat on the barstool next to mine. Jeans, black shoes, black blazer, hip designer T-shirt that had hues of brown and orange to make a solar design, like a smiling sun about to go supernova. He smelled nice. Very nice. He smelled of Egoiste, an aroma that enhanced his masculinity, the oriental and woody fragrance sending his pheromone level into the red zone.

In the smoothest baritone voice he said, "Your hair looks good."

"Thanks."

"All yours?"

"Watered it and grew it myself."

"Are you a model?"

"No. But thanks."

"Buy you a drink, Miss . . . ?"

"Bijou."

"French?"

"My stepfather is . . . was French."

"So you're bilingual?"

"*Oui*. Some Spanish as well."

"Trilingual."

"*Sí*."

"Can I buy you a drink, Miss Bijou?"

"I don't know. Can you?"

"*May* I buy you a drink, Miss Bijou?"

I swallowed sinful thoughts, my leg doing a nervous bounce. "Working on this one."

He asked, "Is Miss Bijou waiting on someone special?"

"Everybody's either waiting on somebody or looking for somebody."

He smiled a confident smile. He had charisma. And he knew he had charisma.

I looked at his left hand, didn't see a wedding ring. Still wasn't sure if he was Karl or Mark, just knew he was one of the twins, all dressed up, in my personal space, engaging me in a flirting game.

I played along, thrilled to be sitting next to him, impressed that he dressed so well. The sense of smell was one to be reckoned with. His Egoiste aroma forever enchanting and maddening.

I asked, "What're your intentions?"

"What do you mean?"

"Seems like you're trying to get me filled with alcohol, mister. And why?"

"Just being a nice guy."

I laughed. "You're being very obvious."

"Am I?"

"Yes, you are."

"No more obvious than you."

I chuckled. "Am I?"

"Very. Your body language. Says you're available. Says come here, talk to me."

My mild laughter ended with an easy smile. "Okay. Then talk to me."

"Things bad between you and your boyfriend?"

"Didn't say I had a boyfriend."

"So you don't have a boyfriend."

"Didn't say that either."

"If you have one, things must be bad."

"And how did you come to that conclusion?"

"You're at a bar. Alone."

"So are you."

"You have that beautiful and sexy dress on, that slit that shows just enough of your leg, a leg that is toned I might add, the cleavage, all of that on display so whoever comes over will know what's up."

"Oh, please."

He asked, "Beautiful woman like you, why are you still single?"

"Just am. No laws against that. Why are you single? Never found the right girl?"

"I've tried."

"Or are you just a guy who can't settle down with one woman?"

"Like I said, I've tried."

"Tell me anything."

"Why would I do that?"

"Because you want an application."

"Would rather have a coochie coupon instead of an application."

"Bet you would love to get a coupon."

"And I'll say what I have to in order to get one."

"At least you're honest."

We laughed, his the laugh of Barbados, mine rooted in the sing-song rhythm of Trinidad.

He said, "Nia Simone Bijou."

"You remembered."

"Of course. Your name has a nice ring to it."

He didn't wear a wedding ring. Didn't seem like the one who would be interested in conversations about Sartre and existentialism. He was the haughty one with the kind hands of an artist.

I said, "Karl, right? I am being sexually harassed by Karl, right?"

"Good memory."

"Hard to tell who you are with your clothes on."

He laughed. "Should be easy."

"How so?"

"I'm the good-looking brother. Mark is the ugly one."

"I'll make a note of that."

His eyes were all over my body, my hair, my clothing. Amazed by my transformation.

He said, "You made it back out. In the rain."

"Was bored, decided to get out. In the rain."

I didn't ask him where his brother was tonight. Wanted to, but didn't.

Bird in the hand.

Still.

Married men were safer. You knew what it was about, so your heart was protected.

I asked, "How was the rest of your day?"

"Spent the evening on the phone with a client. Have to drive to Greensboro to work."

"Greensboro?"

"North Carolina. Other side of Charlotte. New client wants me to come do a photo shoot."

"Louche characters?"

"Probably. Customer wants fantasy shots. Got my info off my Web site, we agreed on a fee for doing erotic shots. Yeah. Louche. Whatever pays the bills, as long as it's legal. I'm not one to judge."

"Bet it would be pretty interesting to tag along and see how you work."

"You could. It's a lot of setup and waiting. It would probably bore you to death."

"Doesn't matter. I'm a writer. We like to see everything."

His cellular rang. He looked at the caller ID, put his phone away.

I chuckled.

Single men, too many games. But it was always a buyer's market for them.

In the end, either you wanted too much or they wanted too little.

Would've asked about Mark, but the flirty game Karl just played, well, it turned me on.

I sipped on my apple martini.

We engaged in small talk. Flirty small talk. Eye contact. Engaged in the kind of conversation that was more about body language than content. Content was irrelevant when body language, the way he shifted, the way I shifted, the way he touched me on my arm occasionally, the way I touched his hand when it was appropriate, the proximity of our bodies, that was the true conversation. Words moved back and forth between us, words that owned no true value because in this moment we were more than words.

He rubbed my leg with his middle finger. "Let me guess."

"What?"

"You were the homecoming queen, right?"

"You're pushing it."

"You look exotic enough to be homecoming queen."

"You are really pushing it."

"Your personality is magnetic. And you're smart."

"And I'm still at a bar, alone, sipping on a drink with a man I met this morning."

"Let me guess."

"Go right ahead."

"Pretty woman like you, bet the captain of the basketball team took you to the prom."

"Football team. Had a thing for football players. He was my first heartbreak."

"Where is that heartbreaking fool now?"

"Who knows?"

"Guess he's not famous, huh?"

"Guess not."

"You dumped him?"

"He . . . he met another cheerleader. New yoni, you know how that goes."

"Yoni?"

"You might know it as a vagina."

"Oh, you're talking about your pussy."

I slapped his hand. "I hate that word."

"I love pussy."

I laughed at him. "Yoni is the Kama Sutra word. Sounds less vulgar."

"You're into Kama Sutra?"

"I'm into a lot of things."

"Are you into vulgar?"

"When I need to be. Vulgar can be good."

"So you call your pussy a yoni."

"No, I just refuse to call my yoni a pussy."

"Sounds like Noni juice."

"Better than Noni juice."

"What do you call a penis?"

"A dick."

"Why no intellectual word for dick?"

"There is. Lingam. One of the Kama Sutra words is lingam."

"Why don't you use the intellectual word lingam?"

"Because dicks aren't intellectual."

"Are you in the castration business?"

"Sure am. Be nice and I'll show you my collection."

He laughed. "You're cool."

"Glad you noticed."

"I've noticed everything about you."

"Have you?"

"Every mole, every freckle."

"I don't have moles or freckles."

"That's what I noticed."

"Is that right?"

"Not many women can inspire a man to hike a mountain to get her number."

"You didn't get my number."

"Night's still young. Your fine ass."

"Okay, change the subject before my head swells up and explodes."

"What shall we discuss?"

"Colonization of our countries."

"Oh, God. We'd be here all night talking about colonization."

Our homelands were paradises for tourists. Violence had grown, guns in places that didn't manufacture guns, killings on islands that never had killings. We chatted about how we had to buy land to keep the English from coming in and taking over, the weight of the British pound crushing the value of the local currency. The English were buying the better parts of our lands one condo at a time, buying land that the hardworking people who lived there couldn't afford to own but were hired to keep clean.

I said, "Trinidad should be owned by Trinidadians. Others who wish to stay there long-term should be able to lease the land, should be able to improve the land and build on the land, but never own the land, because if they do, in the end we will end up leasing our country, our own land, from foreigners."

"I want to see Barbados become more independent. Not so dependent on tourism."

"Well, most of the islands depend heavily on tourism."

"But what's jacked up is, in an effort to keep up with other countries, mainly America, the islands are losing their own culture. The islands import outsiders' culture but outside of rum, sugar, fruit, and a few other things, outsiders don't have to import ours, not to survive. Am I making any sense?"

I smiled and tried to help him make his point. I said, "Cocacolonization."

"What is that?"

"Where a country's indigenous culture is eroded by a corporate mass culture."

"Same as cultural imperialism."

"Only with cocacolonization the people don't have to relocate to the colonized country. But you see the cultural signals, symbols, food, entertainment, and values taking over the colonized country."

"Cocacolonization."

"Yep. Outsiders modify your culture, change you into them, and they never have to leave home."

We became frustrated islanders, talked about how America was an arrogant bitch. How she took football, a game that was played with feet only, called it soccer, then invented a game that used *hands* and called it *foot*ball. Now America wanted to modify the rules of soccer to fit her needs and give it four quarters so they could get more commercials into a game it had shown no real love for since its inception.

Karl said, "You see how they have David Beckham calling football soccer."

"Now that is blasphemous."

"I just hope they keep away from cricket."

"Leave my cricket alone. And don't rename it something as stupid as *soccer*."

Before I knew it I was two apple martinis deep. Conversation flowing, becoming lighter, less political and more personal, personal because now we were comfortable with each other. Inhibitions coming down with every sip. Staring at Karl, unable to stop smiling. While we sipped our mood enhancers, he wouldn't stop telling me how pretty I looked. The heat of July lived between my thighs.

I told him, "Love your tats."

"Used to mess around with this wild-ass girl who loved to get inked."

"This wild-ass girl have a name?"

"Kenya."

"Kenya. The name tattooed on your arm."

"Yeah."

"Is that her picture on your body too?"

He paused. "Yeah."

I asked, "Are you still involved with her?"

Another pause. "Haven't heard from her in a while. Years, actually."

I asked, "Why did you let her go?"

He gave me a damaged smile. "Mind if we change the subject?"

"Sorry. Was just asking."

He turned me on, his vagueness aroused me, made me want to demystify him the way men longed to demystify me. But I didn't want to question him in a way I didn't want to be questioned. I wanted this to remain zipless. Zipless wouldn't drive six hours in a thunderstorm. Zipless wouldn't send six-page letters or text messages. Zipless wouldn't leave anyone with a broken heart.

Yes. Zipless was safe.

I finished my drink, saw an open spot away from the bar, took Karl's hand, led him to the lounge area where we sat on the plush sofa, cuddled up next to each other, in a crowded room, but still alone. My body was tingling, every vein felt electrical, his words, no matter how insignificant, stirred me.

He had seduced me and didn't know it.

I was seduced and didn't let it show.

I asked, "Why did you hike up to the top of the mountain?"

"Had to meet you."

"Did you? And why did you want to find me?"

"You looked so good when I passed you."

"Such a liar. I was sweaty, smelly, skin was dry, wearing mosquito repellant and no makeup."

"Well, what I saw looked good to me."

"Bet you say that to all the sweaty women with chapped lips and dry skin."

"You stand out. Even like that, you looked better than any woman in this lobby."

The tone of his voice. His aroma. The way he looked. I leaned closer to him.

After seeing him, hearing his baritone voice, inhaling his aroma, the touching began.

Four of the five senses had been completed.

The only sense that hadn't been completed was the sense of taste.

He was barely touching my lips. Barely. It was so sensual. I was enchanted. Totally enthralled. His eyes made me believe he was just as spellbound by my gentle touch.

"You look good." He grinned. "Didn't realize your hair was that long. Or that wavy."

"Why, thank you."

"Nice hair. Like it wavy. Au naturel. Feels good between my fingers."

"You are on a roll. More, more, more."

"You smell wonderful."

"Envy Me."

"Envy you?"

"My perfume . . . it's called Envy Me."

"I'd rather eat you than envy you."

"You are so nasty."

"I can stop."

People were near us; talking, drinking, seductive music playing over transpicuous stares.

I said, "I'm trying to stay a good girl."

"Nothing wrong with that."

He leaned in to kiss me.

I didn't stop him. Didn't encourage him. Didn't stop him either.

Tongues danced a slow, unhurried dance. We kissed endlessly.

His hand moved to my breasts, touched the right one, then his finger circled the nipple on the right. I shifted into his naughtiness. His hand moved down my body. Settled between my legs. Massaged my heat. I pulled my bottom lip in, bit down, tried to ignore the fire down below.

He whispered, "Wish I could kiss these lips . . . and . . . taste . . . those lips . . . at the same time."

"Say what you mean. And mean what you say."

"Wish I could eat your yoni . . ."

"Eat my yoni."

"Wish I could tongue you down and eat your yoni."

I shivered, mental images creating soft moans.

"Would you like that?"

Again I shivered, euphoria rising.

"You ever had your yoni eaten while somebody else kissed you?"

I shook my head, licked my lips, his words like cocaine, his words making me high.

"Think you'd like that? To have me kiss you like this . . . and to have your yoni licked like this . . . to have your clit sucked . . . the way I suck your tongue . . . get finger-fucked . . . all at once."

"Maybe."

Moans joined with my shivers. His language was direct and barbaric, stimulating. He was Henry Miller, his prose a stream of vulgarities. He kissed me, his kiss brief and poetic, an erotic haiku.

Our energy exchange was disrupted without warning. Someone stopped and stood over us.

Black suit. Black shirt. Nice shoes. Expensive shoes. The type of shoes Logan wore.

In an angered tone he snapped, "You're in a hotel cheating on me?"

SIX

With reluctance I looked up, nervous, trembling, not knowing what I would do.

He snapped, "Who is this ugly sonofabitch you're snuggled up with?"

It was Karl's brother. The developer. The married twin. It wasn't Logan.

My frown became a smile of surprise, then belly laughter.

Karl said, "Thought the wife wasn't letting you out to play tonight."

The hater in Karl came to life. Childhood envy existed in his eyes.

I said, "Well, hello, Mark."

Mark laughed at me, ignored his sibling, did that as if he wasn't in the mood for rivalry.

I scooted over and Mark sat on the other side of me.

As the techno music changed to R&B, I inhaled him. Everything about him was fresh and crisp and sophisticated. His scent was that of a man who had just stepped out of a shower and sprayed AXE Phoenix all over his toned body, his aroma magnetic and stimulating, crisp and green herbal notes with warm undercurrents of sandalwood and spiced rum. I breathed him in, felt heady, an invigorating rush.

Just like that, I was turned on even more.

Was turned on by Karl. And by Mark.

I became so nervous. So nervous I had another drink. Karl drank Hennessy. Mark had Riesling.

So many lines had been crossed, but I was far from the point of no return.

I slowed everything down, removed myself from Karl's heat, again being cordial.

I asked, "Which one of you was born first?"

Karl pointed at Mark.

I asked, "What sign are you guys?"

Mark said, "I'm a Libra."

Karl said, "I'm a Scorpio."

Laughter rose from me as I leaned back, waiting for the punch line to the joke.

Mark said, "I was born at 11:58 P.M."

Karl nodded. "I was born at three minutes after midnight."

I said, "You guys have different birthdays?"

They nodded.

Karl said, "I held out a few minutes so I could get my own friggin' day."

I laughed.

Mark asked, "What's your sign?"

"Gemini."

"The sign of the twins." Karl laughed. "Now that's funny."

The photographer touched me with his Scorpio hands. Tingles spread like a wildfire.

I touched the one born under the sign of balance and invited him into our world.

First we were laughing.

Flirting.

Drinking.

I asked, "Where did you guys go to college?"

Karl told me he went to Morehouse. Mark went to the University of Georgia.

I said, "Surprised you two didn't go to the same college."

Mark said, "We had to get away from each other."

Karl nodded.

I sensed something going on between them, some darkness beyond the playful banter.

I said, "It's hard to tell the difference between you two."

Karl said, "Told you it was easy. He's an ugly version of me."

"You wish. I was born first."

"I'm taller."

"Bullshit."

"I beat your ass around Stone Mountain."

"I can bench-press two-seventy. What you pumping, Karl?"

I jumped in, laughing, "Boys, boys. Take it down a level, can you?"

They laughed, but that brotherly tension remained.

They talked to me, laughed with me, acted like two teenage boys who had a crush on their teacher. They gave me so much attention. I loved it. Absorbed it as I evaluated them. They were the same, yet different. The conversation shifted from us and we began talking about people. A hundred conversations were going on around us. Men who looked like clean-shaven relatives of the Confederate leaders carved in Stone Mountain, old white men who had to be here on business were doing their best to get conversations with the melanin-filled women, blue eyes focused on the ones that had at least a twenty-inch discrepancy between their waists and asses. The astonished looks on their faces said they were in a sizzling hotel and would love to sample forbidden fruit, at least for one night, and would pay whatever it cost just to have it. Most were visitors from other states, from other countries, would never see each other again, so it was on, full speed ahead, only an elevator ride away from a nice bed, an overnight fantasy that might become a regret brighter than tomorrow's sun.

We engaged in light touching, nothing too obscene, started talking dirty after dark.

I said, "Like I said before, I'm trying to be a good girl."

Mark smiled.

Karl sipped his Hennessy. "She wants to kiss, have her yoni eaten at the same time."

"Yoni?"

"Calls her pussy her yoni."

"Is that French?"

"She says it's a Kama Sutra thing."

"Yoni. Sounds like Noni juice."

"Same thing I said."

"So she calls it her yoni."

"Check it out. She wants every lip on her body kissed at once."

"Hypothetical." I laughed, felt exposed. "That was hypothetical."

Mark asked, "Are you a good kisser?"

"Only one way to find out."

His hand came up to my face, to my chin, brought me to him.

Then I was kissing the married twin. Was slow-kissing a married man in a lobby filled with music, colorful lights, and a million conversations. I was deep into a fantasy, moaning and groaning, my heat exposed. His kiss was pure cane sugar. Sweet enough to give me diabetes.

When we stopped, I fanned myself.

My eyes went to Karl, these lips curving upward, gave a picture-perfect smile to the photographer. Karl smiled, his smile telling me he was waiting on the verdict, who was the best kisser.

I said, "What the hell is this, some sibling rivalry issues or what?"

Mark said, "He's hated me since he lost the race out of our mother's womb."

Karl huffed. "You did a Zola Budd and tripped me."

"Whatever."

"You tripped me and I went down like Mary Decker Slaney did in the '84 Olympics."

We laughed.

Mark rubbed my leg, rubbed it up and down, thought he was about to ease up my dress and try to stir me with his finger. He took my hand and we stood up. Chills moved up and down my spine.

I asked, "Where are we going?"

He winked at me, then took me out on the floor.

I asked again, "Where are you taking me?"

"To dance."

"Nobody's dancing."

"I'm not a follower."

We danced to a slow song . . . my arms around him . . . rocking back and forth . . . him holding me close like he was claiming me . . . let him put his arms around me . . . we danced and danced . . .

He said, "Have you ever seen the play *No Exit*?"

"Sartre?"

He grinned. "Yeah, Sartre."

I smiled. "No. But I've read *No Exit* and *The Devil and the Good Lord*."

We chatted about Sartre without really talking about Sartre, our words hot and flirtatious despite the conversation being about an atheist, a communist, a man who rejected the Nobel Prize for Literature.

We held each other, whispered things about Sartre, then whispered back and forth about Simone de Beauvoir, our conversation remaining on the Ambassador and Ambassadress of Existentialism.

My mind was on fire. Mental orgasms unseen, coming in rapid succession. My body reacting to the stimulation that was occurring inside my head. My mind being seduced one whisper at a time.

I remained exhilarated. I was wet. I was tingling.

The photographer came and interrupted our world ... moved his brother out of the way ... moved intellect and politics out of my way and took over ... gave me lust and desire ... danced with me ... held me close ... my head on his chest ... inhaling his fragrance ... his pheromones ... his sex against my body ... his body chemistry mixing with my hormones, creating a Molotov cocktail of desire.

We went back to the sofa, sat down with his brother, again me in the middle. Each side of the Gemini wanted its own lover. Strange how they felt like, sounded like, seemed like the same person. And at the same time I felt like two people, both in conflict, one wanting to go, one wanting to stay.

I asked, "Okay, which one of you is interested in me?"

The photographer said, "We both are."

The developer shrugged. "It's your call."

I leaned back between them. Let them surround me. It was like being between Apollo and Zeus. I looked at one. Then I looked at the other. Identical. It was the same man twice.

I said, "What if I don't want to decide? What if both of you are like ... one person to me?"

The developer gave me an understanding smile. "But we're not one person."

The photographer nudged me. "It's your call."

"What if I want you both? You good at an equal distribution of what is being offered?"

"Meaning?"

"Are you good at sharing? Have you ever shared?"

They smiled slow and easy. Those smiles unreadable, magnifying my nervousness.

I said, "Would be great to have two good-looking men please me."

The developer said, "Whatever you want. Whatever pleases you."

The developer's words made me smile, made nervousness lessen as desire swelled.

I said, "Where?"

The brothers looked at each other. Then they did the funniest thing. Very comical. They did the rock-paper-scissors thing. In that moment I could see how they were as little boys. Always competing. Always trying to outdo. Always trying to get the attention. Karl threw down the symbol for paper. Mark threw down the symbol for scissors. Scissors cut paper. The photographer had lost to the developer.

Karl flipped his brother off, then went to the reservations desk. I saw him chatting with the receptionist, nodding his head, saw her typing at the computer, then he pulled out his wallet, handed her a charge card, signed papers, and she handed him a hotel key.

The center of my sexual being jumped.

I should've excused myself, slipped into the bathroom and masturbated, taken the edge off of this hormonally inspired craving, this horny headache, let some liquor wear off, come, return to my senses.

Mark asked, "You okay?"

I was nervous. "This is . . . I've never . . . this is different. For me this is different."

"Don't want you to be unsure."

"Just let me finish my drink first."

I sipped my mood enhancer. He sipped his, evaluating me, my inner thoughts revealed.

He said, "Go to the ladies' room."

"Why?"

He said, "You seem unsure."

"I'm fine."

Again he smiled. "Go to the ladies' room. Think for a moment. There's an exit down that way. I'll wait. My brother will be here. If you don't come back, it's cool. Just go to the ladies' room."

"Okay."

"And when you come back, *if* you come back, tell me why you want to do this."

"Are you serious?"

"This is your chance to escape. Or affirm your decision."

"You're the logical twin, huh?"

"At times."

I smiled. "The heavy reader."

"When I can."

"The deep thinker."

He winked at me. "I'd like to think so."

"And your brother, I take it he's the impulsive one."

"He does things without considering the consequences of his actions."

I looked at him, then glanced toward his identical twin. They were visual aphrodisiacs in stereo. I saw myself, at times, as the deep thinker. Other times I was the impulsive one. Two women inside one body, sometimes at conflict with myself, most of the time living in harmony. Today was not harmonious.

I asked, "What's it like being a twin?"

"If I had my choice, wouldn't be a twin."

"Really? Thought you would love it."

"Would you love it?"

"I think it would be great."

"You have brothers and sisters?"

"No."

"That's why you *think* you would love it."

He chuckled, as if his words were to be taken lightly. But jokes were used to hide truth.

I said, "Guess we always want what we don't or can't have."

"Yes. We do. We always want what we can't have."

He was right. I didn't have siblings, so I didn't understand the type of rivalry that went on between siblings. If it was as competitive as most said, I couldn't imagine what it was like between twins. It had to be magnified. Maybe that need to have your own personality fostered resentment. Nobody wanted to be a copy of anyone. When I thought about it, I didn't like to see a woman wearing the same dress I had on.

I asked, "Is being a twin different from having a regular brother?"

"Being identical is. You're half of the same egg. Harder to define yourself as an individual. People confuse you for being your brother. And they see you as bookends. People stare all the time."

"Never would have guessed you felt that way about it."

He shrugged. "It is what it is."

"Bet you and Karl are used to getting a lot of attention."

"Growing up, Karl was the one who needed all the attention. People thought we'd make the same grades, that we processed everything the same way, but I was a little smarter. More focused. He was a little better at sports. In tennis summer camp, we were like Venus and Serena, always in the finals against each other. He played offense in football, so to keep it from being a war, I played defense. I played baseball. He didn't. He ran track. I didn't. At home, we had a lot of fights."

"Sounds like an ongoing competition."

He nodded. "Who has the better house. The better car. The better job."

"You don't like your brother."

He smiled. "I love my brother."

"But do you like him?"

His smile weakened. "Karl is Karl."

"That's not an answer."

"I know."

I smiled at him. "Would choosing both of you to be with tonight, would that be a problem?"

"Sure you'd want to take that route? I don't want you to end up . . . regretting your decision."

"Maybe you and Karl can compete in a different kind of way."

"And you would benefit from the competition."

"Of course."

He smiled. "Take a stroll. Get some air. If you come back, we'll take it from there."

I nodded, sipped my martini, gathered my things and headed through the crowd, went down the hallway, left the kennel and eased inside the ladies' room, joined the clowder as they prepared to rejoin the party. I walked in on two women, one blond with Swedish features, the other dark-skinned with her hair in a perm; both had nice, full figures. They had a small bag on the counter, were dipping the edge of a platinum American Express into white powder, then sniffing the powder from the edge of the card.

The one with the perm looked down and saw her left breast had escaped, was out of her low-cut top, hanging like a watermelon would hang if watermelons grew on trees. A watermelon that had the tattoo of a scorpion forever inked in its flesh, staring at her areola, an areola that looked like the landing pad for a helicopter.

She laughed so hard it frightened me. Laughed and made her breast dance.

Her friend looked at her renegade breast and laughed just as hard.

"One of my girls trying to get out and get her party on. You wanna do the chicken noodle soup for momma?" She made her boob bounce. "That's right, baby—pop, lock, and drop it."

Her girlfriend went to her, took the breast in hand, licked it twice, laughed, and made it bounce like a toy before she tucked it back in its proper place. That let me know they were real good friends.

Heads thrown back in inebriated laughter, they sashayed out the door.

I stood in the mirror, looked at myself, and imagined the developer and the photographer.

Wondered what kind of lover Karl would be. What kind of lover Mark would be. Wondered who would be the best. Who would eat me out. Who would lick figure eights around my sweet yoni. Which tongue would go inside. Wondered if they ate yoni the way I loved my yoni eaten. Wondered if I would reciprocate the oral gratification. In between blinks I kept imagining that magical moment when an erection danced at my opening. Wondered who would get inside me first, who would penetrate me first, Mark or Karl. Imagined hardness breaking the skin, stretching my walls and filling me up. Imagined riding Karl. Then riding Mark. Imagined them taking turns riding me. Wondered who would come first. Wondered if they would do it more than once. Wondered if they would want to do it again in the morning.

Imagined so many pornographic scenarios.

My mind returned to Anaïs Nin. She was always with me. But those thoughts of her gave way to Henry Miller. Her married lover. He had loved his wife, June, and Anaïs. How did Henry Miller love two women? How did he balance his desires? Maybe desires were not balanceable. Love between two people was never equal. Love between three, that had to become an emotional catastrophe.

A scale balanced two things at once. Maybe balancing three things was impossible.

I shuddered and shook my head.

This was too much for me.

I whispered, "No more one-night stands."

It was time to go home, go inside my closet, and unlock my file cabinet.

I slipped out of the W unseen, the rain falling at a peaceful tempo, the night air thick and humid, hot and moist, like the heat from an aroused lover's breath, his breath covering all exposed flesh.

I made it to my car, keys in hand.

I was too restless to go home. All I would do was end up in bed, tossing and turning, a pillow jammed between my legs, wishing I were anywhere but home alone. Maybe I'd drive to midtown, or ride over to Apache Café, listen to spoken word and poetry, find somewhere to sit and let time go by, let sleepiness find me so when I made that journey back home loneliness and desire would not assault me.

My cellular rang. A text message from Logan.

I'm sorry for the way I behaved. Please except my apology.

I sent him a text: *Where are you?*

Passing through Chattanooga.

That was four hours outside of Georgia. I felt relieved. So fucking relieved. Not until then did I realize I had been dreading going home, kept having a feeling that he would be on my porch, waiting.

I sent him a text back. *Take care.*

I muttered, "*Accept,* not *except.* Hire a freaking editor. Asshole."

I turned my cellular off, remained in the darkness forever. Under dark skies, I stood in the parking lot, not moving. I'd had too much to drink. Not too much to hang out, not too much to lime elsewhere, just too much to drive. It would be foolish to drive, APD peppering the streets. I'd wait it out, sit in my car. But for now I stayed where I was, enjoying the lightheadedness, enjoying the night.

The twins. They had smiled identical smiles at me, expressed dual desires for me, now I was engaged in a battle with myself, with my sensual self, struggling to keep my eroticism from taking over.

Mark, the considerate, deep thinker, had sent me to go consider the consequences of my own desires, to myself become a philosopher. We'd had very little contact, yet he affected me in a way I could not control or describe. I took a deep breath, one that was supposed to be sobering, and then I pondered a woman's love-hate relationship with men, and all women had love-hate relationships with men.

I loved handsome men. My femininity loved the masculinity of the alpha male. And I hated that I loved them so. Men were a necessary evil. I hated anything that was necessary, hated needing anything beyond my control, hated needing anything I could not control. And men had love-hate relationships with women. We were their necessary evils. We were their yang. They wanted us. They needed us. And they hated us, always trying to maneuver and outsmart the enemy. We were *frenemies*. Friends and enemies.

But with us, with women, it was different.

Men came inside us. They marked us. After sex was done they remained with us, dripping out of us, each trickle like a thought, or an unanswered question, our insides, our sexual muscles still feeling their presence, still experiencing the thrusts, twitching from the aftershocks of pain and pleasure, feeling that beautiful intrusion that sent us toward what could only be heaven, left us tasting the liquid desire they had left behind, the come that left us awake and alone with our thoughts. While they felt nothing more than sleepy and tired and thirsty, same symptoms of an allergy attack.

I had learned that when I was at Hampton. I had learned that lesson well.

They moved inside us, moved inside our wombs, pushed our insides and disturbed the beats of our hearts. I didn't want to take the chance of having the beat of my heart made uneasy. Women were excited after sex, wired, because in their minds the relationship was only beginning. Men went to sleep because for them the orgasm had arrived and the relationship was done.

I took a step and paused, tested my sobriety, my lightheadedness remained.

Before I could return to my apple-martini-inspired philosophizing, I heard footsteps and murmuring. Someone was coming my way. I imagined Mark or Karl, maybe both, looking for me.

I heard a deep male voice, one that had radio quality. In the next moment I saw his silhouette hurrying by me. I was shorter than the

SUVs in the lot, my Z4 one of the smallest cars, so as he rushed deeper into the parking lot he didn't see me. But I had a clear view of him. It was the lothario I had met when I first arrived at the W. The arrogant and attractive light-skinned man who wanted me to come up to his room on the fifth floor so he could drink my bathwater. I stayed still until he made it to his car, didn't want any kind of conversation or confrontation with him. I was going to be still until he left.

The lothario unzipped his pants like he was about to relieve himself of his drinks.

He said, *"Hurry up, baby. Get your fine ass over here and suck this dick."*

My mouth opened, about to curse him, thinking he was talking to me. He wasn't aware of my presence. Footsteps rushed from the other direction. He had stopped one car over, was standing between parked cars, whispering to someone else. He was creeping out to meet somebody.

"You have a beautiful mouth."

Weed. I smelled weed coming from his direction. Good, strong weed.

"That's it, baby. Hell, yeah. Suck the nut out of this dick."

I moved toward the back of my two-seater, moved deeper into the shadows.

He was moaning, the sexual sounds hypnotic and arousing, the sound of pleasure, the beautiful timbre of a rising orgasm. I took slow, curious steps, was as quiet as I could be in heels, a mouse walking on cotton, the beat from the music inside the W smothering the echoes of my footsteps.

I heard the sound of wetness, that kind that came from practicing the art of deep-throat.

Somebody was tasting his pre-come and trying to suck an orgasm out of his body.

"Goddamn, you can suck a dick."

I held my breath. Moved slowly, my curiosity leading me into the land of the voyeuristic. I wanted to see her. Wanted to see which woman had been brought outside in the name of pleasure. Wanted to witness her technique. Then I saw his lover. Saw his lover taking him in smooth motions, quick motions, making that part of the arrogant man vanish like an exotic sword swallower, the sound of his mouth loud.

His lover was a well-built man in oversized jeans, his head shaven bald. A bona fide thug was kneeling, his hands on pretty boy's thighs, his bald head dipping and taking cock in his mouth as the yellow man moaned his beautiful moans and smoked a joint, its scent spreading in the damp air.

My cellular chimed and I jumped. The theme from *Sex and the City*. My mother's ring tone.

I turned the phone off as fast as I could, looked up, and saw the arrogant yellow man.

He was looking my way. He saw me. He saw my face as I stared at his.

He smiled at me.

That wasn't the reaction I had expected. I had anticipated shame, not pride.

His smile widened, then he put his hand on the back of his lover's bald head, kept his lover bobbing at an anxious pace, and stared at me, smoke streaming from both his mouth and nostrils.

His lust moving in and out of another man's mouth, he smoked and licked his lips at me.

As if watching me watch him turned him on, intensified his corrupt sensations.

He jerked, grunted, his eyes rolled into the back of his head, and his body stiffened.

Despite my phone ringing, his lover hadn't lost his enthusiasm.

I broke from my trance, turned around, my heels clicking across the parking lot, ran away from the moans that were behind me, the apple martinis stealing some of my grace.

That shouldn't have surprised me.

I'd seen muscular men cuddled up with feminine men in Piedmont Park. The biggest gay club in Atlanta was Lennox Mall, the section of Atlanta that stretched between Buckhead and midtown destined to be renamed Tops and Bottoms. In this segment of the Bible Belt it seemed as if desirable men sampled semen more than ravenous women. Probably served fellatio with the fervor of Superhead.

Moments like this were disturbing, beyond depressing.

Yet they owned ecstasy.

They owned it without shame, without denegation, as if it were their entitlement.

I was entitled to ecstasy as well.

I went back inside the W, my sensual self inspired to pursue my own sexual fulfillment.

I had a pleasant buzz. Needed to clear my head. The music rolling through my body, stimulating me, drawing me into the lobby, I inhaled the scent of mixed drinks and alcohol. I returned to its sexual energy. Not the place to be if you were any kind of addict. Sexual compulsion had these beautiful pretenders exorcising their sexual demons in the parking lot and the bathrooms with people they'd known for less than an hour, only God knew what was going on in the five hundred rooms they had upstairs.

I saw it everywhere, heard crackling in the air, the décor of desire, whispers from Eros, witnessed the sensuality of submission, saw people in search of love, romance, and lust. Saw women evaluating men, choosing mates, deciding if he was Mr. Right or Mr. Wrong, others in search of Mr. Right Now. The energy in the room was strong, as if canisters of silent and odorless gases that triggered dopamine production had been released, desire making everyone bold, act out of character, physical attraction being desired more than intellectual stimulation, women with body language saying they were ready, they were open to being opened. I stared at a constellation of needs, the need to copulate being the strongest.

I stood in a room filled with people who needed Prozac to dull the keen edges of their libidos.

But there was no Prozac to smooth out lust, alcohol and music being the opposite, doing the opposite, not dulling the senses but enhancing humanness, making everything exciting and exhilarating.

Mark was across the room, waiting. He smiled when he saw me. Smiled good and hard. His smile created erotic turbulence. A startling need for intimacy. I reciprocated, my stare incendiary. We engaged in mutual objectification, our erotic smiles created exotic secretions. It remained my right to choose. Lust was a sin worthy of hell, temperature rising as I headed deeper into the furnace, went toward his outstretched hand, moved through the collective consciousness of the room until my hand touched his, flesh experiencing flesh, the sense of touch so strong, held hands as if we were on the same page, as if we had signed a contract. He made me feel comfortable. Made me unafraid to try something new.

He said, "You came back."

I paused, whispered in order to conceal the nervousness in my voice, "I came back."

"You decided?"

I was hungry for knowledge. Treading in a lake filled with desires unknown.

Nervous, yet anxious to try new things.

I took a breath. "I've never done this before. Not with two men. I want to try . . . want to do this because I've never done this before. It could be horrible, it could be great. Doesn't matter. Either way, it'll be my experience. The memory will belong to me. Maybe it will give me something to write about."

"Tell me what you want."

"I've never . . . two men . . . fantasized about it . . . but never."

"As much as you want. As little as you want. Just enjoy."

Karl saw us, made a head motion.

Moments later we were walking past the bar, past reception, moving by the anxious crowd, to the hallway that led to the quarters made for relaxation and sin, then we were getting on an elevator.

My easy banter and relaxed attitude belied my anxiety. I looked back at the people to see who was spying on us. There were a few intoxicated eyes, a few knowing glances upon a woman who had been flirting with two men, now all of us heading toward an elevator inside a sensual hotel during the hours of mass copulation. I swallowed. Wanted to jump off the elevator before it was too late.

When the elevator door closed I was standing between them, silenced by nervousness.

The photographer was in front, facing me, touching my breasts, his hands soft and his grip intense. His erection rubbing into my leg. He was more aggressive than his brother. Not a bad thing, just an observation. His aggressiveness was wonderful. He had the look of a man who was a dramatic lover. Good in bed. Not the perfect lover, but the one who took a woman and with his sex he pleased her into submission, made her go insane with orgasm, then walked away beating his chest as he grunted.

The developer moved closer, was behind me, kissing my neck, his kisses soft and sensuous.

It was like he was following his brother's lead. Hardness startled me for a moment, the thickness of his erection rubbing up against my ass. An erection my body moved against, automatically, as if I was in a club and soca music came on, the movement, the wining and rolling my hips done without thought.

He moaned as I moved up and down against the stiffness of his blessing.

I was surrounded by the hardness of sex, by the hardness of desire, each breath as stiff as lust.

I closed my eyes in surrender. The world fell away. Began gasping like I was underwater.

Oh God.

A smooth hand went underneath my dress, teased my flesh, touched my legs and butt. I pulled my lips in, stifled a moan. Hot hands on my burning flesh felt so good, so nice, so needed. Another hand went to my inner thighs, a rougher hand that possessed a gentle touch, the juxtaposition of tenderness and gentleness turning moans into submissive groans. Fingers teased me. Each touch intoxicated me, stirred me, inebriated me to the point of defenselessness, leaving me unable to protect the outer layer of my hidden emotions. My sex was wet, my clit firm. My lips were swollen, opening like a flower, opening wider as an ambitious finger moved to and fro across its moist petals. Throbbing overwhelmed me, my erratic breathing betraying my body, twitches telling them I needed this, that every part of my body was begging to be touched and touched. My yoni told them her needs, wanting to be more than stroked.

Asking to feel tongue, pleading to be licked.

Fire.

I was on fire.

SEVEN

Thirty minutes passed with me living on the edge of madness.

One hundred and thirty-three . . . one hundred and thirty-four.

Mark, the married twin, he licked me deep and I twitched, released moans, deep breathing, a symphony of sounds, the foreground sounds, the echo of foreplay, no longer supping on popcorn, but not feasting on the steak I desired either, feeling tongue but wanting a deeper pleasure, a pleasure that went inside the depth of me, wanting that badly, yet remaining nervous about crossing that line.

One hundred and thirty-five . . . one hundred and . . . and . . . and . . . thirty-six . . .

Don't stop counting, Nia Simone.

I was inside a suite on the ninth floor on a yielding bed, the pillow-top mattress elegant and royal, made for a queen, created for sin and satisfaction. My hands gripped the featherbed as my yoni was being licked, grabbed the soft linens as I moaned and groaned and struggled to count each lick, a struggle that had already moved the fluffy goose-down duvet and plump down pillows to the carpet. The lights were low, romantic, enough to illuminate the room and reveal everything was saintly, the whitest of whites.

My flesh was a contrast against the whiteness as I moaned, as I struggled to count each lick. The whites in the room, the dim lights, I was inside a contemporary heaven, moans echoing as the heat in my body continued to rise like the sun, heat that made me dance, heat that made me wine and squirm.

The scents in the room, the hints of orange and cinnamon, the way the aromas seduced my sense of smell one inhale at a time, adding to the perpetual stimulation I was receiving, the mind-blowing foreplay that had taken me from the elevator down the hallway and to the bed, the high intensity of sexual chemistry that was consuming me, an out-of-control blaze moving through a forest.

One hundred and forty . . . one hundred and . . . and . . . and . . . forty-one . . .

The spirits in my blood made every touch more pronounced, the alcohol had enhanced every stroke of his tongue, every time he grazed my sex, licked my sex, sucked my sex, small eruptions happened inside my body, eruptions I wrestled with, fought with, danced with, moaned with.

I felt fantastic.

I felt free.

But still I was nervous.

One hundred and forty-seven . . . one hundred and forty-eight . . . one hundred and . . . and . . .

Rain falling outside, its cadence peaceful and inspiring.

Wind blowing, whistling against the windows, its song in accordance with the rain.

The music was as soft as the bed, jazz and a yielding mattress pulling me into rapture.

Forty-nine . . . one hundred and forty-nine . . . fifty . . . fifty-one . . . fifty-two . . . one hundred and fifty-three . . . fifty-four . . . oh God . . . fifty . . . one hundred and forty-five . . . I mean fifty-five.

My legs were open wide, secrets revealed. My nectar being savored by a skilled tongue. With each lick the developer had me kicking my legs, had me rolling my hips.

Karl, the twin with the angelic tattoos, the bad-boy photographer, he was good. He was near my head, leaning over me, massaging and licking my breasts, sucking my nipples, keeping me squirming in the middle of the bed.

They had taken off their jackets. Taken off their shirts. Flawless physiques surrounded me.

Don't stop counting, Nia. Count every lick. Count until you come.

Okay okay fifty-six . . . fifty-seven . . . fifty-eight . . . fifty-nine . . . sixty . . . one hundred and . . . sixty-one . . . sixty-two . . . three four five six seven eight . . . oh God . . . oh God . . . you're licking me so so so fast . . .

I moaned endlessly. No two moans were the same, they had similarities, but each was its own song, its own length, incredible, unending, a singsong melody reminiscent of the beautiful accents in Trinidad. In between my delectable sounds, as I writhed and surrendered, became more submissive each time his tongue painted my sexual canvas, my submission evident, deepening with my every tattered breath, every singsong moan a testament to my acquiescence. When there was a pause between the sounds, my unwavering sounds, as my chest heaved, as my swollen breasts ached, my sense of sound returned and I heard a noise so orgasmic it almost pushed me over the edge. That sound of carnality created poetry. In that moment, heat rising like the sun, I listened to sounds more stimulating than my own arousing singsong moans, my ears savoring the sounds of his tongue against my wetness, enjoying the sound of his passionate breathing, the music from his song, the melodious sound of his moan.

His brother was not to be outdone, did not stop stimulating me as my yoni was being licked, savored, tasted, sucked. Karl's tongue moved from my breasts to my neck, suckled my neck, drove me crazy in his own way before moving on to my earlobes, the center of my sexual arousal, the one place more sensitive, more arousing than the licking of my yoni, the combination of their passion making my singsong moans desperate and strong, desperate and elongated, my moans being stolen, my ability to sing my song being stolen as Karl sucked my tongue, his sucking equal to what his brother was doing to me. I moaned a thousand times. Every moan as soft as a snow-flake, beautiful and unique. The sounds I made were called *moans*, but the description of a sound so exciting, an arousing hum that was rooted in bottomless pleasure, I found that description inadequate, not marvelous enough to describe what was being created by my entire life force being stirred, the marvelous being inspired by the marvel of lust.

They had undressed me. My skirt was gone but I still had my high heels on.

This was wrong. And what was wrong was amazing.

I was entitled to wrongdoing. I deserved amazing. I deserved what was marvelous.

My face dank with the dew of ecstasy, my gaze went to the photographer, witnessed him smiling at me, the dank of lust and desire shining on his skin, saw the need to orgasm on his handsome face, in the way he licked his lips, in the way sexual tension had manifested itself in his forehead, in his brow. His expression became intense. As dark as his erection was hard.

I struggled with myself, my words riding on the winds of moans. "What are you doing to me?"

Karl kissed me again, his tongue deep, his breathing extreme, excited. "Keep counting."

"I can't count . . . not while you . . . not while Mark is . . . what are you doing to me?"

Mark rubbed my legs, his breathing heavy as well, echoing his aroused state. "Want us to stop?"

I swallowed, twitched, struggled to find my lost breath. "No."

I suffered, my punishment being to endure the heat of the three fires burning down this room.

Mark stopped licking me, began kissing my belly. "You're sweeter than a Bajan cherry."

Karl whispered, "Did you know that, Nia? Your yoni is sweeter than a Bajan cherry."

"Her skin is just as sweet."

Mark eased his strong hand under my backside, his hands touching my lower spine, drawing me closer . . . closer to him . . . first his tongue on my inner thigh . . . his breath on my clit . . . my legs opening wider . . . wider . . . feeling him kiss my clit . . . him tasting me as he squeezed my ass . . . held my ass as if he adored and appreciated my blessing, spread my cheeks and whispered my name as he tongued, licked, sucked, hummed on, and kissed my skin. Karl sucked my nipples, his sucks, his suckling magnifying every sensation. But Mark . . . his passion was killing me . . . his tongue sliding between my thighs, moving in and out of my yoni . . . now flicking over and over . . . devastating my senses. I jerked and freed sacrilegious phrases when his tongue moved inside me, as it flicked my clitoris, as he pulled me to his face and made figure eights, as he licked the center of my humidity, held my ass, and savored my sex like he owned my yoni.

It became too much goodness at once, I became overwhelmed, felt myself becoming free and primal, wanted to stop before I exploded, had to cry, beg them to slow down, to let me breathe.

In the kindest voice Mark asked, "Are you okay?"

I nodded, body twitching, eyes closed tight, this moment so personal.

"Want us to stop?"

Unable to form words, I shook my head.

They did what my body language asked, remained gentle lovers, moving slowly. Kissing my lips . . . sucking my breasts . . . licking my nipples . . . kissing my forehead . . . massaging my body . . . tracing my lips with tongue . . . playing with my hair . . . again kissing my face . . . my eyes . . . my nose . . . my eyelashes.

Again I surrendered to my lovers, gave them my body to do whatever they wanted to do.

Pleasure was like love, subjective, personal, not the same for any two people. Like the interstate in the morning, many on the same road, few taking the same journey, only cars passing in the sunrise. Thinking these thoughts, listening to my desires, allowing them to whisper in my ear, give me mental images, all of that led to the inevitable. Acting on these thoughts created a transformation.

I desired transformation.

But I fought the change, battled like a caterpillar resisting becoming a butterfly.

The conservative one, the married one, his adulterous touch became a little rough, the strength of envy, his touch very competitive, demanding my attention. My moans were as profound as his touch.

It was so good I lost my smile.

He was rough. I loved rough. Loved gentle. But needed rough too.

Needed yin and yang. A rough touch. A gentle touch.

It equaled out, both sides of erotic pleasure being given all at once.

I started sucking my fingers . . . oral fixation taking on a life of its own . . . but my hands were taken . . . moved away from me . . . as if I wasn't allowed to pleasure myself in any way . . . more kissing . . . more licking the flames . . . more sucking my swollen clit.

They savored me like I was chocolate-covered strawberries, salmon filet, wild rice and fresh vegetables, licked me like my skin was covered with home-cooked macaroni and cheese baked in my mother's casserole dish, had me intoxicated like I was inhaling mango martinis, mint juleps and red wine.

Deeper twitches rose with urgency. Wicked singsong moan followed wicked singsong moan.

My breathing, so ragged, suffocating in a room filled with air with my eyes closed tight.

The sense of sight shut down so all others could be enhanced.

Oh God oh God oh God.

Hands on my breasts, squeezing nipples, then licking nipples.

Again my hands went to my breasts. I squeezed them, tried to lick my own nipples.

I heard one moan. Then the other moaned. A powerful song. Turned on. By my sensuality.

Karl moved my hand, licked between each of my fingers, sucked my nipples again.

Oh God. Oh my God.

My yoni was being licked so fucking good. Mark's tongue lagged around the edges. Made figure eights. Darted inside. Then, while I was being licked, two fingers were eased inside my wetness. Two fingers took me closer to orgasm. Breasts were being sucked while I was being finger-fucked and licked.

I was moaning. Suffocating in pleasure. Licking my lips. Sucking my fingers.

I reached up to the one on my breasts, to Karl, found his penis, held it, tried to stroke it.

I tried to reach down, find Mark's erection, wanted to feel his penis, but he was too far away.

Karl said, "Want this, baby? Want to feel this big dick inside your mouth? Want to suck this fat dick and make me come?"

I moaned, his vulgar words direct and unambiguous, scaring and exciting me all at once.

That moan ended when I felt his erection at my lips, easing inside my mouth, at the back of my throat. I sucked him. I sucked him like I was famished. I sucked him so good he had to pull away.

I licked as I was being licked . . . was close to orgasm . . . didn't want to come . . . yet . . . tried to push it away . . . keep it at bay . . . but the orgasm . . . it had power . . . Mark's sucking . . . orgasm inevitable . . . his tongue . . . as I was trying to suck the honey out of Karl . . . my orgasm was being unearthed by rapid licks . . . being pulled to the surface by the flicking of a tongue . . . it was being sucked . . . fingered . . . oh God . . . coming . . . was coming hard . . . body went into convulsions . . . legs trembled like they had a life of their own.

My singsong moan was longer than all other moans, my vision becoming so sensitive as I came, as if I had been licked and fingered and touched and led into a sexual concussion. Every nerve was alive and blazing, senses exaggerated. My soft, singsong moans magnified. My soul was floating through a surreal whiteness, a version of heaven on earth. My orgasm arrived in wonderful degrees of pleasure. A thousand little deaths caused me to arch my back and release a stream of beautiful vulgarities.

I was being pleased. By two men. Men who came from the same egg.

Identical sins.

E I G H T

An orgasm erupted like thunder.

That loud, sensual outburst that came from the heavens seeped into my dreams.

With a start I awakened, naked, soft covers on my legs, on a yielding bed, the side closest to the windows, curtains pulled back, sleeping on my side, so as my eyes opened momentarily I witnessed it all.

The whiteness of the room remained remarkable, ethereal, both surreal and heavenly.

My eyes closed again.

Again thunder erupted like vocalizations at the end of long-overdue sex, as if the damp sky was experiencing muscular spasms, those spasms sending shock waves through me, a euphoric sensation.

My eyes opened in degrees, small degrees, barely open enough to realize my new reality.

In a daze, somewhere between sleep and consciousness, I became a voyeur, watching, imagining all the angels having simultaneous orgasms. Nonstop sonic booms created endless chills. Explosions rang out like orgasmic echoes. I was afraid of thunder, but it didn't scare me this time.

Body relaxed and warm, I gazed out the window, in a trance, unmoving, still barely conscious, mesmerized by flashes, that light event better than the Fourth of July laser show at Stone Mountain.

I shifted, consciousness trying to take over, assaulting my sleep, reality and my five senses returning to my world in degrees, like a sunken ship being raised to the surface against its will.

I had been abandoned. Left alone in a vast bed.

I was free. And inside that relieved feeling lived a house made of sadness.

When I shifted I felt warm skin resting against mine. Felt firm muscles against my skin.

I wasn't alone.

I pushed up on my elbows, looked at his hand, no wedding ring. Inspected his arms, saw his untold story in indelible ink. I moved a bit, he reached out, held me closer. He was sleeping, holding me in his dreams. He was unaware, but that mannish part of him was awake, poking me in my back.

He aroused me. And that arousal disturbed me.

There was something so erotic about middle-of-the-night sex.

And it was the middle of the night. Those bewitching hours had arrived.

With the exception of the flashes of light, it was dark out, like power was out in the city.

When the explosions paused I could hear the soft drumbeat of the pouring rain.

Was almost put back to sleep by the sounds of that slow and easy rain.

That peaceful moment allowed me to hear sounds slipping from the bathroom.

The shower was on. His brother was in the shower.

They had pleasured me into sensory overload, had sexed me into a coma.

The married one was in the shower. That meant he was leaving.

Married men made love on borrowed time, always had to rush back to the woman who wore a matching wedding ring.

I wanted him to stay. Wanted him to penetrate me. Wanted him to penetrate me first. Wanted him first because he was married. Wanted to corrupt someone for a change. Wanted him first because I would be emotionally safer with him. Wanted him because I knew I couldn't have him. Wanted him because I knew a married man would be a cushion to my already damaged heart.

They had given me oral pleasure, but my body wanted to be penetrated. Needed more than oral penetration. Desired more than fingers. My yoni was screaming, begging to be infiltrated by delight. Screaming so damn loud.

I moved, looked at the twin next to me. Karl, his energy so shady. That of a player. That of a man who'd had many sexual experiences. I wanted him too. I wanted to absorb his knowledge.

This was wrong. This was so wrong. But it was so good. So damn good.

I should choose. One. I should choose one. Women always had to choose one.

At that moment my eyes went to the bathroom door. Toward the married one.

He was the safe one. I couldn't get hooked on a man who had obligations. And even if we did engage in an affair, it wouldn't last long. It would be a fling that I would endure no more than a season.

I looked at the man with the tats. The single man who relished being single. I looked at the twin named Karl. He was the kind who could break my heart. Just the thought of being powerless, being under his control, that made me dislike him.

I was scared. These thoughts weren't appropriate. This was supposed to be zipless. A one-time exchange of pleasure, then back to our normal lives, as if we never met.

His angel was staring at me, her body wrapped in wings. Kenya was watching me. Her image was so clear, as clear as photos taken by a professional with an expensive Nikon. As I stared at her unmoving face, I listened to the thunderous orgasms, imagined each orgasm belonged to her.

I imagined she belonged to him.

Part of me wanted to gather my clothes, dash out of this room. Maybe just slip out quietly, shut the door on this experience. My fear was as dark as the city outside, trepidation crackling like its thunder.

That other part of me.

That other part of me came to life, the part ruled by desire, and my darkness hushed me.

I had tasted honey and now, before I left this experience, I wanted to possess the honeycomb.

Desire whispered in my ear. I moaned, touched one breast, my other hand touched between my legs. Thunder boomed. Lightning lit up the room. Rain fell with a steady rhythm.

A steady rhythm.

I desired a steady rhythm moving in and out of me.

Dick.

I desired dick.

Not the beauty of lingam, not the crudeness of cock, not a clinical penis, but the stiffness of dick.

I eased under the covers, took that erection in my mouth . . . suckled him slowly . . . became a gentle alarm clock . . . roused him back into this world . . . made him stir . . . suckled him until he let out baby moans.

I scooted over, reached for the glass of Riesling on the nightstand, dipped his penis in the Riesling, made him taste like pears and peaches, then sipped his hardening flesh. He held my face, touched my skin, and looked down at me. I kissed the tip of his penis. Put another kiss between his thighs. Then another soft kiss on his balls. Then I held his penis, blew air on his gorgeous flesh.

I smiled at him, started licking my lips. I looked in his eyes. Gave him that brief look, the one that spoke of desire, my serious look. My mouth was watering, my tongue touching the head of his penis while I was wrapping my right hand around his erection. I started lubricating him, used my saliva, let my natural juices make him wet, started stroking it real slow . . . up and down . . . made circles.

His hand came to my head, eased me down on his hardening muscle.

I sucked him the same way he had taken his mouth and tongue and hands to me earlier . . . I felt empowered . . . felt as if I was taking what I deserved . . . I felt entitled to pleasure . . . then . . . his hips moved . . . let me know that he was with me . . . he was growing . . . becoming sturdy . . . his sex achieving girth . . . and weight . . . stretching my mouth . . . filling my hands . . . barely able to make my thumb touch my finger . . . larger than his twin . . . but not as long . . . made him moan . . . felt so selfish . . . taking him . . . with my mouth . . . as if this were my rape fantasy in reverse.

The skies exploded, the reverberation from naughty angels achieving simultaneous pleasures.

The covers moved, slipped away from my feet.

We weren't alone.

I didn't look back. Just moaned and tingled when I felt the chill from strong hands touching my backside, squeezing my butt. Imagined I felt some jealous energy moved from his hands into my body.

That excited me.

I kept masturbating the naughty photographer. Karl's legs tensed, began shaking.

He wanted to come.

I lubricated him . . . as I stroked him . . . licked him . . . his strong hips rising . . . his intensity giving me energy . . . loved how he felt inside my mouth . . . loved his gentle thrusts . . . loved the way he was moaning as I rubbed his hairless balls. The primal side of my brain was alive, the animal side in control of me.

Wished I had one of his cameras so I could photograph his look of pain and pleasure.

Behind me, I felt Mark moving. Had expected Mr. Developer to step back and watch. Maybe leave. But he was touching me. Whispering my name. Bringing me back to him. Demanding my attention. Needing to feel special.

He shifted around, made me get up on my knees, then he was getting up under me. His tongue moved up my thigh. Following the trail of heat. Licking me like his life depended on it. He was killing me. Licking slowly. Licking fast. Shallow. His tongue deep. Eating me into a sex haze.

Oh God.

His tongue went so deep. Felt the bridge of his nose up on my wetness.

Then he . . .

Oh God.

Put his finger inside my chocolate star. In degrees. Testing the limits of his exploration.

Oh God.

He twirled his finger. Felt so good. Worked his finger. In and out of my tight hole.

And his tongue went in and out of my vagina at the same time. So much stimulation. So much pleasure. I wailed and moaned. I purred. I wiggled. His tongue took the place of his finger.

I almost lost it, my beautiful singsong moan masked by the excitement of thunder.

Mark was making me want to come.

Again I fought with the orgasm, wrestled with that beast. Pushed it away. Told it to get the hell away from me. Fought to keep my control. It was a good battle. A battle that I was losing one lick at a time. He was doing what he wanted to do. Making me come. That orgasm being held at the gate.

I masturbated Karl. Made him jerk. Made him moan like he was on fire. Made Karl wail like he was singing the Rio de Janeiro blues. His erection was alive in my hand. Throbbing. Swelling. A separate entity. His hands slapped down, became fists as he pulled at the covers. His erection danced. His moan echoed. His erection seeped. He wailed. He was mine. He was at my will. I owned him.

In that moment I belonged to Mark.

But Karl belonged to me.

His erection was throbbing and seeping a long stream of jism. Like it was crying.

Tears flew high.

Karl's body jerked like he was being kicked, he groaned and coughed, grabbed at the sheets the same way I had done earlier, like he was falling and trying to break his rapid descent, his back arching, his every muscle coming to life, his orgasm a magnificent ride, as if he couldn't stop coming.

Creamy tears oozed down the side.

So many tears. Thick and rich tears.

I watched until his erection began to soften, held its strength as he continued crying the tears of procreation.

I masturbated him so good, made the last of his tears roll down his erection over my hand. Those tears, so hot, so arousing. I closed my eyes, imagining, wishing I had taken every orgasmic tear in my mouth, wished I had made them disappear, swallowed his jism, left him clean, as if his orgasm never existed. Those thoughts aroused me even more. Caused me to lose my breath while my heart beat at an unbridled pace.

My desires took hold of me, led me. I did not struggle with my needs, this time becoming submissive to myself. I took him in my mouth, tasted him. He held my face as the last of his come warmed the back of my throat, his come so warm and sweet. I swallowed the sweetest nectar I had ever tasted. I moaned, devoured him as if I were starving, as if I were dying of thirst. Years ago I trembled at the thought of giving oral sex. Was terrified to taste the seeds of a man.

Now it was an acquired taste and I hungered after it the way a career smoker craved nicotine. I enjoyed the sensation of feeling the sweet, warm, creamy fluids as they left a man's body, loved the way a man felt against my tongue, loved creating the magical explosions that went down my throat.

The things we craved. Our silent desires. Our little addictions.

Karl jerked a hundred times, jerked like he was in the middle of intense physical pleasure, pleasure that was out of his control, his nervous system leading him through the gates of euphoria. He was strong, the way his solid muscles contracted, the way his pelvic muscles did the same, the way he clenched his butt and strained, all of that was breathtaking. He slowed down. Found control of his muscles. I kept stroking him until he let go of the sheets, until he put his hand on top of mine. Stopped me from stroking him. He was sensitive. That part of him softening and throbbing like a rapid heartbeat.

I licked my lips.

Smiled because I loved that I was giving satisfaction and I was being pleasured.

Mark . . . I felt the bridge of his nose . . . he was licking me like ice cream . . . tasting me.

Karl moved out from under me, breathing hard, touched my body, touched my face, kissed me, soft erotic kisses, whispered how beautiful and sexy I was, talked to me and held me while his brother's tongue licked my sex, opened my sex, went inside my sex. It was impossible to concentrate. The way I was being licked and sucked and fingered . . . couldn't concentrate. I held on to the one I had

pleasured. Held his strong body against mine. I was being licked . . .
over and over . . . he was playing that same tongue-song over and
over . . . like my favorite record on repeat . . . heard sweet music as
I floated away . . . beautiful music . . . heard guitars and mando-
lins . . . couldn't do anything but shake my head left to right.

Oh God.

The one I was holding, Karl, the one with the angel tattooed on
his flesh, he was stroking my hair, touching my face, sucking my
neck. Too sensitive. I was too sensitive. Had to . . . had to . . . I
pushed him away. Pushed him away and pushed up as I wrestled
with the tingles that were driving me up that winding road to paradise. I put my hands over my mouth, muffled my moans.

Karl moved my hands and kissed me. He eased his tongue inside
my mouth.

I sucked his tongue, kissed him as I made obscene sounds, then
I stopped kissing because I was about to come, unable to breathe, as
if the fire had stolen the oxygen from the room.

Karl eased away from the bed, left me whining and wrestling
with Mark's fingers and tongue.

As pleasure moved through me, I turned my head, stared through
the darkness in the room, looked through the sheer white curtains,
saw the lightning doing a sweet dance in the distance, inhaled and
imagined I could smell and feel the dampness brought on by the
rain.

I was looking for Karl. He was gone.

Had left me holding his brother's head between my legs, left me
getting licked to high heaven. I jerked and moaned and trembled
like my San Andreas Fault was coming undone. My hands went to
the top of Mark's head, pushed him deeper, pushed his tongue toward the epicenter of that violent pleasure.

He slowed down. As I was about to come he slowed down.

Kept me at the edge.

Mark whispered, "You like that?"

All I could do was whimper, so I whimpered and made crazy, sexy sounds.

Again he whispered, "You like that?"

I moaned so damn loud.

Karl touched me. He had come back. He put his hands in my hair, touched my face. I thought my photographer, my bad-boy lover, thought he had deserted me.

He was right there. First his face was near mine, then his tongue was on my ear.

He whispered, "Open your mouth."

I did what he asked. Readied myself to receive girth. Length. Hardness. Wanted to experience and take pleasure in more than a skilled tongue. Breathing labored, I licked my lips, made them moist, and opened my mouth wide. My heartbeat sped up. He put his fingers inside my mouth. Three fingers. I sucked his damp fingers. Mango. His damp fingers tasted like ripe mangos.

I gazed toward him long enough to see he had a bowl in his hand. He took a slice of mango from the bowl. Eased it inside my mouth. Fed me. He fed me as I was being eaten.

He fed me mangos. Slice after slice. I moaned and he fed me.

I ate as I was being eaten, mango juice dripping from my mouth down my neck, down my chest, across my breasts, my hands grabbing sheets, back arching, tingles growing.

Lightning, thunder, and rain were outside the window, coming down harder and faster.

Karl whispered, "Open your mouth, sweetie. Open your mouth for me."

My breathing was choppy, erratic. Felt like a thousand orgasms were kicking at my door. It was a struggle, but I did, I opened my mouth. Karl put slices of mango inside my mouth, ate the slices with me, and kissed me. Mark was loving my vagina, eating my yoni like he was trying to prove a point. The twins were competing. And it was a wonderful competition.

My eyes were rolling into the back of my head. My mouth was barely open.

My pre-orgasm face betrayed me, my expression extremely unpretty, like that of a woman crying. My hands became fists. Muscles tightened. Spasms rolled through my body in gigantic waves. Thunder boomed and *Oh God* I was shuddering uncontrollably. I told everyone in the W that I was coming. I told everyone in Cherokee, Gwinnett, Paulding, and Fayette counties I was coming.

I announced to the world I was coming.

Sucking the nectar from Karl's fingers and coming.

N I N E

A sweet tenderness existed where a raging fire had once resided.

My yoni was sore, that mild ache reassuring me this surreal moment was true. So was my right knee, it was sore as well, injured. I ran my finger across my pain. Traces of blood ran from my right knee toward my shin, my injury fresh and tender.

I was smiling as I exited 285 and took Spring Road back toward Park at Oakley Down, Carina Ayiesha's CD playing loud on my sound system, singing along with the song "Siente La Musica Dentro."

With passion I whispered, *"Cosmological Eye."*

I felt glorious. The lewd and vulgar acts had been astonishing. Both men had been amazing lovers. And I had pleased them as well. There was satisfaction in pleasing. Everything had been so smooth. So balanced. As if the sex gods had sent four strong hands and two skilled tongues to move across my breasts and my yoni, all of that happening at once. The sensory overload was breathtaking.

Their aromas were on my damp flesh, the fragrances of AXE Phoenix and Egoiste mixed with hints of my perfume. A tongue on each breast, then tasting lingam while I was given cunnilingus.

Mango stained my flesh from my neck down across my breasts, their tastes still on my tongue.

I held my steering wheel as if I had them in my hands.

The echo of baritone voices moaning out of sync sent shivers down my spine.

I smiled so hard it hurt my face. I sang so loud. Felt like dancing in the thunderstorm.

When I entered my subdivision and turned on Oakwood Trace, my smile vanished, all hints of ecstasy were replaced by fear and disbelief. It was near the hour of sunrise and Logan was waiting for me to come home. He had found out where I lived. His Range Rover was parked in the middle of the slender cul-de-sac that led to my townhome. My weary eyes went to my mangled dress, a dress that was dripping wet, draining over my leather seats, creating a puddle between my legs, cool water keeping my yoni calm.

I sped by his Range Rover, hoped he didn't see me, hoped he had fallen asleep waiting for me, tried to speed away, then his headlights came on. His engine started. He was awake. I wanted to turn around and leave my complex, figure out what to do, but he'd seen me before I could escape him.

I hit the button on my car's built-in garage remote, made the garage door go up.

The rain was coming down hard, water dripping from my hair, across my face, down over my wet dress. Logan trailed me down into the cul-de-sac and parked outside my garage, his radio up loud, the type of thing that was embarrassing in a white middle-class neighborhood—unless somebody white and middle-class was making the noise. It was the blues. Slow and sexy, Bobby Blue Bland sang a woeful song, "Memphis Monday Morning," talking about the summer rain coming down, he keeps reaching for his baby, but his baby's no longer around, left him without giving a warning, and now he was going crazy because his baby was nowhere to be found. The engine and the music died. Logan got out of his Range Rover and walked toward me, his face down low and umbrella up high.

Love was mental illness, an obsessive-compulsive disorder romanticized.

He said, "Somebody has had a long night."

"How do you know where I live?"

"Internet. Pulled up info on your property."

I wanted to scream, wanted to release vulgarities, but I looked at the townhomes inside this peaceful community, my neighbors' units only feet away. I refused to become that kind of neighbor. *What the fuck are you doing at my home?* came out as a frustrated "Thought you went back to Memphis."

"What happened to your dress?" His eyes were all over me, inspecting me, the look of a man who wanted to sniff a woman's panties to confirm his insecurities. "*It's torn. Your knee is bleeding.* Your makeup . . . it's messed up. What the hell happened? *Why are you wet from head to toe? Your shoes are wet and scratched up.* Where are you coming from at the crack of dawn looking beat-up like that?"

He looked at me as if he knew, as if he had seen what had happened to my dress.

I snapped, "How did . . . how did you get my information from the Internet?"

A half smile and an I'm-smarter-than-you-think wink was his answer. It didn't matter. It didn't fucking matter.

I pulled my damp hair away from my face, a face that had to look like I had been through both heaven and hell, and evaluated my dress. My dress now nothing more than rags, unfit for the homeless to wear.

My flesh smelled like two men, two lovers. Tongue prints and fingerprints were all over my skin.

"Logan, this is not appropriate."

"You're soaking wet. Your dress . . . what happened?"

"Getting my information . . . showing up like this . . ."

"What happened to your knee?"

Logan's reaction to what he saw was extreme, as if he thought I had been in a car accident, or mugged. He was rushing toward me but I put both hands up, palms out, telling him to keep away.

"Don't worry about my knee."

"Something bad happen? Somebody do something to you?"

My irritation intensified. "Why are you here? *Why?*"

"I want it to go back to being the way it was before."

"It won't go back, Logan." I pulled at my hair. *"You can't put toothpaste back inside the tube."*

He frowned. "Then I guess I have to do this."

Logan scowled and reached inside his pocket. He was about to take something out.

A gun. A knife. I didn't know what he had hidden.

My insides jumped. Fear assaulted me.

Logan was about to kill me in my driveway.

But when he reached inside his pocket he took out a small, velvet box.

I asked, "What is that?"

He opened the box and as the skies rumbled and rain fell, my eyes witnessed the most beautiful engagement ring I had ever seen, the kind that would normally make a woman shiver with delight.

He said, "Diamond and sapphire."

"Where did that come from?"

"I brought it with me. I didn't . . . things didn't go so well between us at Wal-Mart. I prayed. Asked God what to do about this thing I have for you. It's heavy on my heart. I've been downhearted ever since you left. Had to come back. I couldn't go back with this in my pocket. I couldn't go back without knowing I had made things right between us. Nia, I came down here in the rain to ask you to be my wife."

The skies flashed and roared as I stared at the stunning ring. Platinum. Art deco. At least two carats. The type of ring that would capture a jewelry whore. I looked at it without touching, afraid that touching it would imply commitment. This was painful. I wanted to lie to him, wanted to save his feelings, wanted to do what needed to be done to keep this volatile situation stable. But I couldn't lie.

He said, "It cost twenty grand."

I shook my head. "I can't accept that."

"Did you hear me? This is a twenty-thousand-dollar ring."

"I can't accept that."

"The rest of my family will be in Memphis next weekend. I've told them all about you."

"I can't accept that."

"My great-grandmother will be there. She's about to turn ninety. She's old and sick. This reunion is for her. Her way of saying good-bye to everybody. Wear the ring. We can make the announcement if you want to. Come up. It would be important to me. If you'd think about it."

"No. I'm telling you no. Don't you hear what I'm saying?"

"Why not?"

He wanted justification, my rejection requiring explanation. But there were no words to make him understand what he refused to understand, not when all that mattered was him getting his way.

I said, "Didn't you hear what I told you before?"

Rain fell between us.

He repeated, "What do you need? What can I do to make this work between us?"

"Logan . . . if you're not happy before you get married, getting married will not make you happy. I'm talking two-people happiness. Both parties have to be happy. If one is unhappy, then the marriage is unwell. Unhappiness infects, spreads, and kills. We are so not on the same page. And you know that."

Thunder boomed. Rain came down so hard it was impossible to see more than a few feet beyond my townhome. We were incarcerated by precipitation. I felt like a prisoner.

We had two distinct views of what we were doing. For me, knowing him had been a brief part of a long journey, this part of my journey now over. To him this journey between us was only beginning, and from the look in his eyes, based on his determination to win me over, I was his final destination. In my world he had been but a brief layover.

He asked, "How did you get soaking wet?"

"Wait here."

My heels clicked over concrete as I hurried to the back of my garage, went near the water heater. I picked up the cardboard box that had LOGAN written across the top. I carried that cheap box to him.

I put the box down between us. My eyes went to him.

I said, "Good-bye."

He shook his head. "No."

"Please . . . just say good-bye and—"

He pulled me to him, forced his tongue inside my mouth. He held me with passion, his tongue tasting like cinnamon gum. He breathed heavily, savored me. I didn't stop him from kissing me. I let him taste me, my tongue not helping, but not hindering. His dick was getting hard. My body was rejecting him and his penis was becoming engorged with desire. He groaned like his erection was so hard it hurt. My tongue had given him priapism while his kiss diminished my urges to ever have sex again. When he was done, he let me go. He smiled as if that kiss should have modified my religion. Like he had seen one Cary Grant movie too many. When the kiss was over, Logan smiled and extended the ring again.

In his eyes I was a woman. And to a man, a woman must have a man, or she's not fully a woman, she has no value on her own, only has value when she is with someone designed to lead her. And in his mind, because he is financially capable and popular in the 901 area code, he was the ultimate man.

This was very sad.

He wanted love. I wanted fun. He had fallen. I had walked away.

I had desired what he couldn't give me.

Too bad people didn't fall in love at the same pace, at the same time, for the same reasons, and too bad those emotions didn't move simultaneously. But each act of madness moved at its own pace, one not dependent on the pace of anyone else. It wasn't like tandem sky-diving, where you were connected as you fell, where you were forced to fall at the same rate and use the same parachute. Falling in love was a solo act. I knew that, had learned that the hard way. You just jumped and hoped your parachute opened. Sometimes you looked up and saw you were falling by yourself, the object of your desire still on the plane, not interested in jumping, watching you descend into that scary place alone.

I had done that years ago, jumped and found myself falling, the man I loved still on that plane.

In this case Logan had looked down and seen I had never left the ground. Logan had fallen from the ionosphere while I hadn't considered leaving the ground, jumping the last thing on my mind.

He wanted more than I was willing to give.

I stared at the ring Logan had offered. I saw it for what it really was, saw its truth.

That ring he had wasn't a ring; it was handcuffs for a criminal.

He wanted to tame me, tame my desires, visions of a barefoot and pregnant wife dancing in his head. That would never happen. He wanted me forever when I'd only been willing to give myself to him when my needs had become unbearable. Even when we were together he never possessed me more than a few hours at a time, never twenty-four-seven. He didn't want more than I was capable of giving, just more than I was capable of giving him. I felt like a man, my energy so masculine, so curt and cold at this moment.

He said, "I love you."

"You hear me?" My tone remained rational. "I don't feel that way. I'm not emotionally receptive to you. You don't turn me on. And the longer we have this conversation, the more you turn me off."

"But can you love me? Eventually? Can you?"

I shook my head, rubbed my temples. Frustration rose, strangled sanity and logic.

I wished he hadn't come to Atlanta. I wished he would stop watering dead flowers.

Being nice wasn't working. I had to be brutal. I had to become a mean bitch and be honest.

I said, "I just had sex with someone."

"I knew it." His tone blackened. "One of the guys you were with in Memphis lives here, right?"

"Someone I met today."

"You're lying. Please tell me you're lying."

"I'm serious. I was out running, met these brothers. We hooked up tonight."

"Why?"

"Don't ask me that."

He snapped, *"Why?"*

"Because I wanted to."

Truth flowed from me like I had autism, incapable of lying.

Then I was afraid. But I told myself I could be strong and do this.

I could be honest. I wasn't being brutal. Only being honest. Had to be honest. Because for some people the soft breakup didn't work. Some people only understood the hard breakup. Logan was six-four. Played football at U of M during his college days. I didn't want to provoke a man his size, didn't want to insult his brain and irritate his brawn, because at moments like this a woman realized how much bigger a man was than she was, how much stronger the masculine creatures had been built, developed fear because those muscles that used to protect her could now become weapons of instant destruction.

But I needed this over. I wanted to get away from this pain.

Thunder. Lightning. Rain.

All of it seemed so different when I was at the W. At the W it was stimulating.

Now it all seemed unfriendly, so deadly. This was horrifying.

He asked, "Why, Nia? Why would you go to somebody else?"

"*This isn't about you.* I sought pleasure. None of that had *anything* to do with you. This is who I am right now. This is who I am. Let me be me."

He put the ring back in his pocket. "I'll give you some time."

"I'm not *asking* you for time. This shit is over. I'm *demanding* my freedom."

He leaned against his damp SUV, his umbrella over his head, his box at his feet, that box getting soaked. He looked like he had been punched in the throat. His face, he looked nauseated. He looked like he wanted me to come put my arms around him. He looked like he wanted to strangle me.

I said, "Let me go along my path. If I find myself thinking about you, if I find myself missing you, I have your number, I have your e-mail address."

I stayed at the back of my car, its wetness against my legs, arms folded, shaking my head.

Across the way I saw lights come on in three townhomes. Eyes were in windows.

The smell of two lovers comforted me. Their fingerprints, it was as if they were holding me.

Logan snapped, "Are these *sexual experiences*, is *fucking* around, is it simply about the *experiences* and being with a bunch of men? Do you think you'll be able to settle down with me and become a respectable woman once you've *experienced* enough men? How long will you be a whore?"

"If I behave the way you behave, and I am *honest* about it, why am I a whore?"

"Because that's what a *whore* does."

"Don't talk to me like that, Logan. Don't you *ever* talk to me like that."

He looked me up and down. "I guess that explains why you look the way you do."

"What's your excuse? I got caught in the rain. You look like you forgot to take your meds."

"You look like you've been rode hard and put up wet."

"I was. I was rode damn hard. And I enjoyed it. You have no idea how I enjoyed it."

"Is that right?"

"And you know what? Since you have to know, I was with two men."

He chuckled, not believing me. "Takes two men to replace me?"

"Would take *two* of you to do what *one* of them did to me."

Logan glared like I was both a liar and a whore, like he wanted to slap me down because in his mind this yoni was his. He glared like he was about to rush over and mark this territory with his seed.

He asked, "Why are you doing this to me? Why are you *lying* to me?"

"I was with *two men*. At the same time. *And it was wonderful.*"

"What, you think I'm not a man? You think you can just say any kind of shit to me?"

He stared me down, now beyond angry, a little boy with his feelings hurt, his emotions extreme.

Like my mother, when riled, my words were irrational. I couldn't hold my tongue.

Defiant, I said, "Did you like the way they tasted?"

"What?"

"When you kissed me, when you put your tongue inside my mouth, did you like the way the men I was with tasted? Did you like the taste of their dicks? Did you like the taste from their come?"

My words were surgical, each syllable sharper than a tool used for castration.

His mouth dropped open, his face in shock.

I wasn't done. He had *pushed* me, cornered me in my own life, and I wasn't done fighting. This argument was a reprise of an *uncompromisable* situation, and I wanted the battle over right now. My adrenaline was pumping, my clarity had evaporated, and all I had was unmanageable anger.

I asked, "Did sticking your tongue down my throat and tasting come, did that taste good?"

He let his umbrella fall, rain falling and assaulting his face, dampening his senses.

He growled. "Tell me you're lying."

"How does it feel to taste the come of another man?"

He spat hard, retched like he was about to regurgitate a lung, then wiped his mouth and came toward me. Then it came hard, it came from within me. Regret. It arrived. And with regret came fear.

"If I went upside your head a time or two, your ass would see Jesus and start acting right."

"Are you threatening me?"

"Lot of places to bury a body between here and Memphis."

His out-of-control expression combined with those deadly words, that terrified me.

I bolted away from Logan, hurried to the back of the garage, ran out of my heels, fled in bare feet.

He cursed me.

I saw my face on CNN, MISSING underneath my photo as police teams, cadaver-sniffing dogs, and volunteers walked through woods looking for my remains, what hadn't been eaten by wildlife.

I pushed the button for the Liftmaster, made the garage door go down.

Logan remained in the rain, water soaking him and the cardboard box at his feet.

I went inside, ran up one level, went to the kitchen window, saw Logan wasn't leaving.

He stood in the storm like he was that mentally imbalanced man from the movie *Psycho*.

My heart was on the verge of exploding.

Moments later he started ringing my doorbell.

I screamed, "This is the reason why I don't want to be in a relationship . . . too much damn drama . . . people like you create so much drama . . . people like you . . . you suck people into your goddamn drama."

The doorbell rang a thousand times.

"What the hell is your problem? Showing up in Atlanta . . . in *my city* . . . expecting a compromise in your favor . . . trying to get me as if this were some game . . . this isn't a damn game . . . this is not about us being in a stupid competition . . . you expect me to sacrifice . . . to have the kind of responsibility *you* want me to have . . . shit . . . you're here . . . a damn storm . . . wrote a six-page letter . . . a damn six-page letter."

He knocked on the door, told me he wasn't leaving. I dialed 9-1-1. Minutes after that, Smyrna PD showed up. As soon as one squad car pulled into the cul-de-sac, another one appeared.

It had come to this. I didn't want to create a public, shameful moment, but it had come to this.

There was no justification for Logan's actions. The meter on his intelligence was showing one bar, if that. Some men only took seriously the words and advice that came from men carrying loaded guns. I felt a deep sadness inside, tremendous pressure on my chest, a shortness of breath.

I felt the opposite of pleasure.

Two officers stayed downstairs, detained Logan, who was now ready to leave. Two officers came to my door. I told them what the problem was, told them he was an ex from Memphis, told them I had moved to Atlanta to get away from him, told them I hadn't seen him in months, told them he had come to Atlanta uninvited and had been harassing me all day, told them I hadn't called him in months, told them he had somehow obtained my address and now I was scared for my life, told them I wanted this on record in case anything happened to me.

They asked, "Did he assault you, ma'am?"

My hair was wet. My makeup horrific. I looked down at my tattered dress, at my scarred knee.

My appearance was that of a traumatized victim.

I had been assaulted. But not by Logan.

Uncomfortable with the truth, I had to manufacture a quick lie.

I told them I had been out drinking, got locked out of my car in the rain, and I had fallen down, stepped off a curb and tumbled. Their eyes told me they didn't believe my stammering falsehood. All I had to do was nod my head and point at the big black man who was about to join history with Rodney King, and say Logan had done all of this to me, and have him incarcerated and put on a chain gang with the rest of Georgia's black men, men the system would rather pay tax dollars to keep incarcerated than send to college. But I didn't. I emphasized that Logan had threatened me. I told them he hadn't touched me, just threatened to do so. Told them he had threatened to have someone bury my body in the woods.

They said, "Ma'am, we have to take into consideration your appearance."

He said that to me like I was an irrational battered spouse living knee-deep in denial.

I folded my arms across my breasts, nipples standing tall.

I said, "I just want him off my property. I just want him to leave and not come back."

The good old boys went to have a man-to-man talk with Logan. He was surrounded by the officers, blocked in. They made him face the first police car, rain falling on his head as they searched him from head to toe, then they put him in the back of one of the police cars. It made me feel uneasy, but this was his doing. He had pushed it to this. All he had to do was leave me be. Now he felt like I did, like his freedom was being taken, like he was a prisoner. I should've lied. Should've said he pushed me, assaulted me, made me fall and scrape my knee. But lying like that, that wasn't me. I watched. Four white officers were detaining one black man. Flashing lights. The neighbors saw. The neighbors would talk about this amongst themselves. Once again the darkies were entertaining the white folks. Once again they would be worried about their property values going down and the safety of their children.

Lights were on in the homes of neighbors. The president of the homeowners association appeared, a bearded man who took his gerbil-size dog with him everywhere he went.

Forever eased by. The rain died down.

Neighbors stared from windows, cups of tea and coffee in their hands.

They let Logan get out of the police car, escorted him back to his Range Rover.

He frowned up at my front door, shook his head, like I was the bad guy in this madness. Like I was the evil one because he came here on bended knee, his fantasy to take me back to Memphis and make this wild horse a tamed, uxorial mare. I'd stab myself in the heart before I took that ring and pledged a lifetime of meritorious service.

I saw inferiority raging in his eyes. I was powerful beyond my wildest dreams.

Now I saw the real Logan. The man who thought he owned a Mercedes dick, but his shit was equipped with a Pinto engine. If I stood next to him in the mirror all he would be able to see was himself. He was a narcissist—spoiled, arrogant, haughty, snobbish, and downright bitchy when things didn't turn out in his favor. He was used to hiring and firing. And for once he had no say in the matter.

Badges and guns followed him out of the community. I hoped

they trailed him down Atlanta Road and made sure he got on 285. Hoped they made him cross the state line and go back to Tennessee.

Shoes off, I still had on my wet black dress, that wetness now cold and clinging against my skin.

Logan was gone. I hoped that sonofabitch was gone for good.

I rushed through my home.

I hurried over all three levels, looking for any gift from Logan, any card, any present, tearing up anything I found, breaking what was breakable, throwing anything that was connected to him in the trash, throwing things into the garbage violently, like I was a goddess gone mad.

I lost it, yelled like he was still here, still in my face, my voice echoing, "I don't want to be with you. You know I don't want to be with you. You are too controlling. You don't fucking please me. You don't fucking fulfill me. You never have pleased me. *Never*. Do you hear me? *Never, never, never.* Do you feel me? Could you understand that? Of course you don't. Narcissistic bastard. Why in the fuck did you have to write me a damn six-page letter? A fucking six-page letter. Who does that shit anymore?"

He made me curse. He made me curse a lot. He pulled me to his level and made me vulgar.

He had too much power. Too much.

I removed my damaged dress, threw its remains into the bathtub.

I stepped into the shower, washed away the wonderful scents from my identical sins. Men I would never see again.

Not long ago I was in my car singing. Dancing in my spoiled dress. Happy. Until I had seen Logan. One glimpse of him and my happiness had been reversed. This was a crime. I had been robbed. He had robbed me of the elation and positivity that had been flowing through my body.

I closed my eyes, wished myself back in time.

Wished myself back to experiencing the praises of four hands, two tongues.

Wished myself back to bliss, couldn't let Logan make my wonderful experience end like this, couldn't let him dilute my night of satisfaction. I went back to the moment when Karl walked into the W, relived the night until I made it to my car, body soaked with rain and my dress mangled beyond repair.

T E N

Three hours ago I was inside a luxurious suite at the W, one that looked like an extension of heaven, a suite in paradise decorated with whiteness that glowed underneath dim lights and a dark sky.

It was raining, heaven-sent tears inspired by our moving exchange of desire and passion, tears inspired by what was marvelous. The sky thundering, applauding the wonderful sex it had witnessed.

While Mark washed his face and prepared to go home to his wife, I dressed without showering, prepared to return to my life, left Karl sleeping in the bed. My eyes stared at Karl's tattoos, at the name Kenya inked in his flesh, at the image of her as an angel wrapped inside beautiful wings. My voice whispered a soft good-bye to him. I eased out of the room, left with Mark in the middle of the night.

During the elevator ride to the lobby Mark kissed me.

He held me and kissed me like he was still hungry for me, like he hadn't been kissed in years.

He whispered, "I wanted you to myself."

I smiled, flattered and surprised by his desire for me, but didn't reply.

Men didn't have to have just one lover. If a man only had one, he was defective.

To choose. Or not to choose. I didn't want to choose.

In the W, I had been pleasured by four hands and two tongues.

That was the way I had wanted it. That was my fantasy. To have them please me with hands, mouths, and tongues; and to please them with hands and mouth and tongue. Mark and I made a left out front, headed toward the visitor parking lot.

Mark said, "I did it for you."

"Did what?"

"Made sure you got what you wanted."

"Yeah, that's what I wanted."

"I did it for you."

He kissed me again. Kissed me like he couldn't get enough of me. Kissed me and I felt his desire swell, harden against me. I had come many times in a couple of hours. He had only come once.

The rain was pouring down on us.

Lightning flashed. Thunder boomed. The skies roared.

He kept kissing me.

Without warning, with so much passion, he turned me around. Hurried to unzip his pants. He lifted my dress, dipped and put his erection inside me. I moaned a singsong moan of pain and pleasure, an encouraging moan as he went deep inside me with urgency. Like he had to get inside my warmth or he would die. He tried to crawl inside me, pumped himself inside me. His jealousy was set free.

Deep inside me, as I embraced this sensation, he asked, "Who made you feel better?"

"You. You. Mark."

He was confident in the way he took me. Skilled. Bold. He knew how to move, wining and moving his hips like he was indeed from the islands, indeed the dance of a Bajan man. He penetrated me like he was trying to get me hooked, to make me move from a zipless affair to his mindless whore.

He growled. "You like the way I'm fucking you?"

I moaned, his words vulgar and strong, demanding, no longer polite, no longer the philosopher who read Sartre and cared about existentialism, all of that gone, the caveman in him remaining.

"Harder . . . harder . . . give me that dick . . . give it to me."

"Like this? You want it like this? Want me . . . to . . . fuck . . .
you like . . . *this.*"

I moaned. "Don't hold back. Don't you fucking hold back."

He growled.

I said, "Let go. Don't be afraid to let go."

He pumped harder. The sex he was giving me was as brutal as
life itself. Removed of all idealism. Still, it was poetic. It was brilliant. It was beautiful.

I said, "Fuck me like you want to come."

He pumped and pumped.

He gritted his teeth as I moaned louder and louder.

Thunder boomed.

We were doing it, having passionate sex in the pouring rain,
parked cars our only witnesses.

His blessing was swelling. Getting wider. Opening me up. He
was going so deep. He held me so tight. Growled. He pumped and
pumped. Then he stopped, turned me around again, sat me on top
of a stranger's car, sucked my tongue as he opened my legs. He
pulled my legs apart, forced me to lie on my back, held my waist and
yanked me toward him, went deep inside me again. All I could do
was hold on. My hands reached out, grabbed the part of the hood
where it met the windshield and held on the best I could, held on
until he stroked me so hard I had a spasm and had to let go. He pulled
me into his lingam with force. *Oh God.* He fucked me hard. Had been
months since I felt lingam. Even longer since I felt good lingam. And
this lingam was damn good. Better than tongue. Better than fingers.

"You're so deep. So deep inside me."

He pumped me hard, relentlessly, like he was trying to make
Kunta Kinte call himself Toby.

I held on to him as he bucked into me over and over.

All I could do was hold on and let my wild Mandingo fuck me
insane.

He shuddered. His orgasm was about to explode. It was at the tip. Feeling him about to come made me come. I didn't want to come. Just wanted him to come. Just wanted to please him. Wanted to end this zipless night with him satisfied. I'd come enough. But I was coming again.

I was pulling him closer, my hands gripping his ass as he gripped mine, my nails going into his skin and marking another woman's territory, giving him pain, encouraging him to go deeper. I slipped and reached for his neck, grabbing any part of him I could grab, grabbing and wanting more and more of him.

Sex always felt like love, but in my world love never felt like sex. For me, love only felt like love.

Mark moved, kept shifting, kept stirring me. He was remarkable, had more gears than an eighteen-wheeler. This was what I needed. This was what my yoni needed. Not fingers. Not tongue.

This.

Not toys. Not an inanimate object that couldn't hold me, kiss me, feel me, not something to put inside my body and play sexual make-believe with. I wanted this. To be held. To be overpowered. To be controlled while I felt orgasm rising, an orgasm that didn't come from my own hand.

My body craved this. Not tongues. Not fingers.

This this this.

Some of my choices would lead to regret, but that would be my regret.

The absence of regret marked the absence of life.

I wanted to live my life.

And I'd never felt more alive than I did at this moment.

The skies roared and I moaned. I experienced weightlessness, the brightness behind my eyes more beautiful than the aurora borealis. My head was back, rain falling in my mouth, my hair wet and heavy, my nipples pushing through the dampness of my black dress. Mark was moving like he couldn't get enough of me. He kept me in zero gravity, kept making me float. My moans were like a creature in the wild. His animalistic groan told me he was about to come. He held me like he was insane, held me tighter with every thrust. My delirium refused to let him go. Selfishness refused to let him seed the ground, jealousy wouldn't allow me to share anything he had to give with Mother Earth. He leaned back, his eyes tight, his head up to the sky, rain falling on his face, and he moaned so loud, and that pre-orgasmic outburst was followed by a keen whimper, like he was becoming weak.

We were out of control.

He fucked me too hard, almost fucked me off the car, fucked me so hard I had started to slide. He reached for me as his orgasm pulled at him. In the middle of the madness, the car we were on was well-waxed, and Mark slipped away from me as I slipped away from him. We began to detach. Maybe he pulled out before his river started to flow. But he was no longer inside me. Left my yoni hollow, left me struggling to pull him back, but I couldn't. He fell away from me calling my name. His come spewed and mixed with rain with him calling my name like he wanted me to get back to him before his orgasm ended.

He shuddered, twitched, collapsed, went down hard.

Even on the ground he was still moaning, breathing in hard, breathing out the same way.

As was I. I owned no strength, no coordination, my legs as limp as overcooked spaghetti.

Rain battered me, the sky soaking me with its own liquid release.

I held on to the car as long as I could, had tried to keep from sliding to the ground, but I was covered with bliss, my thighs slick with jism, too weak to stand. I struggled to hold on to the car's waxed bumper, neither gravity nor friction working in my favor, and had to let go, the convulsions in my body too strong, let my body find its way to the asphalt between parked cars.

I was soaked head to toe, and I was panting.

Rain fell on us hard. The sky lit up with electricity.

The car I was leaning against, its alarm started going off, its lights flashing. It didn't go off until now. As if it had been a voyeur, waiting for me to come, waiting for Mark to come, maybe frozen in awe of what it had witnessed, now so excited by what it had witnessed it had somehow pleased itself, was coming for us as we had for it. I expected all the cars to start coming, waited to hear alarms going off one by one until the parking lot was filled with automobiles and SUVs having orgasms.

But only one car screamed.

I looked at my partner. He had made it up on one knee, like the orgasm had taken his strength.

The car wailed, its lights flashing and betraying us to at least half of the five hundred hotel rooms.

I moaned his name, my voice more sound than an actual word. He didn't answer my call. I managed to get to my feet, staggered over to him, shook him. He didn't move.

I leaned against the wailing car, my hands holding on to whatever I could hold on to, my body was struggling to recover. As Mark raised his head, rain drained down his face, his expression so intense.

He struggled to his feet, pulled his soaked and wrinkled pants up, the change in his pockets jingling. The flashing lights showed his suit was ruined. Revealed my black dress ruined beyond repair.

Hand in hand, soaked head to toe, we laughed and staggered away from the wails and flashing lights. Mark escorted me to my car, our walk that of two drunkards leaving a bar at last call.

He panted as he asked, "Are you all right?"

I panted in return, moved my hair from my soaked face and nodded. "Scraped my knee."

"How bad?"

"Not bad. Will put some Neosporin on it when I get home."

Mark nodded. "Think I pulled a muscle."

We sat in my car, rain draining from our skin, water dripping across my leather seats.

I didn't care.

He held my hand and talked to me.

I didn't expect that part, conversation after sex, endearing words after intimacy, not at all.

I asked, "You do this often?"

"Do what?"

"This."

He yielded a weak smile. "Marriage changes everything, including your sex life."

"If I ever get married, I want both to change for the better."

"Idealistic."

"Every woman wants a fairy tale, even though we know there are no fairy tales. There might be fairy tale moments, but there are no fairy tales. Dopamine dwindles and the energy lessens."

"Dopamine. Where did you read that?"

"*National Geographic*. Yeah, I know. I'm a part-time nerd."

He chuckled. "Well, FYI. Twenty percent of married couples only have sex ten times a year."

"Since losing passion seems inevitable, maybe people should just keep dating."

"Maybe. Once married life begins, your sex life ends. Stop laughing."

"What about you and your wife? Ten times a year."

"We had sex four times last year."

"Four times?"

"That last time was on Valentine's Day."

"That was in the winter."

"I know."

"It's summer now."

"I know."

"Sex four times a year is not sex."

"What would you call it?"

"Hell, if we're having sex four times a year, we sure as hell aren't in a relationship. I mean, if we were only going to do it four times, give it to me over one weekend so I can have the next fifty-one weeks to do my own thing. Don't have me sitting around wondering if I'm going to get lucky. Sex four times a year, you're nothing more than roommates. Friends get more benefits than marriage."

"It wasn't always like that. Once we had sex twenty-one times."

"In a month?"

"Over a weekend."

"*Twenty-one times?* What did you do? Drink a gallon of Irish moss every day?"

"You know about Irish moss?"

"Island girl, baby." I chuckled. "Honeymoon? Were you on your honeymoon?"

"Before we married. Over six years ago. We were on holiday in Jamaica."

"What part of the island?"

"We moved around. Mo Bay. Ocho Rios. Kingston."

"And you gave it to her twenty-one times. One weekend. Twenty-one times."

"I think that's where our problems started."

"That's where your problems should've ended."

"It's what she wanted." He smiled, but sounded solemn. "I just gave her what she wanted."

"Okay, let's change the subject. Twenty-one times. I'm getting jealous."

"Sure."

I smiled. "Tell me about you. Never been to Barbados."

"You should go to Barbados with me. Come down for Crop Over."

"Typical Bajan. You are really trying to sell me your island."

"If you come to my island I'll take you down to Oistin's on a Saturday night and show you a great time. Some of the best entertainment and fish fry in the world could be had there."

"Be careful what you ask."

"Bajan Roots and Rhythms. Or Back in Time at the Plantation, could take you to that."

"You been to our Carnival?"

"Man, do people from Trinidad ever talk about anything else besides *their* Carnival?"

"I'm sorry. Was there something else *better* than *my* Carnival to talk about?"

He laughed. I laughed too.

He spoke with pride and detail as he told me they grew up in Barbados, in Redman's Village, but had relatives all over, some who lived in chattel houses right on H7 on the way into Bridgetown, still had relatives who worked at the bus terminal, at stores on Broad Street, at Digi-cel, Shell Gas, Cave Shepherd, at the sugar factories, at Banks brewery. He could ride the ABC Highway and half the local people on the packed Zed-R public transportation van would speak, same for the sweating people packed like sardines on the yellow minivans, which would modify their route to get him where he needed to be on time. He could get off the plane and bypass customs at Grantley Adams International Airport.

He said, "I'm talking because . . . rambling . . . I don't want to leave you yet."

We kissed again.

He kept his lips on me, his voice soft and seductive, still yearning. "Glad you came out."

"Same here."

"I would've been home reading."

"Is that right?"

"That's right."

"What are you reading?"

"Just finished *Quiet Days in Clichy*. About to get started on *Cosmological Eye*."

"Heavy reading."

"Stimulates my mind."

"Have you read *Sexus*?"

"*Sexus, Nexus,* and *Plexus, Tropic of Capricorn*."

"You have no idea how hot you're making me right now."

"Show me."

We kissed and kissed, his tongue moving around my lips, putting soft kisses on my lips, my cheeks, my eyelids, sucking my earlobes, his eroticism causing me to jerk, making me throb again.

He said, "Nia Simone. Nia, as in purpose. Simone as in Simone de Beauvoir."

"That's me."

"So your name could mean the purpose of a writer."

"It could. Loosely translated it could."

He kissed me again, this kiss being his final farewell kiss, not knowing if he would ever see me, touch me, feel me, taste me, hear my voice again, hear my singsong moans, my singsong orgasm.

When we were done he traced my face with his fingers, touched my nose, and smiled.

I smiled in return.

He said, "I'd better go."

"Before we start having sex again. Or end up talking literature and have a book club meeting."

That gave him laughter.

He said, "I'd love to have a book club meeting with you."

"A nerd after my own heart."

"I'm serious. That could be fun."

"Can we be naked?"

"Sounds even better. We could start our own naked book club."

He slipped out of the car, rain beating down on him, walked a few steps before turning around and walking backward, an enormous smile on his face, that elation for me as a downpour made him so wet he looked as if he was a God risen from the seas. His smile never wavered, telling me he didn't care about the weather, because in that moment, despite the storm that covered our world, everything was peaceful.

I made sure he made it to his car, waited until his headlights came on.

Then I drove away, exhausted, water draining from my body down over my leather seats.

Satisfied beyond my wildest dreams.

Hours after Mark had given me unadulterated bliss, Logan had stolen what felt good.

I tossed and turned, the ceiling fan spinning over my naked body. My eyes went to the floor-to-ceiling mirror to the left side of my bed. I looked at me. At my tense expression.

My home glowed with the light of a new day, but remained tainted by unwanted feelings.

It was morning but my insides were decorated with shadows darker than midnight.

I turned the television on. Atlanta news came to life. Jewell Stewark was reporting. I gazed at her blond hair, at her beauty, and her Julia Roberts smile. She was wonderful, articulate, well-educated, the Oprah of the city. She looked as if she lived in a perfect world, a world she controlled.

The girl with ancestry in the West Indies, the woman who was in search of her roots.

The Jewell of the South was telling the people in the surrounding counties that despite the heavy rain, restrictions on watering lawns remained. A drought existed and heavy fines were being enforced on all violators. Lake Lanier, the city's main supplier of drinking water, was dropping to dangerous levels, was expected to continue its dehydration, yet car washes were open and working overtime.

Hypocritical priorities existed all over the world, none more extreme than in the Bible Belt.

I stared at The Jewell of the South and agreed. Rain had come, but all had not been relieved.

There still was a drought.

ELEVEN

I had to keep running from her.

It hurt. I couldn't breathe. But I couldn't stop running. Had to get away from her.

She was behind me, a long-bladed knife in her hand, the kind made for hunting wild animals.

The kind of knife made for gutting and killing beasts in the wilderness.

And that evil heifer had been chasing me for almost two miles.

The trees were knobby and bent, worn and abused by strong winds and rain in the summer, snow and ice in the winter. I hiked over a fallen tree and negotiated another steep incline made of wet ground and jagged stone. I heard her coming after me. I looked back and saw her. Saw her young face and short hair, her mane as black as pepper. I didn't take in her features, just looked at the knife she carried. A knife with an eight-inch blade. A knife that could kill a bear.

I started running again, ran through this section of the Blue Ridge Mountains, took it uphill at a strenuous pace, almost slipped on a section made of soapstone and dunite, recovered, then hit a stretch of flat ground that led me to another precipitous section made of earth and rocks, a section that slowed me down to a strong walk. I kept panting, pushing branches out of the way when I had to, slipped on jagged rocks that were still along the pathway, muscles burning, and I grunted and panted and attacked another steep section, one that made the final hills at Stone Mountain seem like mild inclines.

I had to stop again, couldn't tell which way to go to get out of this jungle. Looked back and couldn't see her. I was beneath a northern hardwood cloud forest made of huge, old birches that covered the north face. Legs ached. There were too many rhododendrons and mountain laurels and shrubs to get a view of her. Hoped she had given up. I stood still on the cold soil. Listened. I saw her again. Saw her before I heard her. She was closer than I had realized, running through wildflowers, coming up one of the longest, highest ridges in Georgia, closing in.

Sweat covered her face and she looked evil. The knife in her hand made her resemble the legendary, horrible, sharp-clawed, winged beast who attempted to steal and eat Indian children.

God, I was hurting.

She was going to catch me. I heard her knife, heard it cutting anything in her way.

My legs were trying to cramp up on me.

Then she dug in deep, came after me again.

She was determined.

I ran. Ran through trees and foliage that were as old as time itself, ran and I could no longer hear the echo of traffic creeping through the trees, coming from everywhere at once, giving no true sense of direction. Town and Union counties were beyond the wilderness. I couldn't be that far from where the forest opened up into the paved area that led to the summit. Couldn't be that far from people who were up by the wagon trail that used to be part of Georgia Route 66.

She was getting closer.

I had gone up five hundred feet in half a mile. It felt like I was dying. Felt like I had never worked out a day in my life. I looked back and saw her coming around a wicked turn, her blade in her right hand.

I started back running, my face orgasmic, sweat first falling like gentle tears, then like a torrential storm as I panted and pushed on toward the Hiawassee Ridge. My pace not as fast, but I kept fighting that uphill battle, kept pushing past foliage on a narrow trail that led me toward the highest in a spine of mountains called Wolfpen Ridge.

As I panted, I looked back.

There she was, breathing hard, sweat running from her pixie cut down over her brown skin, her red T-shirt soaked with sweat, her painful grimace no more than twenty yards away from me. She struggled with the terrain, chased me through a dwarfed red oak and white oak forest, I felt her getting closer as I sprinted by trees that were old, twisted, and limby, heard her getting closer as I frowned and trampled dwarf willow and red-berried mountain ash.

It surprised me when she caught me.

She grunted.

I dug in deep, sprinted, left her huffing and puffing.

Once I made it out of the forest, I stopped and waited on her.

She jogged until she caught up to me, put her hand in the air, and I gave her a sweaty high-five.

She struggled to breathe. "Don't believe that fat ass of yours beat me."

I panted like I was dying. "Whatever."

"God, your ass is spreading."

"At least I have an ass."

I laughed. At least I tried to. Was in too much pain to express the joy of winning our race.

She asked, "What's our time?"

I looked at my watch. "Fifty-one minutes, forty-seven seconds."

"Hoped we could break fifty."

"Five miles up the side of a mountain in under fifty-two minutes."

"Not bad." She nodded. "Not bad at all. Not my best time, but not bad at all."

"Welcome to Brasstown Bald."

She took a digital camera out of her backpack, made me take a picture of her in front of the Jacks Gap Appalachian Trail marker. She made me pose next. Next she held the camera at arm's length and took a picture of both of our sweaty mugs, both of us making silly faces like we were two-year-olds.

We jogged another half mile across the parking lot, made it in four minutes, slowed to a casual walk as we passed other tourists, followed the slow-moving families and eased onto the paved trail, then we picked up our pace, kept it a decent power walk as we maneuvered around people. The civilized part of the trail was wide enough for four people and led up to the visitor center and fire lookout station. We were approaching the highest point in the state of Georgia.

She panted and sped up, again challenging me as she said, "We ran up a mountain."

"Since we're out of the woods, do you mind losing the knife?"

She put it back in its sheath, tucked it in her backpack.

I said, "Running around acting like you're the last of the Mohicans."

"Your fat ass. Don't believe you put on that much weight."

I sped up on the last section of the trail, after we crossed roadway 200, left her aching.

I waited for her at the top, waited and jumped up and down like I was Rocky at the top of the stairs of the Philadelphia Museum of Art, hummed Rocky's theme song with a smile on my damp face. She showed me the middle finger of love when she caught up.

That got a laugh out of me.

She said, "Somebody's showing off today."

We went to use the toilet at the visitor center complex then stepped into the Mountaintop Theater and sat down so we could regroup, chilled out during a fourteen-minute video program before walking around the outside observation deck and taking in the three-hundred-sixty-degree view of the surrounding areas, the hills of Georgia and parts of Tennessee.

She said, "Cold as a witch's tit up here."

"Yeah."

"Feels more like Massachusetts than Georgia."

I nodded. "Temperature dropped at least twenty degrees."

"Did you know Georgia was named after George II of England?"

"Didn't know that."

"And Tennessee, that name is Cherokee."

I smiled. "Somebody's been doing their homework."

She frowned. "I read some of the revisionist history on the walls."

"Uh-huh."

"They make it sound like the Cherokee just packed up and peacefully moved away one day."

"We live in a country filled with people who think they did Africans a favor by making us slaves."

"The British did the same thing."

"My point exactly."

I wanted to take her up into the fire lookout tower, but it wasn't open to the public.

We found a spot on the observation deck and stared at hundreds of miles of trees.

I had stopped moving. I had stopped running and climbing. I was at peace.

I loved nature. Loved being in the mountains more than being in the city. So quiet. So calm. Loved coming to the summit so I could look down at the trails that passed remarkable cliffs and boulder fields, places where rock tripe, lichen, reindeer moss, old-man's beard, and club moss flourished.

But right now my mind wasn't on nature. At least not Mother Nature.

My thoughts caught up with me. Thoughts I had wanted to let go of but was unable to flee.

My mind was back at the W.

I felt them touching me. Felt four hands and two tongues on my heated body.

I felt them giving me pleasure, felt them making me come.

My mind was one hundred miles away from here, every thought on my identical sins.

I stared out at the rolling mountains, at the real estate formerly known as Mount Enotah, and imagined being out there, running up the mountain, racing for my life, only this time Mark and Karl were chasing me through the land that used to be owned by the Cherokee Indians, shoving each other, tripping each other, competing to get to me, the winner knowing he had earned the right to fuck me in the forest. I would run, but it would not be my best run. They would run naked, wearing nothing but socks and running shoes. I'd run the same way, naked except for my Nikes. One of my Mandingo warriors would catch me and I'd close my eyes, not look to see if the winner wore tattoos that symbolized a lover gone by or if on his left hand he carried the burden of a wedding ring, not caring about anything but the moment, just playfully fighting like I wanted to be liberated, but not really fighting for my freedom.

He would give me sex alfresco.

The battle would turn me on and I would come fast. I would come hard. I would come so loud that the locals would think the legendary creature that haunted the mountains had returned.

As one brother was about to come, his twin would pull him away, leave him wailing and trembling and spewing jism across the colorful forest. The other one would enter me hard and fast, make me come hard. When my orgasm died I would once again hear insects singing as I leaned against a tree and listened to their identical ragged breathing, listened to them pant as I listened to my own breathing.

Underneath the shadows created by the trees, we would stare at each other.

Standing on come-stained leaves they would glare at me, lust in their eyes.

They would growl at each other, their stares and deep frowns once again competitive.

I would run away from them, would race across stone and leaves and broken branches.

Once again they would chase.

Those thoughts had me so horny it hurt. My rabbit couldn't ease the pain, couldn't find anything in my File Cabinet of Pleasure to remove this carnal suffering, not the way they did.

I rubbed my eyes, tried to get them out of my mind. Tried to move their tongues from between my legs. I couldn't stop thinking about them. If I didn't think about Mark, my mind was on Karl. But most of the time I thought about them together, as if they were one unit, the same person split by nature.

I had enjoyed them. Enjoyed them too much. That new experience left me yearning to find out what else could happen between us. And I missed them. Missing them was a sin. A sin worse than the sin we had engaged in underneath thunderous skies illuminated by streaks of lightning.

She said, "Penny for your thoughts."

I laughed. "We better go. It's cold up here. Need to get back to the bottom and warm up."

On the way down the hill a middle-aged man was taking a picture of his wife as she sat on a bench. He was blond, hair long. She was a redhead, hair short. Her wrinkled T-shirt said "HELP I'M

TALKING AND I CAN'T SHUT UP!" His said "YOU MESS WITH ME YOU MESS WITH THE WHOLE TRAILER PARK." The woman asked if I would take a picture of both of them. I took their digital camera and snapped two shots.

The woman said, "You two look so much alike."

I shrugged. "Unfortunately I've heard that a time or two."

The woman asked, "Sisters?"

"Why, thank you. You hear that, Nia Simone? I look like I'm your sister."

"Don't get her started." I laughed and playfully nudged her. "That's my mother."

The redheaded woman turned to me. "Your mother looks so young."

The long-haired man asked, "Where y'all from?"

That question had been thrown out there because of my mother's singsong way of speaking, her singsong accent. Or because the man had read the front of our T-shirts, both of ours promoting ICC Cricket World Cup West Indies. My mother told the curious hikers that she was born in Port of Spain, but lived in Los Angeles, that she was visiting her daughter for the weekend, told them I lived in the Atlanta area. They were so amazed by my mother, stunned by how toned her body was and how youthful she looked. Mother told them we had hiked up from the bottom of the mountain, our trek being over five miles, had made it to the top in less than an hour. They were blown away. Mother loved the attention.

Over and over the red-haired woman said she couldn't believe my mother was almost two decades older than me. She was so astonished and impressed that she had to photograph us to show their friends.

While the strangers chatted, they held hands like they were a couple for life.

Part of me envied that, how they had bonded, endured the years, defied the odds.

When that was done we headed back down the paved portion, took it across the parking lot, and entered the narrow trail that led first up the mountain for about a half mile, then the rest was all downhill.

She had her hunting knife out again, slicing at branches like she was the queen of the jungle.

I said, "Must you be so dramatic?"

"Nia Simone, there could be a bear or a snake in those woods."

"And what are you going to do with that ten-dollar knife?"

"If a bear comes after me, I'm not going to be the only one they find dead."

As we walked the narrow trail, once again, my imagination took over, and for a moment I saw Karl and Mark. They had me against a tree, both touching my body, both kissing my flesh, pleasing me. I was sandwiched between them, one deep inside my yoni, and the other sodomizing me. I saw pain and pleasure in my face. I saw me coming so hard it looked like I was dying. The orgasm I saw my twin self experiencing was irrepressible. That vision terrified me and excited me. I'd done that with a single man and a vibrator, had two orifices filled at once, the pleasure so extreme. Imagined what that would be like with the identical sins.

"Nia Simone."

I jumped, saw my mother was a long way ahead of me, looking back, watching me stare at a tree.

I jogged and caught up with her.

We hiked for about half a mile before we stopped to catch our breath. I went to an ancient tree, gave my attention to a huge, black caterpillar trekking across moss. The caterpillar looked like a moving penis. I wondered what it would be like to feel Karl inside of me, to feel him moving across my fleshy fold, opening me up at an un-hurried pace, moving like that caterpillar, easing deeper and deeper a little at a time, not rushing to fill me up, the sweet torture so gradual it would feel like sensual madness. I wondered if Karl would feel the same as Mark. Or better.

I blinked away from that image, from those thoughts, then searched for my mother.

She was staring at me, giving me that stern mother look.

I said, "What?"

"So, Nia Simone, my mysterious daughter, blood of my blood, what's the problem?"

"Nothing, O ye queen of the dramatic words."

I led the way back down the mountain, our pace easy on the knees.

She asked, "What was the deal with Logan?"

"Was wondering when you were going to bring that up."

"Why did you let him go?"

"Why do you sound so disappointed?"

"I'm not disappointed. I'm very proud of you, Nia."

"Thanks, Mom."

"You've done well for yourself."

"I'm doing okay."

"You're the most successful non-famous person I know."

"And I love it that way."

"You're not foolish with your money."

"I'm working hard, just not as hard as I did the last two years."

"You made four million one year."

"Only made three."

She let a moment pass. "That why you didn't want to marry Logan?"

"Wasn't about money, if that's what you're asking."

"Was money part of it?"

"He has no idea of my true income. He thinks I live paycheck-to-paycheck."

What I needed, it was hard to articulate. This was my mother.

Not my girlfriend, not a stranger on a plane. We had closeness, but she was still my mother. I'd never tell her about the W. Would never tell her how I met two handsome men that morning and allowed them to seduce and please me in whatever ways they saw fit that night. Wouldn't tell her how I craved doing that same thing again.

In a Trini accent I said, "He no ready."

"He no ready?" Her Trini accent came to life for a moment. "He couldn't satisfy you?"

"I tell him it good eh but you not ready for this Trini yet. I tell him he boring."

My mother asked, "Were you on the phone?"

"Nah woman. We face-to-face."

"Are you mad? You could've just sent him a text message."

She waved her hand, tightened her lips, and didn't push the issue after that. She knew me. Half of my DNA had come from her. The honesty part of me came from her, imported from Port of Spain.

"Listen to me, Nia. Every man is different. Just like every woman is different. Sometimes you have to train them, tell them what you want, show them how to make you happy in that way."

"I'm not a sex-ed teacher."

"Nia Simone, do not look at me like I'm crazy."

I wanted to ask her about what I was feeling, wanted to ask her if she ever felt this way, if this was normal, if this was a part of growing, a part of a person's evolution, this discontent and need for personal fulfillment being the wall between selflessness and settling for what the mind knew was best. But I didn't feel comfortable talking to anyone about my desires, about the making of me, not on that level. What I was feeling, even now, I didn't feel safe writing about those sensations in my diary, didn't want to journal this portion of my life for fear that the journal would be found.

I didn't want to die a sudden death and leave words behind that exposed my world.

I didn't want to be looked upon as a Sodomite who provoked the wrath of God.

Memories of the W refused to let me be.

I wanted the same experience with them again, wanted that level of satisfaction, if not more.

But that wouldn't happen.

I had to think like a man; fuck, then release. Like they were *Fucker*men. Sexual fisherman, casting their bait, reeling in women for zipless fucks, engaging in orgasm and immediate release.

TWELVE

As we left the mountains, I had the top down on my convertible.

Sirius was on classic R&B, Chanté Moore singing love had taken over as we left the mountains and headed south, rode alongside the Chattahoochee and came up on what used to be a logging municipality, a city that had resurrected itself by becoming a replica of a Bavarian alpine town.

We passed by a string of horse-drawn carriages riding Main Street in Helen, Georgia. Some of the carriages were pumpkin-shaped. I looked off to the side, saw a group of women, most had on tight jeans with huge belt buckles, biker boots, and breast-tight tank tops. Harley girls until the day they died.

The sun was still high, streets packed with tourists of all nationalities, and kids and adults were floating down the Chattahoochee in pink and green tubes. A block later we eased by mom-and-pop stores that had Confederate flag swimsuits, Confederate flag biker jackets on display in their Main Street windows. I saw three more people wearing T-shirts that read "WELCOME TO AMERICA. NOW SPEAK ENGLISH." I saw the same T-shirt in the front window of every novelty shop; the locals were sending a message to the Spanish-speaking newcomers whose population had doubled over the last five years.

There were no Harlem Bars up this way, no Compounds, no W

Hotels. I doubted that I would be able to find *Essence* magazine or any of the kind of hair care products I needed within fifty miles.

Harleys roared up and down Main Street. Bruce Springsteen was screaming he was born in the USA. Good-old-boy music poured out of Dutch-style buildings, one of the restaurants having a large windmill in its structure. It was an Alpine village complete with cobblestone alleys and old-world towers.

My mother said, "I'm putting the word out about the sci-fi book you're doing."

"Who did you talk to?"

"Few actors. Will Smith's production company. Put the buzz in Angela Bassett's ear. I'm going to shoot the word to Don Cheadle too. And I'm working on getting word to Leonardo DiCaprio's people."

"You really liked my idea?"

"I *loved* that idea. With points, a producer's credit, and residuals we can retire off that idea."

"*We?*"

"Where you go, I go."

"And where you go, I go."

We made our way back toward the other side of the world and connected with Georgia 400, rode that autobahn down to Alpharetta and stopped at J. Christopher's, a friendly place with healthy food. It was too humid to sit on the patio, so we took a booth. Mom sat facing a ten-foot-high rustic, gold sun-devouring-the-moon sculpture on a gigantic wall. Behind me, up high, was a painting of JFK on the cover of *Life* magazine, August 4, 1961, back when the magazine cost twenty cents.

My cellular rang once. It was a text message from one of my identical sins.

Flashbacks of four hands and two tongues made my yoni shiver and swell.

My mother asked, "Who is he?"

"Guy I just met. Met him a few days ago. After Logan was here."

"You know what you are? Sneaky. Hard-headed. Stubborn. Mysterious."

"I'm so much like you, it's scary."

She switched gears, her momma face being replaced by her serious face. "I was thinking. And this has been bothering me. I think it's time. We have to open a business in Trinidad."

"We?"

"I know we have a home there, will always have a home there, but we need to come up with some idea, nothing extravagant, and open some business, something where we are helping our people and contributing to Trinidad. Nothing where we would have to be there for the daily operations."

"And I thought I had problems with Uncle Sam."

We laughed.

She asked, "Well, what do you think? Maybe open a Rituals. Start with a coffeehouse."

"Sounds good to me."

We ate pancakes and planned out our evening and our tomorrow.

Later on we'd ride out 75 to the Auburn Historic District and chill out at the Harlem Bar, pig out on the ambrosial skillet-fried chicken, chew on moist cornbread, and fill up on the cheese-encrusted mac 'n' cheese while we nursed lime martinis and listened to a band throw down some neo soul. We would be there until the music died and the lights were turned out.

My mother lost the race up the mountain, so all of that would be her treat.

Tomorrow morning we planned to drag ourselves to Cumberland Mall for manicures, pedicures, and massages at Spa Sydell. No running or working out, just have a spa morning, then shop at Phipps and Lenox, make a mad dash through DSW for shoes, then hit another shoe warehouse on the east side of Piedmont Park on

Amsterdam Avenue, then go out for dinner, drinks, and desserts at Café Intermezzo.

All of that would be my treat.

After Café Intermezzo I'd leave midtown, hop on 85 South and take her back to Hartsfield-Jackson Atlanta airport. I'd kiss her good-bye and cry when I dropped her off, then would sit in the parking lot and talk to her on my cellular, wouldn't hang up until the plane was about to take off for LAX.

The family side of me would be satiated. And the dark side would be ready to take control.

That would happen after we hung out tonight, after we had our mother-daughter day tomorrow.

But now as we sat in J. Christopher's and broke our fasting, butterflies lived inside my belly.

Our conversation was nothing more than white noise, my mind somewhere else. My mother was talking, eating, flipping through the pages of *Creative Loafing*, her cellular constantly ringing.

My mother looked at her caller ID, frowned, and clicked her phone on. "Hazel Bijou-Wilson."

She always said her first and last name when she answered the phone. Hollywood trained.

After my mother started chatting, I looked at my cellular phone.

Every sensuous word of the text message pulled at me. He gave good text-sex. Logan's text-sex was horrible. His spelling was horrible. That destroyed the flow, having to fight the urge to correct spelling and fix word usage didn't stimulate me. These messages were hot. As if I was there with him.

My mind went back to the W.

Back to a night that should have been a zipless night, filed away and forgotten.

I wasn't sure if I had a guilty conscience, or was experiencing the consciousness of guilt.

One of my identical sins had contacted me, had sent me a text message first. A simple message that had more power and created more stimulation than a six-page love letter. I glanced down at my phone, read part of the message again, read the part that made me think things I shouldn't be thinking.

Did you enjoy having your velvet yoni savored while you were being kissed?

Velvet yoni. Those words read like the sexiest shit that I had ever seen. His words created the image of a red velvet glove. Just the thought of it made me suffer the start of a provocative wetness.

I sent him a text back: *Can you make that happen again?*

I can make that happen.

Then make it happen. ☺

I imagined four hands on my warm skin. Felt two tongues tracing my flesh.

In the back of my mind I heard a smooth baritone voice whispering, *"Open your mouth."*

Flashbacks created a Pavlovian response; I opened my mouth, anticipation so strong, my breathing catching my throat. Imagined pleasing Mark while Karl watched, masturbating his angst away.

My mother finished her call about ten minutes later, the closing of her phone breaking my trance.

We talked, ate, laughed, both laughs created in Trinidad, mine nurtured in the California smog.

Masturbatable thoughts created a spasm, and that tremor rolled through me as my nipples betrayed my secret desires. It took all of my energy to keep my eyes on my food as I laughed and talked with my mother, afraid to look at her for fear that she might see something that I didn't want her to see. I tried to force my memories out of this room. I swallowed pancakes and tasted mangos. Imagined mango juice dripping all over my skin. Remembered how his come was so warm and sweet. His nectar had been as sweet as syrup. Two tongues had been kind to my yoni, had savored my yoni, had licked my yoni like she had been twice as sweet.

Minutes later we were on GA 400 heading back toward Cobb County.

Mother let her seat back, closed her eyes, the top down, the warm wind blowing over us.

I received another text message from one of my Bajan lovers.

I'm naked.

Are you? Doing what?

I'm imagining kissing and touching you.

I asked myself why I didn't want to talk to my mother about what I was going through. I rationalized that it was because telling her about what I was doing, what I had done, would leave me up for judgment. In reality I would be asking for her permission. I wasn't in search of validation.

Are you touching yourself?

Yes.

What are you trying to do to me?

I want to make your clit swell.

It's swollen. Are you really hard?

I wasn't in search of validation. I loved Hazel Tamana, but I did not need my mother's permission. I turned to her, looked at her to see if she was staring at me, somehow stealing my thoughts. Mothers had those types of powers. They were walking lie detectors, superheroes without capes. Hazel Tamana was asleep before we made it to 285. She was so relaxed. She worked hard. She played harder. She was the woman I wanted to be when I grew up. I let her be. She needed the rest.

My cellular buzzed again, sexual messages stirring me as I drove, the part of my brain linked to reward and pleasure creating enough energy to light up a small town.

I want to fuck you from behind, bend you over, and go inside you a little at a time.

Damn. I'm driving. Don't make me run off the road. Text me later.

Until then . . . one hundred kisses and one thousand yoni licks.

Damn.

I drove licking the corners of my lips. Imagining. As I passed by Ashford/Dunwoody, the exit for the W Hotel, another ripple rolled through me, made my toes curl inside my hiking shoes. Pleasurable waves and tingling sensations moved through every part of my body, my yoni being the epicenter.

I looked at my mother, looked to see if she was reading my mind. She was still sleeping. And I was glad she was exhausted, probably more from working long hours and jet-lag than the hike itself.

There was a war going on within me. The logical part of me wondered if we were all created this way and unaware, unconscious of the hardwiring, all prone to some sort of serotonin imbalance, all prone to love and obsessive-compulsive acts, all prone to madness. Because obsession was madness.

My thoughts of Mark, my thoughts of Karl, they were never-ending, my yoni perpetually moist.

I struggled, my struggle both terrifying and exhilarating, enhanced by a gathering of fantasies.

I wanted to know if my mother had done battle with self as well.

I wanted to know if this sensation of restlessness was inherited.

But there were things I didn't want to know about my mother.

And there were things she probably didn't need to know about her daughter.

No way could I smile with joy and tell her about my night of exquisite sin at the W.

The memory of the W was resplendent. My smile was victorious. The sperm was chasing the egg. The sensual fantasies that had consumed my imagination at Brasstown Bald lived inside my mind.

I couldn't wait to see them again. Just one more time. And we would be done.

Once again I was seven years old, and it was Christmas Eve.

* * *

A huge bouquet of flowers was waiting for me at my front door.

I thought about my identical sins. I smiled. Smiled because it was the largest bouquet I had ever seen in my life. The delivery company was on Spring Road near Cumberland Boulevard, A Petal Pusher.

It came with a Hallmark apology from Logan.

I saw his name and a migraine took root.

Just seeing his name put my body in distress.

The wind left my body. I looked around, expected to see his Range Rover. While my mother went inside through the garage, I took the arrangement to my car, sped Oakwood Trace to Oakwood Way, burned rubber getting to the Dumpster near the entrance at Campbell Road, and shoved them in the garbage, not wanting any scent associated with him inside my home.

But the scent from touching what I didn't want to touch remained on my hands.

The aroma had seeped inside my physical being, had tainted and violated my skin.

Unseen, Logan remained with me, a tick attached to my flesh, sucking away my happiness.

THIRTEEN

It was early morning and the Southern sun hadn't begun baking the humid air.

I was driving fast, cellular up to my ear, making a call I didn't want to make, but had to.

"Logan, this is Nia. But you know that. Flowers. Why? Four days in a row. This madness has to end. This is over. Please. No more flowers. No more text messages. I ... I ... I don't know what to fucking say at this point. I don't love you. Will never love you. Move on. Let it end. Just let me be me."

I took another hard breath, anger rising like the sun.

A second arrangement of flowers had arrived after my mother left town. Then two more arrangements followed, each larger than the one before. Then the text messages had started again.

Irregardless of the hurtful things I said, your the one for me. Please except my apology.

This was nerve-racking. This was beyond ridiculous.

Then came the nightmares. I started dreaming that he was outside my door, in the rain, banging hard, ringing the doorbell, screaming, "Open the door. Let me in so I can fuck you like you're a whore. My whore. You can't make love to a whore ... whores only understand a good hard fuck."

I had let him get to me. Allowed him to torture my soul, drag my naked body over flaming barbed wire. I'd blocked his numbers.

Blocked his e-mail addresses. I'd taken him off my friends list on MySpace. Shit. He'd never been in my "Top 24," so that should have been a clue to him right there.

How did you break up with someone you weren't with? How did you break up with someone who didn't want to see you happy without them? I wanted to call my mother, but the sun wasn't up in L.A.

He wouldn't let it end. He'd lost the battle and was too narcissistic to tuck his tail and walk away.

But under all that puffery, Logan was a child. This was about reclaiming his esteem.

He had told me I was his fantasy. And that was frightening.

I should've turned around. Should've called, canceled the meeting, and turned around.

I didn't.

I was nervous. Beyond tired. I'd spent half the night writing, this time skipping the stimulating and masturbation-provoking smut in order to slave over my sci-fi novel, a project that sounded better with each idea I wrote down. I'd stayed up working on the outline, setting it up in three acts, Hollywood-style.

I knew I should've turned around, but I was beyond the point of no return.

I had to continue my journey, let no one turn me around.

I merged to the far right lane, whipped by three eighteen-wheelers, and left I-285 at exit 7, Cascade Road. At the bottom of the ramp I made a left and went inside the perimeter. The directions said I had to go past Kroger, Bank of America, and at least three gigantic churches. I followed the two-lane road up a street lined with older single-family homes. Where I was going was supposed to be exactly two miles from exit 7. If I remembered what he told me, if I passed by J.R. Crickets or Big Daddy's Café, I would've gone one block too far. As soon as I crossed Willis Mills I slowed down, looked to my left, and I saw a community of huge homes tucked behind the trees. I pulled up to the security gate, saw a real estate box, and pulled a flier out. *Audubon Estates. Custom homes starting at one million. Twenty-one wooded half-acre to one-acre lots.* One home was under construction. Four levels. Elevator. Two libraries. Three kitchens. Media center. Finished basement that had two bathrooms and a kitchen. At least ten thousand square feet. The perfect house to have if you were married to someone you couldn't stand. Plenty of room so you'd never have to see each other. The backs of most of these starter castles faced the woods, so there were plenty of places to bury a dead body.

God, my morbid sense of humor was in rare form.

I backed up to the buzzer and looked up his name. I pushed the button to call the house.

The phone rang three times before he answered, "Hello."

"It's me."

"Okay. Hold on." Sounded like he was pushing buttons on his phone. "Did the gate open?"

"Nope."

The buzzer was malfunctioning; he gave me the private code to his gated kingdom.

I said, "Where do I go?"

"Come around to the end of the street. On the left side. Garage door is up."

He hung up and I entered the code.

The buzzer went off and the dramatic metal gate eased open, parted like a woman's legs.

I had the secret combination that allowed me entry to his kingdom.

I entered his domain, drove slowly, looked at eighteen of the starter castles, nine on each side, before I came up to one on the edges of the cul-de-sac. The community only had one narrow street. One way in, one way out of an area lined with million-dollar homes. In the better parts of L.A., one million dollars would get you a one-level home built in the '40s, no security gate, no yard. Two million would get you a nice home in a neighborhood that was bordered on four sides by a wonderful ghetto.

This was ridiculous.

Now I knew what Dorothy felt like when she stood before the Emerald City waiting to see the wizard.

It looked like the trees in this area should sprout money instead of leaves. I'd never live this way. I admired those who did, but it wasn't my thing. I leaned toward quiet, discreet, and being as invisible as possible with my money. I was too busy admiring the homes and went too far, had driven to the end of the cul-de-sac and had to turn around. As I turned I saw him waving. He was coming out of the garage, smiling. He wore khaki shorts, camouflage tank top, Birkenstock sandals. I forced my mind back to Karl.

After a night fueled by fantasies and alcohol, I didn't know what realities soberness and sunlight would bring. I didn't know if this was a good idea, or if I ever should have accepted this offer to hang out. I was nervous. Hoped I looked good. Hoped he still found me attractive. Hoped I didn't end up thinking he was a jerk. This was daytime. No colorful lights and apple martinis to create a fantasy world.

This was creeping beyond zipless. The hotel was neutral territory, but now I was at his home.

I was supposed to fuck, then release.

He had a three-car garage that faced the side of his home. I pulled up the steep incline that led to his home, was about to park in his extended driveway, but he motioned at the open garage, waved for me to park inside, right next to his Jeep. When I got out of my car, before I could say hello, he was kissing me. He tongued me for a long time. He kissed my face, my eyes, my neck, sucked on my lobes, then put his tongue in my mouth again, made me dizzy, and it felt like I was in a formal dress, dancing to a classic love song, that kiss making me crazy, making me hot, filling me with an unexpected desire.

I was inside a garage, wearing jean shorts, strappy sandals, T-shirt from Trinidad's Carnival. But I felt like I had on a full gown, Cinderella at the ball, knowing I should leave before the clock struck twelve.

He said, "Good morning."

"Morning to you, too."

Karl held me close and kissed me like I was his preferred lover, like my tongue was flavored with chocolate-covered sin. Guilt rose inside of me. I tried to pull away from him, tried to slow this down, but we kissed again. I melted into him, so close we were one body with two heartbeats. I sucked his lips, tiptoed and brushed my tongue along his neck, touched his chest, tasted his shoulders.

Any problems I had before I came here didn't matter anymore.

My exhaustion ceased to exist.

If this was how brothers competed, let the competition continue until my last breath arrived.

We separated reluctantly, both of us smiling like teenagers. Just like that, I felt like calling him names like sweetie, baby, honey. But I didn't. I tried to keep it cool as I followed him up the three steps that led inside his butler's pantry, then we went left toward his kitchen. Dark wood floors and cabinets. Stainless-steel appliances and a Sub-Zero refrigerator. The television was on in the living room, its sound coming out of the walls. I expected him to be up watching CNN, but he was looking at *Smallville*, he'd recorded that on TiVo. He turned the flat-screen television off and came back. Told me he hoped I was hungry. I was. He'd made a simple, healthy breakfast. Turkey sausage. Oatmeal. Fresh mangos. My tattooed Mandingo had given me mangos. The fruit of the islands. The fruit of passion. I put a slice of mango in my mouth and a memory returned. In my mind his brother's tongue was stirring me while he fed me. Karl smiled at me. His eyes telling me he was reliving the same carnal moment.

I said, "I thought most photographers were starving artists."

"I thought most writers rode public transportation."

That got a laugh out of me. "Touché."

Karl aimed the remote at a sensor on the kitchen wall. Music came on all over the house. Roger and Zapp were telling me that they heard it through the grapevine. When that song ended, Karl used the remote and changed the CDs in his system until he found what he was searching for. Then all over his home a woman was singing, her timbre making the atmosphere double in its eroticism, some moaning and wonderful singing, her voice hot like morning sex.

I asked, "Nice song. Who is that?"

"Simfani Blue."

Karl's wicked kisses had started something. The music he had on was dragging in the same direction. I wasn't expecting this. Not this fast. I sat on a barstool, humming and shifting like I was trying to contain a wildfire. Simfani Blue continued singing, continued moaning like she was on the stairway to heaven. Her voice was orgasmic, like she was singing as a lover ran his tongue down her spine.

Karl was looking at me, smiling as he ate his oatmeal.

I ate the last of mine and said, "This is a very nice home."

"Thanks. Mark built it for me about three years ago."

"He built all of the homes in this development?"

"He built three. There have been several builders up in here."

"Nice area."

"Lots of break-ins. Everyone in the community has been hit at least once. Some twice."

"You've been hit?"

"Twice. Mark's been hit once. Guy near the entrance was hit three times."

I shook my head.

He said, "Black-on-black crime ain't no joke in the ATL."

"Same in L.A. My mother lives in View Park. Everybody out there is getting burglarized."

He used his fork to pick up the last slice of mango. He put the mango to my mouth. I let my tongue trace the fruit, let the juices ease inside my mouth before I savored the entire piece.

We stared at each other. In that moment, we were back at the W.

After we ate he loaded the dishwasher. While he did that I picked up what looked like an invitation to a party. What caught my eye wasn't the beautiful colors on the flier, but the sexy woman who was naked on a bed, her breasts nice and large as she sucked her finger and looked directly at the camera, her expression like she was in the middle of pleasure. She had long, dark, curly hair, her race ambiguous, but she looked familiar, very familiar. There was nothing vulgar about the photo, made her look human, feminine, like a professional woman celebrating life in her birthday suit. WEDNESDAY NIGHT HOOK-UPS. It was a newsletter for an adult club called Trapeze. The flier promised 100% PURE SWINGING. A second newsletter for Trapeze was under the first, that one advertising TROPICAL HEAT SATURDAY. Couples had to pay thirty-five dollars to get in. Single males had to pay seventy-five. Single females ten.

"Nia Simone."

When Karl said my name I broke away from the newsletters, divorced myself from my overactive imagination and looked at him. His air conditioner was on, his home lukecool, but my face and neck became warm. Our eye contact was strong, direct. I wondered if he had left these out for me to see.

I asked, "Ever been?"

He nodded. "You?"

I shook my head. "But I heard about Trapeze."

"It's all about the women. Where women go to celebrate their sexuality. It's an environment where women are in charge. It's not always about having sex. Do as much or as little as you like."

I nodded like I understood. "You have these fliers out because . . . ?"

"I photographed the women in the shots."

"Oh."

"Was reviewing my work."

"Looks good to me."

"Not my best. Was a rush job. Could've been more creative."

I put the flier down, pulled my eyes away from the invitation to be open and participate in clandestine transgressions with professional strangers, my mind craving to be in an adult playground where women were in charge, a place where I could do as much or as little as I desired.

I said, "Let's see the rest of this castle."

I took Karl's hand, and he gave me the tour.

The living room was lovely, great modern furniture set off by a huge oriental rug. The family room had a stone fireplace, another oriental rug, a large flat-screen television mounted off to one side, yet everything symmetrical. A wonderful walk-in pantry was between the kitchen and the formal dining room.

Houses like this made me want to get naked. Not for sex, at least not right away. Every room was so large, so open. His back deck spread half the length of the house, nothing outside the windows but trees and privacy. And with Simfani Blue's voice following me from room to room, I wanted to hibernate, stay all week, at least a weekend. Have sex, eat, sleep, shower, and watch films.

And listen to Simfani Blue moan like she was in *9½ Weeks*.

Turtles made of mahogany, golden cricket players made out of one continuous strand of wire, wooden plaques showing the natives climbing coconut trees, some plaques with flying fish, marlin, pictures from their carnival, images from their beaches, his entire culture was represented throughout his home. The representation wasn't overwhelming, was just enough to give it a subtle Caribbean flavor.

Karl also had sculptures, framed art by African American artists like Bibbs and Gatewood, but what caught my attention were the family pictures. Most I didn't really see. My eyes went to a picture of Karl and a stunning woman. Smiling. Him in a tuxedo. Her in a wedding dress. Newlyweds. She looked similar to Mariah Carey and Alicia Keys, as if someone had blended their DNA and created his spouse. I stared at her eyes, slanted eyes the color of new envy, and she stared at me in return. I wondered if she was Kenya, his angel.

I said, "You were married?"

"That's not me."

"Oh. Mark?"

"Yeah, that's that ugly motherfucker."

"Language."

"Yeah, that's him."

I studied the photos again. I studied Mark and the stunning woman who was his wife.

I said, "Nice photos. Your work?"

He shook his head.

I said, "You weren't the photographer at your brother's wedding?"

Again he shook his head. "Nah."

I studied her again, looked at her eyes, her nose, said, "She looks very familiar."

"WBS-TV Atlanta. 'The Jewell of the South.'"

My mouth dropped open. "Mark is married to Jewell Stewart?"

"Yeah, that's little Miss Pussy Controller."

"She looks . . ." I caught myself, made my excitement fade like smoke in a strong breeze. "I never would've recognized her from this picture. Her face . . . it's the same . . . she's older . . . hair's different now."

"That's her with darker hair. Copying Halle Berry's cut. Looked horrible on her."

Karl would reveal nothing about his brother, as if there were some familial code, maybe part of the unwritten code of silence that existed between men, but he would chastise and verbally humiliate his brother's wife. *Little Miss Pussy Controller.* Blood was thicker than water. Whatever bonded twins was thicker than blood. Mark was married to Jewell Stewark. "The Jewell of the South."

I said, "She's Jamaican, right?"

"Her grandparents were."

"Well, to me if she had Jamaican roots, she's Jamaican."

"Okay. She's Jamaican."

"Married herself an island man."

"Yeah. That hater married herself an island man."

Jewell Stewark. Mark's wife.

I said, "Something else is different."

"Rhinoplasty."

"Wow."

"Made a difference in her career. Got that fat nose trimmed down to a decent size and dyed her hair."

I stared in the eyes of the woman who had Mark in a horrible marriage. Never would have thought it was her. I wondered if she was awake when he came home, his suit damaged, smelling like both rain and left-behind lust. The feelings I experienced were not the feelings that came with a zipless night. I moved my eyes away from that photo, felt stirred by a twinge of jealousy as I took Karl's hand and put my eyes on other photos, particularly those of Ali and other boxers. Karl was in the photo with Ali.

But I didn't see Karl in any of his brother's wedding pictures.

He said he wasn't the photographer at his brother's wedding.
I didn't ask, again not wanting to get too personal.

We rode the elevator up two levels to his office, which was almost as large
as the main floor of my townhome, had its own giant bathroom. A
family room was on the top level too. Mounted big-screen televisions
were in each room. Great art from Puerto Rico, Barbados, and Antigua were on the walls. After that we rode the elevator down to his
basement. The entire basement was his studio. Wide-open spaces.
Lots of professional lights. At least six rooms. Had sections set up
for doing studio shots. He showed me some of his work. A lot of it
was erotic, beautiful women in very creative poses, made up in body
paints, some in very creative settings, like abandoned warehouses,
or on stark white sheets.

He said, "You should come over and let me shoot you one day."

I shrugged. "Don't think I could do it."

"It'll be just us. Every shot will be tasteful." He paused talking
long enough for him to gather lenses and another Nikon, no doubt
his backup camera. "If you don't like the shots, we'll delete them
all."

I stared at his creativity. Vanity rose. "I'll think about it."

"Let me show you the rest of the crib."

The bedrooms were two levels up, above the main floor. His
master bedroom was so large that the fifty-inch television over the
fireplace couldn't be seen from the bed. But it was laid out so the
television was for the sitting area, and the king-size bed was for
other things. It gave the feeling that seduction started in the sitting
area, on his big red lounger, then moved deeper, as if there was an
imaginary line that separated the sitting area from the fucking area.
His bed was huge, pastel colors, lots of big pillows. I wanted to run
and dive on the mountain of pillows, bounce on the mattress like
I was a little girl, maybe have a pillow fight that evolved into some-

thing else. He took my hand and for a moment I thought he was going to lead me to the leather bench at the foot of his bed, do creative things and take his pleasure at sunrise.

I wanted him to. I wanted him to make love to me like I was his wife, his brand-new bride.

With that thought I brought my hands to my face, tried to rub the green out of my eyes.

Overhead, in between the lyrics, Simfani Blue moaned, echoed sensuality.

I thought Karl was about to turn his master bedroom into his own private Trapeze. Maybe blindfold me, start making love to me, then have Mark sneak out of the closet, change up on me and see if I could feel the difference. But he showed me the oversized bathroom, the oversized bathtub, walked me through the his-and-hers walk-in closets, then we left, took the stairs back down to the main level, then to his garage.

He had to get to his client in Greensboro, the drive being at least three hundred miles.

That disappointed me. Leaving without marking territory in some way, even if it was a quickie.

I put my overnight bag in his Jeep, got inside, and we were leaving the land of starter castles. As we exited Karl's community, Simfani Blue's voice remained in my head, her sensuality stayed with me.

The image of Mark and his wife lived inside my head.

I wished I hadn't seen that picture. My inner hamster was running fast, making that wheel spin, giving undeserved energy to the part of me that produced envy.

But maybe it was for the greater good. A reminder to not get caught up.

As we were leaving and came upon the largest of the mini castles, I saw her.

If I hadn't seen her wedding picture only minutes ago, I would've been excited to see her. I recognized her face better now, six years older than her wedding picture in Karl's home. Her hair no longer dark, no longer in the trendy Halle Berry cut, now golden and long and straight, the same as Calleigh Duquesne on *CSI: Miami*. That Swedish color change and the rhinoplasty made the unspoken half of her heritage become bold, highlighted, and underlined. Her small eyes and oval-shaped head were on billboards all over Georgia, part of the award-winning local news team, her striking face always up front.

She was standing in the driveway of a four-level home on the left. Jewell Stewark was dressed down: tight jeans, sling-backs, and a white short-sleeved blouse. She was with the gardener, pointing at her landscape, her face showing her displeasure with his work. That wasn't the face she showed the rest of Atlanta. Jewell Stewark filled my sense of sight; my other senses denied their rampant curiosity.

Karl blew his horn as he approached her castle.

Drawn by the noise, she looked up, her face in an abrupt smile, like she was prepared to wave and say good morning to one of the kings and queens of the chocolate village, but she saw it was Karl.

Her smile vanished. There was no wave. Karl's sister-in-law's lips tightened and went south. Her charm-school posture and body language reeked of self-importance, like her name should be on the Walk of Fame. Her eyes came to me. Anger eclipsed her mixed beauty. Felt like I was looking directly into the sun with my naked eyes. I couldn't stop staring at Mark's wife. Couldn't pull away. That's who Mark was intimate with. His tongue on her yoni. Her mouth on his lingam. His thick dick pounding her into bliss. Her riding him, coming down hard, making him come for her. I imagined it all. Before I could be blinded, she turned away, as if looking in Karl's direction would turn her into a block of stone.

She didn't yield the Julia Roberts smile that was on billboards.

She didn't look friendly and professional like she did on television.

Jewell Stewark looked cold-blooded, like she came from a long line of evil bitches. Like her heart was damaged and impenetrable, her soul made of ice. She looked like instant hatred, just add water.

Karl chuckled and mumbled, "Yeah, fuck you too."

He had blown his horn just to force her attention, did that to rile her, I knew that.

I didn't ask what that family feud was all about.

Anxiety rose like humidity.

I reminded myself that this was supposed to be zipless. But this had moved to the far right of zipless. I felt its fever, the heat of infatuation, it warmed my nervousness. Too much was on my mind as I rode in silence. On satellite radio, Aaliyah began telling the world that she was writing a four-page letter and sealing it with a kiss. Her four-page letter made me think of Logan's wretched six-page manifesto.

Karl asked, "Your book is going to be like *War of the Worlds* meets *Children of Men*?"

I shifted. "Plus *Lord of the Flies* and *Something New*."

Jewell Stewark remained with me. I wondered what it would be like to break up a marriage. I wondered if that was empowering. Or just plain mean. Either way, I didn't want to find out.

Karl said, "I'll be the first one in line at the bookstore."

"You might be the only one in line."

"After I buy it, I want you to sign it."

"Feel free to buy more than one."

"What got you into sci-fi?"

I told him my French stepfather was a sci-fi aficionado, loved stories set in the future and on distant planets. He loved Heinlein's work to death. My stepfather wrote stories filled with sophistication and realism as a hobby, and reading his work, reading the books he left on my desk, books which made me think outside the box, it inspired me to play that *what-if* game and taught me how to manipulate everyday situations. And my stepfather loved *The Twilight Zone*, loved the twists and the statements that were made about mankind, our frailties and fears, a theme that was in almost every episode.

Karl said, "So he's why you became a writer."

"He gave me the love of reading, the love of writing."

"Why do you ghostwrite?"

I smiled, almost didn't want to answer, didn't want to get too personal, but it was too late. Karl was touching my leg, that rubbing being the equivalent of taking sodium pentathol. I gazed at his kissable lips and told him that when I grew up in Los Angeles, I was always around Benzes, Bentleys, and the self-important people in the movie industry who spent their lives drinking, sniffing cocaine, and popping antidepressants in between taking their bipolar dogs to therapy. I knew preteen actors and actresses who went to work in chauffeured limousines. I knew kids who threw temper tantrums on the set and had adults kissing their spoiled asses. My mother had a stage built in our backyard in hopes of me becoming an Oscar-winning actress. Being on stage never interested me. Being famous never interested me. I was too private to want to live my life in the tabloids or on the world's hypocritical stage. Acting didn't interest me because actors didn't interest me. What interested me were the people who created the words the actors brought to life. The writers. The unsung heroes whose names only a few recognized.

My words were in another place but my mind was on The Jewell of the South.

Karl asked, "Have you ghostwritten any sci-fi?"

I answered, "Did some work on a couple. Nothing major. Mostly been getting contracts to do smut. You know, sexy bathtub masturbation books. Erotic books with weak plots and soft endings."

The way Jewell Stewark had scowled at Karl was both intrigu-
ing and disturbing.

I said, "I did a few projects in Hollywood. Screenplays."

"How was that?"

"Hated it. They Michael Jackson your work."

"Michael Jackson?"

"They take the original and do so much surgery on it that the
final version isn't recognizable."

He laughed. My mind remained on The Jewell of the South,
wishing I didn't know she was Mark's wife. She was the woman
Mark had given mind-bending orgasms. The woman he honey-
mooned with and fucked so good her Jamaican moans could be
heard through wood and plaster. She was his wife. And he had given
her twenty-one orgasms over a weekend.

Karl continued laughing. "They Michael Jackson your work in
Hollywood."

"Yup. Lots more freedom in what I do now."

"Less compromise."

I nodded. "Less surgery."

I touched Karl's leg as he drove, only for a second. Needed to
touch him so I could purge other thoughts. Thoughts of getting my
own twenty-one orgasms. His leg was strong. Part of me wished we
had left a record of our ecstasy drying on his sheets. Him not trying
anything when we were in his bedroom, him only being aggressive
in the presence of his brother, that bothered me. Had wanted him
to want to seduce me. I wanted him to lose control, want me as
Mark had wanted me. Wanted him to fuck me. Maybe that wish was
more about validation and acceptance than sex itself.

I slept alone. Sleeping alone left me anxious. And that anxiety
created an emotional duress. I desired human contact. Needed to
feed on the energy that radiated from another. Needed that the
same way Superman needed the energy from the sun to maintain

his powers. If I tried to count the number of nights I'd longed to feel the warmth of a man's body next to mine, I'd have to count beyond infinity. That restlessness had left me open to Logan. That restlessness had allowed me to wallow in mediocre sex just so I wouldn't have to sleep alone.

Never again.

I told myself that Mark was unhappy. I allowed that to justify my behavior with him.

I was lonely. He was unhappy. We could steal away and give each other happiness. And I could give Karl what he wanted. Fun and pleasure without the feeling of restraints, that too being temporary, that too being what I wanted. That was all I wanted at this point in my life. Fun. Pleasure.

I asked myself why I continued justifying my behavior. I knew. Guilt forced justification.

Karl's cellular sang. He read the caller ID, then chuckled before he answered, said a couple of brusque words, then handed the phone to me. It was Mark. Guilt bloomed in an exponential fashion. I'd kissed Karl this morning. My yoni had throbbed for Karl to put me on his bench and fuck me. Not make love. Maybe fuck like we were making love, but still fuck. Pull my hair, slap my ass, be out of control. Now Mark was on the phone. It felt as if I had been caught cheating. Maybe Mark was inside my head; maybe he had found a secret tunnel that lead to my brain, my most clandestine thoughts revealed.

I took a breath and said, "Hey, Mark."

Mark said my name in return. He sounded angered.

"So you're hanging out with Karl."

I paused. "Yeah."

He paused. "That's good."

Another pause.

I asked, "You okay?"

"Work stuff, that's all."

"I meant your leg. When you pulled a muscle . . . at the W."

Karl chuckled. I wondered if he knew. Wondered if his older brother had told him, had given him the details, told him what happened stroke for stroke.

Mark chuckled. "It's fine. My leg is fine."

"You sure?"

"That was embarrassing."

"Never experienced anything like that."

"Me either."

Karl was rubbing my skin, his hand tracing my flesh, creating sunlight between my legs. Mark's voice was in my ear. Karl's hand on my flesh. Paradise was returning.

Again we were on the elevator in the W, my senses being stimulated in so many ways.

I asked Mark, "Where are you?"

"Heading down 75. I have five houses I can't get closed. Built a home for a preacher out in Gwinnett, had it in escrow, and the reverend cut me a ten-thousand-dollar bad check."

Karl's hand moved up to where my legs met, competing with his brother for my attention.

Tingles rose as I told Mark, "I don't know what to say about that one."

"And the business is slow now. Gets any worse, might have to get a job at Wal-Mart."

"Buyer's market. Over one hundred thousand properties on the market."

"It's killing me."

I pulled my lip in, suppressed a moan.

Mark went on, "This morning I have to get over to Midtown so I can meet with some investors and look at building some properties down at Atlantic Station."

"Okay. Anything I can do to help?"

"Yeah. Buy two or three million-dollar homes from me and all will be fine."

"Sure. Let me borrow the reverend's checkbook."

He laughed. "Wish I could kiss you right now."

"Me too."

He asked, "How's that scrape on your knee?"

I chuckled. "It's fine."

"Hold on, Nia. Got another call. Guy I've been trying to reach since yesterday."

"Okay."

The phone clicked.

I looked at Karl. He winked. Mark stimulated my heart. Karl kept me moist.

Mark's voice came on the line, said, "Hey, buddy, thanks for getting back to me so fast. Here's what I needed to know. If you had to do a subpanel, what's the additional cost, just for my knowledge? Also, I need the numbers on you pricing out that basement with a full kitchen and marble."

I said, "Same line, Mark. Your phone didn't click over."

"Sorry, Nia." Mark chuckled again. "Look, I'm having a hard time getting this phone to click over and I really need to catch this guy and get this issue resolved before I get to this meeting."

"Handle your business. Wish you were rolling with us."

"Me too." I heard some envy in his tone. "Have to run."

"Talk to you soon."

"Miss you."

"Will I see you anytime soon?"

"Things are crazy right now."

I sighed. "Miss you too."

With reluctance, trying to hide my longing, I clicked the phone off.

Karl continued rubbing my leg, kept me aroused.

I smiled. I felt better. Hearing Mark's voice had made me feel better.

This was strange. What I felt was strange.

I felt validated. He had put himself out there, expressed himself emotionally.

He had told me he missed me. That was better than a huge bouquet of flowers.

"Miss you."

As we moved down Cascade Road and away from Audubon Estates, those words stayed with me. Simple words that were a powerful magnet against my moral compass.

FOURTEEN

Reggae played as we left the city, my Carina Ayiesha CD putting sweet reggae in the air.

Karl and I chatted, talked nonstop until we were on the part of I-85 North that led into Franklin County. I saw her face three times. The Jewell of the South. Three billboards with her image smiled at me along the way. As if she was following me. Time went by fast and before I knew it, we were sixty miles outside Atlanta. Jewell vanished as did my guilt. It was me and Karl.

No Mark.

Thinking about what I couldn't have was wrong. I needed to shift my focus.

The CD ended and Karl switched to satellite radio.

I turned and inspected Karl's body art as he drove. His tattoos were dark and very unique. They amplified his physique. What used to be a symbol of sailors and criminals was now a fashion statement embraced by doctors, lawyers, and engineers. Getting a tattoo was another rite of passage.

I asked, "Ever been married?"

"Never." He paused for a second, thinking. "You know what marriage is?"

"Okay. What is marriage?"

"Marriage is when a man stops disappointing many women and focuses on disappointing one."

"Is that what happened to Mark and his wife?"

He paused, masked whatever he had with a thin smile. "Ask Mark."

"I'm asking you."

He paused again, nodded like he was debating giving up government secrets.

I said, "Not asking for details."

"I've seen them go from being elated to emotional and motivational erosion."

"Now who's getting all Dr. Phil? Just when I thought you didn't read."

"I read. I don't read the shit Mark reads, but I read."

"So you've had a front-row seat watching your brother and his celeb wife."

He took a breath, thinking. "I've watched them live in hell forever, since before they married."

I asked, "If the marriage is that bad, why don't they end it?"

"I guess some motherfuckers like living in hell."

"But why?"

"Maybe they think they are in Palm Springs."

Karl's hand came to my leg, once again making me tingle from my yoni to my heart. I moved my legs apart. He massaged me while Ricky Nelson sang about going to a garden party where nobody knew his name. Then we were sixty miles away from Greenville. Billboards for Café Risqué, the 24-hour strip club, were posted every mile, maybe less, letting the truckers know the pole dancers were corralled at exit 173.

By then I was sucking my bottom lip, trying not to moan.

Karl tugged at the top of my jean shorts.

He said, "Take these off."

Without hesitating I wiggled out of my shorts, left my thong on.

He said, "Those too."

I arched my back, eased my thong off, put it in my bag.

His fingers found the edges of a swollen clit. A clit that throbbed against his hand.

I cursed.

Billboards advertising Ben Zack's fireworks popped up.

Karl's finger slid inside me as we crossed North Fork Broad River. He put his fingers inside the flames, stirred the fire, moved deeper inside my cul-de-sac, sent trembles up my spine. I cursed louder. He stirred me senseless. RaceTrac gas station went by in a pre-orgasmic blur. I rode the edge of the orgasm, a surfer on waves, my hand grabbing the roll bar to keep my balance, hips moving into his fingers. He fed me my juices. I asked him to finish, told him to make me come. He refused. I demanded for him to give me an orgasm. He laughed. I cursed him in English, Spanish, and French, cursed my identical sin like I hated him. He laughed harder.

We crossed into South Carolina. Abbott Farms fresh peaches for sale every half mile. Shelton Fireworks, a red and yellow building, stood sentry on the left side of the interstate.

He moved his hand and I touched myself, I stirred the fire, my moans arousing him.

As we passed by the Peachoid, one of Wal-Mart's eighteen-wheelers pulled up next to us as I touched myself. The trucker blew his horn. I stopped long enough to pull a towel from the backseat, then rolled my window down enough to put that towel in the window, created a hiding place, then letting my seat go all the way back I reclined as far as I could. Eyes closed, I continued massaging my aroused sex.

Karl groaned. "I wanted to eat your pussy when you were at my house."

I trembled. He was rough, coarse, direct with his language. He was my Henry Miller.

His hand moved between my legs, stirred me. I couldn't take any more. I pushed his hand away. He laughed and changed the radio to Sirius 106, took me to Foxxhole. I cursed. My fever was so bad I wanted to break down and cry. I reached my hand to him, made him suck the desire away from my fingers. I should've stopped then. But I couldn't. The battle had begun.

Driven by passion, I reached over, undid the zipper on Karl's khakis, took his penis out, masturbated him. Karl grunted, gripped the steering wheel as we crossed the Saluda River, kept suffering and took us toward Spartanburg. He moaned like he was speaking in Italian and Spanish. I undid my seat belt, leaned over, took him in my mouth, felt him straining to keep control of his Jeep, loved how his hips rose into my face.

Another trucker blew his horn as he passed. Karl sounded his horn in return.

I pleasured Karl off and on until we were sixty-nine miles from Charlotte.

We passed Crossroads Baptist Church, breezed by a billboard advertising a warehouse that claimed to have fifty thousand rugs in stock down at exit 90, on the other side of Prime Outlets.

I masturbated him, held his thickness as if it belonged to me, imagined it fitting inside me. I closed my eyes, made a frustrated sound, and squeezed my legs tight.

"I want to come, Karl. Damn. Need to come real bad."

"You and me both."

Karl exited the interstate without warning.

At the end of the off-ramp we were greeted by a big cross with a white angel.

Karl headed back over the interstate, passed by a beat-down building that sold fast food, and pulled into the parking lot of the place that sold the rugs, a huge warehouse-type building on the op-posite side of the highway. The parking lot was empty. Didn't think the place was open, but it was. We spied inside. There weren't any customers inside the warehouse, only three employees, the one be-hind the counter being an elderly white woman who never looked up from whatever crossword puzzle she was doing. We went upstairs toward the restrooms.

Upstairs was an empty space, spacious with abandoned shopping baskets.

We were alone. Karl and I stared at each other at the same moment, in the same way. His look dared me as my expression triple-dog-dared him in return. He took my hand in his, pulled me along, dragged me down the empty hallway. First I followed him toward the bathrooms, then I gripped his hand, picked up my pace, and led him. Two runners at the end of a race, sprinting for the finish line.

The men's room smelled of cheap cleansers. The tile directly underneath the urinals tinted yellow, piss from men who either had bad aim or had stood too far back, thinking their dicks were bigger than they really were. The toilet was to the right, away from the urinals, in its own little room that had a real door, not like I had thought it would be. It was a separate room, not a stall. We would have privacy, wouldn't be seen at all. We rushed in there, shut the door fast, made sure the door was locked.

This was inappropriate. This was adventurous. There was a chance we could get caught.

I laughed like I was sixteen, a Catholic school girl doing wrong in the name of romantic love. I undid his khaki shorts, pulled up his camouflage tank top and licked his nipples, gave him the seductive powers of Eros. His breathing was out of control. He pulled down my jean shorts in desperation, raised my T-shirt, unhooked my bra, licked and sucked my breasts. Just like that, laughter ended. Oh God. I wished I could get both breasts sucked at once. Wished I could feel four hands ravaging me. It felt strange, being with Karl, it only being us two, knowing it was his brother I craved.

One leg out of my jean shorts, one sandal kicked away, I held that rigid part of him in my hand, again at a point of no return. He stiffened and filled my palm with hardness and heat. I straddled him, my left knee bumping into the dull wall, my right knee bumping into a dirty sink, wiggled in that tight space as I put the tip of him at my opening, my left hand on the wall for balance, and I moved him back and forth, teased him across my dampness, refused to allow him to burglarize himself inside me.

He moaned, that sound communicating his excitement, his need for pleasure. So did I. I moaned like we were inside a room in a five-star hotel. I moaned and bit my lip, thought about Mark once again. Didn't want to think about him, but I did. It felt like I was cheating on Mark. It felt as if I was betraying him. That feeling of sin excited me. I had seen Mark's wife. Had seen who he went home to after experiencing me, after loving me in the rain. In its own way, this moment felt like a revenge fuck.

Revenge fucks were always good. Revenge was its own aphrodisiac.

Karl wasn't fully erect, but he was thick enough, he had risen enough to fill desire.

A winding moan slipped out of me, long and thin, like air leaving a balloon.

Karl's hand came up to my mouth. I bit down on his fingers as I eased down on him, my nails digging into his arms as he filled this void. He was penetrating me. His brother had penetrated me. And now he was pushing inside me. Brothers. Twins. I'd been penetrated by brothers. By twins. What was done couldn't be undone. I didn't want it undone. That moment when Karl broke my skin, astonishing. I absorbed the length, width, and weight of his manhood. I owned his erection. What was inside me belonged to me. His mouth hurried to mine, his hand taking the back of my neck, his starved kisses moving from my face to my ears, to my neck, to my breasts. Karl loved sucking breasts. My breasts felt huge, heavy and filled with desire. He licked my breasts and made them feel beautiful, cupped them in his hands, sucked my erect nipples.

I moaned.

He didn't feel like Mark. His anatomical blessing was different. Not as long, but had more girth.

Girth was good.

The toilet was situated low enough for me to plant a foot on both sides of Karl, low enough for my heels to touch the floor, low enough for me to be able to do squats over and over, made it easy for me to hold the wall and move up and down on him, low enough for me to work my quads and hamstrings. I found a rhythm that was smooth and steady, the beat to this song inside my head.

I was high over the ground, flying through clouds, a member of the mile-high club. My body moved through warm air, took me to a tropical land, so much sweat on my brow. My feet touched the ground, toes sunk into the warm sands. I was on the Fijian Island of Taveuni, standing naked and free on the old International Date Line, my spirit and soul existing in past and present at the same time.

Karl took out his cellular. Fucked me as he made a phone call. He put the phone up to my ear.

I moaned my singsong moan, cooed my singsong coo. "What are you doing?"

Karl whispered, "Tell him what you're doing."

I trembled, turned on and troubled by his boldness. "No."

He pumped me hard. "Tell him."

I was dying a wonderful death, head back, singing my sensual song.

Mark answered. "What's going on, Karl?"

I tried to hold it inside me, but I moaned my unique moans, gasped like I was drowning.

Mark asked, "Who is this?"

I struggled to breathe. "Nia Simone . . . it's me."

"Okay. So . . ." He paused. "What's going on?"

"Karl . . . he's making me talk to you . . . he . . . he . . . he's doing something to me."

"That's nice to know." He said that like he was around people. "What's going on?"

"Fucking me. He's fucking me."

"I'm sorry. What was that?"

"He's fucking me and . . . he's fucking me and making me talk to you."

There was a pause, a pause filled with my moans.

Mark said, "I'm in a meeting with my investors. Hold on a second."

Karl moved in and out of me. I cringed, held the phone to my ear.

Karl was smiling. He was smiling hard, stroking me harder.

Mark came back on the line and asked, "What is he doing to you?"

"He's . . . he's fucking me. He made me sit on his . . . he's fucking me and making me talk to you."

"Where are you?"

"Don't know. I don't know. Some warehouse . . . off 85 . . . place that sells rugs."

"Don't let him make you come."

"Okay, baby, okay. I won't."

"Who are you thinking about?"

"Thinking about the W."

"Say my name."

"*Mark.*"

"Say my name again. Look Karl in his eyes and say my name."

"*Mark.*"

"Louder."

"*Mark.*"

Karl took the phone from me, hung up on his brother.

"Oh God. Why'd you make me do that?" I moaned. "That was mean. Just plain mean."

"That turn you on?"

I swallowed and smiled. "*Yes.*"

He fucked me into a hundred new paradises. Like his brother, he had so many moves, so many gears. Fantasized about them being inside me at the same time, pleasing me like this, concurrent pleasure. My body took on a life of its own, buttocks clenching, every part of me trying to tighten around the girth of his anatomical blessing, moving up and down, making him plunge into me over and over.

I didn't want to feel this way, but I did. This was not of my design. This was how I was made.

We moved like we were animals born with the purpose to make love and procreate. Fucking to procreate was in our nature. And the urge to seek pleasure, the need to give pleasure, the urge to replicate pulled us together, raised hormones and . . . and . . . Oh God . . . Oh God . . . Oh God.

He fucked the stupid thoughts out of my head.

He fucked me away from Mark. Each stroke was a riptide, pulling me out to sea.

He growled, "Say my name."

"Karl."

"Who do you want?"

"*Karl.*"

We moved and sucked tongues, sucked lips, sucked fingers.

Giving up sex was like giving up food and water. Sex should be listed with life's basic necessities. Sex, food, shelter, clothing. In that order. Fuck me, feed me, take me inside, and dress me.

Pleasure had not been mine for so long. Once desire was turned on, combustion gave it a life of its own. Once it was turned on it tended to become a raging wildfire, uncontrollable and uncontainable, the type of conflagration that had to be allowed to burn itself out.

The handle on the bathroom door shook hard and fast.

We jumped, but didn't disconnect, stared at each other, sensual expressions laced with surprise. I swallowed, sweat on my neck, my mouth shaped like an orgasmic O.

The handle on the bathroom door shook again, shook harder, shook faster.

Panic rose in his eyes. My hand went to my mouth, muffled a nervous laugh.

"Is somebody in there?"

"Yeah." Karl yelled back. "Somebody is in here."

"What?"

"*Somebody is in here.*"

I stayed still. Cringing in silence, living in pain and pleasure, Karl filling me up so damn good.

"*Sorry about that.*" The man was yelling through the door. "*Take your time.*"

That voice was old and Southern. The outside bathroom door didn't open and close again.

The old man wasn't leaving.

Karl pumped into me. Made me cover my mouth to muffle my scream. I tried to stop him, but I gave in, moved with him. He was switching gears again, each gear sending me to faraway places. I was making the crying face, not coming, but pleasure was galloping on the horizon. It was too much. Had to end the madness. I tried to get up, but Karl pulled me back down. Slammed me down hard. I shivered with pleasure. Right then I couldn't imagine my life before Karl and Mark. Couldn't imagine what my life would be like after. Had all sorts of crazy thoughts. Needed to come. Orgasm brought clarity, and now I was going insane. Orgasm brought reality, now I was fucking deep inside a fantasy.

Outside the door, the old man coughed. That cough brought me back to reality.

Orgasm was the great deceiver. It was the master illusionist.

I tried to free myself, but Karl wouldn't let go.

Karl and I kissed, labored breathing, manly grunts and kittenish cries. Sweat dripped from my face, landed in the river that was already streaming down his neck. I needed to release a thousand voluptuous moans. Needed to moan so goddamn loud. My right hand moved by Karl, flushed the toilet to hide my sounds. When the water filled, I flushed the toilet again, did that over and over.

I stopped devouring him, stopped moving, this feeling too good.

Karl grabbed my hips, tried to raise me, tried to force me up and down. Sweat rose on his face, on his neck; liquid flowers in a garden of lust. His pleasure rose and what was hard became harder, elongated as if it had a life of its own. I moved his hands away from me, stood up, my vagina open, wanting more.

His erection stood strong, like a pole, his vulnerable expression a flag of surrender.

I stumbled in the small room, too stimulated to move with any real control, fell against the wall, pulled my shorts back up, pulled my T-shirt down over my breasts, my nipples sensitive to the cotton as it glided down.

Karl remained on the toilet, pants at his ankles, erection reaching up like I was a bandit and he was being robbed with an invisible gun. Robbed of pleasure. Robbed of his release.

I pulled my hair back, the loose strands that had come free and glued to my sweat.

I leaned into Karl, my tongue easing out of my mouth, and kissed him again.

He moaned and tried to yank me back on him; with urgency he reached for my shorts.

As I kissed him I flushed the toilet. With the noise at its peak, I moved his hands from my body.

He reached for his erection, his expression saying he needed to get this voluptuous orgasm out of his body before he went insane. I slapped his hand out of the way, watched him struggle.

He gritted his teeth, his chest rising and falling.

I opened the cheap wooden door, faced an old man with liver-spotted skin.

A man who was rocking side to side like his insides were about to explode.

Behind me Karl was doing the same thing, rocking and trying not to explode.

I spoke to that Southern-fried Christian with a smile and hurried out the door.

I didn't know if he heard me, his flesh-colored hearing aid might not have been turned up to the proper volume. Outside in the hallway was an older woman dressed in pink, her neck slipping, her marsupial features in need of a facelift, wrinkly knees, body ravaged by sun damage, age spots. She saw me come out of the men's toilet, then her mouth opened, she looked at the sign on the door again, then tried to understand why I was coming out of that water closet.

She was the wife of the man who needed to ease his troubled bowels.

Desire and arousal ravaged me, and I passed by her without speaking.

I stopped halfway down the stairs, fanned myself, adjusted my clothes, my body tingling like fire.

Only a few seconds went by before Karl appeared. Skin damp. T-shirt soaked and wrinkled. His lingam thick and long inside his wrinkled khakis. Bet the old woman got a kick out of seeing his potency.

Karl stared at me. His stare intense, like he was about to lose control.

I felt like a woman who made her own rules; the woman desired.

I moved ahead of Karl, motivated by the mean look in his eyes. He hurried after me, the darkness in his beautiful eyes saying if he caught me he would fuck me on the dingy tile floors in the lobby of the rug warehouse. He would fuck me, then grab my hair and drag me back inside and fuck and sodomize me on each of the fifty thousand rugs, would abuse me until my body was covered in rug burns.

Hands over my top to stop my breasts from bouncing, I ran hard, laughing.

Unfulfilled desire motivated his chase while blue balls slowed his stride.

He could've caught me if he wanted to, could've caught me the way a parent caught a child, but he let me stay just out of his reach, every now and then speeding up like he wanted to capture me and make me his P.O.W. Each time he sped up I jogged a few feet, laughing, refusing to be trapped.

He chased me because that was the way it was designed.

The sperm always chased the egg.

FIFTEEN

Sexual scents rising from heated bodies, we continued our journey on I-85 north toward Greensboro. Karl was on his cellular talking to a relative in Barbados, giving directions.

"They live on Golf Club Road . . . yeah, mon. Where you? Quayside Center . . . okay you're by Accura Beach . . . go toward St. Lawrence Gap . . . *toward* not *to* . . . turn left at the Shell station . . . after Cave Shepherd . . . yeah, mon . . . and before you leave the area run in Chevettes and buy me a roti."

He laughed.

I checked my messages.

I had six missed calls, all from the area code 901. Memphis. Shelby County. Logan.

Karl ended his call and looked at me. "You okay?"

"Why did you do that to your brother?"

"Because he's my brother."

"Has he ever done that to you?"

"Ask him."

My phone flashed. This call from DNA: LOGAN. Just like that, I saw a flash from my nightmare again. Logan banging on my door. Telling me he wanted to abuse me like I was his whore.

Karl said, "Was that Mark calling up to give me some hate?"

I shook that nightmare from my head. "Not Mark."

"Uh-huh. Boyfriend?"

"Getting personal, are we?"

He chuckled. "My bad."

"Hey, you wouldn't happen to know where I can find some parametboxyamphetamine."

"What the hell is that?"

"From what I hear, it's better than Ecstasy. Maybe just pull over and get me a forty ounce."

He asked, "What's the problem?"

I waved my cellular to indicate what the problem was. "Just this jerk up in Memphis."

"Giving you grief?"

"Some men have a problem with women being free thinkers and being equal."

"So he has a problem with the good old concept of egalitarianism."

I laughed. "Egalitarianism."

"Morehouse, baby. I might not read the books Karl reads, but I read."

He put his hand back between my legs. Tingles rose again. My problems vanished.

I embraced this libertine sensation.

Soon I saw signs welcoming us to North Carolina. Signs for Kings Mountain National Military Park. Black billboards with white letters: NEED DIRECTIONS? was the message. In the bottom right corner it was signed: GOD. I put the towel back in the window as we crossed Dixon School Road. Another sign came up that said the cigarette outlet was at exit 3. We passed a river basin, moved into Gaston County, Bessemer City, Cox Road, South Fork River, Sam Wilson Road, Little Rock Road, Beatties Road.

I kept having flashbacks of three in a bed. Then my imagination created different scenarios. Imagined Karl's passion taking me from one end, Mark's fervor taking me from the other. My hands moved up my neck, through my hair, down my T-shirt, across my breasts, eased down my belly. Again I patted my fire, touched myself. Touched myself from exit 49 and Speedway Boulevard until exit 54 at Kannapolis Parkway, then I leaned over and took Karl in my mouth again, tasted myself on his flesh as I suckled him, tasted and licked him until we crossed Dale Earnhardt Boulevard and entered Rowan County, now close to three hundred miles from Atlanta, the entire journey made on one tank of gas.

I stopped sucking him, sat back, smiled, licked my lips, and chuckled.

His smile was broad.

I stared at Boyles Distinctive Furniture. Fell quiet as we passed exit 11, didn't laugh at Mo'Nique's jokes on Foxxhole, held the roll bar as if the Jeep might lose control or flip without warning. Guilford County, Cape Fear River Basin, Deed River. We came up on exit 119, Groometown Road, made a left at the top of the off-ramp, went over the interstate and pulled into Citgo. It looked like a great place for truckers to buy Preparation H by the case. Karl took out his American Express, swiped it at the pump, spent over sixty-five dollars on premium fuel, went inside, came back and handed me a blue Gatorade.

We'd been riding over five hours. Three hundred and thirty-two miles of excruciating foreplay.

He asked, "You okay?"

I smiled a painful smile. "I want to come so bad."

After he filled up, he moved his Jeep, parked on the side of the building that housed the newspaper racks for *The Charlotte Observer*, *USA Today*, and *News and Record*. I sipped my blue Gatorade as I looked out at the lot, the far edges of the lot gravel and rocks, the cabs of eighteen-wheelers and older cars parked in that area. All around were signs encouraging blue-collar workers to play the lottery. Neon signs for beer were placed in the windows, positioned like they were bright lights to pot-bellied bugs. I'd bet my town-house that inside that gas station, condoms and stay-hard pills were sold behind the counter, probably in plain sight, right by the Marlboros and jarred pig's feet.

I twisted the cap back on my Gatorade, made sure it was on tight before I sat it down at my feet.

I asked, "Where is your client?"

"She should be here."

"She?"

"Problem?"

"Just didn't know it was a she. I mean, I figured it was a she, just wasn't sure."

"You do makeup?"

"I can."

"You're hired."

"Who said I was looking for a job?"

"I'll pay you in orgasms."

"Will I be allowed to work overtime?"

After we exchanged soft chuckles, again I fell quiet.

On satellite another black female comedian was on, at some point they all started to sound the same, all of their jokes having the same rhythm and subject matter, this one loud and doing a routine about fucking white men, talking about a white man she had fucked, de-scribed how his pink dick curved to the right, described its huge mushroom head. So much laughter from the black crowd. She talked about how hard he fucked her, how he fucked her like he hated her. She screamed how she loved it.

The audience laughed so damn hard. The women could re-late.

I asked Karl to tell me about one of his sexual experiences. One that stood out in his mind. Didn't expect him to respond. Expected him to shut down. But he chuckled, made a thinking sound, like his mind was going through its Rolodex, picking out a sexual adventure, then he nodded and played along. He told me that once he had made love to a woman. He was in a bed with a white comforter and white sheets. And when his lover came, she came so hard her bowels loosened and messed up the party.

I said, "Oh shit."

"Exactly."

"White sheets and comforter?"

I laughed so hard at that one. After I wiped the tears of laughter from my eyes, I told him about the time I was with this guy, things were going great, then I took out a vibrator, wanted him to take the toy and get freaky, please me to a brand-new level, and while I lay there waiting, the guy freaked me out.

He asked, "What did he do?"

"He started using it on himself."

We laughed so hard.

I said, "Didn't matter. His thing was so skinny you could paint it silver and call it a kick stand. So I got more fun out of watching him do his thing than I did out of the two minutes of awful sex."

When he stopped laughing, Karl told me about another sexual encounter.

He said, "She had the hairiest pussy I had ever seen. Was like a Black Panther Afro growing between her legs. And hair traps odors. So, needless to say, her scent wasn't appealing, not at all."

"What, she didn't hear of waxing or razors?"

"She needed hedge clippers and a weed whacker to cut that gorilla hair."

"Damn."

"Last time I saw something that hairy it was getting shot off the top of the Empire State Building."

We laughed.

While we waited, we traded a few more war stories, laughing the whole time.

I was a woman. A curious creature. I said something that only a woman would say.

"Karl, how do you see me?"

"What do you mean?"

"You know what I mean. What do you think of me?"

That wasn't a question born from insecurity. I asked because the eye couldn't see itself.

"Private person. Independent. Confident. Professional. Very sociable."

"Actually I'm an introvert who forces herself to be sociable."

"Introvert? No way. You're too outgoing and exciting. You can talk about any subject."

"Like a nerd."

"Nerds don't look like that. No way anybody will ever confuse you with a nerd."

I smiled. "So me being with you and Mark, what does that tell you about me?"

"Tells me you're open-minded. Maybe ready to explore some new things."

His words made me feel fearless.

I was glad we were alone. I missed Mark, but I was glad I was with Karl.

The power of words. How they fed the ego.

I asked Karl, "Was this you and Mark's first threesome?"

"Nope."

"I could tell."

"How?"

"You and your brother were in sync. The way you two put it down . . . awesome."

He told me that they had been with a woman when they were on vacation. That was years ago with a woman from Los Angeles named Frankie. Hotel ME in Cancún. His room was on the eleventh floor facing the white sands and the clear blue waters. Frankie was on holiday with her sisters. Her sisters weren't interested in either of them, plus the married sister had her eye on some Latin guy, was in a two-piece bikini and was allowing him to rub suntan lotion on her flesh as they laughed and had drinks, her adultery already set in motion by the time they had met Frankie. The third sister was both the tallest and the youngest of the three, very attractive and curvy, stunning even with a small burn on her face, but she was withdrawn, as if she was afraid for any man to get close, her energy the opposite of sexual.

I asked, "How did the thing with Frankie jump off?"

He hummed. "We met poolside. Drinking. Talking."

"Sounds lovely. Erotic. Sensual."

"It was party central all day and night."

"Cut to the chase. Where did all of you hook up?"

"Went back to my suite."

I imagined them out by a pool, sun over their heads, drinks in their hands. Imagined the way she looked at them, imagined how excited she must have been to have been chosen by them. Tried to imagine her mind, her way of thinking, wondered if she was like me. Every lover and relationship—if it lasts—always ended up the same way, with one person needing more. Someone was always unfulfilled.

I wondered what Frankie needed at that point in her life. Sex was always more than sex, always represented some deeper need. Wondered what kind of freedom Mark and Karl had represented in her world, what healing they had done to her spirit. Pleasure was like love, subjective.

I asked, "Both of you were with her?"

"Yeah."

"At the same time."

"Yeah."

"Double penetration?"

"Yeah."

"Wow."

"Yeah. Wow."

The thought of them pleasing her in that way made me squirm. I imagined her, lust baking on her skin, their bodies sliding together, tropical perspiration making everything slippery, three smells blending into one sensual fragrance. I imagined them making her feel so good a million tears were in her eyes.

I squirmed, imagined them holding her, filling two cul-de-sacs at once.

I asked, "Did she have long or short hair?"

"Long braids. Like women have when they go on vacation."

"Was she aggressive sexually?"

"Not at first. Kept laughing and saying she couldn't believe she was doing this."

"She was drunk."

"Not really. Just feeling right."

"Sounds like you had a lot of fun."

"When it got rolling, she stopped laughing, was pretty aggressive, was into it big time."

"What turned you and your brother on about her?"

"Can only speak for myself."

"Okay. Then what turned you on about her?"

"She was professional. Well put together. Articulate. Humorous. Like you."

"Whatever."

"Serious."

I asked, "Was she pretty?"

"Very."

"Short? Was she a short woman?"

"Tall."

"Skinny?"

"Thick."

"What does thick mean?"

"Thick means thick."

"Are we talking Jennifer Hudson, Sanaa Lathan, Jennifer Lopez?"

"More Audra McDonald than anything. A taller version."

A full picture of their lover rested in my head. I shifted in my seat. "She sounds sexy."

"She was."

"One-night stand?"

"Not really. We hooked up two or three more times before she left Cancún."

"All three of you?"

"Yeah."

"So she must've been damn pretty."

"Very pretty woman. Uglies have to go home before the sun comes up."

"You are a mess. You and Mark still in touch with Frankie?"

"We never heard from her after Cancún."

A mild breeze moved across my skin, my imagination refusing to be cooled.

Karl broke our silence when he asked, "Was that your first time doing a three-way?"

"Yeah."

A soft moan escaped me.

He asked, "Sure that was your first time?"

I nodded. "A couple of guys I dated wanted me to try, thought about it, but I never did."

"Ever been with two men on the same day?"

Old memories and sudden embarrassment made me smile. I answered him, "I plead the fifth."

"Come on, Nia. I just answered a thousand questions."

"Okay. Yeah. Once. Was seeing this jock. Football player.

Belizean. There was this other guy. Dominican. Had some overlap.
Woke up with the Belizean I was seeing. We did it. Later that evening, hooked up with the guy from Dominica. The guy from Dominica, I hadn't planned on doing anything. The circumstances
unexpectedly evolved into that. It sort of went on like that for a
couple of weeks."

"How long ago?"

"That was back at Hampton. Twitchell Hall. Room 332. Senior
year. Long story."

"Want to tell me about it?"

I took a breath, released hints of an old pain, felt the sting of a
wound forever open.

I remembered how one man had broken my heart and I'd allowed another to give me solace, had gone to him for solace, that
solace becoming intimacy, pleasure used to smooth over a bottomless pain, that intimacy being used to remove what didn't feel good.
I thought of moments I wanted to forget.

"The Belizean was my boyfriend at the time. The Dominican
was this guy who had been interested in me for a long time. He was
from Norfolk. Or Richmond. Can't remember. It was senior year.
Was about to leave Hampton and go back to L.A. Grad school at
USC. Knew I'd never see either one of them again. Guess I went for
it. Treated myself to the second guy."

I gave him partial truth, decorated it with smiles, left out the
part about my lovers being friends, best friends as a matter of fact,
kept my confession simple, in my favor, no shame or real pain revealed.

Karl asked, "Was that exciting?"

I created a brave smile, one that said I was stronger than I really
was. "Very."

"Stolen fruit always tastes the sweetest."

Karl's hand touched me, rubbed me. I smiled. He was with me.
He accepted me.

I licked my bottom lip. He didn't judge me. I felt both exposed and free.

Otto Rank. Henry Miller. Rupert Pole. Edmund Wilson. June Miller. Artists and psychologists. Taxi dancers. Those were only a few of my literary idol's lovers. Anaïs Nin had many lovers. She had seduced and been seduced, every experience adding to the totality of her being. To her humanness. I shouldn't remain timid when it came to mentioning my lovers, shouldn't be afraid to mention the ones who had been unpretty, ended without kindness and understanding, ended with friends becoming enemies.

I'd almost told Karl the truth, about how one of the men was, at the time, the love of my life. How he had betrayed me for a freshman, a cheerleader, and, in the end, I had gone to his friend in need of revenge. The revenge had been sweet. It had been wrong, but the sweetness was indescribable.

Once revealed, the pain my Belizean lover had experienced, it had driven him mad.

As the pain and heartache he had given me had driven me into the bowels of madness. Madness that had started at Ogden Circle during a pep rally. Madness that had escalated at the Student Union, burgers being thrown like weapons. Madness that continued and had me confronting a cheerleader at freshman talent night, then again confronting her while she was on the football field. A freshman who lived in Davidson Hall, the dorm across from mine. I'd lost the plot. Madness had inspired violence. My final shame had happened during halftime, a girl fight, right on the field in the middle of the marching band. Not one of my finer moments. It had been ugly in the end. When he found out I had betrayed him with his best friend as he had betrayed me, it was so ugly it was Shakespearian. I was surprised one if not all of us didn't end up with our bodies being found floating in the James River, our inconsolable spirits added to those that had haunted Virginia Cleveland Hall since the nineteenth century.

And it had been rewritten in my mind. All history was rewritten in favor of the writer.

Karl kissed me. "What are you thinking about?"

I cleared my mind, lied, and said, "That girl Frankie. The double-penetration you told me about."

"Fascinates you, huh?"

"She's a bad bitch."

"Not as bad as you."

I imagined Frankie cringing, the exotic expression of a sweet suffering all over her dank face.

I licked my lips. "Taking two men at once like that . . . sounds . . . painful."

"She enjoyed it. Frankie came hard. Was shaking for a long time. She started crying."

My yoni moaned a singsong moan.

Karl's hand eased between my legs and my thighs separated, opened like they were waiting for his return, then his fingers moved inside my heat and I was being finger-loved again. My glazed-over eyes and soft moans went to the Carolina blue skies, then to a man in a blue shirt pumping gas as fingers pumped in and out of me.

Karl said, "Don't come."

I was about to come. So close to the point of no return. That edge almost within reach.

He said, "My client's here."

"Don't stop . . . Karl . . . don't."

He took his hand away with quickness.

"Don't come. Don't you come."

"I hate you."

"Don't come."

"I hate you so much right now."

He was gone, leaving me frustrated, leaving me in a horrible state.

I whimpered at his cruelness, again cursing him in Spanish and French.

I swallowed a scream, looked up and saw a black Yukon Ram 3500, its rims shining as it pulled into the parking lot. A horn blew. With the hand that had been between my legs, Karl waved at his client.

I lowered my head and trembled, my ears filled with Eddie Murphy's voice and laughter, my need to orgasm being violated and ridiculed by him doing a routine about Buckwheat, Stymie, and Farina.

My almost-orgasm clawed at me, moved up my spine, forced me to hold my breath. I shuddered, wiped my eyes with the back of my hands. Legs tight, I squirmed in my own dampness. Refused to die a thousand little deaths underneath the heat of this Carolina sun. Sweat running down my head, dripping to my chest, dampness building up in the small of my back, teeth tight, I inhaled through my nose, looked to the skies, and shifted on my passion. I dug my nails in my arms, created pain to control pleasure.

For a moment, as it died down, I sucked air, gurgled like I was drowning.

Now I could breathe again, my breaths remained asthmatic, but I could breathe.

Sweaty and shaking, I could see again, the world fogged over, clouds lifting.

I could speak again. My words as intelligible as a newborn's, but my voice had returned.

Oh God.

It was ethereal, dreamlike, seeing Karl standing at the driver's side of his client's truck.

His client's truck was only a few feet away, parked with her door facing mine.

He was standing between us, off to the side, her view of me unobstructed.

My vision became clearer, my breathing smoothing out, sweat raining from my flesh, everything about me felt so tropical, as if I was back in the islands, standing at the top of Lady Chancellor Road, the sun resting on top of my head as Humidity held me in her loving arms.

Karl was grinning. His client was wide-eyed, frozen, staring at me, her mouth partly open, her expression a combination of fascination and horror, as if she was witnessing a crime, as if my throat had been cut, or I was naked and bleeding to death in the cab of this Jeep.

She stared at me, her eyes never moving away, her mouth never closing.

My embarrassment moved with agonizing slowness.

My mind took her photo, processed it with the speed of a digital camera.

What I could see, her round face in the window of her truck, was tanned, her left hand hanging out and revealing her short fingernails, her face being youthful and mature all at once. She was beautiful. The T-shirt she wore was fluorescent yellow. Her hair was long and red, wavy. Her brows were dark, as black as tar. No makeup on her face, a face that was dank, another victim of the Carolina sun.

She looked like a confident, quiet, easygoing person.

She smiled.

I was angry. Too livid to construct anything that resembled a face of faux happiness.

Karl had his Nikon in his hands, its eye on me, clicking away in rapid succession. My personal moments were being stolen, documented. I didn't want to be photographed struggling with an orgasm as I became drenched with sweat. Words would not come but I shook my head, tried to make a motion with my hand for him to stop. Karl was relentless, continued photographing my struggle to maintain control.

With an audience of one, an audience who refused to stop evaluating me.

He had captured my truth, held it captive inside his camera.

She waved at me.

Karl smiled his beautiful smile, the same smile his brother owned.

I nodded at them, then turned my head away.

I wondered if he had made her come.

Karl's Nikon clicked away, now capturing and documenting anger and jealousy.

His client called out and asked, "You okay?"

I struggled, then yelled back, "Allergies."

"You have bad allergies too?"

I nodded again, realizing my eyes must look puffy, face flushed, skin dank.

"Pollen is real bad," she called out. "Worse up in Yadkinville and Mocksville."

I wiped my face, the smell of my vagina on my hand, now that aroma on my face.

Her white smile flashed out as she went on, "Claritin-D. Try that."

I lowered my head like I was about to sneeze. No longer fighting the desire to come.

I was laughing a shameful laugh, laughing and holding my swollen breasts, my nipples so firm.

With a look of victory in his eyes, Karl called out, "You okay?"

Sonofabitch.

I said, "Eddie Murphy . . . he cracks me up."

I turned down the volume, left Eddie Murphy at whisper level, and looked back at them.

She was staring at me. Intelligent eyes filled with fascination. The sunlight revealed my darkness. She could see as much of me as

I could of her. My skin sweaty, my pinned-back hair, now loose, had fallen in disarray. She saw I had a post-fuck face even though I hadn't been fucked properly. Sweat on her skin, a soft glow in her eyes. I imagined that was her post-orgasm face. For a moment it seemed like she looked at me the same desirous way I regarded Karl. The same lustful way I stared at Mark. The way I gazed at men I desired, if only in my fantasies. That look of evaluation and consideration coupled with contemplation.

She called out, "I'm Kiki Sunshine."

"Nice to meet you . . . *Kiki Sunshine*."

If I wasn't in agony I would've laughed. She had a Bond-girl name. *Kiki Sunshine* sounded like *Pussy Galore*. And *Pussy Galore* was a slick way of saying *Glorious Pussy*.

Kiki Sunshine called out to me again. "Karl said you can help me a little bit with my makeup."

I paused. "Sure. I can help you a little bit."

"Sorry I was late. Just told Karl my beautician gave me the directions and I made a wrong turn, ended up on Randleman Road. I don't usually come to this side of town."

Her voice was sweet and Southern, like an instrument with many strings.

Little Miss Kiki Sunshine eased out of her good-old-boy truck, her movements feminine. Jeans rolled up at the ankles. Yellow flip-flops on her feet. Her frame surprised me. She was a lot taller than she had looked. She had to be five-eleven. That Amazon was close enough for me to see the fullness of her lips, the greenness of her eyes. Hoop earrings and a single coral snail ring on her right hand.

With the fog lifted from my eyes, at last I could see her. Kiki Sunshine was stunning.

I didn't like her. I didn't like the way she stared at me. I didn't like the way she flirted with Karl.

Another truck pulled up on the other side of me, gave me reason to look away, and since that interruption gave me reason to break my gaze, I found another way to occupy myself.

I picked up my cellular, turned it back on. It rang as soon as I did. The number blocked.

I answered, "Hello?"

"Hey, Nia."

"Logan, please."

"I'm just calling to apologize."

"Apology accepted."

I turned the phone off.

I picked up a magazine, *People*, opened it to page thirty, pretended I was more interested in reading about 50 Cent's fifty-three-room house being on sale for eighteen million than anything else.

I raised my eyes from the pages and they were laughing with each other, grinning at me. Kiki Sunshine waved, sashayed her beauty inside the station before I could respond, my eyes trapped on her.

Karl came back to the Jeep, opened the door, and eased in the driver's seat.

His hand rubbed mine, moved across my legs, settled in my lap, rested on my sex.

I asked, "What are you doing?"

"Keeping my dinner warm."

For a woman, the need for love moved us into the realms of sex, took us where we felt good, where we felt special, where we bared ourselves and each moan was a moan of trust, each moan asking that we not be betrayed. My song was soft, yet lyrical and astounding. It wasn't the moans but the space between those moans that told what was truly in my heart, those spaces were my soul.

Kiki Sunshine came back out with bottled water, went to her Yukon Ram 3500, her sashay self-confident and hot, a flame that could create wildfires, each step made for a red carpet.

I felt out of place. Like Cleopatra in Rome, a long way from my kingdom in Alexandria.

She looked back at us, her waist small, her breasts the proper size for her frame, her tall body well-proportioned and blessed with curves, a body that owned some size, but not looking unhealthy, not fat in any unflattering way.

Kiki Sunshine winked, then hurried her Amazonian body inside her good-old-boy truck.

Again I wondered what she was to Karl.

As the sun kissed Kiki Sunshine's flesh, jealousy rose inside me. A jealousy I didn't want. A protectiveness I didn't understand. Maybe being territorial was innate, tattooed into our DNA at birth.

It was the sex. Sex made us territorial. Sex made us primal.

If I hadn't experienced Karl, what he was to Kiki Sunshine wouldn't feel like an issue.

A woman let a man penetrate her and emotions fought with logic. That was our faulty wiring at work. That was our never-ending struggle with nature. At least it was mine. I could only speak for me.

Men said they loved you to get sex.

Women had sex hoping love was at the end of the rainbow.

I passed Karl my Gatorade; he took a long swig, finished what was left.

Kiki Sunshine pulled out on Groometown; Karl followed her, made that right turn.

When we were in the left-turn lane, light red, waiting patiently so we could turn onto High Point, I saw his curious and beautiful client looking back in her rearview. Her eyes were on mine. Her gorgeous smile was unhidden.

I closed my eyes on her happiness, wondered if she had smelled my scent on Karl's clothes.

Wondered if she had smelled my arousal on his breath.

Wondered if she knew this territory had been marked.

I wondered if she knew that Karl was fingering the jealousy out of me as we rode.

SIXTEEN

We followed Kiki Sunshine to Big Tree Way. She headed inside Hunter's Chase apartment complex, led us beyond swimming pools and a tennis court. Lots of trees. Well-maintained grounds.

Kiki Sunshine parked her black Yukon near building K; Karl parked a few spaces over.

Karl eased out of the Jeep and went to Kiki Sunshine. They conversed, nodded, and then Kiki Sunshine pointed back toward the direction we had just come, made a few more gestures. Some agreement was made, then she waved good-bye to him. Her eyes came to me and again she waved good-bye. Southern people were so courteous. I returned the gesture. She hurried toward building K and Karl came back to the Jeep.

I asked, "What's going on?"

"We're going to check in, freshen up, then come right back and pick her up to shoot."

Karl took us to the Hilton Garden Inn, no more than two minutes from Kiki Sunshine's apartment, the hotel being right before Wendover Avenue, a main street that had all the restaurants and Wal-Mart.

We headed to 427, a room with a small living area and two queen-size beds, the suite facing Big Tree Way, a Waffle House, and K&W in view. I had a feeling that this was the side of town were NASCAR and Marlboro lovers considered Hooters and Red Lobster fine dining. Nothing like sipping on a Budweiser while eating fried wings or a plate of fried fish swimming in a lake of butter.

We showered then headed back to pick up his client.

En route I said, "What kind of name is *Kiki Sunshine?*"

"What do you mean?"

"*Kiki Sunshine* sounds like the name of a woman who does tricks on poles. Like an announcer in a club should call out, '*Now coming to the stage, Kee-Kee Motherfucking Sunshine.*'"

He laughed. "Language."

"You're rubbing off on me. You're corrupting me."

Karl parked in front of building K, the midday heat unbearable. I didn't want to sit in the Jeep. I grabbed my purse and went up to the third floor with Karl, decided to get out of the sun and help him collect Kiki Sunshine. When she opened the door, she wasn't dressed, had on a housecoat.

I went upstairs because I was nosy. I wanted to see what her apartment looked like.

I didn't expect much. Expected her living space to be furnished like a college dorm.

There was a fireplace facing a leather sofa that looked too pretty to lounge on. The red love seat was made of high-grain leather, so soft it was like resting in a tub of warm butter. Her ceiling fans were spinning on low, and when I looked up I saw that those weren't the standard apartment-issued fans, even those had been replaced with designer, high-end fans. Her furniture was expensive, too nice for an apartment, every item meant to be in a very nice home, every piece sexy and inviting, like being in the W on a Friday night, apple martini in hand. Her patio was small, filled with terrace furniture that was just as high-end. Her dishes were Mikasa, Mikasa clocks, same for her candleholders and picture frames. Even her kitchen garbage can shined, that being made of stainless steel. This furniture, her oversized truck, no house to put the furniture inside, no garage to shelter an expensive truck, that told me a lot about her priorities. She had invested in a lot of things that depreciated, not a single item that grew in value in sight.

Kiki Sunshine gave us glasses of water, used her Mikasa glasses, then she hurried and changed. I sat and waited for Karl to load his camera with a new memory card, then he sorted through several lenses, picked one, and attached it. Karl said he liked her space, asked her if she wanted to take a few shots up here before we went to find locations for outdoor shots. That excited Kiki Sunshine.

Moments after that Karl had brought some equipment upstairs, things to create the proper lighting, and was doing a photo shoot starring Kiki Sunshine, her apartment having great colors.

Kiki Sunshine wore a dress that showed off her legs, moved with charm and grace, like she was on a fashion runway in Paris. She posed for the camera, remained natural, never seemed uncomfortable.

She asked me, "Did you know Fantasia was from around here? She's from High Point."

I asked, "Who?"

"Fantasia Barrino. *American Idol* winner. She's from High Point. That's around here."

"Oh. Didn't know that."

"She's in *The Color Purple* on Broadway."

"Good for her."

"Fantasia grew up right around the corner. Our American Idol. Fantasia is blessed."

"Yeah, she is."

"There should be no doubt in anyone's mind that God is in the midst of that girl's career."

I looked at the photos on her wall. She had a few family photos, but most of the images were of herself. Poses in bathing suits, stunning gowns, she had many. In some she had big glossy lips. There was a series of her naked, her body painted like it was a work of art. Very creative. The kind of photos that left me speechless. One was blown up and had its own wall. She had on a black suit, big-collared white shirt open to her waist, exposing the edges of her breasts, cigar in her right hand, a whip in her left, her pose very masculine, very sexy. The shadows and colors in that photo were awesome.

Her pictures went against the grain of Southern traditions and supposed values. That motivated me to turn to our host. I asked Kiki Sunshine if she was born in Greensboro.

She shook her head. "I was born in São Paulo."

"You're Brazilian?"

"Momma is. Daddy met her on the beach in Casablanca, fell in love, hung out with her for a week, got Momma pregnant with me, went back before I was born, married her, brought us back here."

"Romantic."

"The way they fought and cussed at each other, I wouldn't call that romantic."

"You speak Portuguese?"

"Not a word. The only thing that looks Brazilian on me is my hair."

"Red looks good on your skin."

"Thanks. Colored it last week."

Karl had Kiki Sunshine step out on her patio for a few shots. When she stepped into the light, I saw the mixture of several bloodlines in her exotic features. Native American. African slaves. Spanish.

While Karl catered to her vanity and beauty, I stayed inside, evaluating, judging.

Her space was awesome. But I came to the conclusion that she wasn't money-smart. She had upgraded somebody else's property. Not a good move. Her life was filled with a lot of feel-good stuff. Immediate gratification that didn't last until the next sale started. On her kitchen counter she had boxes of champagne. Bollinger Blanc de Noirs Vieilles Vignes Françaises. Dom Pérignon Rosé. Salon Le Mesnil.

When the impromptu shoot was done, I helped Karl take the equipment back down to the Jeep, then he turned the air conditioner on high while we waited for Kiki Sunshine.

Kiki Sunshine hurried downstairs. She had changed, was wearing white flare pants, the wide legs almost covering up her golden shoes, sexy shoes with high heels, silk chiffon top with flowing prints, wide belt to cinch her waist, making her shape pop. She had two big Louis Vuitton bags with her. One was her makeup. And she was carrying a champagne box, the Dom Pérignon Rosé.

Louis Vuitton and Dom Pérignon.

Kiki Sunshine loaded her things into the backseat and then eased inside the Jeep, sat behind Karl, getting comfortable where her eyes would be on me, forcing me to look at her.

I glanced back at her, saw her putting her seat belt on, exchanged smiles, then we were on the road, Karl taking me toward newness, likable or not, this being the continuation of a novel adventure.

Kiki Sunshine asked me, "Are you related to a girl named Yasamin Kincade?"

"Never heard of her. Why?"

"You favor her. She's black and Lebanese."

"Never heard of her."

"So you're not related to any of the Kincades from over in Charlotte or up in Detroit?"

I shook my head.

Karl made a right on Big Tree Way, passed by our hotel, then made a left on Wendover.

Kiki Sunshine told Karl, "You're going to make a right on Market."

"Is that after Friendly?"

"Before you get to Friendly."

Karl headed toward downtown Greensboro, passed another section of town populated by the privileged, those old-money people out walking dogs and riding bicycles, a couple were cutting their lawns, quite a few were teeing off on their local golf course.

Kiki Sunshine said, "Nia Simone, how you like living in the ATL?"

"It's cool. Been there?"

"Few times. Went to M Bar. Pearl. Slice. Verve. Two Urban Licks."

"You got your party on."

"Boyfriend took me down. Well, that ex-boyfriend was two ex-boyfriends ago."

"Uh-huh."

She asked, "What part of ATL you stay in?"

"I live in Smyrna."

"I was in that area once. This guy took me to dinner at Tomo Japanese Restaurant."

"Same ex-boyfriend?"

"Different guy. I met him on the Internet. Yeah, we kicked it in Smyrna."

"Small world."

"You have a house?"

"Townhome."

"I'm saving to buy a house. Used to stay near Bennett and A and T, but man, they kept breaking in. Lot of the guys who do the break-ins stay over that way. The guy everybody said who broke in my apartment last time works at Food Lion. I know that was the guy who did it. His ass smiled at me. I lost three televisions last year. Where I stay now, no problems. At least I ain't had none yet."

I said, "I heard that."

Kiki Sunshine shook her head. "Damn shame that black people have to stay by white people to feel safe. Well, that depends on the white people, because some of them are crazy, acting like they still mad because slavery is over. But it makes me so mad when black people treat each other that way."

I said, "Uh-huh."

"You know what the Bible says, what God said. 'My people are destroyed for lack of knowledge; because you have rejected knowledge, I will also reject you that you shall be no priest to Me; seeing you have forgotten the law of your God, I will also forget your children.'"

We passed Greensboro College, Moore Music, Jimmy's Corner Café. The moneyed real estate changed, the big homes vanished. We cruised into a downtown lined with banks and mom-and-pop businesses. Not long after, we were in the zone where men wore their shirts so large they hung longer than my grandmother's Sunday dress, the laces in their pristine white Air Jordans undone, their super-sized pants hanging below the lowest part of their butt cracks, a style that in prison meant you were gay and willing to copulate. The ones who wore belts had buckles so large they rivaled a WWF championship belt. I knew that we were heading toward poverty, just had no idea how deep into the land of the forgotten children we were going to ride. My eyes went to the door, saw it was locked.

Even with the door locked and Karl nearby, I felt afraid, as nervous as Sandra Bullock's character in the movie *Crash*.

We looked for spots to shoot, nothing stood out, at least not right away. Karl rode up and down the one-way streets until he found what his artistic eye needed, an area that was the opposite of safe and clean. An area I never would have stopped to visit, but it excited him to no end. He parked, removed equipment, and we walked down an alley. Karl wanted the contrast between her over-the-top beauty and the ghetto, the juxtaposition of heaven and hell. Kiki Sunshine had a train, a makeup box the size of carry-on luggage, filled with top-of-the-line products, at least three thousand dollars' worth of products.

I envied that. She had the best makeup I'd ever seen.

Three thousand in makeup, a brand-new truck with sparkling rims, thousands spent in her apartment, and she chose to do all of that over using that money to buy her a piece of land first.

To each his own.

If that was her addiction, it was her right. Not the smartest thing, but still her right.

I touched up her makeup, the same for her hair, neither really needing anything done, just playing my part. Karl took a few shots while I worked on her face, a face that didn't need much work at all. Kiki Sunshine loved the camera, was smooth, seemed like all Karl had to do was point and shoot.

Around thirty shots later we were on the road again.

Karl asked Kiki Sunshine, "You grew up over here?"

"On East Florida Street and South Benbow Road."

"What's over that way?"

"Nothing much. Barber Park."

"Cool park?"

"I can take you over to Barber. Should be empty this time of day."

Her cellular rang. She looked at the number and answered.

"Hey, Momma . . . uh-huh . . . yeah I heard Rose Furniture was about to close for good . . . okay . . . I can run you out there . . . okay . . . working now . . . let me call you later . . . love you."

She hung up.

Kiki Sunshine said, "That was my momma. Always wanting to go shopping. Working my nerves."

I asked, "You went to school around here?"

"Went to Bennett for a while. Started off in arts management with a minor in psychology, then switched to mathematics with a minor in computer science, wanted to run a web-based service, a Yahoo! or YouTube kind of thing. Ran out of money at the start of my senior year. Family drama and stuff left me in a bad way. Got into entertaining. Never made it back."

I didn't ask her to expound on what field of *entertainment* she had ventured into.

We rode around the neighborhood, Kiki Sunshine pointing out different landmarks, telling who used to live where, this side of town being the area where poverty ruled and white people looked like an endangered species, riding and listening to Eddie Murphy on Sirius, laughing at his Aunt Bunny Gooney-Goo-Goo routine. We rode to East Florida Street, ended up at Barber Park. We passed the entrance, driving slowly, looking for spots. Karl parked in an area that had foliage on both sides of the road, giving us shade and about thirty yards of privacy before the street ended at another major intersection.

Very scenic. Lots of tree coverage at the mouth of the park. Rolling vegetation that went on for miles. Kiki Sunshine went into the trees, the sun high, creating slivers of light on her commanding body as she stepped over branches, leaves, went deep enough into the thicket to be unseen from the road. She took her clothes off, swapped her high heels for Roman sandals.

Kiki showed her sunshine with no shame.

She was as naked as Eve. And comfortable with undressing in front of strangers. Karl was at ease, as if a beautiful woman being unclothed in front of him was part of the business.

She asked, "How's this?"

Karl laughed a small laugh. "You could've waited to get undressed."

"Don't want to get my clothes too dirty. Those pants came from Dillard's."

Karl nodded. "Give me a few minutes to make a call and get what I need out the back."

I asked, "Want me to carry anything?"

"Just take care of the talent."

"Okay. I'll be the good little assistant and have Miss Kiki Sunshine ready."

I made my way over the grass, moved over limbs, went to Kiki Sunshine, took her clothes from her, let them rest over my shoulder, played the role of assistant, the role I was, at this moment, enjoying.

I told her, "Let me check your makeup."

She had too much shine, this humidity being impossible, and I powdered her skin.

She continued to stare at my face, continued dissecting me.

I asked, "You okay?"

"Do you model?"

"Nope."

"You look like a model."

"Be still so I can get rid of the shine on your nose."

I used my fingers to pull her hair back into a low ponytail at the nape of her neck, let it rest slightly off to one side. Used a rubber band that matched her hair color to hold the style in place. Added rose hair-pins. She owned beautiful jewelry. Pearl chokers, tapered gold rings, golden shoes, three-row crystal head wraps, so many headbands I thought she might be heir to some headband manufacturer.

She said, "Karl is fine as hell."

"Very appealing."

"Looks better in person than he did on his Web site and MySpace page. His eyes . . . good lord . . . he has to be mixed with a lot of stuff to look that doggone good. Bet he could make some pretty babies."

I didn't respond. Kiki Sunshine was so pretty it was intimidating. She'd have to suffer a severe industrial accident to have her beauty diminished to the level of normal people.

She caught me staring at her. I looked away, made myself busy doing my job.

She asked, "How did you get this job?"

"He interviewed me at the W."

I put a classic band on her, kept it simple, then I painted her lips. Used a hue that worked with her skin's cool undertones. Lined and filled in her lips with nude lip pencil to keep the color from bleeding. Used a lip brush to apply lipstick, then blotted with a tissue. When I was done, I moved out of the way.

I said, "Brazilian, huh?"

"On my momma side."

"You're a beautiful woman."

She paused, then gave me a nervous smile. "I'm not a lesbian, if that's what you're asking."

"Wasn't trying to . . . no, not at all. Was just saying you're beautiful. Not trying to offend."

My defenses rose. Maybe I had been gazing at her beauty the way Anaïs Nin stared at June's loveliness. Her perfection had caused me to pause and appreciate what was before my eyes.

She smiled a little. "Thanks."

I took my eyes off her, then shrugged. "I guess you look like the type of woman that women would be attracted to. I'm not talking about lesbian attraction, I'm talking about heterosexual women would be attracted to you. Like women are attracted to Angelina Jolie or Salma Hayek or Halle Berry."

"Thank you."

"That's all I meant. Your beauty is universal."

"Universal?"

"Men would want you, and women would want to be a woman like you."

"You really think I'm beautiful? Because you are really beautiful to me."

"Whatever. You're tall. You have a nice body. People from all over the world would hit on you."

"Well, since you put it that way, yeah." She winked at me. "Women have hit on me."

"I'm not surprised."

"I love men, but I have dabbled a time or two."

"Dabbled?"

"You know. Dabbled."

"Oh. Dabbled. Gotcha."

"Now you got me thinking about things I shouldn't be thinking about. This girl I knew, she loved to go down on me. Never went down on her. I'd wake up with her face between my legs."

"Sounds hot." I smiled, hummed, imagined. "Outside of the obvious, how was it different?"

"You never dabbled?"

"Never dabbled."

"It's nice. Real nice. Guys fuck you. That's not a bad thing. Nothing like the way a man feels." She laughed. "Chicks caress you. A woman has a smaller tongue, smaller hands. It's different."

I looked at her. Again she smiled at me, her smile unhidden, penetrating.

She asked, "You sure you never dabbled?"

"Don't tell me I look like a lesbian."

"Not at all. Just asking. On the real. You ever tried it?"

I shook my head. "Never dabbled."

"Not even a girl kiss?"

I chuckled. "Why are you looking at me like that?"

"Can't help it. The girl I used to deal with back in the day, you look like her. A lot."

"The Yasamin Kincade girl?"

"Yeah. Freaked out when I pulled up in the lot at Groometown Road. Heart started beating all fast. Thought you were her. Heart was beating too damn fast."

"But I'm not."

She shook her head at me. "Now you all up in my face looking like my girl, got me thinking about my other experiences. Got me thinking about stuff I'd put behind me a long time ago."

"With women?"

"With Yasamin Kincade. My black and Lebanese freak. She used to dance at Baby Doll down off Highway 29 and she sold real estate over in Charlotte. We messed around for a while. Off and on. I mean, I always had a boyfriend. She was in the background. A side dish, not the main course. Didn't want to get hooked on doing something like that."

"Were you here when you were dealing with her?"

"Charlotte. We'd meet halfway, in Kannapolis, or I'd drive down to Charlotte. Never let her come here. She'd put me up downtown at the Omni. Or I'd go to her house late at night, real nice house, but most of the time I'd tell her to get us a room. Greensboro is a small town. People get all in your business. Lot of people from up here drive down to work in Charlotte every day. Word gets around."

"I bet."

"For my birthday, Yasamin Kincade sent a doggone limo to pick me up and bring me back to Charlotte. We spent the night at the Omni, rose petals and champagne all night long, and then she rented a convertible Benz and drove me to Caravelle Resorts out at Myrtle Beach, drove three hours with the top down and the music bumping. She had planned everything, paid for the entire weekend."

"Spoiled you."

"Hadn't thought about her in a while."

"Where did you meet her?"

"Met in Charlotte. During race week. She loved NASCAR, just like me. She was actually flirting with my boyfriend. I thought she was trying to get with him, but she was just trying to get my attention. She gave me her real estate card, tried to get my phone number, told me she wanted me to be with her. She wrote it on the back of the business card she gave me. Said I was irresistible. Said she wanted to be with me."

"How did you end up hooking up with her?"

"Her fine butt kept calling my job. Kept telling me she wanted to French kiss my downtown lips."

"How did she get your number?"

"I slipped it to her that night. She kept getting on my nerves, did it to get her out of my face."

"While you were with your man?"

"Yeah, gave her my number. She kept asking. Worked my nerves. Gave her my work number."

"Damn."

"He was a two-minute man anyway. His cheap ass. Only reason I was with him was because it is so hard to meet good men out here. You have to go all the way to Atlanta or down to Miami to meet somebody decent. And he would fuck me, but he would never re-fuck me."

"Re-fuck?"

"You know. Fuck me then fuck me again. Re-fuck. He never re-fucked the same night. I don't mind a man coming fast, not the first time, but at some point he needs to man-up and re-fuck me."

I laughed with her. Kiki Sunshine was a nomenclator, inventing names for things. I doubted if *re-fuck* would make it into the dictionary, but it definitely had earned a place in my vocabulary.

I said, "Okay. So . . . Yasamin Kincade . . . how did that jump off?"

"She kept calling my job . . . sending flowers . . . sending expensive gifts. Told her I wasn't into women, that I didn't do women, said she just wanted to go downtown on me, I didn't have to do her."

"Sounds aggressive."

"Women always offer to do me."

"And? What happened after the flowers and gifts?"

"She would take me to the best restaurants. Table. Bonterra. The Melting Pot. Café Sienna. Then one night we went out, danced all night, drank, and we went back to her spot. I was drunk as hell, had been doing shots, and no way was I going to be able to make it back to Greensboro without killing myself. Went to sleep. Next thing I knew, I was waking up, sun in my face, her licking me down."

"Really?"

"And the shit felt good."

"Unbelievable."

"Yeah. That was unbelievable. You have no idea how unbelievable. She had me tingling so good felt like every nerve was open, had me aching like I had a T.I.P."

"What's a T.I.P.?"

"A toothache in my pussy."

"That's funny. Aching so bad it felt like a toothache. Hilarious."

"She had me hotter than fish grease. Felt like I was in the devil's living room with a T.I.P."

I didn't correct her, didn't say the proper acronym should be TMP. People in the South had their own style, their own way of pronouncing words, *re*-spelling words, same for making acronyms.

Kiki Sunshine hummed and grinned, said, "She loved it because I come so fast. She used to put three fingers inside me. Her hands were small, her fingers were short, and I would tighten my legs and in no time I would go crazy and come all over her hand."

I looked at her. Again she smiled, this time her smile was accompanied with a raised brow.

She said, "You look a lot like her. You smile like her too."

Wordless stares existed between us.

By then Karl was coming up behind us, branches cracking under his feet. He had a camera and other photography equipment at his side. Kiki Sunshine and I slowed our laughter. Karl showed me how to hold this big round thing to reflect the light that was easing through the trees, that reflection yielded magnificent light that gave Kiki Sunshine a wonderful look. I took instructions and watched Karl do his thing with so much passion, and I watched Kiki Sunshine work it, also with so much passion.

As if she was put on this earth to create priapism in men, she turned up her sexuality, performed, moved her body however Karl told her to move her body, made orgasmic faces, serious faces, laughing faces. She did sensual pictures, then posed where her vagina could almost be seen, showed enough to tantalize, then went all the way and took photos where she was putting one finger inside her hairless yoni while the other finger was inside her red lips; sensuous, naughty-girl poses.

When her finger went to her yoni, I tried to look down or look away when she started doing those stirring poses, had to because I could relate to what she was doing so well that I imagined what she was feeling as she posed, but I kept moving the thing that reflected the light, so I had to look at her, make sure the light was hitting her in the right way. She took photos down on her haunches, took booty shots with her looking back at the camera, took shots with her holding the tree like she was climbing a huge erection, her serpent-like tongue coming from her red lips, her tongue moving like she was licking an aroused clitoris, penetrating a woman's vagina and anus. A wave of electricity swept through me.

She asked me, "Can you hand me my box of Dom?"

I did what she asked, became pauper to the queen, her every wish my command.

When she opened the box of Dom, I expected her to pull out a bottle of French champagne and use that high-class holy water as a prop.

What had replaced the champagne was a nice-sized vibrator. My mouth dropped open. It was a beautiful vibrator, pink and sleek, a feminine color on a mannish device. My surprise changed into a naughty smile as I shook my head at her. She grinned. That was clever. Never would have thought of using a box of Dom Pérignon to conceal a pleasure maker.

She took her tool, then handed me the empty box.

I said, "Pink?"

"It matches my hair."

She held her toy as if she were taking a man orally, stared at the camera with a seductive boldness, gazed at Karl as if he was her fantasy, mouth open as if she was waiting for him to spill his liquid energy, waiting for his strength to become her salvation. The camera shutter echoed.

I was their voyeur. Ashamed and excited all at once.

She asked, "Want me to put my toy here, daddy?"

Karl laughed. "Your pictures. Do whatever you want to do."

She teased the vibrator between her legs. It was as if she was touching me in the same place. I tingled.

Karl grunted, lust halted his breathing, almost lost his professionalism, but snapped back. Kiki Sunshine smiled a victorious smile, one that said she was desperate to corrupt Karl. Karl moved around, got closer shots of her, most focused on her face, the expression.

Kiki Sunshine moaned, bit her lips, faked an orgasm as a mild wind blew through the trees.

Birds were singing overhead, telling other birds to come see the show.

Karl didn't miss a beat, took so many shots, didn't stop until Kiki Sunshine stopped.

We took a break, just long enough for Kiki Sunshine to sip water, long enough for me to dab sweat from her face and touch up her makeup. Karl opened the small ice chest he'd brought.

Kiki Sunshine picked up pieces of ice while Karl started shooting.

She ran ice over her chest and face, lived in a state of euphoria and excitement, made sure her nipples remained hard as she posed making climactic faces, had a love affair with frozen water, made faces like she was having a colossal orgasm, her sounds loud enough to stir the birds.

Kiki Sunshine lost her rhythm and fell into deep laughter, looked like a child who had heard a good joke on *Sesame Street*, so unguarded, so real in that moment, her breasts bouncing along with her chortle. Karl never stopped photographing her, captured those images too. Kiki Sunshine's laughter was sweet and contagious. I swallowed, laughed too. Laughed and fanned myself.

The laughter, like a yawn, became contagious. Karl started laughing.

Karl said, "It's hot as hell out here."

I nodded in agreement and amazement.

Karl said we were done, said he had enough shots.

I took Kiki Sunshine her clothes, gave her a towel, helped her get dressed. She packed her pink toy back inside her champagne box. I followed her back to the Jeep, told her to sit under the air conditioner and cool off while I went to help Karl gather his equipment.

Kiki Sunshine said, "I had an orgasm."

"No way."

"Could you tell I busted a nut? It was a little one, but it was damn good."

"Thought you were acting."

"I'm not that good of an actress."

"Damn. You . . . just like that? Karl turned you on big time."

"I was looking at you . . . imagining what it would be like to feel your fingers inside me."

I smiled at her, nervous and excited.

I backed away from Kiki Sunshine, said, "I'm going to go help Karl with his equipment."

I headed back through the trees, fanning myself, disturbed, barely able to walk without stumbling. I wondered how much money men would be willing to pay to have a few moments with her. She was powerful. Her sexual energy radiated like a furnace. Her ability to create desire in people who shouldn't desire her was strong. Tried to imagine her giving herself, losing her control to a woman who resembled me. Looked at my hand, imagined my fingers inside her.

Once I made it into the woods, when I knew I couldn't be seen from the road, it took control of me, that darkness inside me consumed me, forced me to lean against a tree and loosen my jean shorts. That wasn't me getting undressed in the shadows and coolness created by the trees. It was my rage undressing me, my jealousy tugging at my pants. My insecurity and anger had been lurking, boiling deep inside me, had stirred me and demanded that I regain the attention I was craving from Karl, the attention he had given away as he was catering to Kiki Sunshine.

I whispered, "Karl."

He stopped packing his gear and looked at me, his gaze changing from focus to sheer surprise.

I was naked.

Like Kiki Sunshine. Like Eve in the garden, my secrets his apple. We stared at each other, not a word shared, yet everything being said.

He raised his Nikon, took photos of me, came closer with each shot. Karl went to put his camera down, but I reached out and he handed his pride and joy to me.

I whispered, "Taste me."

Without question, a sly smile rose on his golden skin, his tight eyes on my body as he got down on his knees, as he eased into that position of ultimate surrender, as he did what I needed to be done. He gave me his attention. His full attention. I aimed the lens down, pushed the button to make it steal this moment, did that until it felt too good. Camera in hand, I closed my eyes and imagined while he tasted me, imagined other things as he was licking me with swiftness, power, and grace. My body moved, did erotic poses like Kiki

Sunshine had done when she was engaging in self-importance, releasing my own muffled singsong moans as Karl slid his tongue across my opening. I imagined Mark was here, wanted Mark to be here, his erection moving toward my mouth, my stiff fingers helping make that imagination feel real as I squirmed. I opened my eyes, squirmed while Karl was still licking me.

It felt like Mark was here. For a moment I thought I saw Mark standing in the trees.

Not Mark.

She was there. Watching me. Watching us. Kiki Sunshine was standing at the edge of the woods, spying through the trees. I saw the redness of her hair mixed in with the greenness of the foliage.

I kept moaning my singsong moan, squirming and wining, dancing my yoni against his tongue.

Her eyes had become the camera, with each blink she photographed me over and over. Slivers of sunlight walked across my body. Sweat covered my skin, drained down my back, dampened my neck. Animalistic expressions on my face. I fell into my own fantasy world. Became an erotic supermodel. I wanted her to see Karl please me, wanted to moan like a demented bitch and tell him to fuck me like I was his slave while Kiki Sunshine moaned and watched me get fucked until I came.

She crept closer, found a better view, became a zoom lens, got her close-up.

Her eyes blinking like a camera's shutter.

Birds were singing. Little birds were celebrating life. And so was I. I was flying and singing with them all. Pieces of heaven's natural light fell across my eyes. In my pleasure I searched for Kiki Sunshine. She remained a voyeur. Kiki Sunshine licked her lips like a shiver of arousal was running down her spine. She was bewitched by the affectionate image she was witnessing. She shivered like ice was being teased around her nipples. She shivered like her faux penis was being eased inside her.

She shivered like she was erupting in her loins, shuddered as if she had a severe T.I.P.

She licked her red lips. In response my tongue traced mine, traced them over and over.

While I held Karl's head where it was, while I started to feel pleasure again, Kiki Sunshine remained imprisoned by voyeurism, as I was imprisoned by exhibitionism, my performance for her, a lone witness watching me shudder and sweat my way down the road to nirvana once again.

She took a deep breath. Jerked like she was filled with the Holy Spirit.

Her body leaned forward, she took a step, small branches and leaves cracking under her feet. It looked like she was coming to join us. But she waved a hand to the sky and turned around.

She stumbled, regained her footing, kept moving, her grace gone.

She had won her battle with temptation.

She hurried back toward the Jeep, left me panting as twigs of embarrassment cracked under her feet, left me shaded by a million trees, left me praying to God and his son, my eyes rolling in the back of my head as I tumbled into the brightness of satisfaction.

SEVENTEEN

I avoided Kiki Sunshine.

A drying sheen of sweat covered us as Karl and I loaded up the Jeep. I brought the ice chest back while Karl handled all of his equipment. I waited until Karl was finished loading his things before going to the front passenger-side door. Kiki Sunshine was inside the Jeep, in the backseat, side closest to Barber Park. When I got inside, Kiki Sunshine shifted, moved and sat behind me, did that as if she was hiding. I couldn't see her face as Karl drove down Florida.

Damon Wayans was on Foxxhole, doing a hilarious routine about O.J. Simpson.

But Kiki Sunshine wasn't laughing.

She shifted around in her seat a lot. Moved side to side like she had a severe toothache.

I stared out at the blue-collar section of Greensboro and smiled. My envy of Kiki Sunshine was at rest. It wasn't until then that I was fully conscious of my jealousy, of that anger inside me that made no sense, yet it was there. I had the kind of anger, the uneasiness that came from wanting to control something that was within reach, yet out of my power.

I was jealous, and yet I had fantasized about Karl taking Kiki Sunshine in the woods.

I wanted to understand me inside of this moment.

Karl peeped back at Kiki Sunshine and said, "You said you were a big NASCAR fan?"

I could tell that, despite being with me, he was transfixed by her beauty. The way he looked at her face, if I wasn't here, they'd share the same madness, the kind that would make him cross the line.

Kiki Sunshine shifted again. "Might go up to Charlotte and hang out on Speed Street."

"I like watching the pit crew competitions."

"Yeah, me too."

Karl asked, "Jeff Gordon fan?"

Kiki Sunshine moved around a bit. "Not really. Grew up on Dale Earnhardt."

"Gordon is making the record books in a big way. More than Earnhardt."

"Jeff Gordon can double up on race records and never be half the driver Dale was."

If Karl had heard her in the woods, if he had any idea that Kiki Sunshine had seen us, it didn't show in his actions, he didn't reveal his knowledge either by body language or with his words.

I enjoyed the ride, enjoyed looking at Greensboro for the first time, everything within my sight new, and yet everything in my sight familiar. I smelled the air, its humidity touching my skin with the gentleness of a new lover, let the wind caress me as we rode.

Karl's cellular rang. He answered, started talking, went into his own world.

Behind me Kiki Sunshine was stirring, as if she was on fire, unshielded from the heat of the sun. With a smile I turned around and looked at her, wanted to make eye contact, but her eyes were closed and she was biting down on her bottom lip. Kiki Sunshine's body language said she was riding the waves of our eroticism. I watched her. She was as beautiful as the mythical girl from Ipanema.

I asked, "You okay back there?"

Not until then did Kiki Sunshine open her eyes and look at me.

I stared at her the way men stared at me, nervous because my stare was being reciprocated.

Twenty minutes later we were back at Kiki Sunshine's apartment.

Kiki Sunshine offered us wine. I declined, just took a glass of water. She had left the air conditioner set on high. The apartment was filled with jazz. Smelled of good food. Lots of plants.

Kiki Sunshine said, "Y'all want some leftover fried chicken and okra? I have stuffed pork chops and corn on the cob. And I got some macaroni and cheese, potato salad, watermelon . . . plenty of food."

Karl and I thanked her for the offer, but declined.

She left the music playing and turned her television on, news she had TiVo'd this morning, left the television muted with captions on. The top story was about the locals struggling with the concept of the Koran being used to swear in a black woman at their courthouse. Old-school Southernites only wanted the King James version of the Bible used. ACLU and the Muslim woman had been denied the use of the Koran, that issue had been in court for years. Christians against Muslims, the things that unnecessary wars were made of.

Kiki Sunshine said, "Her being black *and* Muslim probably didn't help."

Karl said, "Says she won."

"State of Carolina is going to appeal it."

"Why?"

"Because she's Muslim. You know how they hate Muslims."

Karl nodded in agreement, then asked, "Where's your bathroom?"

Kiki Sunshine pointed down the hallway.

While Karl was gone, she looked me in my eyes, held that unreadable stare until she lost the gazing contest and looked down at first, then looked the other way. Our host moved to the other side of the living room, looking like she was on fire, stimulated, unable to turn the heat down.

Kiki Sunshine whispered, "Didn't know you and Karl were . . ."

I lowered my voice, matched her clandestine tone. "We just met."

"Did you?"

"Met him and . . . he was with his brother . . . I had a severe toothache that night."

"Karl's sexy butt looks like he has suicidal dick."

"What does that mean?"

"Suicidal dick. You know, the type of dick that makes you sacrifice yourself, makes you give up all your hopes and dreams, dick that makes you quit your hobbies because you wanna spend twenty-four-seven making his world better. That's what I call suicidal dick."

The bathroom door opened and our clandestine conversation ended.

Kiki Sunshine and Karl went to the dining room table, looked at some of the digital shots.

My mind was elsewhere, on my own desires.

On Karl. On Mark. On fantasies that concerned both men, fantasies unfulfilled.

But there was more to me than orgasm.

Much more.

Next week my concerns might evolve to the spiritual, or revert to financial trepidations, or my anxiety might switch to heath issues, but I couldn't predict that. All I knew was this week my hormones were high, I was almost as wild as Georgia wildfires, out of control, desire the beast that raged inside me.

I asked myself how important sex was. In the big picture, how much did it really matter? Sex marked the beginning of a romantic relationship. I didn't want mediocre sex. Or a mediocre marriage.

I was thirsty for the marvelous.

That reminded me of what Karl had said. Marriage was when a man stopped disappointing many women and focused on disappointing one. There was a lot of truth in that joke. Disappointment came when things that were spectacular ceased to be marvelous. Reality yielded boredom.

Here I sat in a room with two other people. A handsome man who had the sweet taste of my yoni in his mouth, on his breath as he held a meeting with a woman who was aching for intimacy so bad every nerve in her vagina was alive. She was beautiful beyond reason, had the kind of beauty that disrupted common sense.

Karl's cellular rang again. He stepped to the side to take the business call.

Kiki Sunshine eyed me once again. Her glance was tepid and damp. She licked her lips and my body temperature rose to that of the devil's home. A sensation ran through me. I glowed like a red light in Amsterdam. I turned away from the sight of her. Now she had taken control.

It was the same sensation I had experienced when I saw a shirtless runner hiking the steep part of Stone Mountain, coming for me. A sensation that doubled when I saw that runner came as a pair.

I took out my cellular, checked to see if I had missed any calls. I had missed a few. A couple of friends had called. One was from a blocked number. But there weren't any explicitly from the 901.

I sent my mother a text message, just a smiley face.

Karl told Kiki Sunshine, "I need to get to the room so I can get your disc together. Won't take long to burn a CD. Pick the shots you want enlarged. I'll FedEx those back to you in a day or two."

"What are you and your assistant doing the rest of the evening?"

She was looking at me, so I took that to mean she wanted the answer to come from me.

I said, "I'm going to go work out. Going to run a bit."

"Well, from your hotel back this way to Guilford College Road is probably a little more than a mile. Down and back would be over two miles."

"I need to run farther than that."

"No wonder your legs look so good."

Karl's cellular rang again. Again he answered, then stepped to the side.

Kiki Sunshine looked at me, her look both inviting and nervous.

I asked, "You getting out tonight?"

"Might stay in and deal with this toothache."

"Dentist coming by?"

"Nah. I might have to improvise."

Karl hung up his cellular, then said he was ready to go.

I stood up, told Kiki Sunshine that it was nice meeting and working with her.

She shook Karl's hand, then she came toward me. I wanted to run away from her, run like that bitch had run from her aggressors at Stone Mountain. I extended my hand but she moved closer and hugged me, my breasts pressing into her, her breasts pressing into me.

When she was done she held both of my hands, her right hand sneaking a small card into my left. She kissed my cheek, again smiling, and then she walked us to the door.

Whatever else was said I didn't hear, I couldn't hear, every sound becoming a low hum.

My heartbeat had deafened me.

I had to focus in order to make it down the stairs.

I hopped in the Jeep with Karl, but I wished I could walk it out.

Needed to walk with my thoughts.

Needed to spend three days in fast and prayer.

I looked down at the card in my hand, a business card that had the name Marie Adams on the front, which had to be Kiki Sunshine's real name, then I flipped it over, saw a message to me.

You're irresistible. I want to please you.

Those simple, straightforward words made my breathing halt, made me feel loose and wet. I owned a constellation of emotions. Those emotions had me terrified. Lust was sitting on me, as heavy as a three-hundred-pound lover, yet as light as a cloud. If only Karl could hear my heart beating fast.

I was shaking my head left to right, the movements so subtle, my legs crossed, squeezing them together, speechless, dehydrated and in the need of liquid desire.

I reached over to Karl. Put my hand on his thigh as he left the complex. The hotel was a two-minute drive away, right up Big Tree Way toward Wendover.

I touched him and his erection returned, strained against his pants. I rubbed that hardness, my fingers tracing its length as his Jeep crawled down the two-lane road.

You're irresistible. I want to please you.

Kiki Sunshine remained with me. Her nakedness. Her daring.

Her smell lingered inside my nostrils.

You're irresistible.

My skin tingled where she had touched me.

I want to please you.

Her voice had become a song that refused to leave my head.

I had to run.

You're irresistible. I want to please you.

I had to outrun this wildfire before it consumed me.

E I G H T E E N

Naked.

Karl and I showered. Kissed and touched, then ended the shower by switching the hot water to cold, letting that calm my sexual tension. Cold water on my desires created cumulus clouds.

Thoughts remained uncontrollable, unsteerable, mental needs unrequited.

I dried Karl off with a towel. He went to the computer to handle his work. I put on lotion and then dressed in my running shorts, sports bra, and T-shirt. Karl put on jeans and a T-shirt, no shoes.

I hid behind a smile. A deceptive smile. A smile masked so many things, kept thoughts and intents unknown. Living in L.A., the land of pretentiousness and falsehoods, watching my mother interact with Hollywood, the land of a thousand smiles, the land of backstabbers, I learned the value of a smile.

I dug inside my backpack and took out my laptop so I could get online. Not being connected to the Internet was aggravating. It was addictive. I tried to give up the habit. I failed miserably.

There was an e-mail from Mr. Overworked and Underpaid New York Editor. Forwarded jokes from my mother, the Queen of Forwarded Messages. E-mails from Web sites offering me Viagra at a discount and penis enlargement. That's what I get for going to porn sites on nights I needed visual stimulation. I had at least ten e-mails from Logan. I deleted Logan's e-mails without opening them.

I checked my messages. Special Delivery's song "I Destroyed Your Love" had been left on my voice mail. The entire song, parts one and two, all six minutes played as Logan sang along. The singer telling the world that since his woman left him, all he felt was emptiness and pain from losing her.

That stressed me out. Tried not to let it show. But that bullshit stressed me out.

Logan created no fantasies. None that didn't involve restraining orders or paid-for violence.

The television was on local news. Vandals had terrorized downtown Reidsville, surveillance cameras were being installed. A North Carolina man who was on trial for killing his father wouldn't have to face the death penalty. Bad news plagued the mean world. None of it seemed as important as my personal problems.

I went over to Karl. He had hooked his Nikon up to his iMac, was downloading images of Kiki Sunshine, the shots taken in the woods, her naked, artistic, sweating, provocative. She was a pretty woman. Uninhibited and secretive all at once. Mysterious. Like Josephine Baker. Her images were bold. Like she loved herself so much she didn't care what anyone else thought. Staring at her images derailed the aggravation Logan's message had caused. The images went by on Karl's computer, hypnotizing me, trapping me where I stood. My breasts felt heavy, swollen. Despite the air conditioner being on high, I felt my skin change from warm to hot. Urges rose. Those urges created distress.

She had put that card in my hand, expressed her desire for me, simple words expressing her need to share with me her secrets, she had awakened a new kind of curiosity, magnified my frustration.

I had to pump my brakes, control my libido, not let this new inquisitiveness control me.

Karl glanced back, saw me standing, looking over his shoulder. He turned to grin at me and I shifted away, moved my eyes away from the images that were going by on his computer screen.

He asked, "Which way are you running?"

"Not sure." I swallowed, adjusted my sports bra. "Any suggestions?"

"How long or far you want to run?"

"At least an hour."

He told me a route that would take me around the area, down Guilford College Road to West Friendly and back up to Wendover. Or I could do the reverse, jog Wendover to Friendly.

He asked, "In case anything happens, like heatstroke, which direction are you heading?"

"Guess I'll jog toward Guilford College Road."

"Toward Kiki Sunshine's apartment."

I lowered my eyes. It was as if Karl was reading my thoughts, my struggle feeling transparent. As if picking my direction to run was more of a metaphor than a geographical choice.

A year ago I never would have imagined I would be doing the things I was doing now.

Karl said, "If you run that way you start off with downhill. More shade that way."

"Yeah. More shade." I shrugged like I hadn't thought about that. "Yeah, I'll run that way."

"Sun should be going down by the time you get down to Friendly and Wendover."

After I stretched, I did a slow trot out of the hotel parking lot, heavy thoughts slowing my stride. I went to the left and jogged down Big Tree Way, again passing Georgetown Square, the Camden, Extended Stay, a small park, and then I was in front of Hunter's Chase.

I paused at the driveway, gazed toward building K.

Madness and sanity battled inside my body.

I was contemplating, intrigued, attracted to the thought of crossing new boundaries.

This was a city where no one knew me. Kiki Sunshine was

someone I'd never cross paths with again. She was a face I'd never have to see again. She was a stranger. I'd leave Greensboro late tonight, maybe in the morning. And I'd never have to come back this way again. Would never have to see Kiki Sunshine again. There was safety in knowing that anything I did would be deniable.

I shook my head. It wasn't going to happen.

I refused to be a slave to what she had stirred up inside me.

I kept going, left any feelings and fantasies I had behind, ran toward Guilford College Road, but only made it a quarter of a mile before I slowed down, before I stopped running.

My throbbing made my legs heavy, refused to let me move another step.

Unless I turned around.

I looked back toward Hunter's Chase.

I struggled.

I bent over like I had run a hundred miles, face cringed, hands on knees, panting like I was being attacked by emphysema. Hands on my hips, I stood up, put my hands on my hips, eyes closed until my breathing evened out.

You're irresistible. I want to please you.

I ran back toward the Hilton Garden Inn. Ran back to be in the room with Karl. Ran back to a man who looked like Mark. Ran back toward tattoos and broad shoulders, ran toward strong arms.

But I didn't make it beyond Hunter's Chase.

Maybe like Anaïs, it was not one, but my combined love affairs, my combined friendships, my passion and desires, maybe all of that combined defined me as a woman.

Defined me as Nia Simone. I was a unique woman. I was me. My experiences my own.

I walked inside Hunter's Chase. Went toward building K.

Forever went by as I climbed three flights of stairs. I climbed her stairs like I was hiking up a mountain in search of the gates of truth. Truth had its own watch. I climbed after Kiki Sunshine the same way Mark's and Karl's desire and curiosity had compelled them to come and find me, as if I held their truths. Now I stood at Kiki Sunshine's door winded and humbled, as if I had come in supplication, aching for answers, my eyes beseeching her tolerance, in need of answers to questions only she could reveal.

I rang the doorbell. I lost my breath. My nipples hardened. My heart wanted to explode.

One thousand one.

One thousand two.

One thousand three.

One thousand . . .

The door opened and there stood Kiki Sunshine.

Skin damp, water dripping from her skin, a towel around her body.

Behind her was the sound of jazz and her shower was still running.

The scent of her melon and jasmine body wash filling up one of my senses.

Our eyes met.

She stared at me. A deity stared at me, a woman who felt like a humbled mortal.

I waited for her to accept or reject me.

That rejection could come with a laugh, a shaking of the head, or the slamming of her door.

Forever went by as she studied me, as she evaluated me.

I waited for her to determine whether or not I was worthy.

One thousand one.

One thousand two.

One thousand three.

Kiki Sunshine extended her hand.

Boulders rolled away from my shoulders and I lifted my arm, gave her my flesh.

When our flesh made contact, my flesh became her flesh; whatever she held belonged to her.

NINETEEN

Kiki Sunshine darkened the apartment, pulled the shades, then faced me.

Kiki Sunshine dropped her towel, unwrapped herself, humbled herself as if she was making an offering to a queen. She showed me her nakedness. Same breathtaking body I'd seen in the forest, only different now. She wore no makeup, no mask, stood before me as her true self, naked for me.

I swallowed.

She smiled.

She came to me, her fingers touching my erect nipples, traced both at the same time.

Kiki Sunshine leaned into me, put her warm breath on my neck, her tongue and her teeth on my skin. Her mouth was small, delicate, gentle, the sensation causing me to shiver.

She stopped, withdrew her mouth from mine, smiled at my longing.

Kiki Sunshine went to the bathroom, turned off the shower, and when she came to me, again she touched me, this time touching my face with the back of her hand before putting her mouth to mine.

My mouth opened. With ragged breathing, as I shivered, I offered her my tongue.

The first kiss was on the horizon. A girl was about to kiss me in a sexual way.

A woman was about to add the sum of me to her experience.

And I was about to add the sum of her to mine.

Her tongue eased inside my mouth.

I was a shipwreck, the shivering refusing to end, my breathing refusing to calm.

I slowed down. I tasted her. I tasted Kiki Sunshine. I tasted another woman. Sweet tongue, slight minty taste. She touched my face with the tips of her fingers, sucked my lips, kissed me again. She was tender with me. It wasn't like kissing a man. Her lips were softer, no facial hair, she held me in a different way, softer, gentler, not aggressive, as if she was paying attention to how I felt, worried about my happiness, my pleasure. Her taste, it was warmer, a warm feeling that was hard to describe, her tongue was warmer, as warm as her fevered skin that was rubbing against my body.

She began undressing me.

This was very different. Being undressed by a woman. Very different.

She pulled my T-shirt over my head.

I hadn't been drinking.

She took my sports bra off.

I was fully aware.

She smiled at my breasts.

There was nothing in my blood to dull my senses.

I kicked off my running shoes.

There was nothing in my body to cause me to forget any individual moment.

She pulled off my running pants and panties.

A woman had undressed me, a woman had put her mouth on the hidden spots where clothes had been. Teeth and tongue were on my flesh, her tongue moving to my thighs, her hands held my ass.

Her tongue moved across my flesh and created an unimaginable heat.

I was dying, being slain by a new brand of ecstasy.

When she came back up, my hand touched her hair, hair that I held in my hands as her mouth went to my breasts. The shock of her mouth on my burning flesh made me jerk, made my knees grow weaker. She nursed my breasts. Nurtured my breasts. She became a baby being nursed by her mother.

Her other hand went between my legs.

Kiki Sunshine's fingers tried to work their way inside me.

A woman's fingers were on my wetness, trying to finger-fuck me.

I jerked, tensed, took a breath and relaxed, let inhibitions and forbidden feelings go.

I took a deep breath and moved my legs, allowed her fingers to find their way in my wetness. I was so wet it was embarrassing, ashamed because she would know this wetness was for her, because of her. She touched me there, her fingers tracing my fleshy folds, and I held her close to me. Held her and breathed on her warm skin. The sense of this being taboo heightened every sensation.

Butterflies invaded my stomach. The same nervousness I had the first time I had sex, those virgin-like sensations were alive inside me. Her touch was sensual, more erotic than any man's touch I had ever experienced. She touched me like she understood. All sorts of thoughts went through my head. *What if she told someone?* Women were territorial and vindictive and possessive. Women were emotional. I was emotional. I wanted this favor, but I didn't want her love, not the way I wanted it from a man. I had heard it was different with a bi woman. But a lesbian would claim you, same as a man.

I opened my eyes, found us in a mirror. Saw that I was being touched by a woman. A woman's arm was working back and forth in slow motion, her fingers moving like lingam. I tensed, closed my eyes. Needed to relax. Needed to trust. Kiki Sunshine had lied a wonderful lie. We all lied about things small and large. We all lied in order to not reveal our true selves. Kiki Sunshine had led me to believe she had never pleased a woman. Her touch. The way she knew how to seduce. That was her tell. She had experience doing this. She knew how to make this situation work. I needed to stop thinking, just let her guide me through this sexual encounter. I wasn't this tense the first time I gave myself to a man.

I didn't know how to touch a woman, how to give sex and pleasure and ecstasy and orgasm to a woman. Didn't know who was supposed to do what to whom. These feelings were different. A different set of sexual feelings. A new set of emotions.

She touched my chin with her hand, brought my eyes to hers, checking on me.

Despite my shivering, my shuddering, my moaning, I nodded that I was okay.

She smiled at me, rubbed my hair.

So unrushed. So unlike the first time I was with a man.

This was about me.

She had made this moment all about me.

She eased me down to the floor, down on the carpet, opened my legs and moved her mouth and tongue across my belly, made a trail toward my yoni. My shivers increased, the shivers of fear, the shivers of excitement, the shivers of anticipation. Tried not to tense, but I did tense. First I felt her breath. Her gentle exhales blew on my opening, that warm stream being the herald to what was about to come. She licked me. My ass clenched. She gave me another lingering lick.

I had to ask myself if this was really happening. Was I dreaming? Was I still out on the hot streets of Greensboro and this was my imagination taking over after I'd had heatstroke?

My hands went to Kiki Sunshine's red hair. My fingers played in her hair.

I touched her face.

This was real.

That beautiful woman born in Brazil licked me, and licked me, and licked me.

A woman was tasting my yoni. A woman had her tongue inside my yoni.

Oh God.

She licked me like she knew the way I was designed, like she knew how to move pleasure from my labia majora to my labia minora. She licked me like she had invented the clitoris. Even if she stopped now, it was done. If she never licked me again, I had done this thing. She licked me again and again. Each lick brought a brand new singsong moan, a new shudder. Then she came up over me, her nails tracing my skin, her mouth back on my breasts, then she kissed down my belly, slid her tongue down my hips.

I moaned. "You've done this before."

"I dabbled."

"Thought you said your lover wouldn't let you please her."

"She didn't."

"You dabbled with other people."

"I dabbled a few times."

"Did what you had to do."

"Yeah. Did what I had to do."

After that there were no more words. Just the language that was spoken with moans.

Kiki Sunshine's lovemaking radiated elegance, beauty, and sensuality.

Her body was so hot, so light. I touched her face. Touched her breasts. She moaned as soon as my hands touched her. She wanted to feel me on her skin. She was sensitive. Very sensitive.

She led me, positioned me, her head near my feet as she put one leg between my legs, scooted down until our yonis kissed, sucked my toes and did a slow grind, made me feel so good, made me show her how a girl from the island did a slow wine, made me show her how to do isolations and make hip rolls. Kiki Sunshine moaned for me, her Southern moans breathy, the Brazilian in her blood percolating, rising in her wonderful song. She stopped sucking my toes and started sucking her own breasts, turning me on in a different way, exciting me and inspiring me to suck my own breast while I rolled into her, while I wined into her, while I grinded into her, while I moved against her as she moved against me.

The mutual stimulation, this pace, this level of attention, this type of loving was so new, so different from being with a man, the way we were grinding our vulvas together, the way my yoni was talking to another yoni, kissing another yoni, sharing wetness with another yoni, it was so unreal.

Couldn't believe I was doing this.

As I moaned, as she moaned, weird thoughts went through my mind. A woman was singing a sensual song with me, a woman was writhing because of me, and I was singing because of a woman. A woman was having a spiritual experience, being familiar with me, bonding with my body. It felt like we were one. Our chants felt like they came from the same feminine place. Our sounds were like those of the same cat, using both sets of vocal cords at once. Wetness against wetness, we moved in unison, squirmed together like we were swimming naked across a lake made of light-brown carpet.

I knew a man's come was strong. A man's orgasm was brutal. A man's pleasure was violence.

A woman's orgasm was the sweetest nectar.

Another curiosity rose inside me.

A curiosity that wanted me to experience the five senses of this illicit moment.

I had relaxed into this experience. I wasn't intimidated. Not like I thought I would be.

There was something erotic about knowing she could please me, make love to me, make me come without ever penetrating me, without fucking me, not the way a man entered and opened a woman.

She changed positions, and I moved toward her as she pulled her loose hair back, was curious how she would feel in my hand. I remembered what she had said. How her female lover used to put three fingers inside her. I wanted to do that to her. Wanted to put three fingers inside her and cup them, do to her what had been done to me by men. As soon as I rubbed her, she jerked hard, like a man who wanted a woman with so much urgency that the moment he was with her in a sexual way, he was so turned on his orgasm overwhelmed him too fast. Kiki Sunshine moaned, held my hand where it was, her orgasm rising to the surface of her being, her face cringing, begging for her orgasm to be released.

I moaned. What I saw, what I heard, what I felt, those sensations made me moan.

Kiki Sunshine was so wet, wet because of me, wet for me, so soft, so swollen. I touched and massaged her, put three fingers inside her and she jerked like the Holy Spirit was going through her body.

Kiki Sunshine was coming for me.

Her orgasm looked painful, excruciating, and marvelous all at once. Her eyes widened like those of an ostrich, and that almost scared me. In the next instant her eyes closed tight. She came praising the King of the Jews and calling my name, my name being moaned louder than the former.

As her orgasm died, she kissed my body in appreciation, went down on me in gratitude.

She licked my yoni and I moved slow and gentle, back arched, my body rose, levitated, like a tidal wave was lifting me up, rushing me back to shore. I didn't want to surrender, didn't want to moan for a woman, but I moaned as that wave carried me, moaned and reached for something to steady myself, grabbed air at first, hands searching until I reached down and grabbed carpet, did that as my other hand found Kiki Sunshine's hair, her long red hair, hair that I used to pull her tongue and mouth deeper into me, encouraged her tongue to go deeper inside me, a tongue that was softer and smaller than a man's tongue, but it was a tongue that was familiar with the workings of a clitoris, a tongue that moved around my yoni in circles, first clockwise, then counterclockwise, a tongue working with small lips that knew how to suck yoni lips, knew how to be gentle with yoni lips, how to be firm with yoni lips, lips and a tongue that knew how to make wicked pleasure surge through my body, a surge that made me moan and twitch like I was being struck by little bolts of lightning, each bolt bringing a new level of pleasure, pleasure that made me so damn wet and set me on fire all at once.

I thought it would be disgusting. Maybe I thought some negative switch inside me would kick in. Maybe I wanted it to be bad so I could say that I had tried it and it was appalling. But it wasn't. It was beautiful, felt wonderful in a different way. I didn't expect it to be breathtaking.

I clenched my teeth, her tongue moving in time with my yoni.

I moaned the sweetest moan as her thin finger entered me, as it made slow, easy movements. In the next moment two small fingers were inside me. My yoni opened up, my singsong hum revealed my excitement, asked for more. She slid three inside me. My singsong moan, so melodic. Fingers moved with an in-and-out rhythm, an unrushed rhythm. She made sweet come-here motions, cupped me, made me writhe and gasp, touched me in the same way I imagined her former lady love used to caress her.

I came, the sensation, the release coming from deep within, escaping every pore.

Her touch made me come in a way I didn't understand.

I came and she held me until I was done coming.

My orgasm was so intense it embarrassed me, yet it left me shivering and enthralled.

She held me and blew her cooling breath over my burning skin.

My leg refused to stop shaking, refused to ease my shame at coming like this, for a woman.

I was having an orgasm with a woman.

I took a deep breath, took a ragged breath, surrendered, felt heady.

In that moment, I understood how it was so easy to mistake orgasm for love.

TWENTY

We sat in the darkness of her apartment, senses returning, jazz on, air conditioner humming, her melon and jasmine smell turning me on, absorbed that moment without talking, our breathing erratic, but calming down, the overwhelming power of my female-induced orgasm at last relinquishing control.

The lips of her yoni were puffy.

Mine were swollen as well.

My hymen was long gone, but it felt like Kiki Sunshine had popped my cherry.

The bag she had taken on her photo shoot, it was on the kitchen table. So was the box made for Dom Pérignon. I went to the box, opened it up, took out her pink toy. It felt real in my hand, like it was made from real skin, had weight, firm without feeling too hard. It felt like a man. With a brief smile I went back to where she lay on the floor. I took control, spread her legs. I was in control of her body. She had surrendered herself to me. That excited me and once again I was nervous.

I had never been with a woman and all I knew was what a man had done to me, all I could relate to was the sensations I had experienced when a man touched me, when a man aroused me, when a man made me feel good, when I made a man feel good. There was no penis to suck and lick, only the mirror image of what I possessed, a duplication of my own femininity.

I gave her what I had learned, shared with her the knowledge and experiences I had acquired from other lovers. I did to her what I imagined, what I loved a man to do to me in my surrender.

I gave her my fingers first. Did what an old lover used to do to me, used my pointer and middle finger, put those inside her yoni, did that as I slipped my pinky in her ass.

Shock was the expression she wore. Shock and pleasure. Kiki Sunshine went wild.

She closed her legs tight on my hand, locked my fingers where they were. She trembled and moved with my fingers as I struggled to stimulate her clitoris and finger-fuck her asshole all at once. What I was doing turned her on. And that achievement, that ability to please turned me on just as much. I watched her grab at the carpet and tremble, watched her in amazement.

Her orgasm was more than an orgasm. It was a total release. I felt her happiness harden her clitoris and at the same time her moans released her deep-rooted pain and sacrifice. She moaned and every sound made sense to me, and in between her moans I felt her thoughts, thoughts that told of her search for love, for a husband, for children, for family, and how that quest had left her disappointed and afraid. I felt emotional. I understood her and became emotional.

Too emotional.

I took my fingers away.

Left her squirming and panting for her yoni to be filled. I couldn't abandon her, not like that. I rubbed her toy against her skin, teased her with her vibrator. I pushed her legs open again, put the tip of the toy against her opening.

She moaned.

I eased her toy inside her a little at a time, watched her respond to that type of penetration. The type a man would give her. The type I was used to.

I moved the pink toy inside her pinkness in increments. Eased her toy inside her with respect. Eased inside her in a way that let her know I'd stop when she wanted me to stop.

Her body language begged for more. Her continuous moans were expressing much excitement. I gave her a little more. She begged with moans and squirms, set free so many onomatopoeias. A little more slipped inside her. I moved it around. Gave her a little more. Moved it around. Gave and moved, complied with her moans until there wasn't another inch of vibrator to give.

In and out I moved it slow, never taking more than half away from her, moved it while she moved against my motions. Her hands came up to her face. She covered her eyes and chewed at her lips. Her sexual tension was working its way out of her body. She moaned loud enough to stir the neighbors. She moaned like she didn't care who heard. She spread open her eagle wings like she was ready to fly. It was time for her back to arch. Time for her insanity to take root. Her turn to grab handfuls of carpet. She shuddered. Her mouth hung open as her legs stiffened, as her ass tightened, as the start of an orgasmic hum grew inside her body. Her toes curled. Her breath caught in her throat.

I moved it in and out of her until my hand grew tired, then switched hands.

She cried, those cries telling me how good I was making her feel. Her pleading eyes filled with tears. And those tears rolled down her cheeks.

I moved the vibrator in and out of her. She bucked against my hand, against her toy. Her expression was so passionate. So beautiful.

Her orgasm was violent and gorgeous, her yoni becoming fire in my hand, her back arching as the tidal wave of pleasure she was riding became a tsunami. A beautiful tsunami.

She came as if doing things taboo magnified her orgasm.

She came as if wrongness magnified her pleasure.

Kiki Sunshine came as if she was once again with Yasamin Kincade.

I smiled.

It didn't matter why she came the way she came, with such power and absoluteness.

I'd made a woman reach the ultimate pleasure. I'd danced with her spirits. I had made Kiki Sunshine experience nirvana. I'd made her experience a release to reckon with. I'd given her a clitoral orgasm. I'd stimulated her yoni and ass at the same time. I'd given her a vaginal orgasm.

I stopped vibrator-loving her, put her toy to the side.

Her long red hair was disheveled. The gaze in her eyes said she was extremely satisfied. Extremely. She kissed my yoni. Then she kissed my cheek. Touched my face. She touched my face and stared at me like I was an old lover she couldn't shake. I held her. I held her because I knew the good feelings that came after sex, held her and breathed with her. Held her and cooled down.

This was different. This passion after the passion. When it was done with a man, in the end, he might hold you, but he always gave you that slight nudge that said enough was enough, yielded a go-to-your-corner-until-the-next-round, or a go-make-me-a-sandwich look.

I held her and felt as if I was holding myself, as if Kiki Sunshine was my mirror, my truth, as if holding her was enabling me to understand myself on other levels. Physically, mentally, spiritually, and sexually. I had experienced something wonderful and new. I had achieved a new freedom. Even if I never did it again, that freedom would remain with me. Only with me. No one would understand me in this moment, not as I understood myself. They wouldn't be able to see the beauty, the bonding, they would blind themselves to the erotic part, to the learning of self, would only see the act of a whore.

A few minutes passed with us lounging in that glorious afterglow, then we pulled our bodies apart, stayed close to each other holding hands, then fingers, then we separated.

TWENTY-ONE

Like Dorothy on her quest down the Yellow Brick Road, I was picking up new companions at every turn, new experiences between the rising and setting of the sun.

I turned left out of Hunter's Chase and trotted toward Guilford College Road, turned right at the intersection, jogged in the same direction as traffic, picked up my pace, passed American Flag Self-Storage. Guilford Industrial Park. Big Dog Motorcycles.

As I pounded the sidewalk I smelled Kiki Sunshine on my skin. Her mango and jasmine fragrance blended with my sweat. It was almost as if she was running with me, leading me, chasing me, touching me.

At least four miles were behind me when I made a right at Guilford College proper, the actual college located across from a Hess gas station. I had made it to West Friendly Avenue, some ache in my legs, wanted to turn around, but was beyond the point of no return, ran toward the Guilford College tower, ADOPT A STREET signs creating eye pollution as far as I could see.

I had done so much in the name of pleasure. So much in the last few days.

I ran with my thoughts, feeling like I had deceived Karl. Like I had betrayed Mark.

Soon I was in the God Zone: Trinity Church, Westside Chapel, Friendly Avenue Baptist Church, church after church decorated the

The jazz music seemed louder now. As loud as reality.

I looked at my pile of clothes. Felt so naked. Felt exposed. Felt too vulnerable.

I didn't want to wake up naked with a woman and experience the first light of a new morning. This was just something to add to my Rolodex of clandestine experiences.

I wanted to hold her all night, but I didn't want to hold her another second.

I undid my hair, then redid my ponytail.

That done, I kissed her on her lips, touched her face, gave her a thank-you smile.

Her thank-you smile was broader, owned more brilliance than a movie star's smile.

Kiki Sunshine pulled the towel up over her body.

I gathered my shorts. My panties. My sports bra. My T-shirt. Socks. Running shoes.

As I dressed, I imagined this was how a man felt when he had sexed and was leaving a woman.

We exchanged sororal expressions. I had crossed the burning sands into a secret world.

At the door I adjusted my sports bra and finger-waved at Kiki Sunshine.

She grinned. Her grin sending a message, saying if I wanted to return, the door would be open.

I grinned too.

My heart whispered thank you and good-bye.

I opened the door in degrees, made sure no one was out there.

Went on the other side, the sunlight seeming much brighter now.

Heart racing, my smile nervous, I closed the door on that sensual and fulfilling fantasy.

well-to-do neighborhood, an area that looked as if it had been built with old money and lined with older trees.

That was when I saw him, first a dot in the distance, coming toward me at an amazing pace. It was déjà vu, just as it had been the first time I had seen him running toward me at Stone Mountain. In black shorts and black running shoes. It was Karl, sweat was dripping from his skin.

He ran to me, then turned around and ran with me, cut his pace in half, matched mine.

He asked, "You okay?"

"Yeah. What are you doing out here?"

"Miss you."

"Missed you too."

"Thought you'd be almost back by now."

I waited for him to ask questions, wondered if he knew, wondered if Kiki Sunshine had betrayed me and called him, and that call was the reason he had come searching for me.

I waited for him to show he had the same anger as Logan.

Karl was shirtless. His eight-pack on display, body so nice it looked pornographic.

Skin glistening like it was covered with the tears of many lovers he had left behind.

We ran side by side, and then I followed him through an area where a lot of roadwork was being done, the city of Greensboro keeping the roads in this area smooth. Karl's pace was challenging, could tell he was running much slower to work out with me, and I did my best to keep it moving, sped up to make his run decent, so much of my energy had been released back at Hunter's Chase, and I felt that missing energy as we paced it past North Holden Road, beyond First Lutheran Church.

I raised my hand to wipe sweat from my face and smelled Kiki Sunshine on my fingers. I licked my fingers. Tasted Kiki Sunshine's orgasm on my hands. I was tasting her desire.

A couple of miles later the Shops at Friendly Center appeared on the left side of the four-lane street. I slowed down so I could catch my breath, Karl jogged on awhile before he looked back and saw I was breaking down, was walking with my hands on my hips.

Karl came back in my direction, but before he made it to me, my ego had me running.

This time he ran behind me, let me set the pace.

We made a right at Green Valley Road, a street that fed into Wendover, ran by a line of large homes that all had the same red and white sign posted in their huge yards: NO REZONING STARMOUNT FOREST. I was dehydrated, muscles burning, about to die, but I couldn't stop running; knew that if I did I wouldn't start back. I pushed it by a strip club, then ran through the scent of dead pigs and cows being barbecued.

Big Tree Way was within reach, saw the Exxon station at the corner, that being the finish line.

Karl asked, "What you got left?"

I went inside myself, dug in as deep as I could, took it in fast and strong, turned right, breathing hard, sweating, dripping from every pore, muscles screaming. As I made it to our stopping point, my right hand crossed over to my watch, making the timer stop on instinct. Karl jogged by me like it was no big deal, like he could keep running for at least another week. I kept it moving, breathing hard, salty sweat in my eyes, the world roaring all around me, everything aching, frowning back down Wendover Avenue.

I wiped sweat from my eyes and checked the time on my watch.

Ninety-three minutes.

I'd run ninety-three minutes.

It had been a little over ninety-three minutes since I had completed that wonderful experience with Kiki Sunshine. It felt surreal. As if I had dreamed it all, her aroma rising from me and telling me it wasn't a dream, could feel her tongue and fingers in that place that men desired.

I asked, "How far is that course?"

"About ten and a half miles."

"Felt like twelve."

"It's the slave heat. And the pollen count is just as high here as it was in the ATL."

I felt like a sexual warrior. A dehydrated, starving sexual warrior who was about to pass out.

I said, "Karl, what are we eating for dinner?"

He looked at me and frowned.

I looked down at my clothing. A strand of long red hair was stuck to my skin. I pulled that hair away, flicked it to the ground. He was watching me. My skin glowed, guilt radioactive.

He knew. He knew about Kiki Sunshine.

Rage, jealousy, all of that was in his eyes. A man's insecurities could be volatile.

I licked my salty lips, took a breath and asked, "Karl, everything okay?"

His frown deepened. Fear rose up inside me. That volatile expression reminded me of Logan. The Logan at my door. The Logan in my nightmares. Fight or flight came alive. But I was too spent to run another yard. My mind roared, became defensive, and I prepared what I was going to say.

Yes, I had cheated on you, in some ways. What I did was wrong. But listen. I cheated in order to gain knowledge of self, a knowledge no man could've given me. I betrayed you. I cheated. And it was inevitable. As I know, if we continued, one day, if you haven't already, you would betray me.

My mind churned at a thousand miles per hour as I prepared my case for the court.

In the end we betrayed each other to satisfy ourselves, we had secret experiences because we were following our own desires. We were all cut from the same cloth. The cloth of animals. Animals that started wars. Animals who sought revenge. Animals that needed pleasure. The only difference was this: deception. Dogs didn't lie, male or female. Only people lied, so, in some ways, calling men dogs, calling women bitches, that was an insult to the honesty and integrity of the true dogs and bitches.

That was going to be my opening argument, a foolish rambling that made no sense.

But I didn't get to say any of that; his wall of anger was too great.

He snapped as he pointed at his face, "Do I look like that ugly bastard?"

"What?"

"Do I look like Karl to you?"

Not until then did I realize he didn't have any tattoos.

Not until then did I see the wedding ring on his left hand.

TWENTY-TWO

In a confused and surprised tone I stammered, "Mark?"

"How in the hell are you going to confuse me with ugly-ass Karl?"

"I'm sorry, baby."

I ran to him, put my arms around him, hugged him tight. "I'm sorry."

"I leave my job site . . . had more meetings with investors . . ."

"I'm so, so sorry."

"I rush to the airport, get on the first plane, fly here to see you . . ."

"I'm really sorry."

"And this is the love I get?"

The man who was cheating on his wife to be with me was here.

I let him go, my smile so wide. "How did . . . how did you know where to find me?"

"I went by the hotel. Karl told me the route you were running. I reversed the course."

He told me that he missed me so much he had come to find me. Had run miles to meet me.

We walked toward the hotel, sweating and cooling down from our run.

I asked, "You okay? You look a little tense."

"Work stuff, that's all."

"Want to talk about it?"

"Little frustrated. The market is rough. Typical for the business I'm in."

"Cyclic."

"Yeah. I'm living on the rough side of the cycle."

"That's life. Things are good, then the rough times follow."

We passed the hotel, kept moving, wiping sweat from our faces.

I swallowed, Kiki Sunshine's scent perfuming my skin, giving me flashbacks and tingles. I was glad Mark was here, glad he had run to meet me. If he hadn't been here, I might have found myself back at Kiki Sunshine's door. I might have gone back to check on her. Might have become bolder.

We slowed our stroll.

He asked, "How was the drive up with Karl?"

"We talked a lot."

"About?"

"Different things."

"Like?"

"He told me about Frankie."

"Frankie?"

"Cancún. The girl you guys met in Cancún. She was from L.A."

"Oh. Frankie."

Again I imagined the three of them, but my mind focused on Frankie, imagined her sensations overwhelming her to the point of sensual madness, a madness that we all longed to feel.

I said, "He told me everything."

"What else did he tell you?"

"What else was he supposed to tell me?"

He paused, now serious. "We were in the islands more than once."

"So there was more than one Frankie?"

He took a deep breath, my married lover now irritated by my curiosity. "Ask Karl."

"You angry about something?"

He shook his head. "Not angry."

"What's on your mind?"

He frowned.

I sensed I was asking too much, that now I was treading where I should not tread.

I understood. There were things about me I didn't want to be pressured into answering.

Karl and I could talk about most things, personal things, laugh about being with others.

Mark and I were different, I felt that.

There was a connection between us that didn't exist between me and Karl. Something logical, something emotional. Something that I didn't want. A connection I didn't need. But it existed. Made me want him to be more open with me, wanted him to do more than give physical pleasure. Then part of me shifted. Part of me wanted to pull away. Red lights were flashing. I didn't need to get caught up. Needed to make sure it stayed at the physical level. Needed to be with Mark the same way I was with Karl. They could compete with each other, but I didn't need to compete with Mark's wife. Once again I had to remind myself that Mark was the safe one, because being married, he could only invest so much. He could only ask for so much.

He said, "That call . . . hearing you sound like that . . . it messed me up."

"He made me do that."

"Did you enjoy torturing me?"

"Not at all."

"Did you enjoy letting him be with you? Did you enjoy making me listen?"

"He made me. He pulled over and dragged me into that place and made me."

"But did you enjoy it?"

"No."

"Sounded like you did."

"I sounded like that because I imagined he was you."

Mark was sensitive, an endearing and appreciated quality that had eluded Karl's DNA.

We paused at the entrance to Hunter's Chase. It all seemed like a dream. My yoni twitched, the memory of Kiki Sunshine, my unfaithfulness keeping my sex awake. Still felt her hands and mouth on my skin, felt her softness, that sensual warmth covering my body, for a moment it was taking over like kudzu.

Having cooled down enough, we turned around, headed back toward the hotel.

Mark asked, "Did Karl make you come?"

"Ask Karl."

"Did he?"

They were of the same egg, of the same father, so I knew they were not like Edmund and Edgar. I wondered if their rivalry was like that of Venus and Serena Williams, or closer to being Cain and Abel.

I said, "Don't make it more than it is."

"What does that mean?"

"We're having fun. It's just fun. I'm another girl for Karl and I'm a distraction for you.

"I want you to be more than a distraction."

"I can't be any more than that."

"Why not?"

"Saw Jewell Stewark today."

My words stopped him from talking. He understood what I was saying. He nodded.

I asked, "I know you said things were tense at home. Are you still sleeping with her?"

"I got your point."

"Answer the question."

"Yeah. Not often. But yeah."

"She's your wife. Having sex with her is part of your husbandly duties."

I said all of that with a smile, but it was still hard to say. Reality was never easy.

When a man went deep inside a woman, it was inevitable, someone would become emotionally trussed, feelings would ascend and someone was destined to want it all.

He said, "It's like I have this unmanageable, overpowering urge to be with you."

"Because you can't have me."

I wondered why it was so easy for a married man to experience somebody else and not worry about the consequences. Wondered why we became so sensitive, why we were affected differently by the same act rooted in nature. They had been inside my body, but now they were inside my head as well.

I was inside Mark's head, deep enough to cause him to travel across three states.

Mark asked, "What do you want?"

That was a simple question that was too hard to answer. I wanted the attention they gave me, I wanted the pleasure they gave me, I wanted the infatuation I saw in Mark's eyes, and the lust I felt when I was with Karl. I wanted them to ravage me. I wanted intellectual stimulation. And I wanted the challenge of pleasing two men at once.

I wanted this to go on forever.

And I wanted honesty. That was hypocritical, but I wanted them to be honest with me. Even if I'd never reveal all to them. We all held secrets. No one was totally honest.

"Mark, I want you and Karl. In different ways. I can't be with just one of you. Not in my head. Not with my body. I know there are two of you, but to me there is only one of you. That's my position."

"But which one of us, if you had to chose, would you chose?"

"It's all or none. That's the only way this can work for any of us. All or none."

Jealousy was flattering. For now. But I knew perpetual jealousy would become irritating. It was a long way from being irritating today. Today it was a long way from being confining, a long way from threatening my autonomy.

He had abandoned his wife, had left The Jewell of the South and come to find me. The king had left his castle with a swiftness, had traveled to rescue me from the evil dragon. It was wrong. That wrongness made me feel special. It was a Pyrrhic victory, but I was happy.

Mark said, "So that ugly motherfucker told you about Cancún."

"Your brother told me about Frankie. Three days with her. Double penetration."

Mark kissed me. The scent of his sweat was so arousing.

When the kiss was done, my smile was as gigantic as my imagination.

He whispered, "Double penetration."

A chill went down my spine.

He said, "Let's go find Karl."

We headed for the elevator, hand in hand. I was not the same woman he had met a few days ago. I was not the same woman I was a few hours ago.

Two hours had passed since I left building K in Hunter's Chase. Two hours since I had been enlightened by the fingers and tongue owned by Kiki Sunshine.

Two hours since I had alleviated her toothache and given her bliss.

He asked, "Why are you smiling?"

"Am I?"

"Smiling hard."

"Happy, I guess."
"Good. I want you happy."
I had grown. And yet I was still famished.
Today I craved things new.
Today I desired abnormal pleasures.

TWENTY-THREE

Karl wasn't in the room. But his cologne tantalized the air. He'd left smelling sensual.

Mark and I showered together, light touches and a few kisses, foreplay that I didn't allow to go too far. We sat on the bed, waited for Karl, assuming he had gone to get something to eat. Mark made a few phone calls, at least one being to his wife. His tone was not happy, as if in a heated debate. Reminded me of my conversations with Logan. I went into the bathroom, gave him space. I made calls too, one being to my mother. Another hour went by. No sign of Karl. No message. His Jeep was in the parking lot, viewable from the hotel window. He hadn't gone far. Wearing babydoll lingerie, I moved by the double beds, stood in the window. Mark was behind me, naked, holding my breasts, kissing my neck, his erection firm against my ass, my nipples hard, my clit swelling between my legs, waiting on Karl, Kiki Sunshine on my mind as I gazed toward Hunter's Chase.

Mark needed to do to me what his brother had done. He wanted me now, wanted me to himself. He was jealous. I was jealous as well. Waiting on Karl, imagining where he might be, jaw tight, jealousy rose while hormones raged.

After the weatherman said that the temperature in Greensboro was sixty degrees tonight, the newscaster said it was ladies' night at

Bowman Gray Stadium; women could get in for one dollar. I wondered if Karl had gone there, to meet new yoni.

He hadn't left a message at the front desk. He had vanished.

Darkness covered Greensboro. Food arrived from a local delivery service.

Mark made me lie down on the bed. He decorated my body, put warm food all over my stomach, all over my breasts, on my thighs, made my body a buffet table. He fed me. Then he started eating sushi off my skin, made me feel so beautiful, like I was a stripper onstage at an exotic club, like I was inside the film *9½ Weeks*. He ate from my body, then licked my skin clean when he was done.

He opened my legs. Then he licked the edges of my yoni, sucked the meaty part of me.

The winds were picking up. The rain started falling harder.

I made Mark stop. What he did felt good. But I wasn't ready to go there yet. I wanted the full fantasy, something he couldn't do alone. I needed Karl here to dilute any real emotion that might inadvertently rise from the type of passion I wanted to give and receive.

That was what I kept telling myself.

There were no promises. No one owed anyone anything. None of us ever would.

The rain was coming down hard and steady, pounding the ground.

Thunder boomed and the skies lit up.

Mark took my foot in his hand, licked my feet, sucked my toes, asked, "You ever switch up?"

I moaned, fire moving up my spine. "What do you mean switch up?"

"You and your girl, on a double date or something, and you and your date start having sex, then she and her date start having sex, then while it's going down you switch partners."

"No." I squirmed, my toes in his mouth, him sucking as if he was giving me oral. "You?"

"Once. College days."

Another moan slipped free. "You're just as wild as Karl."

"Not nearly."

"Sounds like."

"I doubt if you were up for the Mother Teresa award."

I took my foot away from him, the tingles too strong. "I'm talking about you, not me."

He stared at me, his grin thin. "Notice how you get me to talk without talking yourself?"

I reached for our food, then moved closer to him, began feeding him.

I asked, "How did the switch-up happen?"

"The other girl was prettier than my date. She was more attracted to me than she was to her date."

"What happened to that girl?"

"We married."

"Jewell Stewark?"

He nodded.

Twenty minutes later we finished eating, everything was gathered and thrown away.

We laughed and talked, kissed and touched. The rain remained steady. Karl hadn't returned.

Once again I went to the window, the repetitive action broadcasting my obsession.

When I turned around, Mark was watching me, waiting for me.

I smiled an exposed smile. Felt foolish for waiting on a man like Karl.

Mark whispered, "Want me to call and see where he is?"

I shook my head, my gut telling me where he was. "No."

Thunder and darkness echoed and rose inside of me. A different kind of blackness. The kind fueled by a barbaric emotion I despised in others. Mark had brought two bottles of Riesling. I opened one, poured drinks. Kissed him. Rubbed his body. I danced, made it a show for Mark's eyes only. I wanted this to take forever. I wanted to torture Mark the way the passage of time was torturing me now.

My wish, my desire was for Karl to walk in and see us having a good time.

I wanted him to feel superfluous.

Mark said, "You're getting tipsy."

"Would hope so."

He laughed. "I want you so bad it's killing me."

"I can see."

I ran my fingers up and down his bare leg, my fingers moving across his anatomical blessing.

He smiled like he knew he had me. Glasses of Riesling in hand, we sipped awhile, let the spirits take us higher. The phone never rang. The tattooed half of my fantasy remained MIA.

Disappointment festered.

I called downstairs, asked them if they could send up tea and honey.

By the time the tea and honey arrived, Mark was at the end of his second drink.

I asked Mark, "Have you ever heard of the velvet tongue?"

"Nope. What's that?"

I took some of the tea, made sure I had plenty of honey, held it inside my mouth for a moment, allowed my mouth to become hot and sticky, then brought Mark's erection to my concoction, gave him the heat, let him feel the hot tea and melting honey as it smoothed across his hardness, a hardness that I suckled until all the honey was gone. He moaned a thousand times. When the honey was gone, I looked up at him. He was in ecstasy. So far gone from here. His erotic smile told me he understood.

I raised the cup, sipped more tea, added more honey, gave him another velvet tongue.

Mark moaned so loud.

I took control of Mark, took that part of him in my hand, took him in my mouth, began a kind of suckling, stroking with my right hand, my good hand, the one I could control the best, once again doing my technique, moving my hand in circular motions, feeling him inside my mouth, feeling him grow, moving up and down until I felt him rigid at the back of my throat, breathing through my nose and relaxing.

I stopped, moved up on him, climbed him, mounted him, descended, began riding nice and slow.

I looked toward the door, wishing it would open, wanting Karl to walk in and see this.

Mark said, "Count to fifty."

"Why . . . count?"

"Maybe that ugly sonofabitch will be back by the time you count to fifty."

"I don't care if he ever comes back."

Mark moved me, put my ankles around his neck, pinned me down. He entered me, not all at once, went inside me slowly, staring in my eyes, watching my expression.

I looked away.

He began stroking me hard, stroking me fast, going deep inside me.

He growled. "Am I not good enough for you?"

"Yes, baby, yes yes yes, baby."

"You want me to stop?"

I shuddered. "You're going so deep."

"I can stop and we can talk literature, if that's what you want to do with me."

"No, don't stop."

"We can talk Toni Morrison. Gustave Flaubert. Theodore Dreiser."

"You are so fucking deep."

"Do you need me to read you some goddamn Nietzsche while I fuck you?"

"Mark . . . Mark . . . Mark . . ."

"Will that keep you here? Will that keep your damn mind here with me?"

"Damn . . . Mark . . . Damn."

"What in the fuck do I have to do to keep your attention?"

"I'm here . . . Mark . . . God . . . Oh God . . . I'm here."

"Look at me. *Look at me dammit.*"

My eyes went to his, to his passion, to his intense stare, to a level of emotion I could not match. Embarrassed, I closed my eyes. He kissed my face over and over, his kisses patient and telling of a need deeper than sex itself. He made me joyously, drunkenly, serenely, and divinely aware that his need was deeper than sex.

He was that part of me I kept well hidden, that part of me that had been damaged.

"I feel you." His baritone voice was so sensual. "You're coming."

"Uh-huh oh God uh-huh."

He stopped, pulled away from me, left me panting, tingling, sweating, his desire so taut.

Tears were in my eyes. So many tears. He was teasing me. Controlling me. Forcing me to forget about his brother. Forcing me to focus on him. He kissed my face, licked my tears away.

This was poetry.

He whispered, "Tell me what you want. Tell me how to make you happy."

I moaned, told him I wanted to see him touch himself. Wanted to sit and watch him handle himself. Wanted to watch and learn more about that part of a man, about that part of him, the part that created orgasm inside me. He held himself with his right hand, started with slow strokes, moaned, closed his eyes, growing in his hand. I licked my lips. My breathing became disturbed. His strokes became intense, faster, his grunts so sexy. His body began to tense, a thousand little deaths trying to run up and down his spine. I looked up at his lingam, his dick, his penis, his prick, his instrument of pleasure; whatever he wanted it to be called, I would call it that, would whisper it, would moan it, would scream it.

Mark reached for my head, grabbed my hair, begged me as he led my mouth to his fountain. He trembled and cried and shuddered like he was having an aneurism.

When he started to come, I pulled away, watching the fluids flow from his erection. He collapsed, came down on his knees, then used one hand to prop himself up, posed like Atlas holding up the world, his muscles glistening with sweat, his chest rising and falling, his breathing choppy. I watched his orgasm spew, saw his desire weaken him, saw his come, the hue of cinnamon frosting. He coughed on his own saliva. Coughed like he was overwhelmed.

He frowned and cursed, released a thousand vulgarities.

As he coughed and came, again I went to the window, gazed toward Hunter's Chase.

I glanced back at Mark. He was still disabled, panting, eyes glazed over, trembling.

He was calling God, talking to God, praying, his orgasm taking him closer to a spiritual realm. Hearing Mark call out to the heavens sent my eyes to the floors of God's kingdom.

I stared at the skies, looked deep into the darkness, beyond the home of the stars, my gaze unbroken by the blinking of the eyes, my soul on a quest to see God. I didn't think of God as male. Or as female. I thought of God as God. That was too simple, too abstract, too uncreative for most. I refused to remake my deity into my own image, into my own sex, refused to force the color of my skin on

God, never felt the need to express my insecurities or egotistical needs in that way just so that in the end I would be able to wag a finger at people who didn't look like me and say, "Told you so."

I believed in God, my mistrust rested in man's interpretation.

An interpretation that made me *less than*.

I went back to the bed, put my back against the headboard. Mark came to me and I kissed him.

I whispered, "I prefer you to Karl."

Mark's kisses flowed from my mouth, to my neck, to my ear-lobes, to my breasts, kissed me and took his tongue to my yoni, his licks slow, his intent at wooing me, disturbing me, owning me un-hidden, his tongue moving in circles, flicking inside me, doing to me what Kiki Sunshine had done not long ago.

TWENTY-FOUR

We showered. Flossed and brushed our teeth. Washed away our crime of passion.

Body slightly damp, I crawled into the bed with Mark, cuddled with him until sleep found him. My emotions tried to overflow, tears almost came, my emotions almost revealed themselves.

I wasn't in love but I was on its porch, hand raised, prepared to knock, biting my lips as I hesitated, hoping my knock was answered, at the same time hoping no one was home.

I'd been to that house before. My last visit had been so unkind.

Anxiety kept me awake. Thoughts tattered, I slipped away from Mark.

I stood in the window, looked out on Big Tree Way, searching through raindrops, occasional flashes of lightning disrupting the darkness with momentary brilliance.

My body remained filled with conflicting desires.

Inside me lived two women.

I thought about my Hampton days. Back then I had fallen in love with the idea of falling in love, knowing romantic love was brief and fleeting, its damage total, its damage unseen to the un-trained eye.

Beauty was the currency of betrayal. The same went for a man's handsomeness.

I saw her rims sparkling in the moonlight. Saw her coming in this direction, her pace casual. Kiki Sunshine's black Yukon pulled up out front. I shook my head, disappointed, betrayed. I felt *less than*, coldness creating chill bumps over my skin as I murmured many obscenities.

Kiki Sunshine remained parked in front of the hotel. Karl was with her. She had my lover. They were kissing. Touching. Delaying their parting farewells. Taunting me. Torturing me.

Memories of Hampton, of standing on the steps at Virginia Cleveland Hall and watching the man I loved, the man who had fucked me the night before, memories of watching him touch and kiss another woman in public, that haunted me, pulled me back to a time and heartache I wanted to not remember.

That freshman. That cheerleader. I was her tutor. I had introduced them.

Ogden Circle. Confronting a bitch over a man who didn't want me anymore.

A confrontation that took place in front of the world as I knew it then.

The first of many confrontations. The beginning of foolishness.

She had attempted to make me irrelevant. She had mistaken my kindness for weakness.

Men disappointed me and women could not be trusted.

The truth. What bothered me. What intimidated me at this moment.

Karl was indomitable. He was the dark side of me. Me if I was a man. Me if I was free to exercise my sensuality and sexuality without being looked upon as being a whore.

I wasn't envious because Karl had gone in pursuit of a new pleasure.

He had done with me what I had done with Logan.

It hurt like hell, but there was another issue.

I envied Karl's freedom to do so without being harshly judged.

He wouldn't be judged by others. He wouldn't judge himself. Those were fears and realities that plagued a woman, not a man.

I looked to the skies, frowned into the darkness, wiping tears from my eyes.

Maybe I was wrong. Maybe God was a man.

Only a man would allow happiness to continue bobbing just beyond a woman's grasp.

Only a man could allow the life of a woman to be this cruel.

Those were my thoughts as I pulled on jeans and a T-shirt, as I pulled on running shoes and took to the hallway, skipping the elevator and taking the stairs, rushing to run and confront Kiki Sunshine.

TWENTY-FIVE

Four naked people were inside the hotel room.

Beautiful birthday suits everywhere.

Two naked people were blindfolded and tied together.

The two queen beds had been pushed together, creating one huge playground.

Two naked people were sitting on the bed watching the other naked people.

Kiki Sunshine was naked. Blindfolded. Tied to Karl with neckties and scarves. A beautiful woman and a beautiful man were bound together by neckties, scarves, and the sweetness of curiosity. They had become the exhibitionists.

Mark asked me, "How does this little game of yours work?"

I smiled and whispered in his ear, told him that I had read about this in a magazine, one I was browsing on my many trips to This N That in Smyrna. The couple was supposed to be tied together, face to face, naked, breasts against chest, where they couldn't use their hands. They had to be lying on a bed. As they struggled to get out from the ties, the woman and the man get stimulated from the friction.

They struggled to get free.

I frowned, should've tied them tighter.

The binds holding Kiki Sunshine's ankles loosened, fell away, and she opened her long legs. Their blindfolds slipped away, those silk scarves slipping off their heads.

Karl managed to get his head to Kiki Sunshine, began sucking her breasts. She moaned. Karl wiggled between her legs, moved against her until his erection was positioned at her yoni. He tried to get inside her, but she shifted, wouldn't let him break her skin. They wrestled and fought, hands still tied, Karl's erection growing like Kiki Sunshine's moans.

I had tied them together. Silk scarves. A necktie that Mark had in his bag. Told Kiki Sunshine that if she wanted to stop the game, just say *Shakespeare*. That was the safe word. In this game if she said *stop*, *stop* didn't mean *stop*. And if she wanted to get free, her hands weren't tied that tightly.

Kiki Sunshine wanted this.

I whispered in Mark's ear. Told him what to do. Wanted to move this to the next level.

Mark went over, pulled his brother away, put his face between Kiki Sunshine's legs.

Seeing him touch her disturbed and excited me, more of the latter than the former. He was gentle with her, as he had been with me at the W. Gentle and intense. I moaned as if he was doing that to me. Moaned as if he was fighting for the right to fuck me.

Karl wrestled with his silky binds.

Kiki Sunshine was begging Karl to come save her, to stop Mark from licking her, from squeezing her breasts, begging Karl to break free and make his brother take his tongue out of her yoni.

Kiki Sunshine had no control. She squirmed like she was angry, cursed Mark and she begged Karl to get free and come save her from his brother's wretched tongue, but she didn't close her legs, didn't try to get away from receiving oral sex from a stranger. In fact, her body language was completely submissive. Completely vulnerable. She told Mark to stop, told him to stop a thousand times. But she never said *Shakespeare*.

I was aroused.

Kiki Sunshine released kittenish sounds, moans and purrs, soft murmurs that said she was stimulated by the thought of Mark taking control of her even though she was in the power position. Orgasmic expressions and the sounds that came from her made me tingle.

I was wet.

I watched as Kama Sutra and its energy crackled in the warm air.

As Mark ate her out, his erection was growing, dangling between his legs.

I went to them. My body took me to them without permission from my mind.

I looked back at Karl, smiled at his suffering as I touched Kiki Sunshine.

I touched my clandestine lover.

I played in her hair, looked in her face, smiled at her, kissed her eyelids, kissed her ears. Let my tongue roll along the edges of her ear, blew warm air on her damp skin. She twitched and moaned. She was so turned on. I took my tongue and teeth to her nipples, then sucked her nipples while she wiggled. She was being savored by a masculine tongue while a feminine tongue licked her erect nipples.

Fruit. There wasn't any fruit in the room. I craved slices of exotic fruits. But all we had was Riesling. I rubbed the Riesling on Kiki Sunshine's skin, dampened her swollen breasts, her lips, dampened her erogenous zones, made sure her belly button and breasts were flavored, did it like I was preparing to do body shots, then licked the sweetness away. My tongue made its way to her belly button. There was a lot of licking, kissing flesh, sucking fingers, feeling each other up. I kissed down to her thighs. Then I moved away. I teased her like I was going to feast on her yoni, then moved away.

Kiki Sunshine shifted around, her hands still tied, following the rules, living in pleasure, and as Karl watched, as Karl suffered, she kneeled in front of Mark, began pleasing him with her mouth. She suckled him, treated that part of him with love and kindness. Suckling him like a baby in need of nourishment. Suckling him until his strength became his weakness.

She owned him.

Karl stopped struggling for his freedom and watched, his mouth wide open, his expression unadulterated anger. His breathing thickening as Kiki Sunshine took his brother deep inside her face. I watched her. Watched her technique, saw how she licked the tip, sucked the tip, teased Mark to no end.

Karl managed to get free, moaned and reached for Kiki Sunshine's head, tried to pull her away from sucking Mark so good that my married love cringed and moaned with her every move. Karl tried to pull Kiki Sunshine by her hair. She wouldn't let Mark go, sucked him as if this was payback. Karl began spanking her ass, spanking her ass hard. Kiki Sunshine kept giving Mark a blow job. In between moans, Mark took her head into his hands and started to move her to his rhythm. He moved her mouth up and down, made her adjust to his speed, his depth, and his motions.

Karl looked my way, witnessed the heat in my face. Saw lust unhidden.

Karl came toward me.

I backed away from him, ended up in the corner of the bed, my back to the headboard. He attacked me. I struggled with him, telling him to stop, told him to quit, never saying the word *Shakespeare*. Our naked fight was playful, intense, and so damn erotic.

Karl held me down on the bed, entered my yoni with powerful strokes. My legs wrapped around his waist and my nails dug into his flesh. He moved inside me and made the hotel rumble. Mark was being sucked, looking at me while Karl fucked me like I was his woman. Karl fucked me like the devil and I sang like an angel. I fought with him, my face flushed, pores raining, each stroke killing the last of my jealousy, each stroke softening my heart, his pace sending me into a state of bliss and exhaustion. This felt like love. I didn't want love. I called out to Mark. Reached for him. Begged him to come save me. Told him to stop his brother from treating me like this. Mark was calling for me to come save him at the same time.

Kiki Sunshine had pushed him down on his back, mounted him, was riding him reverse cowgirl, her back to his face. She rode him then stopped, backed up on him, took her yoni to his tongue, sat her Brazilian-born blessings down on his face. His cries were muffled by the ass that smothered his words.

A hand pulled my hair. Yanked my attention away from watching them.

Karl stroked me away from voyeurism, had me biting on my lip, sucking my teeth, moaning out my pre-orgasmic mantra. Ecstasy consumed me. My orgasm tried to flow like water, but I wouldn't come. I refused to come. I lost that battle. Just wanted to hold on to the torturous moments that came before the orgasm. He left me there, moaning, wiggling, coming, shuddering, trembling, ripples of leftover orgasm running through my body over and over, aftershocks after the big earthquake.

I closed my eyes.

Moans covered me like a warm blanket.

I opened my eyes.

While Kiki Sunshine rode Mark reverse cowgirl style, Karl stood over her, made her take him in her mouth. She suckled him. She sucked my yoni juice off his flesh. Their movements were slow. Deliberate. No longer fucking. Now making love. Lyrical moans. Calm movements that made me feel like I was standing in the middle of someone else's wet dream.

She owned them. I refused to let her take them from me.

I crawled to them, sat on Mark's face, fed him my yoni, my back to Kiki Sunshine's.

Mark's tongue felt so damn good. It was the best tongue in the whole wide world.

Stolen fruit was always the best.

They controlled us. Mark and Karl. They took control. I was so exhausted, so high on the moment, so orgasmically aroused and orgasmically spent all at once, all I could do was enjoy.

Thunder boomed. Rain fell.

Everything remained slow and easy. The sound of heavy rain blended with moans and laughter.

Mark was inside Kiki Sunshine. Kiki Sunshine had taken Karl in her mouth. Mark was eating me.

This was unbelievable.

Bodies shifted, moved, positions changed and the experience continued.

Soon I was sucking Mark. Karl was inside Kiki Sunshine. Kiki Sunshine was eating me.

A woman was pleasing me as my identical sins watched.

This was unreal.

Lightning flashed, illuminated our naked bodies.

It was too much, I didn't want to come again, and I wiggled away.

Mark came to me, held me, rubbed my breasts, kissed my neck.

He whispered, "You okay?"

I nodded. Held his girth, his length, and nodded.

Karl remained as one with Kiki Sunshine, kept his rhythm, his hips rolling, wining, as if he was dancing inside her womb. Her eyes closed, her hands reaching for his ass, her legs rising to Karl's waist, her knees moving up and down against the rotation of his hips. She jerked like he was massaging her spot. Her head began rising, lips reaching for lips, her tongue entertaining his mouth. She kissed him like she was in love with him. Soft kisses and lengthy moans as he continued dancing, refusing to be distracted by thunder, by lightning, by the presence of two voyeurs. Kiki Sunshine was emotional, vulnerable, a tender lover.

This was like watching a passionate love story.

Mark and I crawled back over, rejoined the party. Mark took me from behind while I held Kiki Sunshine's hand. We held hands while we were being stroked. Her grip tightened. Her moan spiraled. She trembled. Kiki Sunshine came. Karl and Mark stopped moving. I was so far gone, I couldn't hear what they were saying. Karl went to the bathroom, washed up. When he came back, he had wet towels. Karl cleaned me, cleaned me good, cleaned my vagina first, soaped the towel, then cleaned my ass, cleaned my chocolate starfish real good. After that Karl went to Kiki Sunshine, cleaned her just as good.

While Karl wiped us down, Mark was in the bathroom, heard him washing up. Karl took me to a chair. A devilish look painted his face. Karl sat down, had me mount him, face to face, heated breath to heated breath, eased his erect lingam inside my yoni, filled me up, pulled me, made me lean forward.

Across the room, Kiki Sunshine sat, watching.

It was about to happen.

Again I was nervous.

Aroused and nervous.

Mark came back, was behind me, his erection touching my skin. Mark touched my ass, separated my cheeks. I jerked when I felt a warm lubricant going down my butt into my orifice.

My chocolate starfish was being lubricated.

Fear and excitement danced inside me.

Karl moved in and out of my yoni. Kept me stimulated while Mark played with my chocolate starfish, put his fingers inside me, oiled my opening, prepared me for pleasure yet to come.

His fingers felt so good. The way he was sliding inside me. That anal play felt good.

I'd let him do anything he wanted to do to me right now.

I did these things with them because I felt at ease with them. Something about them made me want to take action on my fantasies. Maybe because the intimacy was astonishing. Made me want to try things with them. See how far this could go. But this made me tremble. That moment of truth had arrived. I was scared. Like Betty Wright should walk in the room and start singing "Tonight Is the Night."

Mark whispered, "Relax."

I nodded. "Go slow, Mark. Just go slow."

I said that like I was at the mercy of his imagination. *Do with me what you must.*

I should pump my breaks. I should stop right now. So many thoughts invaded me.

Voice in rapture, I whispered, "Be gentle . . . don't be aggressive . . . you hear me?"

I was in a submissive position, trying to be in charge, trying top from the bottom.

Karl kissed my skin. "Just relax, sweetie."

Mark's lingam, the head, touched me there, slid across the lubricant, found the opening, began working its way inside me. A thousand nerves came alive. My breathing became a series of stutters. I nodded that it was okay, eyes tight, mouth and mind ready to moan *Shakespeare*, knowing I wouldn't. I wanted to know what this was like. I had done so many sexual things. But it wasn't out of being whorish. A lot of it was out of seeking pleasure. Wanting to feel it. Desire it. Crave it. Experience it. Face it. Challenge it.

What I felt was the opposite of whorish. What I felt was the opposite of weak and submissive. I felt entitled. I felt empowered. I felt as if fears were being taken away.

I didn't think it was the people who were being sexual who were the misfits in the world. The other people were the misfits, the cowards. The paranoid ones were spending their days going against the grain of what felt good, of what was natural, denying pleasure, yet desiring it all the same.

They were the ones who had me, even now, defending myself.

I moaned. Karl moaned. Mark moaned. Twelve limbs intertwined. The air conditioner hummed as sweat dampened all we touched, the room as tropical as Trinidad, Barbados, and Brazil combined.

I told Mark, "That's enough . . . that's enough . . . no more."

We didn't move for a while. Curt breathing. Rapid heartbeat. I held Karl while Mark held me. I wanted to stay like this forever. We owned each other.

Kiki Sunshine called my name, whispered my name as she came over to us, to me.

Her mouth was close to my ear. "Just relax, sweetie."

"You've done this before."

"Uh-huh. Just relax. You're too tense."

She kissed me on my lips, a friendly, supportive kiss as she ran her hand over my hair, pulled stray strands of hair away from my face, from my eyes, then kissed me on my cheek again.

She asked, "You okay?"

I took in a deep breath, let it out slowly, put on my brave face and nodded.

Kiki Sunshine dragged her fingernails up and down my skin, made me coo, made me so calm.

I whispered, "I'm okay."

Kiki Sunshine kissed my lips again, then went back to her spot, went back to watch. I wanted her to stay next to me. I didn't want her to go away and leave me alone. One of the twins asked me if I was okay, wasn't sure who asked, everything a dreamy blur. I nodded, told my identical sins that I was fine, that I wanted more, to move some.

Karl moved in and out of me, his level of penetration not that deep, his angle not the best. Mark had the best angle, eased inside some, moaned like the tightness of my chocolate starfish was driving him crazy. While one moved in the other moved out, while one moved out, the other moved in.

They were so smooth, so tender, both whispering to me, making sure I was okay.

I panted, swallowed, told Mark, "Little more . . . just a little more."

"How does it feel?"

"Hurts but it feels good." Again I panted and swallowed. "Feels real good."

"Can you come like this?"

I swallowed again. "Just go slow. Like that . . . yeah . . . keep it slow."

One moving in while the other moved out, then one moving out as the other moved in.

The physical sensations were unique, different from anything else I had ever felt. My brain was enjoying the new sensation as much as my body. It was beyond pleasurable. I moaned and bit my lip, panted, sucked in air, then leaned deeper into Karl, bit him, eyes tight, my sounds trapped in my throat. Mark's sounds were so intense, like he was losing his virginity, like he was on the road to his first true orgasm. I was well-lubricated, but still so tight back there, much tighter than my yoni, his pleasure more tactile than Karl's. So many nerve endings came alive. Then Mark was inside me. Karl was inside me.

They were inside me. At the same time. Like I was Frankie. Like I was in Cancún.

I stared toward Kiki Sunshine, my body moving in slow motion, easing toward a new pleasure.

Oh God oh God oh God.

Kiki Sunshine came over. She kissed Karl. Sucked his neck. She moved and kissed Mark. Mark sucked her breasts while I moved back into him, our connection better now, all the pain gone.

Kiki Sunshine rubbed my breasts, pinched my nipples while I was filled with lingam.

Mark grabbed my hair, led my mouth to Kiki Sunshine. Karl grabbed Kiki Sunshine by her hair, became rough with her, made her bring her tongue inside my mouth. She moaned like that toughness turned her on. I moaned my singsong moan. They made us kiss like lovers madly in love.

Every orifice was filled. So much stimulation at once. A celestial energy flowed through me, made everything kaleidoscopic. It was transcendent. It was a spiritual experience. I was gone to a wonderful place.

My body was here, but my spirit, my essence had sojourned away from North Carolina.

My soul had alighted in a land filled with white sand beaches, crystal indigo seas, a world filled with warm, romantic Caribbean nights. I was in Tobago. I was back home. Could smell the doubles. Could taste bake and shark. Heard the waves crashing into the white sand. Saw coconut trees. I was moaning and moving toward a paradise most of the world didn't know existed. I was back in heaven.

My identical sins cleansed me before cleaning themselves.

Kiki Sunshine smiled at me. Her smile dreamy, filled with unforeseen intoxication.

I smiled in return.

She whispered, "Thank you for punishing me."

I smiled, knowing what she meant.

She said, "I thought you were going to kill me."

"Did you?"

"You looked so mad. I was so scared."

Not long ago I had gone downstairs, jealous and angered, went to talk to her. She had told me that Karl had showed up about thirty minutes after I had left, had brought her a disc of her photos. She fed him. Gave him wine.

Her and Karl. Alone. Inside her apartment.

I had asked Kiki Sunshine, *"How far did it go?"*

"We messed around."

"Define messed around."

"Kissed a couple of times."

"He touch you?"

"He touched me."

"What did he do?"

"You know. Tried to feel me up."

"Did you enjoy it?"

"He started it."

"It feel good?"

"I made him stop."

"You're being transpicuous."

"What does that mean?"

"Means you're lying. And it's obvious."

"Damn . . . Nia . . ."

"Did you enjoy it?"

"I'm sorry."

"No reason to be sorry, Kiki Sunshine."

"I wasn't trying to disrespect you."

"He made you wet?"

"Don't do this to me."

I said, *"I'm going to punish you."*

"Punish me?"

"You heard me, bitch."

I had paused and stared at her. She looked nervous. As if she never would do anything to harm me. She looked at me as if she was in love with me. As if she was mine. That made me smile. She hadn't been pleased, not like I had been pleased. In that moment, I didn't want to be selfish.

I didn't want to be mean.

In that moment I didn't want to go back to what had happened at Hampton.

I asked, *"Would you like to be kissed and have your yoni licked at the same time?"*

That made her smile.

"Stop messing with me."

"*I'm serious.*"

"*Well . . . yeah. I would like that. Hell, yeah.*"

The expression on her face when she saw Mark, it was priceless. I said, "*Kiki . . .*"

"*There are two of them?*"

"*Suck his dick.*"

"*Suck his dick?*"

"*I want to watch you suck his dick.*"

"*Simon says?*"

"*Nia says.*"

"*Which one?*"

"*Pick one. Start sucking.*"

And here we were.

The identical sins took Kiki Sunshine to the chair. They oiled her, prepped her. Her breathing, her body language, she was nervous and excited all at once. It was her turn to see kaleidoscopic lights, to feel pleasure rushing out of every pore. I wanted to go to Kiki Sunshine, touch her face, caress her, whisper in her ear, watch her moan. But I was too exhausted to help. I struggled to crawl to her, but my body owned the weight of a building. All I could do was watch her do what I had just done.

I watched her moan and come and enjoy the Frankie experience.

TWENTY-SIX

Four lovers slept naked.

I woke up first. I was a morning person. I always woke up thinking. Ready to write. Ready to run. But this morning there would be no writing. There would be no running. Only thinking.

Everything about the world seemed surreal, as if I was melting in a Salvador Dalí masterpiece.

Two orifices had been filled by men as a soft tongue danced inside my third orifice. A woman's tongue. A tongue that was placed in my mouth because her hair was grabbed, her face led to mine as, at the same time, my hair was grabbed and my face was led to hers. For the men we tasted tongue. It was poetic. It was eloquent. The sounds we made had been more powerful than the most imaginative prose. I basked in the feeling that came from physical satisfaction. Felt at ease, the spiritual release that came with orgasm, that period of melancholy or transcendence, the expenditure or spending of life force, all of that anchored me in the peaceful place I had awakened, on a queen-size bed in a hotel.

I inhaled pheromones. The room was filled with the scent and power of pheromones.

I had shed all sexual inhibitions. Physically and psychologically, I felt fine.

It felt like I was at a rest stop in an unknown world. A world with its foundations built on curiosity, mutual fulfillment, and immediate gratification. A world built on the need to give and receive passion.

I told myself that I was in control. I told myself that this wasn't self-destructive.

I told myself that my mother would never find out what her daughter did behind closed doors.

Air conditioner on, room cool. Cellular phones started going off all over the room; Karl's phone started the party. Soon mine played the ring tone that had been given to the people in my DNA category. Kiki Sunshine's phone sang a hip-hop song not long after. Mark's phone started blowing up too.

I was in the bed with Mark. Kiki Sunshine was in bed with her photographer.

I was on the bed closest to the window, my body facing the other queen bed. I closed my eyes for a moment. When I opened my eyes again she was rubbing her nose.

Kiki Sunshine was on the side of the other bed closest to me, easing back into this world.

Flashbacks of tribadism entered my mind. Tribadism had never been a fantasy. Never. But I had done it. I had abandoned vanilla sex and given away my chocolate starfish, had received orgasm in a new way. I had disconnected myself from my anchor and sailed away from what was traditional.

Kiki Sunshine opened her eyes and found me staring at her. She came into the world glowing. She returned to consciousness with Karl wrapped around her and happiness all over her face. We looked at each other. We smiled. Both smiles owned hints of embarrassment, vulnerability.

I whispered, "How are you feeling?"

She whispered back, "Like I should write somebody a check."

"You okay?"

"I think I passed out on the re-fuck. Came so hard I saw Harriet Tubman and passed out."

She looked back at the man she was in bed with, her face filled with sheer amazement, then craned her neck to see the face of the man who was in bed behind me.

She whispered, "Twins?"

"Identical."

"You know we going to hell for this, right?"

"And we will have a story to tell. People will gather around us to hear about this."

"There are no heroes in hell."

"Because we're not there yet."

"Heathen."

"Hypocrite."

We laughed.

She looked back at her lover, then looked at me again, whispered, "Which one am I in bed with?"

I lowered my voice to match hers, told her, "Karl."

"You sure?"

"You see the tattoos?"

"Oh. Yeah."

"Karl. You're in bed with Karl. Mark is unmarked. Karl has KENYA on his arm."

"Kenya? They're African?"

"They're from Barbados."

"Never heard of Barbados."

"West Indies."

"Where is that, like over in India or someplace?"

"South of Jamaica."

"So, they're Jamaican?"

"They're Bajan."

"Whatever. Wherever they're from they are fine as hell, that's all that matters."

I laughed.

She asked, "You can tell the difference? They felt the same to me."

"How did they feel?"

"*Good.*"

I laughed.

Kiki Sunshine said, "Hungry?"

"Like you wouldn't believe. I could eat anything you put in front of me right now."

"Wish you had felt that way last night."

"Still got Yasamin Kincade on your mind, huh?"

"If you want this for breakfast you're more than welcome to it."

"Aren't you hospitable."

"Southern hospitality. If nothing else, we will feed the hungry."

We laughed.

I said, "Not ready for that."

"Just playing."

"Let's get some food. Some real food. Hit the cafeteria across the street."

"Oh, heck no. You need some home cooking."

"That would be even better."

She yawned. "I need to go home and shower. Need to do something with this hair."

"I need to shower too. Damn. I need to write. Have a lot of writing to do."

"About this?"

"Nah. Book I'm working on. A sci-fi number."

"Forget that sci-fi mess. You need to write about *this*."

"One day. Maybe."

"Just don't use my name. My momma would whoop my ass across three state lines."

More laughter.

We looked at the men. Nothing but the syncopation of heavy breathing came from them.

We chuckled.

Kiki Sunshine sat up, rubbed her breasts, made a sound like she was old and in pain.

I asked her if she was okay. She nodded and laughed. She was sore. I knew how she felt. I ached the same way. Nipples hurt. My yoni wanted a Motrin. So did my ass. They were satisfied and yet they wanted more. Plus I ached from the ten-mile run. My eyes went to the window. The skies were overcast but the raining had ceased. No more thunder. Kiki Sunshine made it to her feet, yawned, and headed toward the bathroom, her love-hangover sashay making her stagger and use the wall to keep herself up. I found enough energy to sit up while she made her potty call. Sat up and looked at Karl. At Mark. Watched them sleeping so hard. Wondered who would wake up first. Wondered if they woke up, would the Kings of the Re-Fuck want to pick up where they left off last night. Wondered if I could handle any more pain and pleasure. Had to ask myself if I could live this way. Had to ask myself where this would go from here. This was fun. Last night had been fun. Every moment since I had met Mark and Karl had been sexual and fun. But I couldn't live this way. This was too good. This could be addictive.

When Kiki Sunshine came out of the bathroom I went inside and showered.

I ached. God I ached so good. I let hot water burn away my transgressions as I ached.

By the time I came out of the shower, hair damp at the ends, my lavender shower gel releasing sensual aromas to blend with the rampant pheromones circulating in the small hotel room, there was conversation and laughing in the living room area. Mark was up, his jeans on but not buttoned, sitting on a chair while Kiki Sunshine sat on the sofa. Their conversation looked so intimate.

Mark said, "Kiki Sunshine says she's going to cook us breakfast."

She smiled. "That's the least I can do. Forget the fast food. Come get a decent meal."

I asked, "You have time, Mark?"

He nodded. He knew what I meant. A married man's time was always limited. Being here, being away from his wife overnight, that couldn't be a good thing for them.

I had eaten breakfast at Karl's home. I'd been given the tour of his mini-castle.

I'd never be able to feast inside Mark's castle. I'd never be invited inside.

I accepted that.

Mark called out to Karl, "Get your ass up."

"Fuck you."

"Let's get some food and get on the road."

"What she cooking?" That was Karl, in bed with a pillow over his head.

"I make the best pancakes in the world, I kid you not. However you like them. Banana pancakes, blueberry pancakes, whatever kind you like I can make that up real fast. I can run and get some fruit from Wal-Mart. I can get some fruit and make some fresh juice. Won't take me but a minute to throw something together. I have to take my momma furniture shopping this morning, but I have time to feed y'all before y'all get back on the road."

Kiki Sunshine went and sat on Mark's lap, touched his face, rubbed his hair.

Mark looked at me, almost as if he was asking if I was okay with her touching him now.

I smiled, nodded.

Kiki Sunshine asked, "You sure you're not Karl?"

Mark frowned. "Karl is the ugly one."

Karl yelled out, "Like hell I am."

Kiki Sunshine was in heaven.

She said, "Y'all like Deion Sanders in bed."

Karl laughed. "You slept with Deion Sanders?"

"Heck no. I'm saying, on the football field Deion could play any position. Y'all like that in bed. Going downtown. From the back. From the top. Sideways. Upside down. Y'all rock every position. Y'all see an opening, y'all go for it and get up in it before it closes. Y'all like the Deion Sanders of sex."

All of us laughed, but Mark laughed the hardest.

Kiki Sunshine said, "And I'm not letting y'all leave here without feeding you, so both of y'all get up, get dressed, and meet me at my apartment in a little bit. I'm cooking breakfast, that's all there is to it."

It was funny to me. I was born in Trinidad, waved the beautiful flag from the Republic of Trinidad and Tobago, but I guess I was a West Coast girl. A product of the rebellious L.A. mentality. After sex, an L.A. girl didn't cook, but expected to be taken to breakfast. Where a man took a woman after a night of wickedness told her how good her performance was the night before. Gladstone's or some seaside eatery in the Palisades or Newport Beach meant she was the bomb. Being taken to Roscoe's Chicken and Waffles was like getting a C+ on your report card. Denny's or IHOP, well, that spoke for itself.

I guess a Southern girl didn't feed a lousy lover.

Kiki Sunshine was ready to feed three people.

In my mind that was better than Gladstone's.

TWENTY-SEVEN

An hour later.

I sat in an apartment that looked like it was furnished by Pier 1 and Crate & Barrel, designer ceiling fans spinning on low, the room filled with colorful flowers and colorful knickknacks. I had left the hotel with her, became one of the women who went to cook for the men, thought I'd fall into a traditional role, at least momentarily, but ended up watching her work her magic. She may have appreciated a room filled with lovers but she believed in one woman to a kitchen. She didn't share in the kitchen.

I was wearing a Bebe sport racerback tank and capri leggings. Clothes that would be comfortable on the ride back home. Kiki Sunshine had put on a colorful sundress, one that flowed over her figure, had done her hair in a French twist. I doubted if she ever went anywhere in sweats or with her face undone. It was like watching Kimora Lee Simmons playing Julia Child in the kitchen.

It didn't take long for Kiki Sunshine's apartment to smell like pancakes and turkey sausage. The pancakes were made from scratch. Watching her move around the kitchen was like watching my mother make Sunday dinner. Grilled fish and callaloo. Sweet potatoes with pineapples. Rice and peas.

I was craving Trinidad, her sun, her food, her sands, her waters.

Kiki Sunshine made scrambled egg whites spiced up with red

onions and snapper. She took out a juicer, made fresh orange juice. Did the same and made apple juice. She did it effortlessly. Kiki Sunshine had planted some deep-South ways in her Brazilian blood.

I asked, "You ever been to Brazil?"

"Never."

"Your mother never took you back to her home?"

"She don't go back down there. I heard it was real bad down there. She grew up in the places by Casablanca where all the gangs and poor people hang out, forget what they are called . . . fra-villas . . ."

"*Favelas*. They're like shantytowns."

"Yeah, those ghetto places. She said people don't have water or electricity."

I asked, "Don't you wish you knew your way around Brazil?"

"I heard they crazy, hijack buses with the tourists and do all kinds of crazy things to people down there. I don't need to go no place that has it going on like that, especially since I can't speak Portuguese. Besides, I heard that was a place men go to buy cheap pussy. All the women are prostitutes."

"That's not true. They have beautiful areas too. Beautiful beaches."

"If Momma had wanted me to grow up knowing about them places, she would've taught us. But whatever happened to her down there, *why ever* she left, she ain't trying to go back. I wish I knew more about Brazil, but I bet if you talk to the people down there, they can't tell you where nothing is in America. They know Brazil. Because they live there. I can put gas in my truck and get you from coast to coast on any highway that runs through America. I know where I live. That's what's important."

I didn't think any less of Kiki Sunshine, but I found her not knowing about her roots sad.

A flag representing Brazil should've been on display in her home.

Art from her homeland should adorn her walls. Brazilian music should fill the air, as should the scent of Brazilian food. Her dance should own the one-and-two rhythm of her mother's country.

Again I looked around her apartment, this time slyly, with the eyes of a spy, looked beyond all the pictures of her on the walls, beyond the beautiful furniture, saw plenty of magazines, those that were aimed at gossip, fashion, and hair, but hardly a book. She should have Paulo Coelho. Zora Neale Hurston. Langston Hughes. Maya. Toni. I saw all of that inside her, needing to get out. She had yet to recognize her power. Or maybe I was delusional, maybe I was projecting my values onto her.

We talked about men, the subject she was the most comfortable chatting about, the conversation somehow shifting and landing on the man I had left back in Memphis. I'd become conscious of myself now, of my vocabulary, of my not being as earthy and hip as she was. In some ways I felt inferior. I wasn't built for girl talk, for telling my personal life to strangers, but I tried to fit into her world.

I told her, "This guy, Logan, he would stop by unannounced."

"Don't you hate it when they start doing that mess?"

I kept talking about Logan, that angst spilling out of me. "Then his family started doing the same."

"So you broke up with him but he won't break up with you."

"That pretty much sums it up."

"You had his ass pussy-whipped."

"I did all I could to make him go away. Told him I had been with other men."

"Well, when you cut them off like that, it's like they go into denial. They have to go through all the stages. Shock. Denial. Tears and cussing you out. Then acceptance. But in the end they always want one for the road. Have to get that last nut in, then they can say good-bye, and you never hear from them again. But you can't make them do it until they are ready to do it. It messes with your head big time."

"That's why I left Memphis. Felt trapped. Last time I was with him, don't know what I was thinking. You ever have sex with somebody and you know you shouldn't be doing it?"

"At some point we all end up in bed with somebody we shouldn't be in bed with."

"I ended up lying there, staring at the ceiling with him humping me as if it was some sort of perverted necrophilia act, his ass not noticing if I was moving or not, just humping me and I just wanted him to come and get it over with. I went in the bathroom and cried."

"Shit, at least you made it to the bathroom. I usually end up crying while they on me."

"You serious?"

"Been there, done that, bought a post card and two T-shirts." She shook her head like she was trying to shake the memory loose. "What attracted you to him?"

"Not sure if I was ever really attracted to him." I shrugged. "Loneliness has its own needs."

"Got that disease right now. You combine loneliness and horniness and . . . and . . . *BAM!*"

"You end up at the W in bed with identical twins."

We laughed.

I took the focus off me, asked her, "What went bad with the guy you used to see?"

"Guy I used to see, his thing was too little. I could tell because too much air was getting inside and I kept making pussy farts the whole time. If he was big enough wouldn't've been room for all that air."

"Queefing."

"What?"

"That's called *queefing*."

"Well, it sounded like a fart to me. His premature-ejaculating ass."

"Why did you stay with him?"

"He was fine. Not a lot of good-looking men around this way. Not a lot to choose from. Had his own business too. And he was good with his hands. He would use his pointer finger and middle finger, put those inside me, then put his pinky in my booty hole, hold me like he was holding a six-pack of beer."

"That's called two in the clit, one in the shit."

"Whatever." She laughed. "I would come so fast it was crazy."

"You were happy with that?"

"He knew I wasn't happy. So he hooked me up."

"How?"

"He had this friend. One of his business partners. This guy who lived in Jacksonville."

"Florida?"

"Jacksonville, North Carolina. He was stationed at Camp Lejeune with all the jarheads."

"You had an affair with his friend?"

"I wouldn't call it an affair. It was an *arrangement*. Guy I was seeing set it up."

"A guy you were seeing let you sleep with his friend."

"Oh, yeah. He took me to Jacksonville, past all those tobacco fields, and we went to his friend's little party. His friend was looking at me all night. Was ignoring his date and flirting with me. Then the guy I was seeing asked me if I'd sleep with his friend. I thought he was playing. He said he knew he couldn't give it to me like I needed it. Offered me his friend's dick. Told him I would if he wanted me to."

"Damn."

"First he did it for my birthday, had his friend drive up here and meet us over at the O. Henry. Had a real nice suite. Rose petals and balloons all over. His friend did his thing like only a marine can. Yeah, my boyfriend set it up, let his friend get some a few more times. That lasted about three months."

"It got out of control?"

"Not really. The marine got deployed again. Just my luck."

All I could say was, "Wow."

Kiki Sunshine was taking out her Mikasa dishes, her best dishes, as if she was preparing for Thanksgiving dinner with the royal family. As if she rarely had company and this was a special occasion. The air conditioner was on too, had the room cool enough for her to burn candles without feeling the heat.

I said, "Damn, Kiki Sunshine, you had it going on."

"That ain't nothing. I have so many stories I could tell you. But damn. This morning, felt good waking up in bed with a *fine* man. Get tired of sleeping by myself. I missed that. Hard for a woman to find her somebody nowadays. Might have to move out of Greensboro if I'm ever gonna meet somebody worth something. It's hard. Damn hard."

She had loved a good-looking man, despite his faults. We all had our weaknesses. I had succumbed to literature, good looks, Hollywood, poetry, intelligence, and the burning need to satisfy my own lust.

She said, "Hard to believe that girl didn't marry Karl."

"What girl?"

"He told me he was engaged one time. Some African girl. But he never got married."

"I didn't know that."

"He told me that. Said him and his brother . . . there was some big falling out about her."

"When?"

"He just said it was a while ago."

"Never knew he and his brother had a falling out over a woman."

"That was all he said. Told me that last night when he was over here. He didn't get into it. Right then he started getting friendly with me. Put some alcohol in Karl, he gets real friendly real fast."

I thought about the tattoos on his flesh. Thought about the woman named Kenya.

She said, "I have to confess something."

"Okay."

"I saw Karl's MySpace page two months ago. That's how I met him. Saw his page, saw his work, got in contact with him, asked him to come shoot me for this adult calendar I'm putting together. I'm doing a sexy calendar that I'm going to sell at some grown folks' places around Charlotte and up in Virginia."

"You picked him because you wanted to meet him."

"I was going to do the calendar anyway. But when I saw what he looked like, I was like, I really need to meet this man. Had to see him for myself. He has some sexy pictures of him on his page too."

"Uh-huh."

She nodded. "Didn't expect him to show up with somebody who looked like Yasamin Kincade. Wasn't planning on sleeping with him or nothing like that. You the one got me all hot and bothered."

"You're pretty hot and tempting yourself."

Her doorbell rang and stopped me from asking about her conversation with Karl. Her doorbell rang and once again Kiki Sunshine was as excited as a teenager about to go to the prom.

I said, "They're here."

Instead of going to the door, Kiki Sunshine came to me, stood in front of me, touched my face.

She whispered, "Your mouth is so sexy. Can I kiss you?"

The way she asked was so polite, so arousing. So submissive. I nodded.

She leaned over, her breathing smooth, her breath sweet, and gave me her tongue, not her lips.

I smiled. "Are you going to get the door?"

She winked. "Momma told me to never rush to a man."

She kissed me again, her kiss stimulating, touching my face in a gentle way, then she smiled.

She said, "You tasted good. When you were here yesterday, you tasted good."

"Thanks."

"Like honey and pineapple juice."

I smiled with her. Saw that she also loved to be in control.

The doorbell rang again.

Kiki Sunshine asked, "How do I look?"

"You look fine."

"My hair okay? I don't have on too much makeup, do I?"

"Everything looks fine."

She ran to a mirror and checked herself, adjusted her sundress and her breasts before going to the door. The men had arrived. Mark had on Diesel jeans. He came in first, the heat moving with him.

Mark said, "What the hell are y'all doing in here?"

Karl had on cargo shorts.

Karl said, "Hot as fuck outside and y'all have us standing on a damn porch."

Kiki Sunshine said, "Hush. Wash your hands so we can bless the food and eat."

Both had on fraternity shirts. They belonged to different fraternities. That surprised me.

Mark said, "These pancakes better be good."

We ate, talked, laughed. Kissing started. Touching commenced.

Soft music was put on. Games were played, games that created wetness and hardness.

Mark and I were on the red leather sofa. Sexual tension magnified with every breath.

Kiki Sunshine and Karl were in front of the fireplace, her breasts out, being sucked.

She watched us as I watched them.

I thought I would be too sore. But when Mark touched me, when he put his mouth on my neck, when his tongue eased inside my mouth, when his hands touched my breasts, sparks turned into flames.

My moans blended with Kiki Sunshine's, created a lyrical song made of fever, our sounds of pleasure the types of noise that, if a stranger was passing by her front door and paused, could be mistaken for pain and torture. Eyes glazed over, viewing the world as if I was underwater, thirty minutes of lovemaking and laughter equaled ten nights of ecstasy. It was beautiful. It was tender. It was intense. I should have been flustered by what I had done, by the things I had done over the last few hours, things that were new and out of character, but I wasn't.

I glanced at Mark. Asleep. He made love like a philosopher. So meticulous. I glanced at Karl. Almost asleep. He fucked. That was all he did. Fucked. And he fucked well. I glanced at Kiki Sunshine. A woman desperate for love. Her breathing was heavy, her eyes closed. We all lay naked, sprawled across the floor and each other.

Drifting toward unconsciousness. Beaten into submission by ecstasy.

I woke up to the sound of voices and moans. I was on the carpet, in the candlelit room, near the front door. Kiki Sunshine, Mark, and Karl were on the red leather sofa.

Mark was taking Kiki Sunshine from the back as she smiled and gave oral loving to Karl.

They were exchanging pleasure, moving as if they could not get enough of each other.

I tried to move, but my satiated body was so heavy, running and sex had me worn out. Voices were getting louder. The woman who was talking about a furniture sale was the loudest. Sounded like she was on her cellular phone, angry because she had to come find Kiki Sunshine so they could get to the furniture store that was going out of business, heard her complaining about how she had been waiting for her daughter all morning, expected her to come pick her up, but she wanted to get to the furniture store now so she was going to get Kiki Sunshine so they could get on the road before the day was gone.

I tried to call out, but the sounds in the room hid my voice. Kiki Sunshine was moaning. Now she was on top of Karl, had Mark behind her, her yoni and chocolate star being penetrated at the same time.

A key slipped inside the lock. I tried to get up and grab the doorknob. But I couldn't move fast enough. The door opened and daylight blinded me for a moment.

My eyes focused and I expected to see Kiki Sunshine's mother, expected her religious fury. It wasn't her mother horrified by four naked lovers, three in the throes of passion, one at her feet.

The woman who was glaring down at me in shock was Hazel Tamana Bijou-Wilson.

It was my mother.

TWENTY-EIGHT

I jerked awake.

Pulled out of the wretched nightmare I was having.

Consciousness found me first, brought me back to this level of existence in degrees.

I was breathing heavily, drowning in a room filled with air.

The front door was closed. My mother hadn't flown to Greensboro and invaded the room. But the television was on. I had rolled over on the remote, my backside had somehow pressed the on button, the local commercials had wormed inside my dreams. I turned the television off.

Ceiling fans were spinning. The room now cool. Darkness being broken by melting candles. My eyes adjusted to this new reality. I saw Mark. Kiki Sunshine was in his arms, her palms against his chest. Warmth was next to my body, a hand around my waist. Karl was wrapped around me. One by one, they woke up. Thirty minutes had passed. My identical sins needed to get back to ATL. So did I.

Kiki Sunshine pulled her red hair from her glowing face, glanced at the Mikasa clock and yawned. With a broad smile she looked at me and said, "Damn. Too bad I have to take my momma furniture shopping. I'd hop in my truck and follow y'all back to ATL and hang out for a while."

Kiki Sunshine wanted more. When it was good, you always

wanted more, no matter how tired you were, no matter how sore your yoni felt.

Five-minute showers were taken, lotion was smoothed on flesh, clothes were collected from the living room, distributed, and everyone dressed as if the sandman was trying to hold them down. We said lethargic good-byes to Kiki Sunshine. She was dressed, ready to go get her mother.

In the parking lot, I pulled my hair back, gave her a hug, her telling me to keep in touch, me saying that I would, knowing I wouldn't. We lived in two different worlds. It was time for me to go back to mine and leave her to hers.

Mark looked at me, checking if I was okay with him being close to Kiki Sunshine, then he kissed her on her cheeks. But she held his face, gave him her tongue. She went to Karl. Karl held her ass and gave him his tongue until she laughed and pushed him away.

I sensed that Karl did that for my benefit, to rile me, still in competition with his brother.

Karl would never want me in the way I would eventually want a man.

Yet he did things, said things, looked at me in a way that could create false hope.

Karl threw Mark the keys, told him to drive the first leg of the trip, maybe change at the Peachoid water tower or if we grabbed a bite to eat at Fatz Cafe, then he'd drive us to Atlanta's Hartsfield so Mark could collect his car from long-term parking. I crawled into the backseat, separating myself from being in reach of any man, removing myself from temptation and pleasure. But Karl eased in the backseat with me, which surprised me. Mark drove toward Big Tree Way and Kiki Sunshine faded from our world. She was gone. I felt her handprints on my flesh, her tongue and fingers inside me, but she no longer existed in my world. I leaned against Karl and yawned. He put his arm around me and closed his eyes.

Mark entered I-85 and drove us back toward Atlanta, the city formerly known as Marthasville. A city that had gone through so many changes before finding itself being called Atlanta, Georgia. We all went through changes in search of self. We all had our civil wars. Just like Atlanta. Named for the Western and Atlantic Railroad, which in turn was named for the Atlantic Ocean. And the Atlantic Ocean was named after the Titan Atlas, who was condemned to carry the world on his shoulders for eternity.

It felt as if I carried the same weight. Only mine was the weight of desire.

Jewell Stewark's face came to mind, so clear and filled with disdain as she scowled at Karl. I imagined a thousand reasons for her to look at Karl that way.

But only one made any sense. One that was rooted in jealousy.

That was my guess. I had no information to support my hypothesis; it was just a feeling.

In some ways I knew Mark and Karl. In many ways I didn't.

Maybe we were carnal versions of the fictional character Walter Mitty, escaping from intolerable reality into fantasies, our rampant sexual needs being a way of validating self, our free-loving and pleasure-sharing being the response to the stress of reality of four people who were a long way from senescence, but realizing we would slide in that direction if we lived long enough, and these memories would slide with us. This was physically satisfying, but in the end could become emotionally dangerous.

TWENTY-NINE

The temperature remained near the century mark, humidity extreme, pollen count high.

As Mark drove, he adjusted the air conditioner, set it on high, pointed the vents toward his skin. Satellite radio was put on jazz. Mark looked at me in the rearview. And I looked right back at him.

Silence rested between us.

I wanted to be sexually adventurous without experiencing the emotional baggage.

I wanted to swim and remain untouched by water.

But I was drowning in my own emotions.

This was what happened when the sex was good. That air of possessiveness. I tried to separate the two but sex came with emotions. Not always love, but there was some level of possessiveness, and if the sex was given often enough, entitlement. Sex led to drama. I didn't want any drama.

I told myself I didn't want Mark, repeated that in my head over and over, my mantra, my denial.

Karl was comatose, an overworked Greek God who was dehydrated and sleep-deprived.

I whispered his name a few times. No response.

Mark was a married man, late getting home, anxiety showing in his face as he drove.

I said, "Kiki Sunshine enjoyed you."

He turned away, put his eyes back on the road. "Not as much as you enjoyed Karl."

Silence returned.

I said, "And I guess you did Kiki Sunshine for me too."

"Of course."

"You're so kind."

He winked at me. "I did that for you. I did it all for you."

"Bullshit."

His words terrified me. His words delighted me.

Karl, I analyzed him. I think he admired intelligent women, but was afraid of intelligent women, couldn't handle us beyond sexual acrobatics and yoga-inspired positions created in an act of passion. In the act of the zipless fuck. After the intimacy was done, after fucking, he had nothing to offer. No, I stand corrected. He had plenty to offer. But after the fuck was done, he offered nothing. I gazed at his arm. I gazed at his angel.

I asked Mark, "Where is Kenya?"

"Kenya? Who is Kenya?"

"The woman tattooed on his skin."

"Oh. Kenya."

"They were engaged."

Mark grunted. "He told you he was engaged to Kenya?"

"What happened?"

Mark looked at his sleeping brother, looked concerned, then put his eyes back on traffic.

I teased, "Did she get the Frankie treatment too?"

He snapped, "Is that really any of your business?"

His tone hurt my feelings. Made me want to judge him. I asked, "Was I your first affair?"

"No. Not the first."

"Have you always been unfaithful?"

"No."

I paused, took an intense breath as I pulled at my hair, twirling my mane around my finger.

I whispered, "Do you ever feel guilty for cheating?"

"You feel guilty for sleeping with a married man? Am I the first married man you slept with? You want to get into asking those kinds of questions right now? Is that where you want this to go?"

I stopped there. Stopped and shifted against Karl's weight, swallowed.

For a moment I thought Mark was going to screech to a halt and throw me out.

For a moment.

He had backbone. I had crossed some line and been put back where I belonged.

He cleared his throat, his face lined with the beginnings of an apology, said, "Nia . . ."

"It's cool."

"I'm sorry about—"

I snapped, "It's cool."

That ended that.

I had become emotional. That was a crime. His life wasn't my business, as mine wasn't his.

He didn't need to know about Logan. Or any of my other lovers.

I didn't need to know about The Jewell of the South.

We all had secrets. Everyone had their right to own their secrets. I was his secret. I knew I'd become his secret before he penetrated me the first time. Penetration. Men penetrated women. They knew they did. Each thrust was like a sledgehammer trying to break down an emotional barrier. I had felt Mark inside me, touching the bottom of my true feelings.

I had felt Karl inside me, widening my emotional walls.

Still I felt them both, as if only the combination could shatter my emotional barrier.

Anaïs's affairs with men outside her marriage, no matter how it was romanticized, ended in pain, if not for her, then for her lovers, for her husband, the man she cuckolded with her other lovers. Involvement with a married man never had a happy ending.

I was angry at Anaïs. Angry at the way she never stayed to explain everything to me.

We passed the largest city in the Carolinas, then put Charlotte in the rearview mirror.

I was an hour away from Kiki Sunshine. I wanted many hours, many miles to come between us. Mark pulled off the interstate, stopped at a gas station, went inside, came back with a can of Red Bull, bottled water, and a blue Gatorade. He handed me the Gatorade. I couldn't suppress my smile.

I didn't ask him how he knew that was my favorite, didn't ask if his choice was random.

Maybe we had a stronger connection than either one of us realized.

That was better than sending me flowers every day for a week. Better than him bringing me an engagement ring. Better than sex.

After that we were back on I-85, the heat horrendous and the humidity close to one hundred percent, each minute taking me closer to Atlanta, moving me away from Kiki Sunshine.

Mark smiled and shot me a playful wink. "I love you."

"Love spoils sex. Don't spoil the sex."

"Why combative all of a sudden?"

I drank more Gatorade, thinking. "Do you love Jewell Stewart?"

"Is she an issue?"

"If this continues, she will become an issue for me as I will become an issue for her."

"Only if you make her an issue."

I chuckled. "If you don't tell me, maybe I'll ask Jewell what I want to know."

"If you want, I'll set up the meeting."

"Fuck you."

"All that education from Hampton, can't you say something a little more profound?"

"Fuck you."

I was getting emotional. Mark was getting emotional.

And Karl was being Karl. Working hard, fucking harder, going with the hedonistic lifestyle.

I didn't want to have the Logan disease where infatuation led to love and love spoiled the party.

Mark said, "I saw you first. Karl beat me to you. But I saw you first. Whatever I have, either he imitates or tries to steal. He tries to steal whatever I have. He ruins everything. Always has."

"Why?"

"Because that is who we are. We were born minutes apart. No one understands us but us, and even we don't understand ourselves. Our lives are separate, but they are the same life. Our bond is unbreakable. If he died, I would know it and in response I would die within the hour."

He said that and I wanted to cook for him, watch him eat, bathe him, make love to him, give him orgasm, then send him home to his wife, pleased in all ways, leaving nothing left for her to do but suffer.

But I had seen the way he enjoyed Kiki Sunshine. I'd invited her, yes, but I had seen Mark with another woman. Maybe I wanted to see him in that way, needed to know how special I was to him.

Kiki Sunshine had taken him in her mouth, was trying to suck the life out of his body and leave a husk of a man where a man once stood. I had seen them soldered together in a perfect blend of hardness and softness. His orgasm was a volcanic outpouring that erupted across her stomach.

It was never safe to invest in one love. Love needed to be diversified. When we made it to Atlanta and I relinquished him to his wife, I hoped a vast emptiness wouldn't consume me.

Mark had had sex with Kiki Sunshine as if I was nothing special.

Had to keep it real. There was no relationship here. This was still zipless. It was just the extended version, the remix of a zipless affair. The emotions were high, but nobody wanted a commitment. We all wanted to use each other to achieve and give satisfaction. We were filling voids, releasing stress, fucking. And they had fucked Kiki Sunshine the same way they had fucked me. I was just another woman. New yoni turning old. For them this was still zipless. I didn't need to get caught up. I didn't need to become to them what Logan was to me.

But still, it was part of me to always want to feel special, even when I wasn't.

Maybe that came from being a woman. Maybe that came from growing up in L.A.

I closed my eyes, tried to make myself blind. Pretended I didn't have the ability to see beyond the moment, pretended that down the road I couldn't see red lights flashing.

Again three phones rang at once. Mine flashed DNA: LOGAN.

Maybe Kiki Sunshine was right.

Maybe men needed to get in that last fuck so they could say good-bye.

THIRTY

Birmingham, Alabama.

In the heat of the morning sun I had traveled east to west to meet with Logan.

He was coming from Memphis, a four-hour ride down Highway 78 to get here.

I was nervous. Felt like I was standing in a bed filled with spiders.

He had left me feeling uncomfortable in my own life. I wanted it to end.

I wanted the dreams about him to end.

The best way to deal with fear was to face the nightmare. So I was here to deal with my fear.

I was on 11th Avenue South, in the Five Points South district, the center of Birmingham's nightlife. Daytime was filled with people who loved to eat and shop. The Original Pancake House, a place to get smoothies, a tattoo shop, and a decent hotel, all of that was right here.

I was at Starbucks, sipping on an iced green tea when I saw his Range Rover pull up and pause, looking for an open parking meter, finding none, then circling the block.

I crossed the street and waited in front of Surin West for a moment, but the heat was not to be reckoned with, so I stepped inside, the smell of Thai cuisine welcoming me like an old friend.

Today I was dressed chic and Hollywood, sporting sunglasses with huge lenses, wearing white pinstriped slacks with a wide cuff, yellow charmeuse top that had short balloon sleeves. Sling-backs with a nice heel, and a large Gucci handbag that was black and white with red trimming—a bag to die for.

My appearance hid my true angst. My palms sweated. My heartbeat was fast. Veins rose in my neck. I trembled. I shifted from foot to foot. Moved my bag from hand to hand.

Dealing with Logan had created nightmares.

Last night I dreamed I had come home from running the Silver Comet Trail and saw a trail of milky white substance on the concrete stairs leading to the flowers that were waiting at my front door. That same milky substance was on the doorknob. I had opened the door and Logan was inside my home, naked, sitting in a chair facing the front door, masturbating, gallons of come at his feet. He was coming nonstop, his thick, milky come oozing across the carpet and hardwood floors. His come was oozing toward me, covering my feet, each seed alive, moaning my name.

He looked at me with red-rimmed, tear-filled eyes. "See how much I love you?"

I tried to move, but I was trapped, his come thicker than honey, gluing me where I stood.

I woke up screaming, a cold sweat dampening my neck, hair, and pillow.

This morning I had gone to my front porch to get my morning paper. I smelled his unwanted gifts before I opened the door. Another arrangement of flowers. Each arrangement more expensive than the last. I had called the initial flower company who delivered the sweet-smelling annoyances, told them to not deliver any more to my address, only to have Logan contact another flower company, this one black-owned and out on Cascade Road near the HBCUs. It was getting ridiculous. I picked up my morning paper, left the flowers sitting there. For the last two weeks an arrangement had arrived every day. And every day I would go to my mailbox and find that he'd mailed a card with a different message. *I miss you. Your my heart. I will always love you.*

Despite his grammatical flaws, he was persistent, if nothing else.

His persistence had forced me to agree to this meeting.

I whispered something I had heard on television, Glenn Close on the show *Damages*, "Taking power from a man was always a dangerous thing. Someone always pays."

It was over ninety degrees before nine in the morning. Now it was noon, the temperature at least ten degrees hotter, the humidity strong enough to rival the dankness of Trinidad and Barbados.

It was the kind of heat that caused delirium, the heat that created madness.

This was the season of madness.

I thought about what I had read in the newspapers and seen online, how Prophetess Bynum and her estranged husband, Bishop Weeks, their late-night meeting didn't end well at the Renaissance Hotel in downtown Atlanta, not for her, and not being able to work out their differences had left her beaten and bruised at four in the morning. When emotions ran high, even Christians stopped being Christians.

Maybe this was what she felt like. Nervous. Afraid. But still had to do this face-to-face.

Logan could lose it. He was a strong man. I could die a brutal death.

I had picked this location not only because it was busy and I loved the food, but there was a police substation only a few feet away, only a couple of businesses over, right near the ATM.

As I waited, a text came in on my phone.

It was Kiki Sunshine. She'd been on my mind, knew I was avoiding her.

Still thinking about me you and the boys. But I'm really thinking about you. They have suicidal dick. But you have suicidal clit. ☺ *I still see you in my mind, when I opened my door and you were there. I was so scared. After all that mess I had been talking in the park, I was so scared. Damn I was scared.*

Her long text message made me smile a bit, filled my five senses. My cellular hummed again, another long text message from Kiki Sunshine.

You tasted so damn good. And your skin, it was so soft. And your body was so nice.

My yoni had marvelous flashbacks.

If you want to hook up, let me know and I'll drive over to ATL. No pressure. Just putting it out there. We can hang and not go there, but I will be thinking about eating your pussy the whole time.

Greensboro had been two weeks ago, but felt like yesterday.

Kiki Sunshine. Kiki Motherfucking Sunshine. We didn't have anything in common, but I understood her struggle. I understood her feelings. Her wanting one thing and needing something else. I understood being torn. I understood needing to feel good.

The way she had savored my yoni was remarkable. She had taken my cherry in her own way. I was her resurrection of Yasamin Kincade. She could become my Pandora's box. Just thinking about it made me wet. Thinking about it too much would make my yoni a waterfall. We'd have to keep away from each other, lest I start appreciating rainbows a bit too much.

Logan was coming. It was too late for me to change my mind.

I saw him as he passed the window and came inside the door. Logan had on a sandy brown suit and a coral shirt, no tie. He was a good-looking man, no doubt about that. Seeing him dressed in a suit reminded me how stunning he was, pure eye candy. In Memphis, whenever we entered a venue on a date, the way people responded to him, you'd think King or Kennedy had walked into the room. Being with him was the equivalent of walking the red carpet in Hollywood, cameras flashing from all directions.

But being handsome only counted for so much.

He smiled at me, his smile civil and uncertain, pretentious, the same as mine. Our public faces on display. The ghost of jealousy had left his eyes with a virescent tint.

He said, "You look nice."

"Thank you."

He apologized for that night when I had to call the police.

With a nod I accepted his apology.

I didn't stand too close to Logan, waited to be escorted to our booth.

Logan said, "Sorry I was a few minutes late. Was hard getting out of Memphis."

"I only have about an hour."

"So much for the pleasantries."

"Didn't drive one hundred and fifty miles in this heat for pleasantries."

"Well, could you at least be pleasant?"

I nodded. "For an hour."

Logan was here but my every thought was on Greensboro. That had been life-changing.

With a gentle smile, he asked, "This booth okay?"

"It's fine."

Logan asked, "You okay?"

"Just . . . tired. Was up late working. Driving on I-20 in this heat, it's draining."

"I promise, I will not keep you long. I just hated the way things ended last time. I got a little out of control. And I just want to . . . want us to not end it that way. I've been praying on this."

I didn't look at him, just bounced my leg and read my menu.

And thought about those decadent hours spent in Greensboro.

Logan was staring at me, his expression very profound, the expression of a deep thinker.

I asked, "You okay over there?"

Without warning he told me his grandmother had died.

That moved my thoughts out of Greensboro, sensitivity rose, gave my aggravation a reprieve.

In a kind voice I asked, "You okay?"

"I'm okay."

"What happened? I mean when? Recently?"

He told me she had died, there had been a funeral, and she had been buried. His nana had been with them at church, went to dinner with them at Red Lobster, went home, said she was tired and wanted to take a short nap before her favorite television show came on, closed her eyes, died without notice.

Not knowing how to respond, death making this awkward, I said, "At least she didn't suffer."

Logan quieted, looked a little emotional. In that moment I became emotional.

I wanted to reach out to take his hand, but I didn't.

I said, "I'm sorry. So sorry. Let me extend my deepest condolences."

"Thanks. I'll pass that on to my family. They still ask about you." Logan rubbed his face, rubbed his eyes, let out a sigh and said, "I'm going to run to the men's room. Back in a second."

"You okay?"

"I'm cool." His thick voice fractured with emotion. "Need to wash my hands."

He left, his steps quick and expressive, as if he wanted to sneak away and cry for his nana.

I didn't want to be here. Would rather be with my identical sins. And if I couldn't have them together, I wanted them one at a time. But I had to take care of this. Had to remain focused. If I was getting paid to make love I'd work overtime. But sex was a hobby; hobbies didn't pay the bills.

If sex became an obstacle to handling my responsibilities, sex would become a burden.

Logan returned, his steps strong, once again the personification of the alpha male. But for some reason I saw him as the omega male. Not alpha. Not beta. Omega.

As soon as he sat down I eased out of the booth, told him I needed to wash my hands. I wanted to get away from him, regretted wasting gas on this trip already. I walked away, my thoughts tagging along, feeling Logan's eyes on my ass with my every step.

Inside the toilet I closed the door, went inside a stall, stood there, breathing.

My cellular vibrated. It was a text message from Mark. This morning all of my lovers were desiring me, their need for me growling like a beast.

Mark wanted to know if I could meet him down at Howell Mill and 75 for indoor rock climbing. I sent him a message, told him I'd be tied up today. He sent me another text, asked me to send him a kiss. I did. I sent Mark another text, a smiley face. Didn't want to overdo it. But I couldn't help it.

I typed: *Send me a picture. Something sexy.*

Despite my amorous smile, I was feeling overwhelmed.

I'd become a woman trying to please two men. A woman with two lovers trying to give the right amount of attention to each. I'd become Anaïs, only my relationship with my lovers was not hidden; no secret marriages, no financial need clouding the true purpose of our relationships. We were known to each other, yet remained clandestine to the rest of the world, our universe our own private playground.

Mark and I had spent some time over the last two weeks as well. We'd met for lunch at Doc Green's near Cumberland Center. Had had Mexican food on Cobb Parkway. Had gone to the movies. Had gone indoor rock climbing. It wasn't always about sex. Each encounter gave inner joy, a different type of happiness, but nevertheless we were creatures of the flesh, our libidos set fire whenever we touched, whenever we sent text messages I was left stirring in my seat, left wet, left wanting. Mark had stopped by my townhome four times. We enjoyed literature, poetry, and laughter. But the language of literature bonded us. His knowledge impressed me, surprised me. Just me and Mark, in my bed, naked, eating lunch, talking about books. He'd never read D.H. Lawrence. So we picked a book, finally started our NBC. Naked Book Club. At every meeting we were to dress according to club rules. He was crazy about me. Did things to my mind. Mental arousal created its own warmth, the warmth of adoration, the herald of love, the need to touch. The discussion of classic literature evolved to soft kisses, to him moving the plates away and getting on top of me, kissing me more and more, kissing me until I reached for him, until I moved his energy against my wetness, put him inside me, owned him as he moved in and out of me slowly, not rushing our orgasms, defying commandments and seeking pleasure. Once I continued reading as he entered me, pretended I could focus on the book in my hand. He moved in and out of me as I struggled, as I moaned, as I read to him pages from *Lady Chatterley's Lover.*

Mark craved me like no other man had ever craved me. The married lover would always crave the yoni because he couldn't have it all the time, because he had to go home to his married yoni.

We always wanted what we couldn't have.

The time of a married man was never unlimited, the way his cellular rang told me that.

I was the fruit he stole, the juices he tasted in the middle of the day.

But Jewell was the last kiss he received at night, the first face he saw in the morning. Hers was the yoni he penetrated after he had left me, maybe hers was the yoni he swam in before he came to experience me.

Mark was daytime. A secret hidden in the hours covered by the sun.

We laughed and talked, had sensual moments, but in the end he went to Jewell.

In the end he left me alone. When the sun set he was gone, leaving me hollow.

Karl was late-night. Karl filled that hollow space Mark left behind.

I'd met Karl in Buckhead, had traveled to Sambuca for dinner and jazz, his hand under the table, his finger rubbing my clit in a swank, dimly lit environment as I tried to keep a straight face, as I died a thousand little deaths. Mark was love and Karl was pure, unadulterated sex. There was nothing else to Karl. He made me come all over his finger, then stirred his drink with that same finger. Made me reach orgasm in a room filled with well-dressed people who were drinking and listening to jazz. With *one* finger. That night I learned it was impossible for me to come with my eyes open. As I came I'd been forced to steeple my hands and bow my head like I was praying, not caring who saw what looked like an emotional trembling inspired by my commitment to the creator of us all, yet if any ear was close, if the jazz had stopped abruptly, the room would have heard the sweetest vulgarities being sung by me.

I'd met both of them at the W for drinks, then watched them engage in rock-paper-scissors again, the loser paying for the room, both of them kissing and touching me like they did the first time.

I'd held their carnal offerings, each becoming hardened fire in my soft hands. I created indistinguishable moans. So many veins existed in each. I masturbated them as they touched me. My moans rose. When four hands and two tongues on my heated flesh became too much to bear, I held on to that part of them, took deep breaths, and tried to feel how identical they were. They were similar, but not identical. The reticulate pattern of the veins in their lingams felt unique, one had more girth, the other more length, making me imagine it would be easy to tell the brothers apart, as easy as identifying a tree by its sturdy branches, as easy as distinguishing a plant by its leaves.

The dueling sides of the Gemini that ruled me were being fulfilled in their own ways.

After I washed my hands, I stared at myself in the mirror.

I told myself that I wasn't in love with Mark. Or Karl. I was not in love with two men.

I felt that unfairness. The unfairness of sex. The way a woman was opened up physically and emotionally, I felt the wonderful sting of penetration, felt what that beautiful violence did to the mind.

I headed back to the table. As soon as I sat down with Logan my cellular vibrated again.

I looked at my phone, opened the photo he sent. A picture of Mark's perfect lingam filled my screen. My mouth fell open, a gasp escaping my surprised expression on shortened breath. I shifted, stared at what had filled my every orifice, what I had tasted, what I had held, what, at this moment, I began to crave. I was thirsty. I was disturbed. I was a mess.

Logan said, "Nia?"

I jumped out of a fantasy, looked at Logan.

He asked, "Any way I can get your attention long enough to order?"

"I already know what I want."

"So do I."

THIRTY-ONE

Soon food was on the table. Logan blessed the meal. I waited out of respect.

Crab angels. Fresh basil rolls. Thai barbecue chicken. Catfish special. Thai teas.

We remained civilized yet tense, ate like normal people, that elephant sitting between us as we dined. Surin West was large, its décor made me feel like I was in Thailand, the place smelling of so many spices, every wall adorned with photographs of Thailand and its people.

Lunch was done, more like we'd eaten all we wanted to eat, had delayed as much as we could.

I glanced at my watch and said, "Thirty minutes have passed. You've said nothing."

He nodded. "I just don't know what to say."

"You have me here. You have my ear. You sent flowers and cards and messages, and you promised to stop it all if I went to lunch with you. If I gave you an hour. Well, I'm here. Stop delaying."

"You make it sound like you're in one of those Hollywood meetings."

"Excuse me?"

"The ones your mother runs. You said she could be brutal. When you walk into her office you'd better have your stuff together. How she gives you one minute, two if she likes you."

"I am my mother's child."

He gave a short smile, one that implied that maybe that was the problem.

I saw a montage of memories in his eyes. They went by like a silent film, each memory in color, each and every one he possessed, the moments he was clinging to, places we had traveled, going to football and basketball games, times spent at Memphis in May, times spent gambling in Mississippi, walking through the Civil Rights Museum, going to the Orpheum, Playhouse Square, Pink Palace Museum, trips to Nashville, watching films, cooking for me, working out at the gym, riverboat cruises. A season of memories went by in his eyes. I had wanted to see Memphis, he was my guide to all things new.

Those were mostly daytime memories. Wonderful experiences, my venture into the unknown.

But I remembered the ones that came at night. The ones that left me unfulfilled.

I remembered opening my legs with him and feeling cheap for allowing myself to do so.

I remembered him coming and me holding him so he couldn't see the disgust in my face.

He lowered his head, frustration so heavy it strained his neck, voice thick and sullen as he said, "When I played for U of M I never fumbled a ball. Why can't I hold on to you?"

"Because I'm not a football."

"Always the smartass."

I paused, let seriousness settle between us.

Without the sarcasm my heart rate would rise, my palms would become damp. Without the use of wit as a defense mechanism he would know I was afraid. Fear was weakness uncontrolled.

He asked, "Do you have to sleep with so many men to find pleasure?"

"I don't sleep with a lot of men."

"How many men will you have to sleep with to find pleasure?"

"And pleasure is more than sex. It's mental as well."

"You said you were with two men while we were together. Was that mental? Was being with two men you didn't know, was being with strangers mental?"

"I didn't come here for you to scold or condemn me at length."

"I'm not trying to do that to you. Just asking. As a friend."

"As a friend? We've never been friends."

"All the shit we did?"

"A friend would listen and try to understand another friend."

"How will you know when you're satisfied?"

"What is this, my inquisition? Do I get burned at the stake after this? Where is this going?"

"I'm just trying to understand."

"No, you're not trying to understand because people who try to understand stop transmitting and receive." I spoke in an angry whisper. "You're trying to make me feel guilty. It's not working. If you had it your way, there would be no questions. When people don't see things your way, instead of embracing and trying to understand another point of view, you try to criticize and dissect and ridicule."

He fidgeted while I once again became agitated, defensive, argued on behalf of me. When I was done, he sat back, sipped his Thai tea, and shook his head like I was way off base.

He said, "It's not about what man wants, it's about what God wants."

"You don't see the difference?"

"There is no difference."

"So there is no difference between man and God?"

He took a breath, his expression perplexed and frustrated. "I'm just trying to understand."

"God?"

"You. I'm trying to understand you."

He took a deep breath, his exasperation rising.

He repeated, "How will you know when you're satisfied?"

"Why do I feel like I'm being persecuted? Why do I feel as if I'm walking uphill carrying a cross?"

"Doing this shit, living this way makes you feel free?"

"Relationships can be slavery."

"Relationships are salvation."

"At least the ones I've been in have felt that way, like slavery."

He cleared his throat, nodded. "So, being in a relationship with me was slavery."

It was my turn to take a deep breath. Aggravated. This had been a mistake. A big mistake.

I'd thought he was going to bring me something new.

He only had one song to sing, and his song made me weary.

We could argue until the sun fell from the sky and nothing would change. He had his point of view. I had mine. It was as if we each had our own religion.

Logan said, "I was dumb to fall for anybody like you. Just dumb. I loved making love to you. Loved being with you. I was very comfortable with you. You might have been messing around, but even now, after all of this time, I'm not ready to let down my guard and sleep with anybody else. Not yet. Love you too much. I don't like the fact that I love you, but I do."

Again I felt rankled. Again I struggled to remain in control.

He said, "I wanted to clear a few things up."

I nodded.

"I never cheated on you, Nia. *Never.* I had plenty of chances to, but I am not about that."

"Okay. You could've said that in a text message."

"Not that. Wanted to look you in your face and tell you that."

I nodded. That didn't mean I believed him, just wanted him to continue.

He went on. "I don't chase women. A man will lose a lot of

money chasing women, but a man will never lose women chasing money. I have money. I have never had to chase a woman."

I didn't say anything.

He sighed. "But I'm chasing you."

I had a moment of empathy for him. He was me when I was at Hampton, pleading for my lover to love only me, asking for the impossible. Logan looked defeated, but remained in battle, determined. Again, as the lunchtime crowd chattered, as silverware clanked against plates, as the wonderful scents of spicy beef and chicken and curry dishes laced with pork filled the air, I gave him my attention and silence. We had only been here a few minutes. Some minutes felt like seconds, these minutes felt like hours.

Logan panted.

I asked, "You okay over there?"

"I'm fine, I'm fine. Just can't . . . what I feel for you . . . it won't . . . I can't stop loving you."

Once again he was getting emotional.

I said, "You will. You will move on and find a better love. A better love is always around the corner. You just have to let go and remain open to the possibilities. You will find a better love."

"When?"

"You will, Logan. Just let me go. Let it go. Part of being in love, if you love me, if you *really, really* love me, is learning to let go. If you loved me you would want me to be happy. No matter what my choices were, you'd want me to be happy. The same goes for any other woman in your life. Love wouldn't want you to make anyone a prisoner. Love is not supposed to suffocate anybody."

He lowered his head.

I felt like I was talking to a grown man whose body had developed, but his mind hadn't evolved, not in a way that would allow him to be able to deal with matters of the heart.

I said, "Sometimes you have to let go."

He paused before he sighed.

He said, "I know."

"Logan . . ."

He raised a finger, did that like he didn't want me to say another word.

I let him have his moment, pretended to live in the land of guilt and shame.

Whatever it took. Whatever it took to end this madness, I was willing to do.

But still, since the eye could not see itself, I had to ask him one question.

"Logan, how do you see me?"

"You really want me to answer that?"

"I asked. Pull no punches. How do you see me?"

"You have to have everything your way. You don't compromise. You're a spoiled brat."

"Spoiled brat? I've worked hard to get where I am. Spoiled? I compromise. I choose who I compromise with and what I compromise about. I compromise every day of my life. You think that because I didn't choose to compromise with you that I don't compromise? And you call me spoiled?"

"I think you're afraid of me. Not me, as in the person I am, but what a man like me offers. I think it's too much for you. I think you're shallow and pathetic. I think real love, pure love, you can't handle that. You need the shallow shit. Men you meet for a night and never see again. You need the lost and shallow people in your life, people like yourself, so you'll feel comfortable. Church or whorehouse, we all go where we feel comfortable. You can be in control with people like that. You can't control real people."

His denunciation ended there.

We stared at each other.

I asked, "You done?"

He cleared his throat, his eyes turning red. "I'm done. A man can only talk to a brick wall for so long before he realizes he's talking to a brick wall."

"It must hurt."

"Saying those things to you? Knowing I still love you. Yeah, it hurts."

"No, not that."

"What?"

"Realizing you can come at me from every angle and it still yields the same result. That must really hurt. A man like you, a spoiled brat who is used to getting whatever he wants, to come up on me, to not be able to have me, knowing I can't be bought, knowing I'm stronger than you, that I'm smarter than you, knowing that I have rejected you over and over, realizing you can't have me, that must hurt."

"Is that how you see it?"

"Tell me this, if I were anything *less*, would we be having this conversation?"

Logan swallowed. He sucked his tongue and rocked.

I tried not to let the tears fall from my eyes, but they were heavy, beyond my control. I cried. Not a hard cry. He had hurt me and now I was being defensive, doing my best to hurt him in return. Reciprocity of angst and misery. I tried to be still, tried to remain calm, but my tongue rebelled.

He nodded. "I know what I don't need. I don't need a woman who behaves like a whore."

My voice remained calm. "I'm not a whore."

"Right, right." He nodded. "Whores get paid. Maybe you're just a pro bono whore."

Nothing was said, his damnation being the soft, cruel words that filled empty space between us.

Whore.

His word had slapped me with scorn and ridicule, had put me into a pillory, the wooden circles tight around my hands and neck, boos and catcalls flying at me from all over the restaurant.

He had called me a whore.

His unmarried mother had seven children by three different men and he called me a whore.

He had an unmarried sister with four children by as many men.

I almost brought his unmarried mother and his promiscuous sibling into this conversation.

I had to remain better than him.

I refused to respond. Because it didn't matter.

I enjoyed the beauty of sex, the energy received and given. And his words were an attempt to cheapen that enjoyment.

He shook his head, wiped his eyes. "End up like your mother."

I gritted my teeth. "What was that?"

"You said you were your mother's child. Maybe that's the problem. I see her picture in *Essence* and *Ebony*. Read about her online. But magazines don't tell the truth. If she's anything like you, I bet your stepdad was glad to get rid of her. Bet she used him and tossed him after she had used him up."

Forks clanged against dishes. The hum of lunchtime conversations filled the restaurant. Waiters walked by. New customers were led to their tables. Customers left. Life moved forward for many.

We had digressed to the language of fools. Educated fools, but fools nonetheless.

I said, "Sex with you owned no poetry, never created all the euphoric accompaniments that would allow it to move from being a pedestrian encounter to something that could be regarded as profound. Your sex was commercial, never literary. Too predictable to ever become mythical. Your physical moves were empty of emotion.

Sex with you was orgasm, but not love. Never erotic. Sex with you was like every one of your trite conversations—mechanical and redundant. Your touch didn't stir my major senses, and that meant it would never be capable of titillating my minor senses. It never inspired sensuality or disheveled my emotions. It was barely sex. It negated my fantasies. It left me feeling so small. It made me feel cheap and dirty."

He stared at me, now offended, now hurt.

I went on, the anger in my voice controlled, said, "When a woman lies down with a man she doesn't desire, *then* she is a whore. I stopped being a whore when I stopped sleeping with you."

He was hurt, but I wanted him destroyed, wanted him devastated by his own inadequacies.

My chest was rising and falling, yet my breathing was controlled, my pains hidden, still aching, stinging, enduring the sensation of a wounded animal. Wounded but refusing to flee. Holding my ground. Remaining in battle. I waited for him to reach into his low-level vocabulary and attack me with his vulgar words. If he insulted me one more time, if he once again tried to slaughter me with misogynistic words, my language would become misandrist, so nasty and profound that my words would violate so many Alabama laws, I would be incarcerated, tonight writing my very own Letter from Birmingham Jail.

But Logan said nothing. His chest was heaving, his words trapped inside his throat, so many phrases struggling to be freed, filling up his jaws, but he refused to open his mouth, refused them their freedom. The dark clouds of animosity didn't pass away and the deep fog of misunderstanding didn't lift.

He frowned at me and shook his head, did that as if he was disappointed with himself, as if he was asking himself how he could have not only fallen for me, but asked a bitch like me to marry him.

Logan opened his wallet, took out a crisp hundred-dollar bill, slapped it down on the table, stood tall, adjusted his suit coat, and strutted away, didn't look back, his head held high, tears in his eyes.

He strutted away as if, this time, he was leaving me.

He left like he couldn't wait to get to his Range Rover and journey up Highway 78.

The door to the restaurant opened, Logan pausing to let a few women come inside first, his Southern hospitality in effect even now, then he went out into the heat.

Logan vanished.

Each insult had cut me deep, left open wounds, left undeserved pain.

I sat alone, in silence, invisible blood draining out of me, leaving invisible puddles on the table and floor. She was there. I didn't see her, but she was there. She was always there.

"I wept because the process by which I have become a woman was painful. I wept because I was no longer a child with a child's blind faith. I wept because my eyes were opened to reality."

I heard Anaïs, her voice as clear as the Alabama sky, looked around, wanted to see her, but she wasn't here. Anaïs Nin wasn't here. She could never be here, not in the physical form. She was dead.

Anaïs was dead.

The voice I heard was my own. I always heard me talking to myself. I heard me comforting me.

Maybe I'd gone insane.

I waited for the check to arrive, paid my part, took nothing from Logan. I left my tip as well. The appropriate amount. No grandstanding by throwing C-notes on a table and walking away as if whoever had the larger denomination had the most power. No, like I had always done, I paid my own way.

At that moment I knew why I had come to meet Logan. I had come for acceptance. I had come because in the end I wanted him to accept me for who I was. For me that would have been a small victory, a small battle won on the way to becoming whoever I was destined to become. I had come because I didn't want to leave anyone in pain. Our last encounter had been horrible. I wanted that to be redeemed for both of us. That was not the last image of him I wanted in my mind. I didn't want to leave thinking of him as a monster. This image was worse than the first. His words had been spirit-damaging.

In his eyes, if I were selfish with him, then I must be selfish with the rest of the universe. Only a moron would rationalize that way. Those were the thoughts of the emotionally immature.

Before today he was aggravation, irritation personified. Now it was deeper.

I hated him.

I would forever hate him. I would never respect him.

Not for what he said about me, that was his right, that was his perspective.

For bringing my mother into this conversation, for being that low.

Tears flowed. Not many. Not a river. Not a lake. A small puddle, dammed by my tenacity. My intention had never been to hurt anyone. My intention had only been pleasure.

Yet hurt remained.

I was parked around the corner, had a space in front of the tattoo shop.

I went to my car, meter expired but no ticket on the window, acknowledged that Pyrrhic victory with the nod of my head, and rushed inside my heated car, left the area, shades on, air conditioner roaring. Tears remained in my eyes, each tear feeling like invisible blood trickling down my cheeks, body temperature up, head aching, sweat on my neck, I was one hundred and fifty miles from home.

Men traveled the world looking for the fountain of youth, werewolves, and vampires. I only wanted peace, space, and pleasure. And in some eyes, that was a crime worthy of burning me at the stake for.

THIRTY-TWO

Two hours and a million thoughts later I was home.

Logan was tethered to my mind. His egomaniacal attitude.

I mumbled, "Asshole. You've never met a woman like me. One who had her own mind."

I changed into shorts and a wife-beater, took the forest of flowers from my front porch, drove them all to the trash bin near the entrance, had to make two trips, arrangements so large I had to leave the top down for them to fit inside. Walking up and down my stairs with those heavy flowers, loading up my car, doing all of that in the late-afternoon sun, the heat beating down on me for ten minutes, that had left me sweating profusely. It was too hot to think right now. The thermometer was bubbling at well over one hundred degrees and there wasn't a beach within three hundred miles.

I showered, sat on the bed naked, putting on body butter, praying for the sweating to end.

My cellular rang again. Marvin Gaye sang "Sexual Healing." His ring tone.

It was Karl.

It was the ring tone of pleasure.

I tingled. The beat of my heart changed, its rhythm that of peace and tranquility. I felt open, senses alive, the sensation that went beyond simple arousal, the sensation that told me I was aware of every incoming feeling, a sensation that made me feel soft, fragile from outside down to my core.

He said, "Hello, Nia Simone."

"Hello, Karl."

"Feel like going for a short run?"

"You're skipping part of our greetings and salutations."

"How was your day?"

"It sucked."

"Too bad."

"Whatever."

"Feel like going for a short run?"

"Define short."

"No more than four."

"A man after my own heart."

"Four miles of hills."

"I hate you."

Laughter returned to my world. Laughter and the promise of exhilaration.

Logan had angered and depressed me.

I struggled to discard all pessimistic thoughts, went to a drawer filled with new things from Victoria's Secret, went to my black file cabinet and packed a bag of satin and sensuality.

He remained inside my head. The scent of his cologne searing the lining of my nostrils.

The man who had stolen the soft words of a poet in order to shield his own inadequate language, to hide his shortcomings, the man whose words didn't have the value of a bottle of cheap wine, remained inside me. Logan refused to leave my mind. Refused to let me breathe, refused to give me peace.

THIRTY-THREE

The sun was setting, smog thick and the pollen count high.

As shadows elongated, the heat wasn't direct, wasn't as torturous as it had been midday, but still the air owned a thickness, a humidity, remained stifling nevertheless. That humidity was the harbinger of another storm. Dark clouds were out in the distance, beyond East Point and College Park. I was riding with the top down, glasses on, a pink Atlanta Braves baseball cap on, hair pulled back into a ponytail.

By the time I had driven I-285 from Atlanta Road to exit 7, Logan had escaped my thoughts. Somewhere on that twenty-mile journey, somewhere between what used to be Bankhead Highway and the exit at MLK, the stench of his cologne dissipated from my nostrils. His scent had faded as I moved closer to Cascade Road. His stench had been replaced by the scents of therapy.

As I put in the code and began entering the gate to the kingdom known as Audubon Estates, on the other side, I saw Jewell Stewark, leaving her empire, her chariot a convertible Jaguar, its top up.

We made eye contact as I eased through the gate, her car no longer moving, sitting there as if she was waiting for me. I slowed and stopped next to her, looked at her, unafraid. I had too much anger—the residual aggression from my trip to Birmingham—to be afraid of anyone. My top was down, my windows down, her view of me unobstructed. Her windows remained up, her beautiful face visible through her lightly tinted glass. The gate on her side was open, poised for her to leave, but The Jewell of the South didn't leave, she remained paused, continued evaluating, but nothing was said.

The woman with roots in Portland Parish regarded me with a disrespect that took me back to Logan. Just like that, unwanted memories returned. Anger magnified. Negativity moved across my skin and consumed me. The glare she gave me was heavily reciprocated, given unabashedly, without fear.

This was déjà vu.

There was no escaping Ogden Circle. No escaping days gone by.

When I'd endured enough of her territorial glare, when I found her no longer entertaining, I drove deeper into her kingdom, penetrated her world at my own pace, went deeper, left her sitting and glaring. She stayed there as if she was damning my existence in her rearview mirror.

I vanished around the curve. Expected her to reappear when I made it to Karl's driveway.

I paused at the bottom of Karl's driveway. Waited for the Jaguar to come this way.

Hands gripping my steering wheel, I waited for Mark's wife to come to me.

She didn't reappear.

Jewell Stewart was aware of me. As I was aware of her.

Karl greeted me with kisses, deep kisses that stirred me and aroused him.

He was dressed in running shorts and a stay-dry tank top.

He said, "How was your day?"

"Long."

"Mine too."

"Just saw Mark's wife."

"Where was that hater?"

"She was leaving, heading out on Cascade."

He shrugged, kissed me again.

I left what was unsaid as being unsaid; I let the unknown remain unknown.

My day had been stressful enough.

He asked, "You bring the photos?"

"Sure did."

I had brought a photo album. Anguilla Summer Festival. Carnival. Casals Festival in Puerto Rico. St. Lucia Jazz Festival. Jamaica Ocho Rios Jazz Festival. Grenada Drum Festival.

He asked, "Who is this?"

"My mother."

"You serious?"

"That's Mom."

I had photos of her biking and ice climbing in the foothills and glaciers of Bolivia's mountainous landscape. She'd been on Bolivia's "Death Road," the world's most dangerous road, an unforgiving road with an eight-hundred-foot drop off the side of the mountain. She'd gone shark diving in Gansbaai, had gone bungee jumping at the Verzasca Dam. She'd traveled to Reykjavik, Iceland, so she could explore the underwater landscape between two tectonic plates in Iceland's crystal-clear waters, had treated herself to a three-day diving expedition. She'd done things people only dreamed of doing.

I told him, "My mother loves to push herself to the edge."

"These are amazing."

I was sharing my mother with Karl. I was sharing my family. I was sharing myself.

I was doing things that had depth, things that would keep me from feeling like a whore.

Karl appreciated the images from the islands the most of all.

We both came from third-world countries that were regarded as a rich man's paradise, heavens that the locals took for granted. The final destination for many of the African slaves, islands formerly under British rule, a place the British and Americans still flocked to during their holidays.

I had to change, put on yellow running shorts and a tank top from Peachtree Road Race.

Ten minutes later we were running down Cascade toward 285, this end a two-lane road with very little sidewalk, running single-file as traffic whizzed by, with Karl in front so conversation wasn't possible. That was good. I didn't feel talkative. I didn't feel like being alone right now but I didn't feel like talking.

We ran past homes and subdivisions on the two-lane section of the road, another road filled with churches, most of the route a mild decline, turned around after Kroger and shy of 285, the return trip being all incline. I loved a challenge. All the side streets had steep hills. We diverted and ran the hills, did a few repeats on Willis Mills, then jogged back into his community, went down to his basement, worked out in his home gym, did a million crunches and leg lifts, suicides, squats, push-ups, pull-ups, bis and tris, worked out until I could barely stand. I showered and cooked him dinner while he went over some of his work, set up appointments. After we ate, I stayed away from him, sat at the kitchen counter writing, checking e-mails, sending e-mails to Meiling, one of Trinidad's top fashion designers, doing my own thing while Karl did his.

Everything was perfect.

Karl put his home system on, tuned our world to tranquil music. It was different. The sounds of harps and flutes, spiritual music, as if we were walking through a wonderful Japanese temple.

The sound of the bathtub filling with water filled the room behind us. Candlelight surrounded us, our shadows dancing on the walls, our reflection in the mirrors as I sat on the counter, he stood in front of me, began kissing me over and over, sucking my lips, sucking my earlobes, touching my breasts.

I almost said I didn't feel like having sex tonight, wasn't in the mood for what Karl had to offer, even though I loved what Karl did to me. I wanted a different flavor tonight. I wanted a deeper experience. But I wondered what it would be like if there were three of us.

Not us and his brother. Kiki Sunshine. I wondered what this would be like with me and Kiki Sunshine taking control of him, owning his pleasure, pleasing him the way my identical sins had pleased me at the W, with touches and strokes, oral gratification, everything erotic, orgasms with no penetration.

I asked, "You heard from Kiki Sunshine?"

"Talked to her today."

"Really?"

"Have to get her those proofs."

"Are you going back to Greensboro?"

"Not sure. Might FedEx them. Depends."

I didn't ask him what it depended on.

He kissed me again, stopped so he could turn the water off before the tub was too full. He held my hand as I eased inside the water, heat rising into chilly air. He climbed into the tub. His erection was splendid, sticking up out of the water, the head thick and smooth. He smiled at erect nipples.

He said, "Your body is so nice."

"Thanks."

The bathtub was impressive, large enough to launch a ship, large enough for all of my lovers.

He put his finger on my sex, kissed me, suckled my breasts, then eased down, went underwater, put his tongue on my yoni, licked me, ate me, then came back up with water dripping from his face. He took a deep breath and went back underwater, licking and sucking on me until I couldn't take it anymore. He came back up smiling, wiped water from his face.

I moved through the water, went to him, took his hardness in my hand, then praised it by licking the tip, kissing the tip, tasting him and teasing him while I looked in his eyes.

He gave me moans.

He said, "Wish I had my camera."

I moved wet hair from my face. "Get your camera before I come to my senses."

While he climbed out of the tub, water raining from his skin, from his muscles, from his taut backside, from his engorged lingam, I saw my reflection, saw that I had forgotten to take my earrings off, pulled my hair back and saw the reflection of diamonds, saw how they caught light, saw how they reflected in the candlelight, how that same candlelight made my damp skin look so beautiful.

The Nikon clicked, flashed.

I looked back at Karl, the image of a naked Mandingo god, still erect, his tool thick with so many veins, strong enough to hold up a towel, hard enough to fulfill my needs, watched him as he came toward me with his camera in hand, aimed at my face, my eyes glued to his erection, his Nikon, clicking away.

He said, "Just your face. Not taking anything more than your astonishing beauty."

I blushed, his flattering words an aphrodisiac, his words like opium.

The exhibitionist part of me broke free and whispered, "You can photograph my breasts too."

"You sure?"

"Let me hide my face with my hair. You can photo down to my breasts."

"Okay. Yeah. That's mad sexy. Tilt your head."

"Wait."

He paused.

I said, "I think I want to see my whole body. Want to see how I look."

"You sure?"

I left the tub, grabbed a towel, walked into the bedroom with him in tow. I sat on the leather bench at the end of his bed. I turned my face away from the camera, let him photograph my body, my legs always closed, my yoni always hidden. I posed, used the bench and created sensual positions.

I did a split on his bench, my face deep into my leg.

He said, "Didn't know you were that flexible."

"Danced as a child. Mother made me take all kinds of dancing."

I took the camera from him. Had him lay down on the leather bench. I straddled him, put his strength inside me, moved up and down on what was so hard, shook my head side to side because its power and energy were overwhelming, and fought my own good feeling so I could aim the camera at his face, photographed degrees of pleasure rising in his expression. It was beautiful. Watching a man so strong look so weak. Weakness being the look of love. I handed him the camera, let him photograph my face and breasts, wanted him to capture me with weakness etched in my face.

As I rode him, as I struggled with myself, the Nikon clicked and clicked and clicked.

He photographed me a dozen more times before moving away from me, left me longing to be filled, and took my hand, led me back to the bathtub.

The spiritual music was so erotic, in tune with my tingling body.

Karl was so excited.

I gave him the warmth of my mouth while I pulled my hair back, took a deep breath, went underwater, holding my breath and suckling him until my lungs were starting to burn.

I came up for air, wiped water from my face, laughed at his amazed expression.

"Shit, Nia. What the hell you trying to do to me?"

I stood up, water dripping, turned around so Karl could see my backside, then I bent over, spread my yoni lips apart, eased my finger in and out of heat, let Karl witness that act of self-pleasuring.

I asked, "You like?"

"Mind if I get my camera again?"

"Not for this."

"Can't see your face."

"No camera. Photograph this moment with your mind."

Water splashed as he began pleasing himself.

The echo of flutes and harps made everything feel so exotic. I moved back to him, sat on his legs, his erection standing tall against my backside, rubbing against the bottom of my spine.

I leaned back into him, whispered in his ear, "I want you back inside me now."

I reached for a towel, used that as a cushion for his head. A sponge was on the edge of the tub. I dipped the sponge in the water, let the sponge expand, then squeezed the water into his hair, let it drain all over his face. His face was wet, reminded me of when I met him at Stone Mountain, when he was running, sweating, looking like a Mandingo warrior in search of his Nubian princess, so damn sexy.

"Damn, Nia."

I smiled, wiped his face with a towel.

This was wonderful. This was pleasure.

Karl was looking vulnerable, so much weakness in his eyes.

I eased up and down on his strength and his weakness. He held me down, made me stop moving, did that like he couldn't take it anymore. I sat there, accepting all of him, holding him, not moving, my desire filled and pulsating. Karl pulled my hair, moved my face until I was looking at him.

He stared in my eyes. I tried to move my eyes. He forced me to look at him. I wanted to look away, but he made me look at him, forced my emotions to reveal themselves. We remained that way, connected, unmoving, water heating our skin. Looking in each other's eyes. I felt something I didn't want to feel. I wanted him.

I wanted Karl.

It looked like he was about to become emotional and say

something foolish, something regrettable. It was there. He had chased me up a mountain. He had taken me to Greensboro.

He whispered, "Say it."

"No."

"Say it."

"Don't do this to me."

He had been pursuing me from the moment our eyes met.

His pursuit of me perpetually interrupted by his older brother.

I moved my eyes from him like I was once again avoiding the truth, began moving up and down as fast as I could. He tried to stop me, but I wouldn't stop. Karl was moaning. I was moaning. The sounds of skin slapping, the sound of splashing water and moans filled the room, blended with the harps and violins, ethereal sounds that, when combined, made us sound like we were in a Buddhist temple.

I rose and fell harder.

Moans grew.

I slowed it down. Slowed us down.

Karl asked, "You okay?"

It took me a moment to catch my breath. "Get your camera."

"Serious?"

"Take . . . take . . ." Tingles overwhelmed me. "Take some more . . . take more pictures."

His camera was on the edge of the bathtub, so we weren't disconnected long.

He sat up and once again I welcomed him inside my love, slid down on his erection, eased down to the sounds of my moans and his camera clicking. A dozen moans later he put the camera to the side. He was begging for me to make him come, trying to hold me down on his erection, clinging to me, cringing, moaning like he needed to experience all of my yoni. I refused to move. If I moved I would start coming. I would lose control. I would lose my power. I would say things that came from the heart. He was throbbing, growing harder, getting wider, and I was leaning forward, making him not move too much, feeling water pressure up against the entrance to my chocolate star at the same time.

I whispered, "Are you okay?"

He moaned, could barely talk, could just release moans and become aggressive.

He grabbed my ass, forced me up and down, did that as he pumped and grunted like a madman.

His legs trembled.

My breasts were against his damp chest, his heartbeat as strong and rapid as mine.

He moaned. "Damn. Shit. Damn, baby."

Karl was coming. His orgasm attempting to induce mine.

My orgasm teased me, tickled me, sent electricity and brushed fire across my damp skin.

I held him until his erection no longer existed, until he was soft.

The camera was within reach.

I took the camera and started photographing him in his ecstasy.

His face was damp with water and sweat. His eyes tight. His mouth open, his breathing intense. I moved away from him, stood up, took shots of his face, from his expression to his stomach. And I took shots of his softening lingam. A lingam that looked swollen and fulfilled.

He was so strong, body so hard, so well-defined, yet after coming he was so weak.

Samson in the hands of Delilah. Adam standing before Eve.

So vulnerable.

I put the camera down, eased back into the water, went to him, kissed his face.

I held him and caressed what was left of his erection, held on until I felt him soften to the point of being unusable. I stood up and turned around, water raining from my flesh, then I sat with my back to his chest. One of his hands found my breast, the other touched my face. The hand that was on my face, the one that touched my skin, I held it, moved it underwater, put his fingers on my clit.

I came for him. My body felt like a rapid heartbeat.

Karl took his hands away from my pleasure, put his fingers inside my mouth.

He reached for the camera again. Held it out to photograph both of us. Took close-ups of our naughtiness. When he was done capturing this private moment, he put the camera to the side.

Karl pulled me close to him, held me like he wanted me to himself.

Held me as if we were both jumping out of a plane, skydiving in tandem.

Falling.

It felt as if we were falling.

THIRTY-FOUR

After, we dried off.

I let him take me into his enormous bedroom, a bedroom that should come with servants, and let him place me facedown on his leather bench, my feet touching the floor as he slid behind me, as he got ready to re-fuck me, as he took me from behind, his hands on my waist.

I moaned, surprised and amazed that he wanted more.

This was Karl. This was what he did. This was how he related to a woman. This was how he showed love. He made me lie flat with my legs closed, he lay on top of me, his legs outside mine, my yoni tight around his erection. With his weight on me, he pulled my hair back, put his mouth and teeth on my skin, was sucking my neck and kissing me, his every move so benign and gracious.

His front door opened, the sensor telling me that someone had entered his mini-castle, felt him holding me by my waist as feet walked across wooden stairs. Heavy shoes echoed. Hurried steps. Then came the hum of his elevator. Downstairs, someone had gotten on the elevator.

Karl continued stroking me. We changed positions, his hands pulling me back up to my knees, my hands holding the edge of the bench as he made me feel like I was on angel dust.

I moaned, moved, but Karl kept me where I was.

Someone was getting off the elevator.

I surrendered to Karl, moaned my sugary and pleasing singsong moans.

Someone came into the bedroom, heard him moving through the music, passing by the flutes, his footsteps blending with the harps. I heard breathing. Passionate breathing. The breathing of wanting. The breathing of envy. I looked up, saw Mark standing feet away from us, watching us in silence.

Candles had been lit, scented the room with lavender. The music was on the sound system, turned low, everywhere at once, the music stimulating. This home had become a tribal sanctuary. A place of healing. A place of love.

Mark swallowed before he whispered, "Hey, baby."

I set free a beautiful singsong moan. "Hey, baby. I called you."

"Was in Peachtree City all day."

"How was your day?"

"Hectic. Had to . . . had to . . . run errands . . . had this meeting . . . took all day."

He had on jeans. T-shirt. His muscles so strong, my sensations making his look pious.

I said, "Come here. Let me please you, baby."

"I can't stay."

"I know."

Mark was taking his pants down, bringing his lingam toward my mouth, allowing me to suckle and please him as Karl pleased me. This had become my need. The abnormal pleasure that felt so normal. With my hands and mouth I gave him therapy, shared my energy with him, tried to relax his troubled center. By way of orifice and lingam, we united, his hardness and my heat. I stopped giving him oral gratification and began pleasing him with my hand. Did that as Karl wined, made his hips roll, took me deeper into my own pleasure, his ebb and flow not hurried, not vulgar, his movements the perfect massage. As Karl moaned and stroked his way deeper into his own pleasure, as he transcended to places unreachable, I smiled at Mark, pulled him closer, took him in my mouth again. Mark was swelling. Karl was swelling. My clit throbbed, was swelling, felt hard, so erect, electricity flowing through my body. I was so wet and on fire. The energy between us could light up Vegas for one hundred years.

I stopped to catch my breath, stopped so I could moan for a while, panted and stared at Mark's lingam, long and hard like a beautiful plantain. It was standing, it was strong, it was erect.

I licked the corner of my lips, ready to praise him.

I took him inside my mouth, used hands and tongue, strokes and savoring. As I mouth-praised him his moans praised me in return. He whispered my name, touched my face. His breathing thickened. His body tensed. His moans trapped in his throat, became a vicious hum. He ran his fingers through my hair. He was gone. He had abandoned this landscape, had been whisked away. And now he was moving through the topography of pleasure. He radiated, his hardness and heat melding with the warmth and tenderness inside my mouth. He struggled to keep his orgasm at bay, but I wanted him to come. Mark held my hair, trembled like he was about to lose his balance, like he was about to fall to his knees. He came hard and loud. He came as I fought off my own voluptuous orgasm. Pleasure left him slowly, then with suddenness, then again slowly.

He moaned throughout his journey into the land of a wonderful orgasm. His orgasm was as sweet as Bajan cherry juice.

I pleasured him until his plantain became a soft, sweet banana.

In that moment I loved him. I loved his brother. I loved them as if they were one person.

And Karl. Was pleasuring me. Seeking his orgasm. His sounds a deep, constant purr. A rumbling moan. He was lost in me. I loved that sound because that purr and hum sounded like it was just for me, each purr or hum telling me how he felt being inside me, an unspoken compliment, better than him saying that the yoni was good, his sounds homage to the yoni. And my sounds were an equal compliment. I was loud. I think I had grown louder over the years, as my body changed, as pleasure became more intense, as single orgasms bloomed into multiples. Mark was still here but I didn't notice him, not then. I was in the moment. Cursing. Praying. Calling God. Allowing orgasm to find me.

Mark's hand touched my face. "Don't come, baby."

"I'm trying not to."

"Don't let that ugly bastard make you come."

"Make him stop treating me like this."

"Show him he can't make you come."

"Let me come for you, baby."

"Don't come."

"Make him stop fucking me like this."

"Don't come."

Karl fucked me so good. Karl fucked me so hard.

I moaned to Mark, "I'm sorry baby he's making me come shit he's making me come."

But using the word *fuck* diminished the power of what he was doing. Calling it fucking gave it distance. That distance made me feel safe. But I couldn't lie to myself. This was better than fucking. Couldn't lie when I knew the truth. Much better than fucking. The connection was beyond physical.

We were making love. Karl. Mark. And I. We were sharing energy, spiritual needs, bonding.

Mark kissed my face, gave me his tongue. With his hand in my hair he smiled at me as another orgasm approached me, my eyes glazed over, the world electrical and ethereal, everything underwater, then he gave me his tongue as I shuddered, he sucked my tongue and stole my wicked moans.

The place they took me was beyond ethereal. Was higher than Strawberry Fields in Jamaica, was twice as lush. It was an unseen room inside the mansion in heaven. A place filled with white sands and warm sun. Karl moved inside me as if being inside me made him feel alive, as if touching me was salvation. He moved as if touching this body, seeking refuge inside this yoni gave him wholeness.

Mark whispered, "Don't come."

"I'm sorry, baby."

"Don't come."

"I'm so sorry, baby."

Karl moved inside me with unadulterated envy, his envy undisguised. His older brother had upstaged him and now he wanted to show me he was better. Each stroke was better than the one before, each stroke deep and synergistic, like he was injecting me with a drug that amplified what I was feeling. His tempo revealed lust and frustration. I was moaning. I was dying, this death wonderful.

Karl was jealous because he knew I was craving his brother more than him.

It was about competition between the two. A wonderful competition that had benefited me to no end. Both wrestled with seduction, as if I had become their femme fatale.

Karl was losing, now he had stepped his game up.

Karl rubbed my back, massaged me over and over as we engaged in congress, rubbed my backside as my eyes went to Mark, moans once again rising as I watched Mark dress, my legs quivering as I watched my married lover pause and stare at us, heart reaching for him as he turned to leave, his footsteps taking him down the stairs as Karl showed me all of his gears, the sensor beeping as the front door opened, then the sound of my orgasm following Mark as he hurried home to his wife.

That was unreal. That was surreal.

As if Mark had never been here. As if I had imagined him here with us.

Karl lost control and came. He came hard. Out of breath he eased his weight down on me. I reached back, patted his skin, patted him over and over. That was good.

He wrapped his arms around me.

Karl held me. As if I was his wife.

Mark would never cook me breakfast in his kitchen. Would never invite me inside his home. He would always check his watch when he was with me, the timer always running as if he was in a race, always minimizing stolen moments, always minimizing our moments of pleasure.

A married man would always have to go.

In the distance, the skies crackled and rumbled.

Rain started to fall.

I wondered if it was raining in Greensboro.

In the middle of the night I woke up.

I had to go pee. I went to the bathroom, relieved myself, washed my hands, staggered back.

Karl was sleeping on his side. Naked. The image of Kenya staring at me, bothering me.

I typed Mark a text message.

You tasted too good. Love sucking your lingam. Wish you could've stayed all night. Would love to watch you touch yourself, make yourself hard for me. Imagine my mouth on you, licking your pre-come, then taking you deep in my mouth. Remember us at the parking lot at the W. Thinking about how you took me, how you pleased me in the rain, that makes me want to touch myself, taste myself.

Message sent, I put my cellular away, had it on silent.

But it lit up within thirty seconds, letting me know I had a message. It was a text from Mark.

Where are you?

Where you left me. Still at Karl's. Wish you could sneak back down here.

Why don't you meet me at Starbucks tomorrow afternoon.

Sure.

Can't wait to see you.

I went to Karl. He rolled over.

He asked, "You okay?"

"I'm okay."

"You've been tossing and turning all night."

"Sorry."

We cuddled.

He whispered, "I adore you."

I didn't answer. I was too scared to respond. But I kissed him. Kissed him and held his face. We kissed until our breathing became heavy, infinity resting between our inhales and exhales.

I opened my legs for him, invited him inside me, and once again we exchanged pleasure.

When we were done Karl slid away, rode the elevator down, then rode the elevator back up, brought me a glass of water. I sipped, shared water with him, then he pulled me closer to him.

He whispered, "If you want to talk, just let me know."

"You do the same."

"Okay."

I would never be able to do this with Mark. What pained me was that the night had been beautiful and I had enjoyed Mark, but strange emotions existed. Somehow Mark had denigrated my experience.

It was something deep inside me that preferred Karl. At least it felt that way tonight. I told myself that those emotions were wrong. Everything was as it should be. Karl was here. I was with him.

I convinced myself that everything was perfect.

THIRTY-FIVE

It was over one hundred degrees by noon.

The humidity was atrocious, the heat index made it feel as if Atlanta had been moved six stories below hell. I was dressed in ripped jeans and sandals, a simple green T.

Thoughts of Greensboro remained on my mind. Kiki Sunshine remained on my mind.

I sent her a text message, told her I'd try to call her today or tomorrow.

She sent me back a smiley face.

It was so simple to give someone hope. So easy to generate a smile.

Last night with Karl, it had been wonderful. In the bathtub, then Mark helping make it a temporary ménage à trois, his energy causing me to take it to another level. Making love like that was addictive. It was pure crack. Then the way Karl held me last night. He was so kind. Which wasn't what I would've expected from a man who was incapable of the type of love it took to sustain a real relationship.

I backed away from my thoughts, felt as if I was transparent, as if everybody could read my mind. My energy felt apparent, had me rocking, as if they could all tell that I had received dick, been fucked so good I wanted to slap somebody. They weren't watching me. They were in their own grooves.

All of that was behind me. It was back to work. Back to reality.

When I left Karl's home I drove to Starbucks on Cascade. Before I headed back to Cobb County I had promised to meet Mark for coffee. I walked into a coffee shop filled with laughter and overlapping chatter. Samba music on the sound system. Members of Delta Sigma Theta were all over, a sea of red and white T-shirts, their red and white sorority insignia on almost every license plate in the parking lot. They were collecting fans for the elderly. Or money to buy the fans to help the elderly survive the summer. Muslims were here. Members of Kingdom Hall were here too. All mixing with the Christians.

All over were front-page conversations about Michael Vick, his illegal dog fighting up in Virginia, his legal troubles, and how this would be the end of the Falcon nation as the fans of ATL knew it. In the background were conversations on New Orleans, how it had become Murderville, USA, since Hurricane Katrina.

Next to me a man and two women were looking at the *AJC* and talking.

One of the women said, "By the way, if Bynum is a prophetess, how come she could not *prophesize* the fact that she was going to get beat down in the parking lot?"

They laughed it up.

"Hell, if they was at a hotel at four in the morning, you know what was up."

"They was fucking, then they was fighting."

"*Hello.*"

A celebrity's pain became the working man's fodder.

I had my laptop out, was in a corner writing. Not ten minutes went by before I had e-mail from my mother. She was sending me photos of us climbing Brasstown Bald, our faces sweaty, our smiles broad.

I went to the Web site for *The Trinidad Guardian*. Wanted to see what the costumes for Carnival were going to look like, saw a beautiful one made of plumes and feathers, very dramatic, the kind of costume that motivated me to keep my body in Carnival shape.

My eyes burned. Working wasn't working. Some days I felt as if my work was powerful and poetic, singing. Other days I wondered why I wasn't working at the post office. This was a post office day. Not enough sleep. Right now working was a lost cause. Would go home and nap in a few minutes.

After I met with Mark. He'd be here soon. He'd stop by for coffee, long enough to chat.

I smiled. Thought about last night, now stimulated by what had happened, how he had shown up, how I had pleased him, how he had left with envy in his eyes, how he wanted me but couldn't have me. But he did have me. He had me and didn't know he had me.

I was so exhausted, so deep in thought I didn't notice people coming in and out of the coffee shop. I didn't know I was being watched, being dissected by an angry soul. I should've felt the radical drop in temperature, the abrupt climate change that had taken everything from balmy to arctic.

First I saw hints of a sundress, one that reminded me of Kiki Sunshine's sundress.

She was here.

I was startled when I looked up, saw unkind eyes, saw the look of malevolence standing over me.

It was a similar colorful sundress, bright hues that looked good on fair skin.

It was not Kiki Sunshine.

It was Jewell Stewark.

Hostility, not friendship, had found me. Once again I existed in a life-changing moment.

She had magically appeared. As if she was the Wicked Witch.

As if she had been looking for me, maybe following me as I journeyed through Oz.

Her scent touched my nose, eased inside my nostrils, became a part of me, a part of my essence, captivated me and startled me. Her perfume was rich, self-righteous, stunning, marvelous. She owned the stance of a diplomat and the scent of a queen, a scent to rival Imperial Majesty.

She looked smaller than she did on television. Television added ten pounds, gave height, and now both of those illusions were non-existent. She had a wonderful shape, a backside that made the men inside the coffee shop pause, but the material on her top was light, see through, showed that she had small breasts, hardly any to speak of, an A-cup in a Victoria's Secret Miracle Bra, a bra that created the illusion of cleavage. Despite her imperfections, the type of imperfections that made celebrities seem human, her face was beyond beautiful. She had curves and plenty of ass, the things that captured a Southern man's attention as she entered and exited a room. But between her neck and waist, she was as attractive as a young boy.

In a harsh, ugly, yet still investigative tone, she said, "Your name is Nia."

Hearing my name come from her mouth halted me.

Inside that moment I went through a range of emotions: shock, fear, embarrassment, envy. I searched for something to say but inside that moment my power of linguistic expression withered. We were no longer in cars, no longer separated by fiberglass, no longer able to push down on the accelerator and leave an uncomfortable or unwanted moment behind us. We were face to face.

All I could do was look around the room with a quickness, see who was with her, see who was watching me. Besides the members of Delta Sigma Theta, at the table two feet away from mine a man in a gray suit was having a meeting with another man in a black suit. Next to them was a woman in white pants, brown blouse, big Louis Vuitton bag at her side, Sony VAIO and papers out, as if she was waiting on a client to come to a meeting. Another woman was sitting in one of the big green chairs, a copy of *The New York Times* in her face. A few more people were sipping iced drinks, listening to iPods, reading books, on laptops, but none acted like they were with The Jewell of the South.

"Yeah." My voice returned. "My name is Nia."

She said, "Nia Simone Bijou."

The landscape of my existence shifted. An earthquake went through my body.

With that second shock I created a modest smile, again looking around to see who was watching, saw a few people who were mesmerized by her celebrity, celebrity that could not generate enough heat to melt a candle in Hollywood. Celebrity that left me unimpressed. Being unimpressed left me unafraid.

The cappuccino machine, the music, the chatter, newspapers turning, that noise filled my pause.

She had the eyes of a hunter. A hunter that had cornered her prey.

I was being threatened. Being threatened made me defensive, made me feel mean. A bag of copperheads were inside me, moving through life that was created at Port of Spain.

She said, "I'm Mark's wife."

She came across as lofty, extravagantly colorful, pompous, bombastic.

"I know who you are." I nodded. "I saw you when I was going to see Karl."

"I'm not interested in Karl or the *women* he entertains."

"If that's the case, why are you in my face?"

"I'm not interested in Karl. I don't give a damn about Karl."

She looked around the room, spied to see who was paying attention to the famous newscaster. Over in a corner there was a man in military fatigues, home from a war nobody wanted, coffee in hand, looking at his watch every minute. In front of the fireplace, two women were reading books. Another woman on her cell phone talking about anything and everything and nothing all at once.

Eyes were on her fame. Ladies of DST were all around. At least five Starbucks workers were behind the counter. Quite a few men were here too. Jewell Stewark lowered her head, tried to shield her tears.

She said, "Do you mind if we remain civil and take this matter outside?"

"Sure."

I followed her out the door, her swift pace being matched by my own. She went first toward Nanston Dental, then beyond Nanston Dental, stopping where the building ended. For a moment I had thought she was leading me through the heat and taking this issue to McDonald's.

Jewell Stewark pulled her hair behind her ears, did that like moving her mane would improve her hearing, as if she had a lie detector installed in her lobes, then she quivered, shook her head before she looked at me again, her bottom lip trembling.

She snapped, "Let's not play games. You sent my husband text messages late last night. He was in the shower. That was *me* on his phone. That was *me* you were texting. I was the one who sent you the message asking you to come to Starbucks. Bitch, don't you dare talk to me like I'm some fool."

I stood there, stunned.

She growled. "Bitch, yesterday he sent you *a picture of his dick*. After you sent that text, I went through his messages. He's been sending you messages *all day, every day*. You've been meeting him at your home for lunch. *Reading books and fucking each other*. Don't stand in front of me thinking I'm stupid. *He sent you a picture of his dick*."

Then she spit in my face. Her spit came quick, venom from a riled rattlesnake, that discharge flying across the four feet that separated us, hitting me hard, echoed like a blow from an angered pimp.

I yelled, not at her, but yelled as if a fist had been slammed in my right eye.

Colors flashed before my eyes, danced and disappeared inside bright lights.

As I recoiled and wiped her spewed DNA away from my eyes, she hurried away, moved down the walkway toward Starbucks, moved through humidity that made free men sweat like slaves.

It felt as if I had been in a car crash, momentarily in shock, momentarily disoriented.

A few people were sitting outside Starbucks, black people not being too fond of the heat and direct sunlight. Mostly men were out, this weather being the kind that messed up a woman's hair. The small crowd that was enduring the heat, they were watching Jewell's abrupt exit, then they were staring toward me. Southern men who had good home training came to me, stepped out into the oppressive heat, handed me the coarse brown napkins from Starbucks to clean my face, asked me if I was okay.

By then Jewell Stewark had fled to her car, was safe inside her Jaguar, and had pulled up to the front of Starbucks. She sat there with her engine running, staring at me as I frowned at her. She grimaced at me, didn't say a word. She stared, cried, and sent silent curses, dared me to step into the streets so she could run me over, her anger saying she wanted to turn me into roadkill.

She had been the one who had read the text messages I sent to Mark.

She was the one who set me up, had me come here so she could spit in my face.

My chest continued its rise and fall, thunder in the background, sweat blooming on my forehead.

She pulled away, drove by the dentist's office, made a right turn before she made it to the McDonald's parking lot, then made another right on Cascade Road, sped back toward I-285.

Everything became a blur. I ran to my car, was going after her, left everything I had brought with me inside Starbucks, hopped in my Z4 and tried to chase her, but she made it to the on-ramp at 285 while I was stuck behind cars at the light right outside Starbucks. She was speeding onto the interstate, making a right turn and heading toward Campbellton Road. When the light changed I sped around cars, made it to the on-ramp, attacked the ramp like I was leading the pack at NASCAR, sped around cars, made it as far as Camp Creek and I didn't see her. Union City, Fayetteville, a thousand destinations were in that direction. As far as I knew she could've exited at Campbellton and connected to 166, could've been heading back toward downtown or midtown Atlanta.

Or she could've been speeding toward Peachtree City. Speeding to Mark's job site.

Anger had me so heated, sweat was running down my face, back, and neck.

In my mind the same video played over and over, her spitting in my face appended with the violent fantasy of me grabbing Scandinavian-colored hair and beating Jewell Stewark senseless.

I turned around, went back to Starbucks, rushed inside and jogged to the toilet so I could take a tissue and wipe her filthy DNA from my face. Nothing was there, but I still felt her refuse on my skin.

I hurried and closed down my laptop, moved by all the ladies of DST, and gathered my things, head down, trying to hurry and leave this place, too angry and embarrassed to speak to anyone.

Again thunder sounded. That same thunder lived inside me.

The skies roared.

Rain fell hard.

THIRTY-SIX

I sped down the back side of Starbucks.

With haste I traveled down the narrow street that had a Murray Funeral Home and a day spa, my car zooming as I took the narrow street behind Applebee's and Verizon that led to the strip mall facing Fairburn Road. I stopped driving. Had to before I hurt somebody. Was too angry to be on the road. I just wanted to be away from Starbucks, away from the people who had witnessed my shame.

I had to get in contact with my lover. I had to warn Mark.

I called his cellular. Wasn't sure if he would answer, maybe Jewell was holding his cellular hostage. But Mark answered. He was happy to see I was calling. Happy until I told him what happened.

"Hold on . . . hold on." My words rocked him. "She spit in your face?"

"She set me up. She came up to me in Starbucks looking like she was about to lose the plot."

He cursed, anger and confusion blooming, his tone pure irritation and aggravation.

"Mark, how could you keep the messages like that? You know how women are. You know how we are. She said she read all the messages I had sent you, all the messages you had sent me."

"I cover my tracks, but you called late last night. You've never sent messages late."

"How in the world could she go through your phone? I mean, why didn't you delete the messages before you walked into your house? How could you be so careless, Mark?"

"Look, I'm about to get out of this meeting and come to you."

I took another hard breath and realized my own weakness. My feelings for Karl were strong, as were my feelings for Mark. But Mark's emotions were an ocean, like still waters, ran deep. Rooted in things that went beyond physical pleasures. There was chemistry. He appealed to the light side of me.

He said, "Nia . . . are you still there?"

I closed my eyes and saw him. Smelled him. Felt his rough hands massaging my body with gentleness as his baritone voice made his presence that much stronger. And I had empathy for him. For my lover who was trapped in a horrible relationship, wishing he lived in a place of beauty.

"Nia?"

What I felt for Mark was what Logan had wished I felt for him, the emotions that made a woman stay where she should not stay.

He repeated, "Wait for me, okay?"

I took a deep breath.

He told me he could meet me on Cascade Road and Fairburn. He said to wait inside Supreme Fish Delight. It was a discreet place, not too far from where I was, that way I wouldn't drive the streets in panic and fury. I went there, holding hands with an unstoppable anger. A place with yellow and blue walls, pictures of the owner and Snoop Dogg enlarged and placed everywhere the eye could see. Reverend Al Sharpton was going off the air as Michael Baisden came on the radio with his grown folks music and relationship topics for the community. Maybe I should've called in, let my world become fodder for the community. While people hid from the forces of nature and ate fried tilapia, okra, and potato salads, I found an empty table near the window, checked my watch, sat there waiting for Mark.

I went through my old messages from Mark. The ones I had sent. The ones Mark had sent.

Love sucking your lingam . . . licking your pre-come . . . taking you deep in my mouth . . .

Jewell Stewark had read them all. She had read all of my secrets.

Remember us at the parking lot at the W . . . how you pleased me in the rain . . .

Inside my head, a bell was ringing, each reverberation creating a massive headache.

Fish frying, hail falling, trees bending in the storm, Michael Baisden on the radio.

Sounds, smells, emotions. My senses were in overload.

My body trembled and I held myself, felt as if I was about to reach critical mass.

Still I waited in both impatience and ignorance. Unaware insanity would follow me home.

THIRTY-SEVEN

Dark clouds followed me.

As did the rain.

The falling of one raindrop caused all drivers to forget all traffic rules. Southern hospitality became Atlanta rudeness. I wanted to send a one-finger message to the discourteous, but giving another driver the finger, unless your car was armored, was a fool's move. Not when so many trucks had Confederate-flag stickers in their windows, not since the Jena Six and Palmdale Four, not since so many had itchy trigger fingers. My frustration was escalating. I checked my rearview, did that just to look back at him.

He was behind me, following me home.

That was my only consolation.

His lights flashed from low to high to low. I called him on my cellular.

He answered, "You okay up there?"

"That *bitch* spat in my face."

I wiped my face, expecting to feel her sludge on my skin. There was nothing.

I looked in the rearview, imagined I could see him as I said, "Thanks for following me home."

"Get off the phone."

"I'm glad you came."

"Focus on driving."

"Okay."

The trip to Cobb County was horrific. The twenty-mile drive took an hour. We exited at Atlanta Road, navigated rising waters to the Park at Oakley Downs. He parked at the end of my driveway, not in front of my garage like I thought he would, did that like he was leaving space for his brother to park when he came, if he came. After parking he ran to me, rain falling on his head, regret on his face, bags of food in his hand.

I said, "She spat in my face."

He kissed my forehead, then followed me inside, came up the stairs to my kitchen.

He put the food on my kitchen counter, turned to me, and said, "Come here."

"The bitch had the audacity to confront me and she spat in my face."

Those words, those phrases had become an infinite loop, my vocabulary suddenly limited.

He kissed me. He came inside my home, and he kissed me like it was going to be all right.

Or maybe that wasn't the first time Jewell Stewark had spewed her venom in the face of others.

Wonderful scents rose from his bags. The scents of the islands.

He'd brought me food. Jerk chicken, rice and peas, from a restaurant in the Cascades.

He was with me. He was taking care of me. He was attentive, rescuing a damsel in distress.

I said, "It's supposed to storm all night."

"I'm not going anywhere. Staying until the storm is over."

I appreciated his concern, this moment, wanted to smile, but I didn't own a smile, not now.

I asked, "Has she always been like that?"

"She's always had her issues."

"She read all of my text messages. So she knows everything I said, everything that was said to me, has any communication between you and your brother. She knows everything."

He carried me upstairs, kept telling me it would be okay, comforting me as he undressed me, whispering in my ear as he bathed me, kissing me, taking me to my bed, putting lotion on my skin.

A thousand times he kissed me, each kiss an apology, each kiss comforting me, each kiss returned, each returned kiss asking him to alleviate my stress, each kiss inviting his body inside mine.

We moved slow, found pleasure without orgasm, kissed and kissed, went close to the edge.

His voice trembled as he whispered, "Don't come. Stay right here. Enjoy the sensation."

We stayed that way, in a state of erotic consciousness, minds navigating, moving down a spiritual path, energies rising from our skin, mild trembles moving through my body, the electricity of eroticism. I had no idea he could make me feel this way. Maybe because my emotions were so intense at this moment, so extreme and out of control that everything about my being felt hypersensitive and enhanced.

I asked, "What are you doing to me?"

"Just enjoy. Let the negative energy go away. Release bad feelings. Enjoy."

I could've cried from his words, could've died from the pleasure.

It was very altruistic. The way he gave me this type of pleasure was so unselfish.

I remained in my weakened state for a wonderful eternity.

Remained that way until my carnal therapy was interrupted by the ringing of my doorbell.

He moaned, sucked my lips, kissed my face, said, "He's here."

"Took him long enough."

"Make him wait."

"It's storming."

"Make him wait in the rain."

"That would be mean."

"I know."

"Cruel."

"I know."

We kissed for a while, the storm intense, the doorbell ringing, reluctant to disconnect.

Moments later we separated, one became two, the extrication of his erection painful.

Thunder crackled in the distance as the doorbell rang again.

I stood up, tingling, naked, moving through darkness, tottering on the edge of nirvana, so distracted that I didn't do what I should've done, I didn't look out the window, just assumed it was the other half of my identical sins, body tingling, anticipating his touch, thinking of Frankie and her experience, wondering, since I would have them together, maybe for the night, maybe this would remain unrushed, thinking but not thinking, caught up in envy, jealousy, my own egotism, the need to have them with me, to have Jewell's husband here while she suffered for what she had done to me.

I went down the stairs, opened the back door, slid my hand out and pressed the button to make the garage door go up, and as it rose winds rushed inside my home, harsh winds that encouraged me to move my nakedness away from the door. I didn't wait for him. My hands covered my breasts as I took to the carpeted stairs, went to the kitchen, heard taps on the door in the basement and called for him to come on in, said the door shouldn't be locked, too busy getting water, thirsty from the heat I had been given, still tingling, so high from the tantric experience I had been given, asking myself if it was tantric, not caring if it was or not because it felt good, so good I didn't hear the door open and close in the basement, didn't hear the footsteps coming up the stairs from the basement, thirteen steps absorbed by soft carpet, not listening, but standing naked in my kitchen, a glass of water in my hand, sipping, replenishing, not until then did I look out the slit in the plantation shutters and see a Jaguar parked in my driveway, not until then did I realize she was here, not until then did I lose my breath, not until then did I turn around and see her wickedness standing in my doorway, her evilness right outside my kitchen, hair wet, rain all over her face, scowling at me, dissecting me with her anger, not until then did my mouth open as I dropped the glass of water, not until then did I realize I had opened my door and invited the devil inside my home.

She had appeared inside my home, had penetrated my kingdom without a word of warning. As if she was magical, as if the powers of righteousness were on her side.

I stood before her, naked and defenseless.

In the deepest whisper Jewell Stewark growled, *"Where is he?"*

THIRTY-EIGHT

He called down, his voice filled with panic, asked what was going on.

Before I could pull it together Jewell Stewark was headed toward his voice.

She held her dress and ran up my stairs toward my bedroom.

I reached out like I was trying to grab her, stop her, but I barely moved.

I stood shaking, shuddering, broken glass at my feet, water all over the floor.

I inhaled, but couldn't exhale, anxiety held me captive as my lungs failed to expel used oxygen. I was drowning, being suffocated by anxiety, until, at last, my ability to breathe returned, not all at once, first a harsh release of air, then came a series of pants, shallow inhales and exhales. I was holding the counter, trying not to collapse on the broken glass, bent over, lungs refusing to allow me to breathe as much air as I needed to stand up straight.

I needed to wake from this abominable nightmare.

He yelled. His surprise sudden and strong enough to shake my walls. Her anger was impenetrable, covered and consumed the reverberation of his abrupt horror. This wasn't a dream. She was inside my home. Upstairs in my master bedroom, she had encroached on my most personal space.

My mind was screaming for me to dial 9-1-1.

My body not moving. Words not coming. Finally the veil of surrealism lifted. Reality gave me fear and anger. Finally, again, I could breathe. The sense of sound returned, the world had been muted by my fear, my panic, my suffocation. I heard them arguing. I heard her shouting. She was in my bedroom, arguing with my lover while I waited in the kitchen, waited to hear the echo of my things being broken, waited to hear the bang from a gun. I hadn't seen a gun, but I knew she had to have one. She would be crazy to walk into my home empty-handed, carrying nothing but attitude and rage.

The echoes of her anger stopped.

The resonance of his horror ended as if it had died an abrupt death.

Silence fell and covered my townhome. I couldn't hear him saying anything.

My breathing sped up, as did the beating of my heart.

She had killed him. I knew she had killed him.

Or he had killed her. He could be choking the last of life out of her right now.

Death was inside my home. Soon there would be hundreds of police.

The knife my mother had brought when we hiked Brasstown Bald, it was on the kitchen counter. I hurried and picked that up, removed the knife from its leather sheath. My hands trembled. Then I heard her voice, sobbing, saying he made her do what she had done. Sounded like she was telling his lifeless corpse that he had driven her crazy, that this was the only way she could be free.

In a terrified voice, I called out to him. I called him over and over. There was no answer.

I kept the knife in my trembling hand and went to the phone, mind ablaze, ready to dial 9-1-1. Again I paused. The idea of the police returning to my home, that was unappealing, would be humiliating.

As would the arrival of a coroner. And the media.

I was naked, wielding a weapon, praying for the peaceful spirits of the Arawaks to abandon me, praying for the hostile spirits of the Carib Indians to rule me, praying for fear to become revenge.

Without warning there was the sound of a blow, the sound of a fist striking flesh. She called out in pain. The echoes of violence filled my home. The startling sounds of insanity and domestic violence permeated my walls. It sounded like he hit her. It sounded like he was slapping her over and over.

The reverberation of unmasked cruelty stopped.

Her weeping continued, the pleas of the wounded, her cries thin and long, the song of pain.

Knife leading the way, I took to the stairs, headed toward my bedroom.

I hurried up the final stairs, ran down the hallway, the carpet stealing all sounds.

I ran to the door, stopped when I saw them, when I saw their vicious battle.

The candles lit the room. The ceiling fan was spinning.

I saw them. I witnessed their fight. I saw their out-of-control mêlée.

What I saw caused me to let the knife slip from my hands and fall to the carpet.

What I had missed was this: the evolution of this lunacy. Missed Jewell Stewark storming into the bedroom, finding him naked, arguing with him as he struggled with his surprise, her shouting and pushing him until he fell, him not wanting to hurt her and not matching her aggression, trying not to hurt her, then him finding himself naked and off balance, falling to the carpet, a slow fall that was delayed by him grabbing the side of my bed, a fall that ended with him on his butt, then on his back as Jewell pushed him and took his lingam to her mouth, trying to control him, sucking him as he struggled to push her away, her anger and jealousy the manifestation of her possessiveness, lust, and need, madness causing her to take what she had been denied, desire making her savor him as he struggled, making her suck him until he struggled no more, until unwanted sensations imprisoned him as her own desire had imprisoned her, until the heat and electricity inside his body overwhelmed him, until he too was lost, was in the realms of her deep-seated madness, his blood flowing away from his brain, rushing toward his lingam like a dam unleashed, thinning his resistance, and in the end, when he finally pulled her away from that strong part of him, she stood, Jewell stood and stared at him, turned around and as he struggled to get to his feet, as he stumbled and growled at her, as she whined back at him, right then, instead of running, instead of fleeing the evil look in his eyes, she raised her sundress, and bent over my bed as if it was *her* bed, raised her ass up high as if this was *her* room, stood on the tips of her toes, held her ass cheeks and pulled them apart, opened herself up, allowed her scent to perfume the air, allowed the scent of her crazed heat to spread, allowed her wild aroma to waft through the air and signal that she was in need.

He stood, staring, inhaling deeply, angry, his blood drained away from his center of thought.

Struggling to walk away from her. Her scent too powerful. Desire too strong, thickening the air.

Her madness was contagious.

Her madness took hold of him, took root and strangled his senses, became his madness.

He went to her, his hands in fists, his jaw tight, teeth clenched.

Stood behind her. Stood behind heat that was hotter than an Indian summer.

Inhaled deeply, her scent creating urgency and hunger.

So familiar, too strong, her scent being that of a wicked memory.

And he grabbed her waist, took her with his jaw clenched and eyes wide, took his madness to her madness. With a growl he fell into her wetness, met her anger with his anger, her pain with his, her scent covering him and his scent blending with hers. He fell inside her trembling as if he was being beaten, he fell into her heat. He fell into her biting his lip and moaning, his eyes watering as he shook his head.

He fell into her thrusting.

Thrusting his way deeper into their truths.

I dropped my knife when I saw Jewell Stewark was bent over my bed. Her colorful sundress was pulled high up over her rotund ass. My identical sin was standing behind her. Abusing her with passion. I remained frozen. Her pain and his agony blended into an operatic duet, like Pavarotti in a duet with Leontyne Price. The barbaric sound of skin assaulting skin echoed with the rhythm of a constant drumbeat. The music I heard, it stalled me, gave me chills.

He growled out his verse. "I don't love you."

She responded. "Don't lie . . . don't . . . don't say that."

"I have . . . never . . . loved you."

He continued taking her from behind, wetness between them loud, plunging into her repeatedly as she gripped the covers on my bed to keep from falling, as she pulled the covers toward her, pillows flying to the floor, my comforter sliding toward the carpet, her hands grabbing at whatever was left on the bed as he grunted and plunged into her with so much force the bed was trying to move across the carpet.

I stumbled around the bed, my reflection all around me, each mirror capturing a scene that was being illuminated by candles, and I went to the opposite side, appalled, angry, ignoring him, staring in her swollen eyes.

My bed had become their stage, their theater in the round.

Dazed, I stumbled in as if I was meant to be the audience, an angered spectator disgusted by the performance being presented. And at the same time I walked in feeling like I was being upstaged by someone who was minor in my world. I had walked into the middle of act one, the performance already in progress. I had missed the moment before, missed all that had been revealed up to this moment.

I only knew what I saw.

I didn't see sex. In this dark and sexual Shakespearean play, I saw him trying to murder her.

She was crying, begging for forgiveness, submitting to him taking her without mercy. So dramatic. As an orchestra filled with instruments from the string family, the woodwind family, the brass family, and the percussion family were creating music for her misery. Cymbals crashed as she cried out his name, did that as if she was ignoring me, as if I was nothing, as if I was not a part of this opera. She was too busy pushing back into him, meeting his plunges with her own aggravated movements.

This could not be happening.

What I witnessed had me in a trance, a state so far from reality I didn't think I would ever be able to find my way back. This madness was happening in my bedroom. On my bed. Her shadows tainting my walls. Her reflection blaspheming in every mirror, as if this was a funhouse of pain.

This was happening.

Something inside me snapped. Maybe madness was as contagious as bird flu.

And if madness was communicable, it was airborne and I had been infected.

She was on my bed, on my private stage, but all I saw was her at Starbucks, humiliating me in front of the world. I lost it. I rushed to her, no longer saw the man who was plunging into her with so much fervor, only saw the woman who had spit in my face, only saw the woman who had come into my home and violated my personal laws. I grabbed her hair, grabbed it tight and pulled hard.

She cringed, her eyes closed tight, her teeth gritted, but she refused to scream.

I yelled, "You spat in my face."

She cried for him, called his name, refused to give in to the pain I was giving her.

"Bitch, you spat in my face."

She reached up to try and pull my hand from her hair, her nails digging in my skin, but I was pissed, had a firm grip, held her mane tight enough to make her wail and cringe.

She was primal. He'd reciprocated and become primal. I'd become primal as well.

If madness were contagious, then she was patient zero, my home ground zero for an epidemic.

He plunged into her, his skin slapping her backside so hard it shook the room.

I held her hair as I crawled up on my bed. This was my bed, not hers. Mine.

She cried and moaned and struggled.

He remained brutal with her.

Her alto curses matched his in both intensity and vulgarity.

We were people with foundations built on higher education, professional individuals, but all of that learnedness was gone, wiped away by anger, by selfishness, by jealousy, incinerated by a brushfire of emotions, dark emotions that made me feel like I was someone else. And in this irrationality, intellectual words and reasoning were replaced by guttural moans and primal screams. Sounds that echoed the psychological pain rooted in the lower brain and nervous system were exiting with every breath.

She had spit in my face. She had humiliated me. Had defiled my existence.

She had invaded Cobb County, shown up on my front porch.

She had hiked up my stairs, forced her way inside my home.

I had no control over me, not now, the momentum was too powerful. I wanted revenge. I yanked her hair hard as he stroked her toward me. With both hands I forced her face between my thighs. I tried to suffocate her. I tried to smother her song of pain and suffering as he plunged into her over and over.

She was struggling to breathe, her nose moving back and forth across my swollen clit.

This was insane. This was unreal. This was ugly.

It felt as if I had devolved, as if I had fallen into a sexually violent novel by the Marquis de Sade. Or I had been sucked into their mesmerizing opera, its cadence compelling, a beautiful violence that was disturbing, powerful. She had invaded my home, marched into my bedroom like she was with the fucking gestapo, had thrown her rage and arrogance and insults from wall to wall, and was getting punished for her unforgivable actions, not trying to escape the insanity, but behaving like she wanted this, complaining and cursing and crying but not fighting, not the way I would battle if I were being taken against my will.

Maybe she was just weak. Weak for him. Weak enough to submit to whatever he wanted. Or maybe this was part of their game, this was the way they lived and loved and hated each other.

She started to come, her mouth opening so she could moan, so she could breathe. Her mouth opened and I felt her tongue and lips on my yoni, her breath so hot, her breathing so intense.

I moaned, attacked by a fury of tingles, each tingle weakening me, distracting me.

I had to get away from her. This was wrong and I had to cease and desist. I had to stop.

This wasn't right.

This wasn't my definition of pleasure. This was sadistic. Masochistic. But it had momentum.

I cursed her. "I should get my vibrator, see how much shit you talk with it up your ass."

She seized my legs, growled, and pulled me back to her, that action catching me off guard. This wasn't The Jewell of the South I watched on television. The grandiloquent persona she showed the rest of the world was gone. I was running from her, trying to get away, but she wouldn't give me my freedom.

I slapped at her hands, called for help, asked him to get her away from me.

But he couldn't stop. His anger was too strong, his rage too full, had to be emptied for clarity.

My reversal of humiliation had been reversed.

He was taking her.

She was taking me.

He cursed her, gave her vulgar language. She reciprocated, cursed him, damned him.

The sounds of her being taken, their skin slapping, the thunderous sounds from his thrusts, the sweating, the curses, the moans, all of that went on as we fought with each other. The mirrors that were on my walls, it showed us taking and being taken by each other from every angle. Her forcing herself on me with her mouth, my hands pulling her hair, trying to push her away, but her lips were locked on my yoni. I despised her because . . . she made me feel fire. Her hands and arms locked around my legs, pulled me back to her. She was strong. Much stronger than she looked. She was being stroked hard and her lips were massaging my yoni, my hands in her hair trying to push her head away from my swollen clit. Our back-and-forth struggle went on and on, the power between us shifting with every moment.

With a moan and an utterance of the Lord's name, I surrendered.

I was underwater, drowning, stopped pushing her away, pulled her to me, pulled her with urgency. Pelvic muscles, my yoni, my ass, everything was tensing, my body contracting as spasms made my toes curl, every sound I made, everything about my existence out of my control. I held her face, pushed her tongue and mouth deeper into my tingles. She tried to pull away, tried to push me away from her, tried to abandon me. I held on tight, pulled her into my fire.

Powerful burning, tingling, moaning, gasping, eyes rolling in the back of my head, no control over my body, those sensations lasted a lifetime. This could not be happening. But it was. I couldn't stop coming.

My anger returned, its intensity beyond reason.

I tried to suffocate her as I came. Did my best to asphyxiate her. I struggled to regain control, but she proved she had the power. She came after me again, held my legs, pulled me back to her. She sucked my clit and refused to let me go. With her mouth and tongue she gave me her anger. I came like a flash flood. Came like a man, pleasure and pain squirting from my body. Again I saw colorful lights, a kaleidoscope of colors, every color peaceful.

I fell away from her, legs trembling, moaning, my core shaking like I had been beaten in battle.

She was yelping, moaning her angry moan, vibrating, calling out his name with his every thrust.

He was still battling her.

I moved away from my enemy, left her panting for air, left her being punished.

She was shuddering, her beautiful face so ugly, her mouth the letter O, having an orgasm.

She came releasing a quick vibrato, everything about her looking warm, her moans so soft and feminine, almost childlike, then the quality of her voice took on an extraordinary legato, her moans once again changing, like a singer moving from note to note. She came like she was the ultimate soprano, moaning in high G, those moans brighter than the candles that lit up the room, changing to high C as the orgasm grasped her, then changing to D, and as she shuddered, evolved into E-flat and E-natural.

I was frozen, watching her, looking at her reflection in my mirrors, seeing her shadow against my walls, no matter what direction I looked I witnessed the same thing, watched her orgasm in my home.

I looked at her in the candlelight, and even though I hated her, Jewell Stewark's beauty was that of a goddess. I looked at him, that same candlelight illuminating his Mandingo frame.

And in that same light, this was too unreal.

He too looked angry, possessed, his moans reaching notes I'd never heard before.

He was punishing her. And at the same time she was punishing him in return.

He strained, was about to lose control. His operatic moans dark and heavy, the weight of his impending orgasm deepening his timbre, sounding like he was ready to do his solo in a bedroom revival of George Gershwin's *Porgy and Bess*.

I told him to not put his liquid anger inside her. Told him to pull out of The Jewell of the South.

He did what I said, pulled away from her, his body trembling, unable to go far.

And she went after him, pulled him, wrestled him back to the bed.

She cursed him. "You want me to suck your dick? Is that what you want? Is that all you've missed? Me sucking your dick? Do you miss that? I swore I'd never suck your dick again."

She took him down her throat, held his lingam, masturbated him, made him wail and come as she cried and held on to that part of him, sucked him until he struggled to get free from her hunger.

I moved away from them.

It was just her and him. This was their madness, no longer mine. It had never been mine.

He growled, "You bitch . . . you crazy bitch . . . you . . . you . . . oh God."

She devoured him. In those moments she owned him. Owned what was un-ownable.

The earthquake that shook my world ended.

The pounding he had given had left him sweating like he was in the noon sun, panting like he was exhausted. He collapsed on the edge of the bed, touching me with his sweaty palms, not touching her. She was within his reach, but he didn't reach for her.

The opera had ended.

Panting, I looked at him, saw regret and shame in his eyes.

He saw anger and confusion, a collection of negative emotions in mine.

I shook my head, disturbed and appalled, but still aroused in a strange way. Aroused by darkness. Aroused by guilt. Maybe the greater the guilt, the stronger the pleasure.

He coughed. "Sorry . . . sorry about this."

"On my bed."

"I don't know what came over me."

"In my house."

"I'm so sorry."

"You were . . . fucking her . . . in front of me . . . on my bed."

I struggled to catch my breath. Madness refused to dissolve. This was unreal.

She was in a haze, unmoving, looking as if she had ingested opium sap. Strung out, shaky, her eyes closed tight, her mouth in the shape of a silent scream, the agony of withdrawal.

I whispered, "You and Jewell . . . I . . . this . . . you and her . . . I don't understand . . ."

"It's Jewell . . . she's . . ."

"She's what?"

He didn't answer. His expression was as complicated as the true definition of love.

His angel smiled at me, her gaze consistent, never blinking, unbroken.

I closed my swollen eyes.

He leaned in and kissed me, gave me his tongue, rubbed my face, put his hand in my tangled hair, massaged my scalp before he pulled away from me. Went to the bathroom. Heard him urinating, a long stream that went on forever, as if I was listening to a horse relieve itself. Heard the toilet flush. Water came on in the sink. Water turned off. Paper towel was ripped. Then he came back in the bedroom.

I opened my eyes. Saw the markings on his flesh, his angel staring at me, his sweat her sweat. Her stare was unblinking, unbroken. Bleeding.

The angel stared at me, long scratches across her inked image, as if she had been clawed away during his opening battle with Jewell Stewark.

Jewell Stewark had tried to destroy his angel.

My lover's head was down, shoulders slumped, his eyes avoiding the disgust in mine.

I gritted my teeth, closed my eyes, made them all vanish inside darkness, wished this all away.

I heard him dressing, loose change jingling and his belt buckle clanking as he pulled up his pants. He was getting ready to leave, was about to take her and go back to their land of mini castles.

Jewell Stewark whispered, "Karl . . . please . . . come back . . . kiss me the way you kissed her."

She sobbed.

She whispered, "Kiss me the way you used to kiss Kenya."

T H I R T Y - N I N E

Karl turned away from Jewell Stewark.

Veins in his neck, he growled, "Don't you ever . . . *ever* say her name."

"Kiss me like . . . Karl kiss me . . . kiss me like . . . you used to kiss Kenya."

"You fucking hear me?"

I was confused. I was appalled. I was curious.

She growled, "*Fuck me like you fucked Kenya.*"

"*Shut up shut your fucking mouth shut the fuck up.*"

He turned his back, gritted his teeth, and moved away from his sister-in-law.

"Make love to me the way you made love to Kenya."

She taunted him with the name of his angel, taunted him deeper into madness.

He continued cursing her, threatening her, his threats ignored.

It was Karl. Not Mark. Jewell Stewark said his name. Called his name over and over. She had moaned his name. She had put deep scratches in his arm, had defiled his angel, had left hints of blood on his flesh. There was no mistake. Jewell Stewark knew who she incited, who had taken her on my bed. The absurdity of the moment muted me, my mind trying to make what was illogical logical.

Mark hadn't come to me while I waited at Supreme Fish Delight, the pain and sting of his wife's spit in my eye. Mark had called me back, was unable to get away from work at that moment. I couldn't wait for him, not there, had told him to meet me at my home when he was free. In my impatience, in anger, I had called Karl. He had come right away. Had come and rescued me, comforted me as we waited on Mark.

And now Karl stood before me, the scent of his brother's wife on his lingam, the aroma of her angry sex on his softening dick, the scent of her rage on my bed, the scent of madness thickening my air.

His footsteps were heavy as he walked down the stairs, loose change jingling in his pocket.

She called to him, "Sonofabitch. *I hate you.*"

He yelled, "Why do you do this to me? *Why do you fuck up everything?*"

"I hate you. I hate you more than you will ever know."

Her voice was wilted, that of a tortured soul. I owned no pity for her.

The jingling faded. The front door opened and closed, the momentary sound of wind and rain.

Karl was gone. He had left Jewell Stewark in my home, on my bed, her sundress pulled up over her ass, his liquid anger evaporating on her lips. Her own voluptuous orgasm running down her legs. She was not happy, but she was no longer crying. I was angry. I was insane. Everything about my body felt wrong, too bright, too numb, as if my brain was in a state of hypermetabolism.

I looked toward her. She too looked as if she had suffered significant insult to the body, her insult happening long before today. Her eyes were closed. But she wasn't sleeping. She was hiding.

She was longing.

She wasn't desiring her husband. But wanting her brother-in-law to come back.

She had come here because of him. She had come here to do battle, because him breaking down gave her control. Riling him, getting him aroused, getting him to penetrate her was winning the battle. I'd bet that was what she had hoped. But he had walked out on her. Despite all of her beauty, she had been abandoned. Left sprawled out on my bed, her insides ripped apart like the Scarecrow when the monkeys had torn it to shreds.

He had left both of us. He had been overwhelmed and walked out, left drama behind.

I wondered what I was becoming . . . what I had become.

This was not me. This was not Nia Simone Bijou. This was not the daughter of Trinidad.

This was the animal that lived inside her.

I couldn't focus.

I had to get up. I had to kick this evilness out of my bed, grab her by her hair, and drag her down the carpeted stairs, open the front door, then drag her down the concrete stairs and throw her out on the streets. It was my right to beat her like a slave. I was going to beat her until I became the lead story on the news. I would beat her so bad that Atlanta would forget about Juanita Bynum and Michael Vick.

After I had a little more rest.

Endorphins flooded my bedroom, created a faux sense of well-being. It had been a long, intense workout. Felt like my muscles had used up their stored glycogen, were functioning with only oxygen.

I was floating through the land of the surreal, body heavy, like I was walking through the deadly poppy field, breathing becoming thick, body becoming heavy, despite my mind screaming to not rest.

It was a brief session of unconsciousness.

With the enemy resting inside my gates, that was too long.

I tried to sit up, struggling to become fully awake, but the weight kept me down on the bed.

I couldn't breathe. It felt as if I was suffocating, my lungs unable to inhale any oxygen. As if I was struggling to free myself from a wicked nightmare. I expected to wake up in Karl's bed, or wake up in the bed alone, with Karl in the shower, smiling and waiting for me to join him, expected everything that had happened at Starbucks and after to be false, just my own guilt manufacturing bizarre nightmares.

I opened my eyes. What I saw made my heart race.

Jewell Stewark's eyes were inches from mine.

The eyes of a goddess. The eyes of a tempest.

Her blond hair was wild, hanging and framing her glowering face. The look of beauty gone mad.

The weight I felt was the heaviness of insanity. Jewell Stewark was on top of me, her sundress pulled back, her rotund butt flattening my breasts, knees on both sides of my neck, her yoni at my mouth.

She had my mother's long-bladed knife in her hand, as if the hostility of the Carib Indians was alive in her blood, as if war was her primary goal, as if she wanted to raid my village, torture me with her presence and kill me, slaughter her enemy, her intention being to cannibalize the last of the Arawaks.

This was the end of my opera.

This was my death.

FORTY

Candlelight illuminating the agony in her features, death looked both insane and stunning.

Its striking face forever the amalgamation of two beautiful songstresses, her body with strength born in Portland Parish, long hair dyed the hue of a warrior from Scandinavia, that combination of beauty and strength wrapped in the vilest of angers. Atlanta's pride, The Jewell of the South was poised to take my life. As she held the long-bladed knife, my heartbeat was inside my throat, my breathing nonexistent, my eyes wide and on her wide-eyed glower as I waited, as I watched her consider her options.

I watched her internal struggle manifest itself in her lips, in her breathing, in the way she opened and closed her eyes, it poured from her body in each of her tears, her agony raining on my terrified flesh.

She considered freedom or jail. She deliberated heaven or hell.

Her eyes told me the verdict was hell.

In a moment cold metal would slice my flesh. In a moment I would feel the warmth of my blood.

I waited for the beginning of my end.

She held her eyes open, no longer blinking, no more butterflies, took a few breaths.

She moved the knife. She lifted the blade, moved it away from my flesh. But she didn't move, she remained on me, a question-and-answer session still going on inside her head.

The Jewell of the South shifted, moved away from me, allowed me to breathe.

I panted, my eyes wide, my hands going to my throat, thinking I felt my own blood, discovering that sticky dampness was my sweat. I inhaled a thousand times, smelled her over and over.

Her scent was on my chest, on my breasts, permeating my skin.

As my scent was on her face, her mouth, had mixed with the flavors on her tongue.

We smelled of anger, reeked of madness, disbelief, all of that spiced with temporary insanity.

I could only hope her fury was waning.

I could only hope.

Jewell Stewark stood up, then she wobbled, staggered, leaned against the foot of my bed, tugged at her wrinkled clothing, pulled her sundress down, then struggled to slip her sandals back on, shoes that she had lost during her battle with Karl, shoes that had been kicked away as she took lingam on my bed.

I coughed and struggled to get up, legs heavy, body sluggish, my eyes on her every move.

Her face owned six shades of redness, her hair mangled, some stuck against her dank skin. She looked as if a battle was continuing inside her, as if she was two people, one of light, the other of darkness. She held the end of my bed with one hand, her posture that of a woman who had no energy, of an ultramarathoner who had given up in the middle of a hundred-mile race. She made sounds, soft sounds that no longer reminded me of the opera, sounds that echoed like the mixture of angst and sacrifice.

She stood before me, her hands going to her hair, her hands pulling her hair, wrestling with herself, as if she was fighting with the voices inside her head, a woman haunted by memories and desires. A woman haunted by emotions stirred by Karl, imprisoned by feelings she had for Mark.

She balanced herself against my dresser, attempted to stand up straight.

She asked, "Are you sleeping with both of them?"

"Yes."

She tried to look at me, but she couldn't hold eye contact. Her eyes were swollen, so heavy she couldn't hold her head up straight. I stared at her because she couldn't stare at me. My chest was still rising and falling, lungs unable to fill with air, as if she was still sitting on my chest, but I stared at her, her face the mirror of my emotions, a mixture of anger, fear, and disbelief.

There was no room for flight, if she came back toward me there would be a fight.

But she didn't move in my direction. She didn't move at all.

She asked, "At the same time?"

"Yes."

"You sleep with them . . ."

"Yes."

". . . both . . ."

"Yes."

". . . at the same time?"

"Yes."

She swallowed like she was about to break down.

Her voice fractured. "For how long?"

I told her.

She stood before me raw, the real person who was behind the curtain, the woman who pretended to be The Jewell of the South, it was her lie, her shield, the same way the wizard was not really a wizard at all, just a man behind a curtain. The Jewell of the South was just a woman with a good job.

Billboards had made her larger than life, each advert magnifying the deception.

This was her naked. This was her raw. This was her with her demons unleashed.

Her fractured voice splintered one hundred ways as she asked, "Who do you prefer?"

"Sometimes Mark."

"Sometimes."

My voice cracked. "Sometimes Karl."

"Sometimes."

"Most of the time both."

Her voice thickened, each syllable broken. "All of you . . . together . . . at the same time."

"Yes."

"Every time?"

"Not every time."

"How many times?"

"Ask them."

Her controlled tone vanished, became an abrupt cry. A hard cry.

She vanished for a moment. Jewell vanished and I saw myself in her place, breaking down crying. The kind of cry that owned no sound, that kind that etched so many lines of pain and sorrow in your flesh, the cry that stole all of your breath and left you nothing to make sound, the kind of cry that suffocated you. I saw me crying, I saw me in pain, I saw me devastated when pleasure was gone.

She said, "They share you."

"We share each other."

"Did you *share* each other last night?"

"Yes."

"While I was at home, and Mark went to Karl's home, you *shared* each other."

I didn't answer. Her words seemed rhetorical, the repetition and redundancy that came with shock and disbelief. With denial. She nodded, chuckled, wiped her eyes with the back of her hands.

She said, "Karl walked out on me. Left me here. He made a fool of me and walked out the door."

"Where is your husband?"

"I don't care where he is."

I let a moment pass, enough time for the echo from her voice to wane. "You love Karl."

Immediately and with conviction she said, "Yes."

"You love Mark."

She hesitated, her voice softened. "Yes."

"Same as you love Karl."

Again she paused, looked devastated, her voice splintering. "No two loves are ever the same."

She stood there, the long-bladed knife in her hand. Her swollen eyes followed mine to the knife. She stared at the knife, its handle tight in her hand, her body trembling, her nerves on edge.

She shook her head.

At this point everything was premeditated.

She put the long-bladed knife down on my bed. Then she walked out the doorway, took slow steps down the hallway, car keys in her hand, sandals slapping against her feet with each step, slapping her feet and making that skin-against-skin sound once again. She moved like she was disoriented, as if with each step the landscape of her reality was shifting, as if my words, my testimony, my confessions, my truth had disrupted her senses, as if she could no longer see the world, bumping into the railing, bumping into the walls, each step uneven and uncertain, then slower steps as she took to the stairs, her sandals still slapping her feet, again stumbling as she made her way down the carpeted stairs. I thought she had fallen. Or was about to fall. I thought she was about to spin and fall like that man in the movie *Psycho*. She'd spin and fall and break her neck and her death would get blamed on me.

Silence returned and I hoped Silence was not alone, I hoped it had brought its friend, Sanity.

I waited to hear the front door open and close. But it didn't happen. I heard her crying. I heard her breaking down. Her spirit was shattered, her soul ruptured.

I looked back at my bed. And I saw what could've been me. I saw me with my eyes open, blood everywhere, my naked body lifeless, the sting of death allowing me to receive pleasure no more. The image of my lifeless body in a sea of blood, the thought that my mother would have to see photos of me in that way, would have to clean up this mess I had made, that brought heat to my throat. Brought heat to where, only moments ago, a sharp knife had been.

My hands came to my throat. I held my neck. I shivered.

My eyes watered.

Downstairs a woman was crying uncontrollably.

I pulled on a pair of jeans, the first T-shirt I could find, picked up the long-bladed knife and went looking for her. But she would be easy to find. All I had to do was follow her cries, follow her tears.

My body felt a shock, like a stun gun. I let out a scream. I felt the vibration again. It was my cellular phone. In the pocket of my jeans. My heart raced and sweat formed on my neck and brow. I was on edge, the vibrations from my cellular phone were shooting into my body like an electric shock. After it vibrated three times, the ring tone kicked in. The theme from *Sex and the City*. It was my mother. My spirit was created from her spirit. She always called at the most ill-timed moments, as if my troubled soul nudged her. I tugged the phone out of my back pocket, tried to push the red END button to turn the phone off and kill the music, music that would let the woman in my home know exactly where I was, but I fumbled and hit the green button, the SEND button, and I accidentally answered my mother's call.

The Jewell of the South was in my home. And now my mother was on the line.

I released vulgarities, then answered with a quickness, said, "Let me call you back."

My mother began having a conversation as if she didn't hear me.

My mother was calling me because she was still excited about my sci-fi project. Said she had seen the dailies of *Invasion*, Nicole Kidman's movie, and it was mediocre, a blasé remake of *Invasion of the Body Snatchers*, a remake that had a lame *War of the Worlds* ending.

I told my mother, "Call me back in ten minutes."

"Just letting you know that I want to pitch this one. You just sit back and smile, be your beautiful writer-self and let me sell this project so I can get my percentage and buy another property on the beach."

I rubbed my eyes, tried not to sound distressed. "Call me back in ten minutes."

She paused, her tone changing to that of the concerned mother. "You okay?"

There was a boom. The world lit up, lightning crackling in the sky.

"Everything's okay." Chill bumps raised on my arms. "I'm in the middle of something right now."

"Where are you?"

"My bedroom."

"Are you alone?"

I paused. "No. I'm not alone."

"Oh, I'm sorry."

She laughed.

Head pounding, I hung up, trembling, wondering if I should've told my mother what was going on, that her daughter was in trouble, that she should call the police to come fix this for me. I stayed where I was, listening, hearing nothing. The rain began pouring down. Thunder roared. Lights flickered.

My world had become a Hitchcock movie.

I went down the stairs, took slow and deliberate steps, didn't know if she was hiding, didn't know her state of mind, what level of craziness she still possessed, first peeping toward my sunroom, and I saw her there, standing in the window, not hiding at all, in plain sight, her back to me, her positioning leaving her defenseless. Her body was bent forward, one hand out against the casing for the plantation shutters, the other on her hip, her head down so low it looked as if she was headless. She was sobbing, maybe staring out at the darkness and the trees, maybe staring at nothing. I paused at the bottom of the stairs, the blade bouncing against my leg. Jewell Stewark heard me, turned and faced me, and we stared at each other. There were moments in everyone's life that defied logic and reason. This was one of mine.

"Nia Bijou, if you would like to call the police, I'll wait. I take full responsibility for my actions. For coming into your home and . . . and . . . and acting like a fool. And for the way I behaved at Starbucks, I accept full responsibility. If you want to call the police, if you want to have me arrested, I'll wait for them."

She was crying. Not dramatically crying, it was a stubborn cry, one she was trying to keep at bay and failing, emotions grave, being forced to release the kind of profound cry that came from the heart.

I paused, images of her being carted away, red and blue lights flashing. My neighbors witnessing the scene, this being the second time in a few weeks that the police would have visited my home, lights flashing, a person of color being taken away from this white-bread community, a throng of reporters showing up at my door, all of my personal business showing up on Channel 2 with Fred Blankenship and Pam Martin telling the world of my hedonistic moments. That same news would be on *Fox 5 Morning News* and *Good Day Atlanta*, and on the front page of the *Atlanta Journal-Constitution*. The news would be about The Jewell of the South and some unknown, wayward woman from L.A.

No, this wasn't like the regrettable moment with Logan.

This was The Jewell of the South. This was news for Atlanta.

I didn't want that, not at all.

I trembled. I was nervous. I was afraid to let her go outside in the state she was in, afraid that my curious neighbors would see her leaving here crying, maybe had already seen Karl's abrupt exit. The rain was falling hard. The skies had opened up. The wind was strong, streets were probably flooding, the red dirt of Georgia running down mountains, that same muddy water flooding the urban streets. I doubted if she could make it from my driveway to Atlanta Road without being in a serious accident. And 285 would have to be a deathtrap in this weather, two of the four lanes becoming lakes.

I said, "Are you okay?"

"Shook up. Too shook up to drive. I'm feeling . . . nauseous."

"You need to throw up?"

"I'm . . . it's not that bad. I just need to sit for a moment, if you don't mind."

"Why don't you come in the kitchen, have a seat on a barstool."

I led the way into my kitchen, a kitchen that had wooden floors and rustic barstools at the marble counter, a bistro table in the breakfast nook, white cabinets and stainless steel appliances, all of that facing the rest of the other tri-level townhomes in this cul-de-sac on Oakwood Trace. She took a seat at one of the barstools, had a hard time pulling it out because it was heavy. I went deeper into the kitchen, picked up the broken glass I had left on the floor, threw the big pieces in the trash, swept the smaller pieces to the side, tossed a large dishtowel on the dampness, and went back to the pantry, all of my movements jittery as I took out two red plastic cups, cups I almost dropped trying to handle. I stepped over the damp towel, over bits of broken glass, and went to the refrigerator and took out bottled water.

I became the polite, educated, regal woman from Hampton, poured a cup of water for the prim and proper woman from Spelman, then did the same for myself before I handed her the cup.

"Thank you."

"You're welcome."

I ached. I struggle to drink my water, body dehydrated, extremities trembling.

In the name of self, I had committed a chiliad of errors, and I ached for each one.

Sooner or later Karma arrived. Sometimes with roses. Sometimes wearing a black hood.

Sometimes with the face of loveliness and wearing a beautiful sundress.

Again thunder and lightning came, the winds becoming harsher.

The things that had happened, the hostility, it had become something else, our song had a different tempo, one composed of guilt and shame. Severe guilt accompanied by relentless shame.

I sat down at the other barstool, still waiting to wake up from this nightmare.

She took a piece of ice from her water, rubbed it on her neck, on her reddened face.

I asked, "Would you like a paper towel?"

"No thank you."

Awkwardness remained as the skies crackled.

A moment passed. I said, "You followed Karl here."

She shifted. "Where is Mark?"

"Work. He couldn't get away."

"He abandoned you."

"Work. He had problems at work."

She huffed.

I took a breath. "I called Karl. Karl came. He followed me home."

"Karl."

"Did you follow him? Did you follow us?"

"I followed him. Not today. But I followed him."

"Why?"

"Because . . . because."

I paused before I said, "You prefer Karl to your husband."

"Yes."

"Does Mark know?"

"He knows."

"How long?"

"Forever."

She sipped her water. I felt the heat of angst radiating from her reddened skin.

I paused. "Tell me about you and the twins."

She took a deep breath, put the cube of ice back in her cup, then sipped her water too fast, caused her to cough awhile. She got her coughing under control, swallowed, then sipped more water.

She cried. "This is . . . I am so embarrassed."

There was a big boom, lightning flashing, its electrical power coursing through me, that sonic shockwave shaking the earth. I jumped. Jewell Stewark jumped. Both of us made terrified noises.

She said, "I should go."

"You should wait a few minutes. Let this pass."

I turned the television on. Tornado warnings. Cobb County. Fulton County. A tornado had touched down in Marietta, one city over, and that fury was heading toward Smyrna.

The television went off. I looked outside the plantation shutters. Winds. Rains. Bending trees. Darkness arrived. The blackness told me electricity was out. Thunder roared like a wicked beast. I was jittery, bouncing my foot, shaking my leg. It felt like the storm was marching into Cobb County. The skies opened. It was raining hard enough to create a flash flood. That meant there was no way Jewell Stewark could leave here, not without risk of waters rising and sweeping her and her Jaguar out to the Chattahoochee. Not while the winds roared like a freight train heading our way.

In a trembling voice Jewell Stewark said, "Do you have a basement?"

"Yes."

"If you don't mind, we need to get to your basement."

"Let me get my candles and my flashlight."

I went to the pantry, took out three candles, couldn't find my flashlight, looked in all the kitchen drawers, searched until the skies boomed again, then headed out of the kitchen, to the left, and down the carpeted stairs into my basement, my office space. She followed me, car keys and cup of water in her hands, her sandals slapping the back of her feet, that slapping sound reminiscent of her being in my bed.

I took the candles to my desk, lit them, placed all three on my desk, in front of my computer. Licorice. Lavender. Spicy orange. Scents that reminded me of an apartment in Greensboro. Those scents surrounded us, seeped into the air, air that was warming since the power outage had disrupted all things electrical, had stilled my ceiling fans and turned the air conditioner off.

Jewell sat on the futon that was in my space. She sipped her water, stared at the images on my wall, images of my Trinidadian idol, stared at the many books I had in my office.

She said, "That's Hazel Dorothy Scott."

Her eyes moved across my life, evaluated all she saw. She looked at my collection of books, her eyes moving as if she was browsing a library. My personal library. Her attention moved from nonfiction to mystery to literary to erotica to books translated from foreign languages to books on writing. Her eyes violated all I owned. In the end she stared at the books on my desk. I felt naked. Exposed. As if my entire existence was being dissected and analyzed. We had had sadistic moments and now we were chitchatting, trapped in a storm and being emotional and curious creatures, no men here to battle over.

She asked, "What do you do, if you don't mind my asking."

"I'm a writer."

I imagined Ingrid Bergman. Frida. Dorothy Dandridge. Marilyn

Monroe. And of course, Anaïs Nin. I thought of all the artistic women who had endured complicated love affairs, women who felt deeply, women who made hard choices. Sensual women who refused to let their lives wither into bitter regret and desperation. Women who had learned how painful and complicated the *art of being* was.

Rain fell harder. I was a prisoner in my own home, Jewell Stewark my cellmate.

The winds howled and told me that parole was not coming soon.

I stared through my open plantation shutters, the ones on the back of my office leading to my deck, that part of my townhome facing the cluster of trees that separated my unit from the clubhouse and community swimming pool. Anxiety filled me as I regarded the storm and its fury, every cell in my body unnerved by Mother Nature's attitude. Her mood was ruthless, uncontrollable, her every breath volatile.

Jewell Stewark said, "Keep away from the windows."

Not long ago she was contemplating cutting my throat. Now she was saving my life.

I closed the shutters, sat in my office chair, rubbing my temples, let a moment pass.

The skies remained restless, released loud cracks, never-ending rumbles.

The flames from the candles flickered, their flickering sound adding to the pandemonium. Water dripped from the roof of my townhome, fell from trees weighted down by precipitation. Upstairs food was defrosting in my freezer. Ice was thawing in my icemaker. The windows and doors were swelling from the moisture. A million bugs were moving around outside, bugs indigenous to the South. I could hear the liquid sound of humidity, heard the moisture as it was created and formed. Felt each gland in my body as it produced nervous sweat. Heard sweat forming, heard the salty moisture dripping down Jewell Stewark's back, her breathing uneven, still nervous, so very anxious and uncomfortable, trapped here with me, abandoned by her lover and trapped here by Mother Nature.

I looked across the candlelight, our *scandal* light, regarded Jewell Stewark, her skin damp, her red complexion possessing a post-coital glow of shame, her green pupils surrounded by a deep redness. We didn't break our fatigued gaze. Our worn gazes were more empathetic than antagonistic.

My phone vibrated again. My heart raced, I jumped and cursed.

Jewell jumped, startled.

We both shared embarrassed glances.

After three vibrations the *Sex and the City* ring tone played.

I caught my breath, pushed the END button, sent the call to voice mail.

The storm raged. The rain slapped down in increased anger. The skies screamed their fury.

In a terrified voice Jewell Stewark said, "Bathtub."

"What was that?"

"We should get in your bathtub."

"What does that do?"

"My grandmother made us get in bathtubs during storms like this. The more walls between you and a storm the better. So we might have to go into a bathroom and hunker down in a bathtub."

"Hunker down."

"Climb in. Huddle up. Hunker down."

"I have a full bath down here."

"We should take this with us, to cover us."

She motioned at the twin-size mattress on the wooden frame, the Japanese futon.

She said, "If a tornado hits, we can pull that over us. It will block the flying debris. If it comes to that. I hope it doesn't. But you never know. The way it sounds out there, tornadoes might be all over."

I nodded, lips pulled in, fingers nervously running through my hair.

Together we pulled the mattress off the futon, dragged it into the bathroom, leaned it against the wall. I hurried and got the candles, put one on the sink, one on the toilet seat, one on the tank.

She told me to keep away from doors, windows, stoves, sinks, metal pipes, anything that could conduct electricity. She told me to not use the telephone. Then told me I should've disconnected all of my electrical appliances, even the things on the top floor and in the living room, and I should've turned off all the TVs and radios. I took to the stairs, went up top, unplugging as much as I could but not everything, made it back to the basement, breathing hard and sweating. She was sitting in the bathtub, knees to her chest, rocking.

I said, "Now what?"

"We wait. Wait and pray."

Jewell had put her cup of water on the floor and gotten in with her back at the faucets. Did that like she was being polite, saving the most comfortable end for her host. I crawled in the tub.

I said, "Do we need to pull the futon cover over us?"

"Not yet. Keep it leaning against the wall so we can pull it down if we have to."

We sat there, sweating, our bodies touching, the candles flickering. I felt her trembling, her legs shaking. I smelled her sweat. The thunder, the lightning, all of that had her terrified.

She asked, "Which one of them sent you the flowers?"

"They never sent me flowers."

"I saw flowers on your porch."

"You've been watching me?"

"Not you. Him. I drove by looking for him."

"Someone I used to see sent me the flowers. Guy I broke up with, he sent me flowers."

She nodded. "Did you break up with him because of the twins?"

"No. Other issues."

"The flowers weren't from them?"

"Not the twins. Not them. Not from your husband. Not from his brother."

I remembered the plagiarized words from Logan's six-page manifesto. *How do I love thee? Let me count the ways. I love thee to the depth and breadth and height my soul can reach . . .*

I felt Jewell Stewark trembling. She shifted, bumped her head against the faucet.

I asked, "You comfortable down there?"

"I'm okay."

"Let's switch ends."

"No, it's okay. No need to have you bumping your head."

"You might as well turn around. Maybe we can both fit this way."

She stood up, stumbled as the lightning flashed, eased back inside my tub, this tub not as large as the one in the master bedroom. It was unsafe up there in a storm of this magnitude. She had her back to my front, her back against my breasts, her butt against my thighs, both of us squeezed together in a small space in a small cell, body heat against body heat.

She was praying.

I waited for her to finish. When she was done, I shifted, tried to get comfortable. It was impossible. Soft skin against hard porcelain. Her body was soft, much softer than mine. I was trapped between the softness of her skin and the hardness of the tub. So many scents filled this claustrophobic space. Her skin smelled of perfume and Karl. The scent of the Southern rain. The scent of damp wood. The scents from the trees and the dampness from the Georgia red dirt. The scent of three therapeutic candles. It was here settling on me all at once.

The skies boomed. She shook, moved closer to me, meshed into me, afraid to be alone.

She reached for her cup, picked it up, sipped the water again. A gentle sip before wiping her eyes on the back of her hands. Jewell Stewark finished her water. She put the empty cup back on the floor and remained sitting up. She swallowed hard, shivered, then took deep breaths, her nose flaring each time, her chest expanding with each inhale, her eyes closing with every exhale.

Candles flickering. Electricity lighting up the Georgia sky.

A kaleidoscope of fear was in her face. The same fear etched in mine.

She asked, "How did you meet them?"

"Stone Mountain. Running."

"Who came to you first?"

"Karl."

"I'm not surprised."

"Tell me about you and the twins."

"No. Never."

Thunder boomed. She reclined in the tub, a little girl hiding from God's wrath.

She remained close to me, no longer able to tell where my body ended and hers began.

I had nowhere to put my arm, nowhere for it to be comfortable, so I let it rest on her waist. She patted my hand, then she held my hand, held it tight, her hand trembling, still terrified. I touched her in a kind way. The woman who had married one twin, but loved the other.

This was The Jewell of the South. Democrat or Republican, she was the woman Georgia loved as if she was their local Oprah. Inside the city formerly known as Marthasville she was a deity. Inside my home she was a woman who lost the plot and cried like a heartbroken child.

This wasn't real. As she cried she held on to me, a child terrified of the storm.

The scent of sex rising from her body. That scent was too strong, too moving.

I repeated, "Tell me about you and the twins."

"No."

"Tell me about you and Karl. About you and Mark. Tell me how it came to this."

Her heartbeat was powerful, felt the rapid beating coming through her back, felt her rhythm. I knew she could feel mine thumping. I needed to talk to ease my fear.

The Jewell of the South shivered, her voice cracking when she whispered, "Okay. I'll tell you."

"You don't have to."

"I have to tell somebody. I've never told anyone. Holding this inside . . . it's killing me."

FORTY-ONE

Her words were given to me as if they were the shocking pages from her own diary. The unexpurgated version of a corner of time, a small measurement of what, in the end, will be known as the alpha and omega of her existence.

For her it started in her freshman year at Spelman, when she was a teenager, when sex was new and wonderful and taboo, when love was confused for orgasm. When sex was given, bartered for love.

She told me she had seen Karl first. The boy with roots in the islands fascinated her. He was attending Morehouse, the private all-male liberal arts college.

Those campuses were located in the same area, HBCU central, part of the Atlanta University Center academic consortium of historically black colleges and universities. An area populated with upwardly mobile minds attending Clark Atlanta, Spelman, Morehouse, and Morris Brown.

But still populated by men and women. With raging hormones. Where many love affairs began. Where the first heartbreaks happened. Where people had moments that changed them for life.

Her mother died when she was three, her father when she was thirteen. Her mother was closer to her roots in Jamaica, so when her mother passed, so did her connection with Portland Parish. Her father never took her there. He was a blue-collar worker, trips to exotic islands not in his disposable income. They lived in a paycheck-to-paycheck world. Her father took ill. Died suddenly. Ruptured appendix. She'd been living with an aunt since her father passed, spent four years sleeping in the living room on a pull-out sofa.

All of that prefaced her telling me she was a small-town girl who had made it to a major college. With all the educated black men there, it was a small-town woman's heaven. It was a paradise for men as well, especially since the women outnumbered the men by at least ten to one.

She told me that she had seen Karl around campus, had seen him in Greek shows on the yard. For a girl who had grown up surrounded by the rednecks in Paulding County—her city being Dallas, Georgia, a city where it was reported that a uniformed deputy sheriff stood in a parking lot of the courthouse and helped a Klan member put on his sheets—Karl was unique. He was love at first sight. But Karl was Karl; women could seduce him, but none could tame him. Karl was Karl. And he was attending college in an area that had thousands of beautiful black women. She never dated Karl, not then, just wanted to.

Seeing him made her feel high and excited and want to do crazy things.

She told me how much she loved Karl before he knew she existed. But she moved on to other people, other lovers, bad relationships, one abusive, before being on a double date with a friend in Athens, Georgia. And in walked Karl. Or so she thought. For a moment. It wasn't Karl; it was Mark.

She had no idea Karl was a twin. In her mind it was the same man she craved beyond reason.

She followed her desires, went against all she believed in, and abandoned her lover to be with Mark that night. She broke the heart of a man who adored her in order to have passion with the doppelganger of the man she had desired more than anything in the world. She did what she had to do to find happiness.

* * *

She told me about Mark. In the beginning. When everything was perfect.

His kisses were like oysters and champagne, exotic and intoxicating. Kisses were more sensual and arousing than anything. Her arousal so extreme, yet she was shy, had never experienced anything like that, had never been so astounded. With his fingers he stirred her, and with those same fingers he tasted her arousal, savored her arousal, fed her her own arousal. He did things to her no man had ever done. Made her feel so good, tears fell like rain. He taught his naïve lover how to touch his arousal, how to relish his arousal, how to stir him, and she swallowed his love. She wasn't a virgin, but her experience had been limited, only sex, never seduction, never given pleasure in that way, not in the way that opened a woman up, not in a way that opened her heart, in a way that made her live to fulfill his desires.

He took her away on holiday with him.

Karl came along. The man she had wanted for so long was right there with them.

Karl had a date, but something happened between them, and she didn't come on the trip. An argument. They had broken up. Now Karl was single.

So it was her and the twins.

Jamaica. Kingston. Waking up at sunrise and jogging at Emancipation Park. Then off to breakfast. Akee and saltfish. Lobster omelets. Bammie. Mackerel run down. Steamed fish. Plantains. Boiled dumplings. Callaloo. Pastries. Fruit. Going around the city, exploring her roots. Bob Marley Museum. Devon House. University of West Indies. Eating dinner forty-five minutes outside of Kingston at Strawberry Hill. Partying at The Quad. Catching a taxi to Port Royal, the wickedest place in the world, then catching a boat and riding out fifteen minutes to Lime Cay, a slender stretch of land no more than three hundred yards long, playing in the clear blue waters and tanning until way past dusk.

Lots of touching, water games, eating fish, rice, and peas.

Lots of drinking. Too much drinking.

Red Stripe. She had her first Red Stripe on Lime Cay, standing underneath the thatched hut where everyone congregated to buy fish and chicken. Yachts from Miami and Cuba. Everyone half naked. Music filling the air. The twins in swim trunks, no shirts. Her in a two-piece. A thong. Something she never would have worn around anyone she knew. A life in paradise.

Dripping wet, Mark moved across sand, went to the thatched hut, his turn to buy the drinks.

And Karl went to her. Played with her in the water, lifted her up and she put her legs around his thighs. She felt his erection. She looked in his eyes and felt his arousal rubbing against her.

First his hands held her backside. He held her without shame. Aggressive, yet not.

He said, "You have a nice batty."

His arousal was like wood against her. She wanted to move away from him.

She didn't. Couldn't. She smiled.

She was caught up with the aesthetics of the twins. Every woman wanted a good-looking man because every woman wanted good-looking children. The dreams of handsome boys and beautiful girls lived in us all. She relished her feelings. Was openly searching for true love. Thinking that sex came with emotions and those emotions were the road to love.

She knew this was wrong. She was with Mark. Now she was lusting to feel his brother.

Lusting to feel the man she had wanted from the beginning.

She was curious. And curiosity was a powerful aphrodisiac. She was touching Karl, smelling Karl, looking in the eyes of a man who looked exactly like her lover, but wasn't her lover. She wanted to know how much they were alike, if they were the same in all ways, if she would be able to taste, if she would be able to feel a difference.

Karl squeezed her backside, then one hand came up, touched her face, his mouth leaned to hers. She couldn't resist. She wanted to taste him.

In the warmth of the island waters, surrounded by music and people, tongues danced.

One kiss sent her moral compass spinning.

The touching of the tongues had stirred that part of the female soul that perpetuated lust, desire, the need to procreate with a strong warrior, the alpha male who took what he wanted and protected all he had. One kiss anchored her to the shores of joy and misery, one powerful kiss had started it all.

Her body wasn't that of a virgin, but her mind didn't have experience.

One kiss left her confused. One kissed left her terrified.

Yet she didn't run away.

She wanted to explore her options. Expand her horizons.

She kissed him again. This kiss longer, deeper, soul-stealing. She felt Karl. His hand had gone in the water, first his fingers rubbing across her sex, then she felt his erection, he had taken his desire and pressed it against her opening, pushing hard, the only thing keeping him out was her bikini.

In public. In the warm waters in her homeland. Never in her life, never in her life.

Dizzy, she looked toward the shores, saw Mark standing there, three Red Stripes in hand.

She separated herself from Karl, hurried toward Mark, head down, ashamed, felt shaky, as if she was sleepwalking in paradise. She was nervous and excited. She had coveted her boyfriend's brother. As she left the waters, as she adjusted her swimming suit, as she wiped water from her face and took to the sand, she was afraid to look Mark in his eyes. Afraid to go to him, but afraid not to as well.

She had been enchanted by two men.

Karl stayed in the water, his arousal too obvious to return to shore undetected.

Mark stared at Karl. And Karl returned the stare.

Karl broke his stare first, swam out into the clear waters, headed toward the yachts, toward people being buck wild, enjoying life to the fullest, toward the other half-naked women who were partying.

Mark didn't say anything. Sat on a towel next to her, drank his Red Stripe, handed her one, sat the other next to him, said nothing about her kissing his brother, said nothing about his brother kissing her. She was ready to blame it on the beer, on Karl, on anything that would make it better.

It felt as if hell was about to break loose.

She held Mark's hand, felt his jealousy, afraid he wouldn't like her anymore.

But her eyes were on Karl.

His kiss, his touch, that had stirred her.

Karl looked like Mark, but he was nothing like Mark, not to her sense of touch and taste.

She said, "Mark, your brother is hitting on me."

He nodded. "I know."

"What are you going to do about it?"

"*You* kissed *him.*"

"*He* kissed *me.*"

"If you say."

"The devil made me do it."

"Well, the devil sure has your nipples hard."

She looked down at her top, no breasts to speak of, but her nipples stood tall.

She asked, "What would you like me to do about it?"

Mark sipped his Red Stripe, shrugged. "I could ask you the same."

"What are you saying?"

"Maybe you should ask the devil."

"Are you going to say something to him?"

He shook his head, his voice now sarcastic. "Maybe you should sleep with him."

"I don't want to sleep with your brother."

"I think you want to sleep with him."

"Is that what you would like?"

His voice turned bitter and cold. "Maybe that's what you would like."

Mark stood, finished one beer, started another, headed down the beach, left her in the sand.

Pissed off, she went back to the waters, swam to Karl.

And she kissed him again.

When she looked to shore, Mark was sipping his Red Stripe, his face saying he was unaffected, his body language contradicting the nonchalance of his facial cast.

She didn't understand.

She was traditional. Had been taught that sex was sacred. Sex was to happen between two people. She embraced that school of thinking. Sex was created for marriage, created to help forge a long-lasting commitment between a couple. Outside of marriage, sex was taboo, had harsh consequences. Pregnancy, diseases, guilt, insecurity, and shame. A relationship based on lust could only last as long as the two were physically close and found each other sexually attractive.

That night when they were back at the Hilton, Mark told her he was going to the bar. Said he would be gone for a couple of hours. Was going to sit out in the warmth of the night and listen to the band.

She told him she would be down after she had dressed.

Mark left.

Soon there was a tap on the door.

Karl.

She let him in. She let lust into the room.

She didn't resist. Didn't try to resist. She wanted him too bad.

It was wrong, yet she wanted him.

But that was shallow.

Following lust was shallow.

Still.

She followed her lust.

She confused orgasm with love. Over and over.

She went to Karl's room. Stayed there that night.

Three times that night he took her slow, three times that night he went deep. Kept going slow and deep. Kept taking her from behind, bending her over, and she was feeling all of him, every thrust.

She went back to Mark the next morning.

Found him sitting on the patio, naked as the day he was born, staring out at the sunrise.

He turned and looked at her as soon as she entered the room.

He had been waiting.

He went to her. Touched her face, her hair.

He whispered, "You know I love you, right?"

She nodded.

He smiled a hurt smile. "You can't say it back, can you?"

She smiled, but didn't answer.

He didn't question where she was, just took her, showered her, and gave her orgasm.

Took his orgasm as the bathroom steamed, as moans echoed for the island to hear.

The next morning they were all at breakfast, talking, eating akee and saltfish, bammie, drinking coffee and pineapple juice, the brothers talking as if nothing was different, as if nothing had changed.

As if nothing was abnormal.

Jewell Stewark told me that they moved their holiday to another part of her homeland.

Traveled from Kingston to the western tip of Jamaica, to Negril, again swimming and snorkeling in the coral reef, walking white sand beaches, taking in the grotto-lined cliffs that stretched to the old Negril Lighthouse. Watching the locals dive off thirty-foot cliffs at Rick's Cafe. Barbeques and dancing, a nonstop party. The touching. By then the kissing was open. Done in front of the brothers.

They had a presidential suite. Two bedrooms. Full kitchen. Wet bar. Overlooking the sea.

Mark took her to bed. Undressed her. Undressed himself. Was making love to her with his tongue, and fingers. And Karl came into their bedroom. The door wasn't locked. Mark had left the door unlocked. And the door hadn't been closed, not all the way. Karl looked at her.

As Mark made love to her with mouth, tongue, and fingers, she looked at Karl.

Karl undressed.

She remembered feeling uncomfortable. Scared. Maybe cheap. Being taken advantage of.

Yet she was excited.

Excited to break away from all conventions and play the part of the seductress.

Excited to be the irresistible whore.

It was as if Mark knew she had wanted Karl, had given her space, allowed her to explore, allowed her to experiment, to feed her craving. Mark had given her Karl. Had allowed her sexual freedom.

It was as if Mark had accepted her, had given her permission to fulfill her fantasy with Karl.

She didn't take them at the same time, only one at a time, anything more would have been too much for her inexperienced mind to be able to handle. She did it with her eyes closed. Most of it.

Karl had licked her yoni until she was dripping like a ripe mango.

Mark had done the same.

After two nights of fun and passion in Negril, the last few days in Montego Bay had their own rhythm. She surrendered herself to them, took in all the pleasure they could give her, let them teach her things. With enough alcohol in her, she got in the bed with both of them, tried things she never would have imagined herself doing. They excited her. Aroused her. Had her living an adventurous lifestyle.

Twenty-one times. They gave her what she wanted twenty-one times.

Every time she had sex she wanted more pleasure, and at the same time she needed more than pleasure. They gave her love and sex twenty-one times. With every penetration she became emotional, more vulnerable. She was in a struggle, trying not to lose the plot because she enjoyed the sex, but she wanted more. Twenty-one times, nonstop fucking, countless orgasms, each orgasm feeling like love.

Jewell Stewark said, "But what happened that night might have changed everything."

"I'm listening."

"No, this is too embarrassing."

"Tell me."

"Mark asked me if I loved Karl."

"And you said?"

"I told him to not ask me that."

"And he said?"

"Karl will fuck you, but he will never love you."

"And you said?"

"I cried. The way he said it, the nasty way he said it, he made it sound like I started it."

"What did you say to him telling you that?"

"He hurt me. I know it makes no sense, but his words hurt me.

In anger I told Mark that maybe I would sleep with him and never love him. I would torture him. I told him maybe I'd allow Karl to sleep with me because I felt as if I could love him and the best fuck was the fuck of love. That angered him. I wanted him angry. Him being so willing to share me angered me."

"You wanted him to fight for you."

"Yes."

"But he allowed you to do what you wanted to do."

"He gave me to another man. To his brother. I wasn't used to that, wasn't raised in that way. So I gave in to my anger. I told Mark if he drank Irish moss all day and night, he could build his stamina and could fuck me with all the jealousy he could muster, he could make me climb the walls, could fuck me into being his wife, but he could never fuck me into love."

"What did he do?"

"He tried to push me out of the bed."

"Pushed you?"

"He told me I could go to Karl."

"Did you go to Karl?"

"No. I cared for Mark. I was attracted to Karl, yes, but I was with Mark. The attention felt good, but I wanted Mark to stop it. I wanted him to see it going too far and get upset and make it all stop. I wanted him to not want any other man to touch me. But he allowed it. I was angry that he allowed it to happen. And with forethought he had let Karl come inside our room and have his way with me. Yes, I enjoyed it, but yes I was angry. I just wanted Mark angry. Needed to know he felt something for me. I needed to feel valued, not devalued, feel special when I was in his arms."

"He allowed you to make your own choices."

"I wanted him to man-up and shut it down."

"He gave you your freedom to chose the type of woman you wanted to be."

"I wanted him to claim me."

"But you were with Mark and wanting to be with Karl."

She paused. "Yes."

I felt the weight of her desire, pyramids of emotions built over time.

As I treaded in her deepening emotions, I paused a moment.

I paused because my memories were so heavy that the shelves that held the journals of my mind were about to collapse. Like Jewell, I too had succumbed to an unforeseen temptation.

Jealousy manifested itself, always reared its ugly head when relationships reached the physical. Maybe that was a flaw in the human design, to be possessive, to struggle with the desire to own what was not ownable, a constant need to enslave others and chain them to our own needs and desires. If not to enslave, then to be enslaved, led, given instructions on how to live. Or maybe the emotion known as jealousy was there intentionally, to keep lovers together, to force them to protect their nests with a fury. But still. I wondered. I had been resentful in Greensboro. Envious of Kiki Sunshine. But I felt as if I had overcome that jealousy. I'd been able to remain in the afterglow with my identical sins, but maybe because I knew they were leaving with me, in my mind that gave me control, and my being there, even if Mark was married, even if Karl had Kenya's image tattooed on his flesh, I had earned squatter's rights, had made them my chattels to take along if I chose to give in to my rising emotions and do so.

I'd been jealous of the way Mark made Kiki Sunshine moan, of the way she made him come, jealous of the way she had taken Mark and Karl as if she were destined to win the Frankie of the Year award. She had moaned louder than I moaned. She had come faster than I had come.

In that act, as they were experiencing her body, as I trembled and sweated and recovered from my pleasure, she had owned them both. Because what was inside her body belonged to her.

Kiki Sunshine had owned them well.

As she, in our own secret moment, had owned me.

She had owned me as I had owned her.

That would never happen again.

In a soft voice that masked my swelling envy, I told Jewell Stewark, "Tell me more."

"No."

"*Yes*. Tell me more."

Karl left the next morning.

He said he would be back in a while, took a taxi, and came back with another woman. Jewell thought Karl had gone and picked up a female rent-a-dred, an island girl for hire, but she wasn't. Dark complexion with gray eyes, slender, almost six feet tall, hair black and bone-straight, a tattoo of the sun on her stomach, bangles on her arms, a tongue ring that showed with her every word, like she was an erotic and exotic pirate, a descendant of the people in Port Royal. Her name was Kenya. He had made up with his off-and-on lover girl, flown her in for the last few days of vacation. She thought Kenya was Jamaican, but she was not. Her father was African, from Kenya, but she had never been there. She had been born in Oden-ville, Alabama, but had grown up in Atlanta, for the most part. Kenya was standoffish, vague, defensive. But she did mention her father was in Georgia, lived in Stone Mountain. She said nothing about her mother. Jewell said she met Kenya briefly, their initial conversation, that questioning lasting no more than five minutes. Threatened by her presence, she didn't care for Kenya, was uncomfortable, her jealousy hidden, and in the middle of their tête-à-tête, Karl came and pulled Kenya away from Jewell's interrogation, then he and Kenya vanished for two days.

In between, Jewell left with Mark, had hired a car and driven the rugged roads of Jamaica into Portland Parish, over the bumpy, narrow, and pothole-filled roads that led through the rural areas where African slave labor had once been used to cultivate sugarcane and coffee, was with Mark on a short trip in search of her roots, but her mind was too preoccupied to appreciate the journey and conversations about the Maroons, the runaway slaves who used to live in the Blue and John Crow Mountains, slaves that had stood up for their rights and refused to let the British recapture them and take over the land.

She had felt Karl grow inside her mouth. Had allowed him to fill her in other ways, but taking him in her mouth was so personal, something that should only happen between a husband and a wife, had felt him pulsating, had experienced his taste, had done it for pleasure but also to be pleased.

He had come in her mouth.

She had swallowed his seeds for him.

Then he had moved on.

Now Kenya had arrived and Jewell felt disrespected, felt her heart aching, felt her soul withering because her affair with the love of her life had been obliterated.

She had been effaced, as each woman was destined to become effaced by the next.

So it goes.

Mark was making love to Jewell while she longed for Karl, while she wished she could feel as emotionally and physically connected to Mark as he felt to her. He had been her emotional security.

Karl was fucking her, making her scream and beg for mercy, controlling her while she made love to him, and as she came she prayed for emotional reciprocity. He had been her desires unleashed.

Like tasting heaven and hell.

She had been left to Mark. And her sensation of contemptuousness. Her feelings of betrayal.

What she had done was taboo. Had gone against everything that she had been taught as a nice young Christian girl from the South. Was scared. Tried to blame them. Tried to blame Karl. Tried to blame Jamaica, the land of celebrated hedonism and mass nude weddings, but she knew there was more to Jamaica than perpetual sex. She told herself she had been used, coaxed, and liquored up. That they had planned this, had made her comfortable. And she was naïve, was just going with the flow.

Karl had left with Kenya. The beautiful dark-skinned girl with the wonderful breasts. Karl wrapped himself around Kenya, kissed Kenya in front of her, held Kenya with so much affection. In front of her face. As if she were nothing to him.

Jewell felt ashamed. But she had done something that she had secretly wanted to do.

She had experienced so much pleasure.

Maybe it would happen again. Maybe after Kenya was gone, it would return to normal.

Two days went by.

Back in Negril. Two nights of hearing Karl making love to Kenya were the start of madness.

The next day they were all at the pool. Jewell's mind remained on Lime Cay, Karl touching her, kissing her, that first kiss forever with her, how they had felt in the water, her hands on his back, her legs around his waist. Now Karl was in the pool doing the same thing with Kenya. They were in the pool, in the Jamaican sun, hugging, so close, Kenya putting sweet kisses on his face, water dripping from her hair. Her legs around his thighs. His hands under her ass.

The way Kenya was holding him, how she closed her eyes and kissed him, how she kissed him and couldn't stop kissing him, kissed him as if he was deep inside her, stirring her emotions.

The way she was bouncing up and down, the way they were exchanging deep tongue kisses, they had to be having sex.

In front of everyone they were fucking.

On the third night, after drinks, after partying, Jewell rested in Mark's arms.

Karl's room was next door. An adjacent suite. She heard him with Kenya. Talking. Laughing. The laughter ended. Followed by silence. The hums grew inside the silence. The hums that became a stream of sexual moaning. Every moan fractured her. Soon the love-making sounded violent, abusive, passionate.

She heard Kenya's voluptuous orgasm, heard Karl announcing his love for her as he came.

What had been fractured became shattered.

Her heart was filled with love for Karl. She wanted her wayward lover to come back.

His taste remained in her mouth.

His taste forever lingered on her tongue.

She remained with Mark, pining for his brother.

Brows furrowed she asked, "Who is Kenya?"

"He loves her."

"So she's his . . . girlfriend?"

"She's his fiancée."

"They're getting married?"

"They're engaged."

Her breathing halted. Insult opened injury wider.

She said, "But he wasn't . . . he wasn't acting like that . . . when we . . . when all of us . . . you know."

"Karl is being Karl."

"Meaning?"

"A Bajan man's favorite pastime is making love to beautiful ladies."

"Is it yours?"

"I want you. Just you. Would love you to feel the same way."

"So Karl is just being Karl."

"Karl is being Karl. He'll fly beautiful women with agendas to wherever he is to keep him company. He'll wine and dine them at the fanciest restaurants. He'll share his bed with three at a time."

He'd been with her and now he'd moved seamlessly, effortlessly to Kenya.

She asked, "Have you slept with Kenya?"

"No."

"Why don't I believe you?"

"Guilt, perhaps?"

She swallowed, shifted, knew Mark was being candid, wished he was lying, wanted to hate him.

She asked, "And this is his fiancée?"

"This is the one he's in love with."

"You wouldn't sleep with the woman he loved."

"No."

"That's where you and your brother are different."

"Yes."

She listened to them, their moans slipping through the doors that separated their suites, moans that went on into the night, a moment of peace, then restarting almost as soon as they ended.

Karl was emotionally available to Kenya. He'd only give his soul to Kenya.

Jewell drank another Red Stripe, tried to numb the torture, her world becoming lighter. Done with one beer she immediately took another. Soon she was on her third Red Stripe. The world no longer real to her.

Sipping her lager and distorting what was left of her reality. Sipping and lying in the bed with Mark. Her legs bouncing as he held her from behind. Her eyes were to the wall. Staring. Looking deep into the wall. The sound of Kenya and Karl having sex was too much for her inebriated ears to bear.

It was too strong. The sounds were creating mental images that caused her to sit up and glower at the wall. Her agony so strong that she finished the lager and took to Mark. Pulled him on top of her.

In a weak accent she whispered, "Part mi walls. Give mi a proper fix."

"You're full-blooded Jamaican now."

"Mi always Jamaican, mon."

"What do you want, Jewell?"

"Agony. Mi wan de agony."

She took Mark inside her body but her mind was wanting Karl to fill that heated space with love and lust. Karl was inside her heart, inside her head. She closed her eyes and tried to pretend Mark was Karl. Mark was wicked with her, intense and envious, delivered orgasm with the aplomb of a veteran.

In the adjoining room Karl was doing the same with Kenya, their sounds now peppered with profanity and vulgarities, the kind that came when the loving was good beyond reason. Kenya. A moaner. A woman who released herself and let the world know pleasure had taken over. It sounded like they were making a pornographic movie in the next room. It sounded powerful and inexhaustible.

Mark told Jewell how beautiful she was. In the Jamaican humidity, he kissed her sweaty face, told her she was special. Said he loved the way they fit together. Said it was perfect. The way he touched her face, rubbed her, tasted her arousal, licked her arousal, the way he had given her his arousal as he savored hers, all of those new things had her feeling that this was love, that only a man who loved her would do all of those wonderful things to her mind and body, only love felt that way.

She took to Mark, allowed Mark deeper inside her, wanted him to erase the desire.

Jewell released herself, let her arousal be heard from Montego Bay to Port Antonio.

She was determined to be the last one to moan.

She would be heard last. She would be heard by Karl. She would deafen his ears.

Her voice would outlast Kenya's.

* * *

After the next sunrise they had breakfast and walked the beach, Kenya and Karl strolling hand-in-hand leading the way, creating a path in the burning sand, footprints Jewell was forced to follow in silence. Jewell's eyes were longing for the waves to erode Kenya's footprint from her life.

Many thoughts and feelings went through her mind and body, her emotions on fire as she watched the man she longed for walk the streets hand-in-hand with someone else, her eyes on him, watching him, studying him, darting away to hide shame and guilt whenever she felt Kenya noticing her lingering gaze.

No matter how many orgasms Mark gave her, Karl commoved her.

Small talk with Kenya became difficult. She wanted to dissect Kenya. Pick her apart, determine what made her special. Kenya had nothing else to say, was more interested in Karl than conversation.

And Karl, the way he took his Nikon and photographed Kenya over and over, she was all he was interested in. He photographed every little thing Kenya did, worshipped her with his camera.

Kenya. Her breasts were a strong A cup, not a bad size for her frame, didn't distract from her small waist and ass, but still she had enough cleavage to put on display, revealing their brownness.

Jewell looked at her own fair complexion, at her breasts; breasts that were unable to compete.

She took Mark's hand. Mark held her hand tight.

She moved Mark's hand to her backside, had him hold Mother Jamaica as they walked.

That part of her was born in the islands. That part of her all men praised.

The part of her that, in her mind, owned the least value, yet opened many doors for her.

Again Karl and Kenya vanished.

Hours went by.

Hours that had left her jittery, watching the clock, waiting, imagining.

When Karl and Kenya returned, Karl no longer looked like Mark's identical twin. Karl had returned with Kenya's image tattooed into his flesh, the image of Kenya with the wings of an angel.

Karl had given her attention, made her feel like a woman, then abandoned her.

Left her feeling as if her only value rested in her yoni. Inside her vagina. He only wanted her pussy; liquor and conversation was the road to seduction, his route to it being given willingly.

The moment Kenya stepped away, the moment Karl was alone, Jewell confronted him.

With an angered smile she asked, "Why are you doing this in my face?"

"Doing what in your face?"

"Kenya. Why are you messing with her in my face?"

"I'm not obligated to you."

"So what we did, what you did to me, that meant nothing to you?"

"Don't trip."

"Don't trip?"

"Calm down."

"I'm going to tell her about me and Mark."

"Calm down."

"Let my wrist go."

"Not until you *calm the fuck down*."

"I'm going to tell her about me and you."

"No, you're not."

"I'm going to tell her about all of us. She deserves to know."

"Don't be selfish."

"Aren't we all selfish in some ways, at some time?"

"Then don't be a fucking bitch and start some shit when shit doesn't need to be started."

Karl talked to her without sugarcoating, spoke to her with the same arrogance he spoke to other men, which was the same way he spoke to most women. All but Kenya. He spoke to Kenya with that tone of love and subservience. He would kiss Kenya in front of her, kissed many women in front of her, but never kissed or touched another woman in front of Kenya. He would rub on Kenya in front of her, damn near fuck Kenya in front of her, but when it came to that level of intimacy, before he crossed the line, he always took Kenya away, had her to himself, as if she was the prize of all prizes.

With Kenya it was as if Karl was trying to be who she needed him to be.

With Jewell, Karl didn't hide anything. He put everything on the table.

With Kenya, Karl tried to maintain the image of being the perfect man.

Karl said, "Yes, I enjoy you and I enjoy other women."

Enjoy. His word of choice had been *enjoy.*

Like he had said I *enjoy* Chinese food but I also *enjoy* Italian. I *enjoy* riding in a Mercedes-Benz but I *enjoy* handling a MINI Cooper as well. He had *enjoyed* her and now he was *enjoying* Kenya. He *enjoyed* pussy that originated in Jamaica, but he also *enjoyed* pussy that originated in Africa.

He touched Jewell's face. She was angry, but didn't pull away.

He said, "Keep this between us."

"No."

Karl kissed her. His kiss better than oysters and champagne. His kiss was like chocolate and cognac. His kiss created an earthy high and was as addictive as Lady Godiva.

He whispered, "Don't trip."

The kiss left her disoriented, confused. She asked, "Will we be together again?"

"Not if you tell Kenya."

"So we will be together again?"

He repeated, "Not if you tell Kenya."

He kissed her again, gave her his tongue.

She melted.

In that moment Jewell envisioned her breasts in his pillow, her ass hiked in the air for him. She envisioned his kisses on her skin. She envisioned a victorious return to paradise.

With her. With Karl. With Mark.

She envisioned abnormal desires once again coming to life.

He told her an old Barbadian proverb, whispered, "What she eye no see, her stomach will take."

He was telling her that what Kenya didn't know couldn't hurt her.

When she had calmed down, he touched her with kindness and whispered, his voice filled with caring, filled with unselfish love as he added, "And Mark loves you. Please don't hurt my brother."

"Don't hurt your brother."

"Home drums beat first."

"What are you saying?"

"I have to think about family before I think about myself. You should do the same."

He was asking her, pleading with her to be kind, for Kenya's sake, for Mark's sake, begged her to not be selfish, to not cause pain and destruction, to allow everyone to enjoy living in paradise.

He wanted to elongate the lie they were living, stretch it from here to eternity.

She nodded.

Karl headed back to Kenya.

She went back to Mark.

That dizzying kiss on her lips. That patronizing kiss of hope making her tingle.

But still. You couldn't ask a mongoose to watch a chicken. The temptation was too strong.

She stared at Karl, the wonderful way he treated Kenya, the kissing and touching, the flirting that never ended, saw him treating Kenya how she wanted him to treat her, heard him making love to her and wishing those moans were her moans, and in the middle of the night, as Karl fucked Kenya, as Jewell made love to Mark at the same moment, her moans competing with Kenya's moans, as she held Mark and felt him swelling inside her, as she heard Mark telling her how much he loved her, as she didn't respond to his adoration with reciprocation, as Mark started to moan and come, Jewell couldn't take it anymore, couldn't stand the sounds of Kenya's orgasmic moans, couldn't stand the thought of Karl touching Kenya like that and refusing her in this moment, and she pushed Mark away from her, left Mark sweating and writhing and moaning and spilling his love for her on rented sheets, and she struggled to find her balance, wiped sweat from her eyes and staggered through Kenya's moans, her body naked, defenseless against Kenya's maddening sounds, and Jewell pushed each scream of pleasure to the side, moved through them as if she was fighting through ocean waves, the tides high and strong, fought her way against the undertow of Kenya's rising pleasure, and pushed open the door to the other bedroom, saw Kenya on top of Karl, her head thrown back, eyes tight, mouth in the shape of the letter O, bouncing up and down on Karl, Karl holding her waist, his orgasmic grunts blending with her moans, adding fury to fury, creating the perfect storm, the moans now too thick to swim through, moans that were not only torrent but owned the viscosity of quicksand, moans that were pulling her under in her struggle to regain freedom.

Jewell screamed like every inch of her skin was being peeled away from her body.

Her scream shattered all orgasms.

Her scream made Kenya fall away from Karl, her orgasm interrupted by the sound of horror.

Karl sat up, his orgasm incomplete, but continuing despite the shock in his eyes.

Moans ended, subdued by panic and shock. They saw Jewell in her nakedness, in her agony.

First there was nothing. Then there were the sounds that existed behind sounds.

The sounds of labored and panicked breathing arrived, crashed over everyone at the same time, as if everyone had held their breath and was now breathing once again, all at once, all out of rhythm.

The way Jewell was looking, it was easy to prognosticate what was going to happen next, the outcome of the evening was written all over her face, was held in her hysterical body language.

Jewell said, "Kenya, I *have* to tell you something. About Karl. About us. About all of us."

She heard his heavy breathing first. His hand touched her, tried to pull her back to the other room. Mark was standing behind her. Naked as well. Trying to tow and tug her back to their room.

But it was too late. Red Stripe lager in her veins and envy in her heart, it was too late.

It had been put out there.

Kenya stood up, naked, sweat-ridden, her face reddened by pleasure and surprise, her hands between her legs, hiding herself as she stared at Karl, as she stared at Mark, as she stared at Jewell.

She wanted to know what the *fuck* was going on.

Four naked people.

Coitus interruptus four times over.

The scents of love and shock and fear and jealousy and frustration dancing in the air.

In a court of law, what had happened might be considered an excited utterance.

An excited utterance was something said with spontaneity, an uncontrollable outburst, words that didn't come on the wings of a well-thought-out fabrication, words that flowed from a troubled soul while living under the stress of excitement. Or words that flowed when the pain was too deep to bear.

This was her excited utterance. This was the drunken confession she could not keep within.

Karl tried to drown out her words.

Mark tried to tow her back into their bedroom, that struggle futile, she wasn't moving.

The twins failed.

Jewell told Kenya. She told Kenya what had happened between all of them. She said that she was trying to protect her from them, saying the things all scorned women said, all women who felt they had been made a fool of, trying to spin the situation, give morality to a situation that was never rooted in morality, each word the echo of feeling betrayed, the song of feeling stupid, the voice of revenge.

Kenya needed clarity.

Yes, Karl had been intimate with Jewell.

Yes, right before she arrived.

Yes, Jewell had been intimate with Karl, and Mark knew about it.

Yes, she had made love to both of them, had taken them one at a time.

Yes, consecutively.

No, never concurrently.

Yes, that is what was going on.

Kenya stood near the bed, naked, her trembling hands covering her mouth, her eyes wide.

Kenya screamed. Sweat raining from her flesh, Kenya closed her eyes and screamed. Screamed like she was drowning. Screamed like the quicksand was up to her neck.

This was a moment that would change her forever. A new pain that was a rite of passage.

Karl lowered his head.

Kenya slapped him. She slapped her brand-new fiancé. She slapped him like she was trying to slap the tattoo of her image off his skin. Struck him over and over and over, each slap echoing in the humid room, the dampness from his flesh magnifying each blow, each time it sounded as if her hand wanted to stick to his flesh. She beat him until he was forced to cover his face. Mark took a step into the room, but stopped at the edge of the escalating violence. He knew better. They were twins. This was his brother. But even twins were born separately. They had their own entrances into the world. No matter how close, sometimes they had to do battle alone. Kenya cried and cursed and beat and slapped Karl, jumped on him, pounded him with fists, each blow doing no damage, none that could be seen.

She beat Karl until she was exhausted, her hair wild, sweat dripping from her skin like tears.

Out of breath, Kenya cursed them all, her chest heaving as she called them names that were beyond unkind. Tears in her eyes, Kenya stormed into the bathroom, slammed the door.

Karl and Mark were staring at Jewell. Anger. Disappointment. Jealousy.

Jewell turned away, went back to her bedroom, sat on the bed, wiping her eyes.

Mark came to the room, silent, leaned against the dresser, his head down, his head shaking.

Karl went to the bathroom door, pleading with Kenya to let him in, his pleas unanswered.

Within the hour Kenya had packed, her packing loud and disturbing, filled with curses and speeches and pleas from Karl to at least stay until morning, pleas to wait until then and talk.

Kenya came to the bedroom door, stared at Jewell, that stare filling the room with ice.

Kenya snapped, "You're staying here with them?"

"I was wrong. I'm sorry . . . I never should have said anything. It was the beer. I had too much beer. Don't leave him like this. He's so upset. He's really hurting. You hear him? He's hurting bad. He really loves you. He really does. I'll take the blame for this. I was just . . . just confused. I was infatuated. Mark is my boyfriend. I'm with Mark. Karl means *nothing* to me. We'd been drinking, things got out of control. I knew better. It was my fault. Be mad at me, not him. Just don't leave him like that. Please?"

There was a long pause.

A pause and silence that caused her to raise her head, raise her eyes and look at Kenya.

Kenya was standing there, waiting, wanting to look in her eyes.

The look on Kenya's face, the way her beauty had changed to something vile, her mouth tight, her neck tight, as if her mouth was filled with a mixture of Buckley's, castor oil, and Father John's.

Lips trembling, Kenya stared Jewell down, that stare penetrating Jewell, terrifying Jewell.

"Sick bitch." Kenya growled and shook her head. "Then this is where you belong."

Jewell wiped her eyes, every part of her body shaking, wanting Kenya to leave her alone.

Kenya went off on Jewell, cursed her out, called her stupid, called her a whore, called her jealous, told her she had seen the way Jewell had been staring at her since she arrived, told her she sensed something, but what she sensed didn't make any sense, thought it was jealousy and hatred based on complexion, based on class, never dreamed it was because she was fucking Karl and his brother.

She cursed Jewell as if it was all her fault.

When she was done lashing out at Jewell, she gave Mark the same anger and disrespect.

She cursed Karl, asked him why did he disrespect her by bringing her there, said she had enough drama.

She told them all to go fuck themselves and each other and whatever else they wanted to fuck.

Kenya left the room, her sandals slapping the tiled floor, the wheels of her luggage click-clacking across the grout in the tile, her luggage off balance and bumping the walls, her departure loud and violent. Jewell heard Karl, begging her to stay, to not go, telling her he loved her, that Jewell meant nothing to him, that it was blown out of proportion, saying things that made no sense, desperate things inspired by fear, driven by the fear of losing the one thing, the one woman he claimed to love.

Desperate. Karl had sounded so desperate.

The door to the hotel opened and closed.

Kenya was gone.

There was silence. The silence that came at the end of a tsunami, the silence that arrived after all had been destroyed, the silence that covered the survivors as they stared in disbelief.

Jewell wiped her tears and smiled. Not a wicked smile.

An emotional smile rooted in pain, not victory. She had hurt Karl as Karl had hurt her.

Kenya had left Karl because, as far as she knew, Karl had made one mistake.

But love was like skydiving, one mistake could be fatal.

Karl remained in his room, naked, angered, jaw tight, eyes blood-red, fractured and heartbroken.

Jewell smiled her own heartbroken smile. As if she was his emotional twin.

Mark came back to the room, his head down, disappointed more than angered.

The heat. The excitement. The Red Stripe that had her inebriated.

She ran to the bathroom, fell on her knees and prayed to the porcelain god.

Everything came up. Akee. Saltfish. Plantains. Red Stripe. Bammy. Everything she had eaten came out of her body, left her retching behind a locked bathroom door.

She heard Mark calling her name, shaking the handle on the door.

In between retches, she told him to go away.

She stayed in the bathroom until she was done, stayed in her own smells, her own sickness. Sweat covering her body. Dizziness holding her down inside her nightmare.

When the illness was under control, she cleaned herself up. Cleaned the bathroom. Showered, scrubbed her body with hot water, then let cold water run over her heated body, sat down in the bathtub, let that water fall over her body and through her hair, attempted to baptize herself with sanity.

Then she was scared to leave the bathroom. Scared to go back and see the damage she'd done.

Taps came on the bathroom door, soft taps that sounded like shots from a cannon.

Her head ached. Dehydration was the beast she wrestled with now.

Without drying off, her hair dripping wet, she unlocked the bathroom door.

Mark was in the hallway, waiting, worried.

Jewell kissed Mark. She took him to the shower, had him clean himself, then she took his hand, pulled his wet body toward their bed. She needed Mark, needed to *not* lose him too.

She took to Mark. Made him moan. Allowed him to give her orgasms over and over.

Some real. Some faked.

All loud enough to cause Karl to bang on the door and scream for her to shut the fuck up.

Loud enough to cause Jewell to smile her inebriated smile.

In Jewell's mind, her emotional barometer told her Mark treated her like a lady.

But another part, a deeper part of her spirit, told her Karl had made her feel like a woman.

She had been exposed to both kindness and suicidal dick, the latter having the most power.

She listened to the things a man said during sex as if his words were gospel, his moans the punctuation to the words driven by heat and lust, took his orgasm to be a commitment to nurturing her soul. She didn't understand that men said anything to get sex and hardly remembered what they said during sex.

She held Mark, kissed Mark, made love to Mark with the same intensity and emotion he had when he made love to her, said his name over and over as if language had diminished and that was the only word she knew, the only noun she was capable of uttering, came as he came, then as he held her, she cried.

The tears were real. She made joyful noises but her tears were not tears of joy.

Orgasm had been the great deceiver.

Just because someone made you come, just because you felt like they were making love to you, just because you felt like you were making love to them, just because you called God or saw Harriet Tubman, just because you had visions of Anaïs, that didn't mean it was love, didn't make you special.

She had never been able to separate emotional needs from physical desire, one was tethered to the other. That symbiotic relationship between the physical and the emotional—between her needs and wants—had left her, in some ways, handicapped; had left her brain, despite all of her learning at Spelman and experiences in the real world, incapable of distinguishing between making love and fucking.

Jewell did not travel that road alone.

At times I couldn't tell the difference. At times I was handicapped.

I asked her what happened to Kenya, asked about the woman with African roots whose image was forever a part of Karl's flesh, the image that caused him to pause and think every time he undressed.

She told me Kenya was gone. Had moved on to another man, leaving the engagement ring behind. Her exiting in tears, devastated, ending their love affair without closure, her leaving Karl in the state of love without resolution, he was forever changed, traumatized, shattered, looking and acting like he was ready to commit suicide to ease his suffering. Karl did kill himself. For Kenya he killed himself.

He killed himself the way all damaged men did. By bedding another woman.

First he came to Jewell. Renewed her hope. Gave her his frustrations.

Once again he *enjoyed* her.

Soon after hope was renewed, Karl went back to *enjoying* woman after woman.

Karl and his expensive Nikon cameras, all the wanna-be models that flocked to him, women who, in Jewell's bitter opinion, were vain beyond reason, women who gladly undressed in order to capture their egos on film, women who exposed themselves, women who gave themselves to her lothario.

Karl was being Karl.

Living in pain, he drowned himself in pleasure, as if he was trying to swim upstream and return to the womb, as if he was trying to be unborn, as if he was trying to leave Mark in this world alone.

Mark remained her boyfriend, the one she clung to emotionally. The one Jewell stayed with to be close to the lover she really wanted. To be close to the love she desired. She remained with Mark in order to stay close to Karl. The one whose touch was hotter than a thousand orgasms in the sun.

The one who, despite her common sense, despite her reasoning, continued to commove her.

The one she told herself she would wait for.

But seasons changed.

She wanted a husband. Karl wasn't the marrying type. And

when the time came, he wasn't the type of man she wanted to become the father of her children. No, Karl didn't want her in that way.

Mark wanted to marry her. Had always wanted her to be his wife. Love at first sight.

Every woman had to consider her options.

Karl didn't go back to Barbados to attend the lavish wedding at Sandy Lane. Didn't stand at his brother's side as his best man. Didn't appear at the reception. There were no photos of the three of them together, none since the holiday on the island of Jamaica. He'd declined the invitation to be the photographer. Maybe that was because he had lost Kenya because of Jewell. Or maybe Karl, in his own way, had some morals. Maybe he saw the hypocrisy, maybe he knew right and wrong, despite his choices.

These were Jewell Stewark's recollections. Memoirs colored by obsession were not memories that echoed the truth. Those memories were her truth, but not *the* truth. They were not Mark's truth. They were not Karl's truth. Only her truth. The truth as she saw it; the truth as she wished it represented in moral court.

These were her memories.

Memories were edited, revised, parts of the experience revisited in the mind, but omitted during verbal recollection. Or altered to fit one's needs. A lover who once excited you to no end, when it was over, the memories became rewritten in your mental diary, more than likely in your favor; now the loving that used to make you climb walls and come like crazy was no good, its value diminished by emotional negativity. That was the way it was. We chose the colors with which to paint our memories. With those same colorful words we chose who played the parts of the good and the bad. We chose the scents that brought those memories to life. With words we chose the texture. Whoever told the story owned the words and cast themselves as the protagonist, the victim, the one wronged, the victor.

No one ever saw themselves as the antagonist. No one saw themselves as evil.

We rewrote our lovers. We rewrote our pain. We rewrote ourselves.

We omitted. We embellished. We were all revisionists.

We were all liars.

FORTY-TWO

Jewell Stewark's words had been vivid, intense, and disturbing.

I had expected her to bowdlerize her emotional confession. Her vocabulary had been raw. But it had also been erotic and vivid, just as intense as the thunder and lightning trapping us.

The storm continued to rage, refused to dwindle. Jewell Stewark stopped confessing and quieted. She finished giving me portions of her memoirs, pulled in her lips, and ceased giving me the expurgated version of her private life. A life that included Mark and Karl. A life that had once included a woman named Kenya.

I smelled Karl's cologne, his orgasm mixed with her sex, the perfume on her body. I inhaled their conflict. Heat radiated from her body. Their conflict was thermal, possessed immeasurable energy.

Thunder boomed.

We remained trapped in the bathtub, her body against mine, my every exhale touching her dank skin, my breasts against her back, sweat draining from us, neither of us moving.

She said, "You must think I'm a horrible person."

I didn't answer. I couldn't, not without wondering if she saw me as the mirror of her being.

She said, "You think I'm a horrible bitch."

Whatever existed between them didn't end when Mark took her to the altar. It continued. Maybe not all the time, maybe off and on, maybe with Jewell trying to end it on her end, maybe with Karl trying to end it in his own way, maybe with Mark attempting the same, but they all had failed and it continued. They had momentum. What they were doing had its own life and rhythm. It was its own beast.

It was always hard to stop. Which was why some things were better off never started.

She whispered, "Karl has rejected me. And I'm losing Mark to you."

"That terrifies you."

"Yes. That terrifies me."

"So this is The Jewell of the South."

"And they both have come to you."

"Maybe your husband is tired of chasing a woman who can't fully be his wife. Maybe he's tired of kissing your ass. Maybe you've hurt his spirits one time too many and he's doing what he has to do to remain sane. Maybe he's tired of sleeping with you knowing your mind is in someone else's bed."

"Buy why *you*?"

"Ask Mark."

She snapped, "What is it about you that has Karl parading you in front of me, taking you to work with him, running by my home with you, letting you stay the night, knowing what it does to me?"

I took a breath, let it out slowly, didn't mask my irritation as I repeated, "Ask Karl."

She softened her tone, sounded concerned, gentle, as she asked, "You care about Mark?"

"It's a *physical* relationship."

"Do you care about Karl?"

I smiled an angry smile. "It's a *physical* relationship."

"I saw the *damn* text messages. I read your *damn* messages to him and I read his *damn* messages to you. And I know Mark. Mark is my husband. I know my *damn* husband."

A pause settled between us, silence that magnified the sounds of the wind and rain.

I said, "This is the woman Atlanta idolizes."

"I think . . . I think you're a delusional whore."

"Is that your thesis statement?"

"That is what I believe."

"You don't know me well enough to make that statement."

"You're with my husband. And with Karl. *At once.* I know all I need to know."

I retorted, "You're a hypocrite."

"Wonderful evaluation from a sexual opportunist."

"Karl *fucked* you like a caveman and walked out the door like you meant nothing."

"Must you provoke me?"

"As you have come into my home and provoked me."

"As Karl has provoked me."

"As you have cuckolded and provoked Mark."

There was an abrupt hum, and we jumped, two little girls afraid of the storm. The hum was the sudden sound of energy returning to this section of Cobb County. Energy surrounded us. The lights came on in the bathroom. My computer began to power up. My fax machine began resetting itself. Everything I hadn't disconnected came to life. That meant the clocks on my oven and microwave were flashing, waiting to be reset. The air conditioner kicked on, the cool breeze flowing through the vents.

Jewell Stewart panted, "I should go now."

"Yes." I panted and wiped sweat from my eyes. "You should go now."

We struggled to move, gripping the edges of the tub, bumping into each other. Jewell made painful sounds as she pulled herself back to the opposite end of the bathtub, as she tried to find room to maneuver. She was reaching for something to hold on to, saw her grab the handle, heard it squeal when it turned, and it turned fast.

The shower came on. A burst of cold water rained on our flesh. An abrupt waterfall that poured a sudden chill on our heated skin made us scream like we were drowning. I fumbled, climbed over Jewell, wiggled over her thighs and breasts, almost fell out of the tub as I rushed to turn the faucet back off, but couldn't end the chilly waterfall, not before we were beyond soaking wet.

After that we sat there for a moment, cold water draining into the tub.

The last of the chilly shower water dripping from overhead.

The cold water had shocked my system, awakened me.

We began to stand up, water draining from our hair and clothes, gripping the sides of the tub to keep from slipping and falling, our every move so very awkward, like power had been shut down in parts of our bodies. We moved with caution, released painful sounds as we too returned to life.

A towel bar was at the end of the tub opposite the faucets. I reached over, pulled down two decorative towels, not caring about aesthetics at this point, grabbed the towels and handed her one, then wiped my face and hair, stood up, held the wall with one hand, wiped my legs and left foot before I stepped out and wiped my right foot. She was having a hard time standing, couldn't get her balance. Then she cringed, made a face that could either be interpreted as deep pain or abrupt pleasure.

I wiped water from my face, water that had diluted my sweat, and asked, "What's wrong?"

"Foot fell asleep."

I groaned, again irate and sickened, unable to mask my frustration. "Can you—"

"I'm numb."

"—stand up?"

"Need a minute. Tingling real bad."

She moved from my bathtub, couldn't stand up, eased down on the floor, sandals off, back to the wall, moaning, her eyes to the opposite wall. I extinguished the candles, the heat feeling unbearable, and a moment later I was sitting on the toilet, the lid down, my hands in my hair.

I wanted her gone. I wanted this evil out of my house.

But she was in pain, crippled, her foot numb, that numbness spreading up her leg.

Her colorful sundress was soaked, sticking to her body, showing she had on no bra, no panties, her nakedness pronounced. She tried to wring out her dress, dabbed it with the towel. It was a lost cause. I put towels down on the floor in anticipation of her raining as she hobbled like she was crippled. I moved with pain. Being in that porcelain tub, being huddled like that, I had a new appreciation for all the slaves who had to hide out for days, unmoving, in ungodly places during their quest for freedom.

She groaned, "Despite what you may think, or how it may sound, I do love Mark."

"He's your security blanket. The safe one. The one who loves you more than you love him. It's always better to be in love with the one who loves you more. I don't agree, but I understand. He's the one who can never truly hurt you. He can't break you in two. He can't kill you. That's what you love."

"He's *my* husband."

Her statement was direct and powerful, righteous and spiritual, rooted in morality, an attempt to question my self-respect and self-esteem. Again coming from her—a woman I saw as deceitful—it had no true weight. She wanted me to believe that I was evil, a concept invented by the theological as a form of control. Her words riled me, but did no authentic damage, not the kind that she had intended.

She struggled to get up, now riled and wanting to get away from me. She made it to her feet, stood with one hand against the wall, rubbing her leg, cringing.

I said, "You okay?"

"Let me get to my car." Her tone was terse. "Once I get to my car, I'll be okay."

Jewell Stewark limped from the bathroom toward the carpeted office, her left leg still refusing to come back alive, then limped across the carpet as fast as she could, stopped on the tiled entryway that led to the garage, the tingles trapping her as she leaned against the wall at the bottom of the stairs.

"You don't have to go back up the stairs." I said that fast, my tone panicked, as if I didn't want her violating any more of my space, didn't want her presence and negative energy sullying my townhome any more than it already had, then took a deep breath, one that told me this was finally over. "You can exit this way, through the garage, straight to your car."

She made it to the door and paused, said, "My earring."

"What about it?"

"I lost one. It's a diamond."

I wanted to scream. I was in purgatory and I wanted to scream until the paint came off the walls.

I rushed and searched around the bathroom, didn't find her earring on the floor or inside the tub. So I hurried upstairs to the kitchen and living room, didn't see it there, didn't expect to, then took the last flight of carpeted stairs back up to my master bedroom, turned the lights on, saw sheets that spoke of sex and violence, smelled the perfume of her sex, smelled Karl's cologne, smelled the scent of unrequited love, inhaled the aroma of madness and lust. Her diamond earring was on top of my colorful sheets, teardrop shaped, classy, expensive, lying there like sorrow crystallized, positioned as if it had been sexed off her body. The scents. All of our scents remained. Scents took me back to what had happened not too long ago. In a flash, in my mind's eye, I saw Karl behind Jewell, stroking her with his anger, that earring flying free as she moaned.

Then I felt her angered hands on my skin. Grabbing me. Pulling me. In that moment the world was out of control, emotions had outweighed reason and we had all gone crazy.

I saw Jewell's desperation, saw her giving her husband's brother fellatio, desperate to swallow his ejaculatory fluid as if it was the magical cure for love, heartache, and all that might possibly ail her.

Then I saw someone else. Someone I never wanted to see again.

I saw me when I was at Hampton, after all had been said and done, begging my lover not to leave me. I wanted more than he wanted to give me. Maybe I had wanted too much too fast. I had a lot of love for him. My heart was filled with love for him, overflowing to the point that sanity had abandoned me.

I picked up Jewell's earring, held her crystallized tear in the palm of my right hand, stared at the diamond and contemplated telling her I couldn't find it, that simple act being my small revenge for the things she had done in retaliation for the things I had done as I sought pleasure, but I couldn't do that, didn't want to leave anything open between us, and I held her earring, hurried downstairs, expected her to be looking in my drawers, on my computer, violating my space, but I found her leaning against the wall where I left her, still fidgeting, struggling to get the blood circulating in her extremities. Pictures of me and my mother over the years, always in colorful costumes, me and my mother at Trinidad's Carnival, the best Carnival in the whole world, surrounded Jewell. I gave her that recovered diamond, our flesh grazing.

She stared at me, hair pulled back, wet and disheveled, sweat covering her reddened face, her sundress so dank it continued sticking to her skin, water dripping from its edges, leaving a puddle at her feet.

She whispered, "We are like sculptors. What you said, take heed to your own lexis."

With a trembling lip, a faltering voice, she had given me Anaïs's words.

I stared at Jewell, offended by the revered words she had thrown back at me.

Her pain radiated, came in waves. As did my empathy. But my empathy was not that great. This moment of forced solidarity changed nothing. In her memoirs, her world colored by her emotions, I was her antagonist. In this chapter of my memoirs, on this page of my uncensored diary, she was the Wicked Witch. She was my antagonist. A role she scowled at me and auditioned for the first time she saw me with Karl. A role she had won the moment she was bold enough to step up to me and spit in my face.

I hated Jewell Stewark.

I found her insufferable, detested her pain, hypocrisy, self-righteousness, and confusion.

The things I hated about her were the things I hated about myself.

It was still raining, the storm once again cruel, malicious winds humming, but I didn't care; there was no more hospitality here, the kindness meter that had been filled with coins of foolishness had expired. If the streets were flooded and Georgia's red dirt had muddied the roads, she could drive as far as her Jaguar could take her, or call AAA and let them send a boat, and if AAA didn't show up I didn't give a damn if she had to swim the filthy currents of the Chattahoochee back to her precious Cascade Road.

I just wanted the bitch gone.

Women had confrontations with wives. Women had confrontations with girlfriends.

This had been like having confrontations with both at the same time.

First, as I reached by her, opened the door that led to my garage, my cellular rang.

The theme from *Sex and the City*. My mother. Her timing imperfect as usual.

Before I could turn the cellular off and push the button to open the garage door . . .

Upstairs . . .

My doorbell rang.

Logan.

My every fear told me it was Logan.

He was all I needed to make this insanity complete.

I heard his Range Rover outside my garage.

I knew he was back. Men like Logan never left. Men like Logan never moved on.

Men like Logan had to win.

FORTY-THREE

Logan had been the harbinger of this horrific storm.

This was his doing, his negative energy surrounding and disrupting my world.

His Range Rover would be parked in front of my townhome, covered in Georgia rain.

The anger and insults he had given me, I heard him inside my head, his voice a low hum.

Pro bono whore.

I hurried to the kitchen, picked up my mother's long-bladed knife.

I tried to control my breathing, tiptoed to the front door, spied through the peephole.

He was here. He had arrived.

I saw his face. Rain falling, I saw his wet face. Framed in gloom I saw emotions unleashed.

It wasn't Logan.

It wasn't the manifestation of that subconscious fear.

It was Mark and Karl. Both. That was just as shocking as if it had been Logan.

Jewell's husband and her reluctant lover. The man who loved her and the man she loved.

My identical sins.

I took a deep breath. Prepared for the next level of madness.

Then I unlocked the deadbolt and the security lock, opened the door to the restless storm.

I smelled the dampness of the city, the dampness of trees, of kudzu, of Georgia red dirt. In the distance thunder clapped and lightning flashed, the downpour still intense.

But they had weathered the storm to come and reclaim what was theirs.

They were noble men, driving through thunder, lightning, rivers, and fallen trees to retrieve The Jewell of the South.

As if the storm gods had told them some unspeakable tragedy had befallen their mad queen.

Their expressions were pissed and alarmed all at once. In this moment, with those angered and fearful expressions, with the amalgamation of mixed emotions, they looked the same, they were the same. This was their pattern. Mark stood in front of Karl, the older twin in front of the younger, as if he was paving the way, leading his younger brother out of the womb, winds blowing hard enough to bend the trees, winds howling like the forces of labor, rain pouring behind them like broken water.

Karl's Jeep Wrangler was in my driveway behind Mark's truck. Jewell's Jaguar was in front, all three vehicles bumper-to-bumper.

My identical sins stared at me, startled at the threadbare version of me that stood before them. The twins were frozen and wordless. I was irritated, soaking wet, sweaty, hair pulled back, my wicked ponytail about to come undone.

But that was not what inspired the terrified look on their faces.

Their eyes had moved from my irate expression to the long-bladed knife I held in my hand. A wicked knife that could be used to kill a queen. Their eyes widened, mouths opened in horror.

Both looked like they were face-to-face with the reincarnation of Lizzie Borden.

* * *

I stepped away from the door, allowed them to come inside my home, water dripping on my marbled foyer. Mark's eyes were on mine. I had waited for him on Cascade. Waited and he never came. Karl's expression was downcast, unable to make eye contact.

In a nervous voice Mark asked, "Where . . . ?"

Before he could form his trembling sentence, before his shaky voice could ask where I had buried his wife's body, Jewell was limping up the stairs. At the same moment six eyes looked in the same direction, watching her enter this space through the marbleized wooden door that led to the basement.

Her sundress soaking wet, dripping water, keys in her hand, her hair wet, her makeup and mascara a mess, running down her face as if she was melting, a demon rising from the bowels of hell.

She looked angered, embarrassed, wounded, this relationship of theirs exposed to a stranger.

Even now, in her state of disarray, she was striking in her anguish.

No one said anything.

There was something ludicrous about this moment.

The silence persisted, chilled us, moved between us, dared us to speak.

I stood between two virile Bajan men, between images that inspired visual orgasms. Men who had given me invigorating smiles. And integration of friendship, sex, worship, desire, culture, conversation, companionship, lust, fantasy, entitlement, and now, knowingly or unknowingly, truth.

Maybe Jewell was right. Maybe Logan was right. Maybe I was a whore. Maybe I was delusional. Maybe all we had done was committed fornication. Maybe all we did was fucked.

I had put pretty clothes on the pleasure-seeking experience, given it a sensual soundtrack, a spiritual melody, given it laughter, peppered with deep kisses, helped create a chorus of escalating moans, and ending the act of lust-driven copulation with orgasms for all, its afterglow painted by lustful smiles. Since I left Logan, I hadn't smiled that much, laughed that much, but in the end, maybe every place I had been with my identical sins was no more than being at a brothel, a five-star brothel we had created at the W, a brothel we had moved to hotels and apartments in Greensboro, a brothel that held me under the red spotlight as its center attraction. The Delusional Whore. Maybe they had dumped come in my mouth and body not with love and affection, but had given me their release the way sewage was given to the sea. This had become complicated. In the blink of an eye it had become complicated.

All of a sudden I felt a wave of sadness. I felt sad because I found them sad.

A little pathetic even.

Everything became trivial.

I looked at Karl and knew he'd never want more from me, as I wouldn't expect more from him. Next I gazed at Mark, my heart heavy for him, and wondered why he stayed where he was when he wasn't happy. I wondered where all of their self-respect had gone.

The things I wondered about them, I wondered about myself.

It was in my face.

Mirrors were all around me. All around us. Each one jumped out at me, stood in front of us all. Mirrors reflected this moment and, as always, in its reflection, the truth remained brutal and unkind.

Whatever energy existed between us, it crackled in the air.

Crackled loud enough for Jewell to hear its sound.

She witnessed our familiarity. She looked at us and saw how close we had become. It was there in our glances, in our body language, the adventures we had shared, the intimacy, the memory of the text messages she had read. And my confession to her. This thing we had created stood before her, too real.

There were emotions between us. Emotions she felt. Emotions that told her I was not a whore.

Jewell lowered her head, her body still shaking, madness and emotions overcoming her.

She opened her mouth to say something, but whatever was on her heart was too heavy to find wings to carry the words beyond her bosom, and in the end, she released a long sigh, a stream of air that left her body as if she was exhaling smoke, and she held her wet hair and lowered her head.

All the things she had confessed to me as Mother Nature clapped thunder in the darkness, I remembered her every word, her every pain as we shared a porcelain tub as refugees from the storm.

Mark and Karl were twins. Jewell and I had been twins.

So close our bodies had touched, connected by desires, making us feel like Siamese twins.

Through her confessions she acknowledged her needs and weaknesses.

I had acknowledged my own vulnerability, a weakness driven not by Karl or Mark, for they were only the representatives at this moment. My weakness remained rooted in my fears and desires.

Jewell raised her head. Mark said her name, his baritone voice low yet strong, the tone of a gentle husband. She said nothing. Mark asked what happened here. His wife said nothing.

But she looked toward Karl. His lingam the instrument that had moved against her desire and created enchanting sounds. In her eyes I saw the memory of Negril, Barbados, saw her in my bedroom defiling my bed, imagined there had been many more times over the years, her number of moments with Karl minimized in order to keep her closer to sainthood, I saw through what she didn't say and saw the stolen moments she hadn't revealed. She scowled at Karl. The look of deep love and deeper hate.

Water dripped from her dress as she limped by Mark. By Karl. By me.

She limped out the front door, left Karl as he had left her, left Mark the same way, left the identical sins dripping water on my tiled floor. Jewell Stewark dropped her sandals on the landing outside the front door, hurried to put them on, ignored Mark's calling out to her, then limped down the stairs, those sandals slapping against her wet feet as she struggled to run, as she limped into the darkness and the downpour.

Rain washed away her footprints. The same rain would hide her tears.

The things she had left behind remained.

Her come on my sheets. Her sweat on my towels.

The husband who loved her. The man she loved.

The segments of her life that she had revealed, that portion of her life, of her spoken diary continued spinning, her words, the images those words created, running an infinite loop in my mind.

Mark looked at me, his emotions heavy, his heart being pulled in two directions.

He looked at me and said, "She's my wife."

With that we lost eye contact, his head lowered, as did mine. Mark went by Karl, by me, and followed Jewell Stewark. I understood. He followed his wife, not out of weakness. She was his wife. And he was a married man. He had stood before God and made promises. Some kept, some not.

He owed me nothing. Not even explanation. His wife's car started.

Still, I wished Mark had stayed. I wished he had let her go and stayed through the storm.

Again, with dark clouds overhead, reality rained as the winds of truth roared.

There was a pecking order to emotional entanglements, a hierarchy not always of the heart.

Somehow I felt this one, in the end, despite all that had been said, was of the heart.

Karl stood there, face wet, his shoulders tight, his head down.

In a damaged voice I whispered, "Karl."

He looked at me, his eyes leveling with mine, the position of honesty. He was frustrated and ashamed, his face tight, waiting for me to explode, become typical, say mean and evil things.

I cleared my throat, spoke softly. "Mark and Jewell, they're blocked in. You've blocked them in."

"Let me run down and move my Jeep. I'll come right back."

"Not your Jeep. You've blocked them in."

He paused, evaluating the double meaning of my words. "What are you talking about, Nia?"

"Pleasure has become pain."

"So what are you saying?"

A million thoughts went through my mind. A million questions. I chose one to ask.

I took a shallow breath before I asked, "Will you ever cover up Kenya's name?"

He paused, his shoulders slumping, my question adding weight to what was impossible to carry.

He whispered, "No. I . . . I can't . . . I won't remove my angel . . . for no one."

"Not the angel. Her name. Could you remove her name, or cover it with something new?"

He struggled, and in the end he shook his head, telling me her name was part of him for eternity.

I smiled at him, a man who was holding on to the past, reliving pain with every glance in the mirror, maybe that was his own punishment, his personal hell. Or maybe he was waiting for Kenya to return, wasting time with work and women until his queen came back into his world. Kenya was gone, her relationship with him henna, his image never tattooed in her flesh on that day in Jamaica.

I took a deep breath and swallowed, told him, "Good-bye."

My word was simple, my word was powerful, its meaning unambiguous, and in this moment had the impact of a car crashing into a brick wall. Less was more. Less was what was needed, no long speeches. All I needed to say was good-bye. Karl had said good-bye to many women.

But only one woman had ever said good-bye to him. Only one had truly mattered.

One man had devastated me, rearranged my world with that same two-syllable word. *Good-bye.* Our parting farewell inspired by moments of insanity. By unforgettable, highly regrettable actions.

Karl understood abrupt partings. He had to. He was wounded, too much like me to not understand. He struggled. I saw him wrestle with his emotions, emotions that, for a man like him, for people like us, would be out of place. He pulled his lips inward, stared at me, wrestled with my decision.

Parting was inevitable. For all of us it was as inevitable as death.

A year from now. Or a month from now. Or a week from now. Or a day from now. We needed to let this moment become our now. I needed to let this moment be *my* now. Still, inside I struggled with this decision. Anger. Jealousy. Being trapped by desires. Jewell Stewart was who I would become if I continued down this path. Or Mark would become Jewell once I became bored with him.

And I hoped I never became to Karl what Logan had become to me.

Even Karl and I, as simpatico as we were, the final result was already written.

When restless souls collided, there was excitement, but boredom was inevitable.

I needed to stop. Before my rising obsession spiraled out of control. I admit it. I was human. I was woman. Feelings were present. Emotions rising, but not at the point of no return. Yes. I needed to acknowledge my feelings and stop before I became a person who behaved as foolishly as Logan. Before I lost the plot and acted as irrationally as Jewell Stewark.

I had to be done with Mark. I had to be done with Karl. Had to walk away from ecstasy amid a growing storm. Before giving them up mentally would destroy my spirits. Before giving them up created severe withdrawal. If I had already reached that point of no return, I didn't know. All I knew was that I hurt deeply. I felt the beginning of a bottomless pain.

There were countless heartbroken souls walking the earth. Today there would be one more.

Karl moved toward me like he wanted to kiss me, wanted that kiss to turn back time.

As all men did. As I had done so many times.

I wanted him too. Part of me wanted his lips and tongue and words to become magical.

But I knew one thing for sure. Time always moved in the same direction.

I shook my head. He looked so hurt, overwhelmed, like he wanted to collapse from frustration.

I imagined his expression, his angst was the same he had on that day Kenya took her love away.

I didn't worry about Karl. Karl was Karl. A lodestone for women in need of temporary fulfillment.

I whispered, "Good-bye. Good-bye. I say it twice. Once for you, once for Mark."

Karl nodded, then opened the door, headed out into the downpour; Karl being the one who had everyone blocked in, him being the one who needed to move so all could move on and be free.

I waited until all were gone. A lover and his wife. A lover and his sister-in-law.

Then, when I was once again alone, I showered, lay in my bed naked, on my back, unmoving, ceiling fan spinning, surrounded by the fading scents of old lovers, staring at the rain.

The rain that fell from my eyes rivaled all Southern storms.

I wept.

For me. For them. For all of us.

I held myself and wept.

FORTY-FOUR

Tropical breezes caressed my skin, brought infinite warmth, like the breath of an unseen lover.

The sun was high, clouds few, mosquitoes and sand fleas many.

This was my sun. This was my sea. This was my heaven filled with mosquito repellant.

I'd been gone from Smyrna for two weeks.

For the last three days I had been living in peaceful solitude at Maracas Bay Hotel. Three days of swimming in the sea. Three days of sun. Three days of bake and shark.

Three days of reading.

Three days of writing in my journal, at least thirty pages written between each sunrise and sunset.

That was my confession, my therapy, always on paper, never to the judgmental.

Suntan lotion on my body, flesh that now possessed the hue of the deepest brown, I was on the second largest island in the West Indies. I was in Trinidad. I was alone, but not lonely, not today, not in this beautiful and picturesque moment, because I was at peace, my inner self breaking bread with the spirits of my long-deceased ancestors.

This was my haunt. My special place in the world, the most stunning beach on the island. My towel and picnic basket were underneath the shade of a towering coconut tree, the weather hot and humid, sunglasses on as I relaxed on the crowded coastline, hundreds of locals and tourists swimming, bodysurfing, and playing in the waves. It felt good to be back in the land of Carib beer. Where the steelpan was invented, created by enslaved Africans and Afro-descendants. Looking around, seeing the peacefulness and joy emanating from the children of the West Indies made me smile.

I was on sabbatical, easing away from the undertow of anguish, from my own obsessions, from moments of cruelty, abandonment, and betrayal. This was the cycle of life. This was what Eros brought, the sought-after and the unwanted forever tethered to the pursuit of pleasure.

I went back toward the waters, my feet first walking across burning white sands, then standing where the emerald waves crashed into the shore, let the warm waters wet me up to my waist, diving under the large waves as they rolled into shore, floating on my back awhile, then I decided to blend with the people celebrating deeper in the sea, take one last swim before driving back over the mountain.

They were near me for a while. They were kissing, touching as if no one was around.

He was a young Spanish boy, no older than seventeen. Dark-skinned. Handsome with long hair. Well-built. The girl with him was an Indian girl. A slender girl. Long black hair. Skin well-tanned.

Water rushing up to my breasts, I drifted out to sea, drifted toward them as I watched them. They reminded me of what part of me longed for. To be held without being held captive.

They eased closer to the shores, playfully splashing water on each other as waves rushed in, laughing and diving underneath the larger waves, gradually moving to chest-high waters.

She put her arms around his shoulders, and he lifted her. She held on to her lover, wrapping her legs around his thighs, her arms around his neck as her lover cradled her butt with both hands. They tasted each other, whispered to each other, and enjoyed the five senses with one another.

There was that subtle movement, one that told me her hand was slipping under the sea, easing her bikini to the side, feeling his erection, testing his strength. She spread her legs around him, guiding that hardness beyond the material of her swimsuit toward the lips of her yoni. She shifted around in that way a woman does when she was trying to get the head to break the skin. She was bold, as if it was her sea, as if pleasure in the salty waters was her entitlement.

Hundreds of people were around. Vendors walking the beach selling jewelry and fruit.

Her eyes were closed tight. Her mouth eased open into the letter O.

He had closed his eyes, held her tight, his heavenly moment melding with hers.

I watched them as if I was studying erotology.

They were beautiful.

I left knowing that it wasn't only me consumed by desire.

It wasn't only me basking in my humanness.

Back in Port of Spain I rode around like I was a tourist, drove near Morvant and Laventille, slums and shantytowns, the area where my mother grew up, where my father was killed before I was born, an area the papers said was populated by drug lords, the type of man my father had longed to be.

I wondered who I would have been if my mother had not left here in pursuit of the American Dream. Wondered if we would have ended up in government homes paying fourteen dollars a month as rent, with an option to buy. If I would have worn a uniform and been a bank worker, or an airport worker, or if I would've sold fruit from the side of the road, wondered which noble profession I would have had, or if I would have lived in a shantytown and had more babies than the old woman who lived inside a shoe.

Before Hollywood my mother had labored in sugar fields, killed chickens, and milked cows. My mother had worked hard to improve her life, to make sure my life was better than hers.

I wasn't spoiled. I had been given options, a better way of living, but I was never spoiled.

Tears in my eyes, I called my mother.

She answered on the second ring. "Hello, good afternoon."

"You made a lot of sacrifices for me."

"Who in the world is this?"

"And I love you for that."

My mother moaned. "Look what you did. Now I'm crying."

"Are you really crying?"

"Hell no. This makeup is too expensive for tears. But I will schedule a cry for later."

She laughed. I did too.

I asked, "What are you doing?"

"About to step into a meeting. You?"

"Just left the beach." I wiped my eyes with the back of my hands, imagined my mother was doing the same, her voice telling me she was emotional too. "I'm going to Rituals for a latte, then to the house."

"I should come down this weekend and we could go to Millennium and golf."

"Let me know. I'll make callaloo, maybe cook steamed kingfish and vegetables."

"Check the calendar for fetes."

"Already have the info on all the Carnival launches."

"Make sure you go to Meiling's shop."

"Can't wait to see her new designs. You tell her I was here?"

"She knows. Since I'm such a good mother, buy me some things and I'll pay you back."

"You never pay me back."

"I'm not supposed to."

I laughed.

She laughed. "Talk to you later."

"More important call coming in?"

"This is Hollywood. There is always a more important call coming in."

"Okay."

"But none will ever be more important than yours."

"You are really trying to make me cry, aren't you?"

"Get our book ready."

"*Our* book?"

"I'm talking to Denzel later this week. Might *happen* to bring it up."

"Anything else, o ye mother pimp of mine?"

"Drive to San Fernando. Randy's Doubles. Eat two or three doubles for me."

She was talking about the most popular fast food in Trinidad and Tobago.

I told her, "You're trying to sabotage me for Carnival."

"Your ass is spreading."

"You're trying to make sure you look better than me."

"I will *always* look better than you."

"Time and gravity, mom. Time and gravity."

Again we laughed, hers very singsong, mine the mirror image of hers. Then we parted.

My mother wanted to own the universe.

I only wanted a couple of planets with a moon on the side.

That and a lover who could take care of my needs.

My mother's mansion, our Roots Home, was right below the sun, high enough to reach up and tickle the flames from our closest star. This home cost less but was much larger than the one in Los Angeles, gated, secure, and well-maintained. The view of the sea and the mountains spectacular.

From my large bedroom, at my small desk, I sat in front of my laptop, ceiling fan spinning over my head, my work clothes now furnished by Victoria's Secret, a few of Anaïs Nin's books at my side, my tattered copies, the ones I carried as if they were my Sunday morning Bible, pages dog-eared to my favorite chapters, favorite verses highlighted and underlined, powerful words underlined, and as proof of her inspiration, notes to myself scribbled in the margins. I was taking time to myself, a few days at least, writing more of my sci-fi novel as I looked at Atlanta news, news I had programmed to be recorded on my DVR. I had Slingbox installed at my home in Smyrna. Slingbox enabled me to look at my television on my laptop anywhere I had an Internet connection. In the thick of the night, Jewell Stewart was in my home, found me through my laptop, and she was once again looking prim and proper and in control, so unlike the woman who had left my home on the verge of a breakdown.

Now she was broadcasting, her wedding ring sparkling beneath her virtuous smile.

This was not the woman who had spit in my face, who had come inside my home.

This was her mask and she wore it well.

With her infectious smile, with the award-winning posture and grace that had earned her the title of The Jewell of the South, she was doing a report about the city trying to impose an ordinance to prohibit the hip-hop generation from wearing sagging pants.

I remembered Jewell Stewart, not the well-spoken one on television, but the one whose jealousy and pain caused her to invade my home, the one who was on my bed being sexually impaled by her husband's brother, the Jewell Stewart who had put a knife to my throat.

A knife had been placed at my throat.

I froze on that thought and I shuddered.

I wondered if it was bad for Anaïs.

I thought of Anaïs and one of her lovers, Henry Miller, wondered what it was like for him, the pleasure, the madness, the challenge, the ebb and flow of his spirit as he was, in his heart, loving two women at the same time. A Herculean task in any era. And I thought of Anaïs having affairs with men, her encounters with women, how she lived and loved in search of her own contentment. I wondered if in the end, despite what was written—because I knew what was written was not always true, maybe one person's truth, but not always the truth—I wondered if she found happiness. Or if happiness evaded her.

I wondered if she had found her pleasure.

Pleasure, like the definition of love, was subjective, different for everyone it touched.

Maybe sex was not love and maybe love was not sex. But love was connected to sex as sex was connected to love.

Sex and love were not identical twins. Not born at the same moment.

Not fraternal.

But still of the same womb.

It was inevitable, with the passing of time, feelings would get deeper and deeper. Until the sex was out of control. Until the emotions you owned ended up owning you.

I wasn't ready to be owned.

Alone I was a success. In a relationship I was a failure.

I wasn't ready.

Maybe I would be one day, but right now, with my restless spirit, I was not ownable, not enslaveable. I was an autonomous woman who owned her own libido. The free-spirited way I lived, I wouldn't live this way the rest of my life, for everything must change, evolution being part of life. This was my now, my now being only a few pages in the book of my life. Only a few pages that would remain remarkable to me, understood by me, revered by me, if no one else. Because in the end, in my final days, I wanted to hold the hand of the man I loved more than life. Or have that happen in reverse, be there for him as his spirit left his body, his energy moving through me as he took leave of this world.

I stopped writing my sci-fi book. I stopped because that was not where my heart was.

I stopped because once again I was crying.

I saved my work, then opened a new screen, transitioned from sci-fi to erotica, my mind moving from cerebral thinking to sensuality, to honesty, once again expressing my duality, my being a Gemini.

A title came to mind.

Abnormal Desires, by Anonymous.

As I began writing the unexpurgated version of my private life, refusing to let my lexis become bowdlerized by my inner editor, the thoughts remained never-ending and the words flowed.

The memories were so strong, vivid, breathing as if they had a life of their own.

My imagery was powerful, my words created heat inside me, my words created tears.

My words reminded me how wonderful it had all been.

I'd never forget any of my lovers. A lover was physically in your life for what amounted to a moment in your life, but remained part of you until your bones turned to dust.

Feeling forlorn, feeling more human than I wanted to feel, inspired by heat and self-imposed solitude, that night I met a beautiful Indian man at Zen nightclub. He flirted for a while before I became receptive to his charms. Sending drinks and wicked glances, taking his time approaching. He was slender with golden brown skin, immaculately dressed. His name was Prada. From England. His British accent so smooth and dignified. He was in Trinidad to meet with diplomats, their embassies being in the area, in the ritzy and gated areas right off the Savannah. The joke was you could see all the classes in Trinidad by circling the Queen's Park Savannah, from the mansions on one side to the poverty that stood out, shantytowns carved in the hills on the other side, facing each like they were preparing for a battle at the O.K. Corral. Prada was a classy man. His vocabulary extraordinary. His conversation profound.

We ended up chatting, liming and wining, soca junkies in search of a good time, then standing out front of Zen watching another band playing steel drums in the thick of the night.

I went to dinner with him the next night. Not wanting to be alone. Not wanting to write. A woman in pain, but still a woman with needs. I was still a woman.

Prada told me that two days before he met me he'd just arrived from Kingston. Said he found Kingston unique. In Kingston he and his colleague had sat poolside at the Hilton and watched hundreds of professional Jamaicans congregated to lime at the karaoke show.

In his intellectual British accent, an accent I found to be so smart it was stimulating, he said, "You'd think the locals would sing something by Marley or Tosh, but every Jamaican was singing a country and western song, the entire audience singing along with each tune."

"People in the islands love country western music."

"I've come to find that out."

The following evening I had met the handsome man at the bar at the upside-down Hilton, had dinner at the restaurant below. When we were done eating we moved our conversation upstairs to the bar for more drinks and chatting, eventually going to his room, a suite overlooking the Savannah. On the surface he was a wonderful man, excellent presentation, professional, wealthy, and beyond handsome.

I told Prada that from his suite, in the daytime he would be able to see footballers and people jogging the two-mile loop at the Savannah toward Lady Chancellor Road, pointed out his view, showed most of Trinidad's Magnificent Seven, told him his view extended beyond the Twin Towers, and at sunrise he would witness clear blue skies and the beauty of the Gulf of Paria as far as his eyes could see.

He whispered that nothing was more beautiful than me, that

maybe in the morning as we ate breakfast, as he put kisses on my neck and breasts, I could once again show him all of those things.

It was strong. My need to efface my old lovers with a new one, one who would be easily effaced.

But after a few kisses, a few touches, his hands on my breasts, my hands on his handsome face and strong chest, light touches, then, before hands had drifted to lingam or yoni, I eased away, excused myself to the bathroom. I sat on the toilet. The heat of hell was between my legs. Heat was power. Heat was energy.

Heat made it hard to breathe, and you knew that the only way to feel better was not to move away from the heat, but to move deeper into the heat, find your way out the other side. I fingered myself. I sat on the toilet and fingered my yoni. Made myself come. Made orgasm rise and then I was able to focus on what I really wanted. With orgasm there came clarity.

When I returned I thanked him for the drinks, told him I needed to leave.

I whispered, "I'm not ready."

A smile couldn't hide his disappointment.

He remained kind, walked me out to my car, handed me his card. He owned several businesses, had a chain of stores similar to Cave Shepherd, his businesses scattered from Jamaica to Trinidad.

Then I drove away. Loneliness was an incurable disease. But I wasn't feeling zipless. I wanted conversations and mental orgasms but I didn't feel like having my body penetrated.

I wanted to please but I didn't feel like being fucked.

I didn't want breakfast at sunrise in a swank hotel facing the Savannah and the sea.

I just wanted to understand the makings of me.

I wanted to understand me.

I wondered if I had walked away from Prada because I did not want a zipless night.

Or if my taste for normal pleasures no longer existed.

* * *

Back in Atlanta, beautiful flowers waited for me on my front porch.

Not from Logan. Birds of paradise from Karl. Roses from Mark. One delivery from each. Apologies from both. Requests to please call from each. There were messages from both on my cellular, only a couple, nothing out of control, just enough to make me feel special. Their words were tender and true, words that let me know more than sex had existed between us.

My heart wanted to respond more than my body. Wisdom told me to let it be. So I let it be.

Soon there would be no more notes. No more messages. No more flowers.

There were houses to build. Photos to be taken. Books to ghost-write and edit.

Life went on. Life never stopped, not for the living. Not for the brokenhearted.

We all continued to move toward the moments when our existences were no more.

And in between the alpha and omega of our lives we looked for meaning.

Some of us.

Two weeks later I received another letter from Logan. A wedding announcement. He was getting married to a woman he was seeing before he met me, a woman I believe he kept seeing while he was seeing me.

He had slipped a handwritten note inside the invitation. Red ink on white paper. As if he was bleeding. "Your not worthy. This is not an invitation to my wedding. Only a FYI. Your not worthy."

I smiled. Then I laughed. He still hadn't worked out that *your* versus *you're* thing.

His pettiness, audacity, and ignorance amused me to no end.

But there was joy.

I took a red pen to his letter, corrected his grammar.

After I was done editing his arrogance, I ran his letters through my shredder.

My cellular chimed.

It was Mr. Overworked and Underpaid New York Editor calling. My favorite Brit on the planet.

We said hellos and started talking about another project he wanted to send me.

Then we chatted about work, the craft, the industry.

I said, "I thought writing was supposed to elevate the masses."

"Maybe during the Harlem Renaissance."

"What is it now?"

"Profit."

"Ouch."

"The truth is like my ex-wife first thing in the morning."

"Meaning?"

"Unattractive. Very unattractive."

I laughed at his humor. "You are such a snob."

"I'm not a snob. I'm an editor."

"Underpaid and overworked."

"Must you remind me?"

Again we laughed.

We talked some more, casual conversation that moved from books to movies. He told me he didn't see a lot of movies, didn't watch television, outside of CNN and BBC channels.

I asked him why.

He said, "Actors don't impress me."

"Really?"

"Never have been impressed by those dramatically regurgitating words created by the true brilliant ones, the brilliant being the ones ignored while faces that have been nipped and tucked receive accolades and make a larger profit than the one who initiated the project as a labor of love, the entire movie starting with a writer sitting in front of a blank page asking herself or himself 'What if . . . ?'"

I laughed. "I so want to marry you right now."

"I'm sixty-five and Jewish."

"I'll buy you some blue pills if you buy me a menorah."

He laughed.

I told him I was leaving Georgia. I'd been in touch with my real estate agent. My townhome would be leased out for now, possibly sold when the market was more in my favor. Maybe I'd go back to Los Angeles for a while, let my mother pitch my book to as many people as she wanted, stay with her until one of us drove the other crazy. Maybe I'd return to Trinidad for a while. Maybe stay there until after next Carnival.

He asked, "When will you find you a nice young man and be his wife?"

I smiled, warm air blowing across my flesh, tickling my desires.

I said, "Can I tell you a story?"

"Yes."

And he listened.

I told him that once upon a time, a guy asked a girl, "Will you marry me?"

The girl said, "*No.*"

And the girl went shopping, dancing, camping, drank martinis, always had a clean house, never had to cook, did whatever the hell she wanted, never argued, didn't get fat, traveled, had many lovers, didn't save money, and had all the hot water to herself. She went to the theater, never watched sports, never wore lacy lingerie that went up her ass, had high self-esteem, never cried or yelled, felt and looked fabulous in sweat pants. The girl lived happily ever after.

I was that girl.

I told him I was that girl.

FORTY-FIVE

Yes, I was that girl.

But just because you were that girl, your heart and soul weren't impenetrable.

Because you were that girl, were of the feminine being, feelings were deeper, sex and love didn't separate. You remained a woman. Memories like the W and Greensboro didn't fade overnight.

Men like Mark and Karl, you didn't stop thinking about them immediately.

Their scents were too strong, too penetrating to wash away with a month of baths and showers.

Being licked to orgasm as I counted each stroke of the tongue, being taken in the rain, being seduced for over three hundred miles, and the whole Greensboro experience, unforgettable.

My yoni tingled in remembrance, begged me to go back, gave me heat and torture.

Only time could do what needed to be done. Time and distance.

I remembered how we'd kissed and kissed, those kisses made what we had shared special.

Nothing about Greensboro had ever felt cheap. Every moment had been wonderful.

The look in Mark's eyes when he gazed at me. The need for Karl to express himself emotionally, a desire I had blocked, for things said during heated moments could never be unsaid. And my own emotions, the jealousy.

Yes, Mark and Karl stayed in my mind, remained a part of my restless spirit.

I had the code to their world, a code that would allow me entry to their community of mini castles.

I drove to the Cascades, gave in to my emotions and went to Audubon Estates.

Irresistible impulse. A heart filled with a sense of guilt. Or simply reminiscing about the better moments. That night at the W. No matter the reason, part of me hoped that they would see me.

I passed by Mark's mini castle. The lights were off.

It was the midnight hour. The hour of lovers.

Lights off on my car, streetlights showed me the way as, music off, I cruised to the end of the cul-de-sac and turned around. I slowed at Karl's mini castle, paused at the foot of his driveway. Karl's home was dark.

What I saw caused me to smile.

In Karl's driveway was a black Yukon. North Carolina plates.

She was here. Kiki Sunshine was here.

The thing that drew men to women, that thing that drew women to men, that unseen force that inspired love and madness, it was here, in the air, its energy crackling like an invisible Southern storm.

Without desire, without sex, I still pondered what men and women would be to each other.

I imagined I could hear them, each holding a temporary cure for heartache and loneliness.

I imagined I heard Kiki Sunshine pleasing Karl, his moans rugged, hers as musical as water falling on steel pans, the wetness of her mouth curling his toes, stimulating him toward his release, her head tilted back in anticipation, smiling, eager to drink from the spring of happiness, the start of his orgasm being betrayed by an abrupt groan, spewing the taste of mangos and breadfruit, flooding her mouth, the whiteness of his pleasure like lotion on her beautiful Brazilian skin.

And I could hear Mark, with his wife. Biting her. Spanking her. Pulling her blond hair. Putting her on her hands and knees. Her healthy backside in the air. Making love to her with his eyes closed. Maybe pretending she was me. As she made love to him with her eyes closed. Pretending he was Karl. Maybe taking Mark in her mouth as she had taken his brother, his coarse hands touching her face with so much gentleness.

When they were done.

As air conditioners hummed and sweat began to dry.

Mark would wrap himself around Jewell. He would hold his wife as a husband should.

Jewell would sigh, then rest with her back to her husband, her face toward Karl's mini mansion. Her face decorated with envy and pain, her teary eyes in the direction of her heart's desire. Toward Karl. As her husband held her she would look toward Karl.

Wishing. Hoping. Praying. Thinking, one day it would change.

Karl would sleep facing Kiki Sunshine, his new lover, his back to Jewell's misery. He had misery of his own. A misery he drowned in sex and pleasure and work. His mind was forever on Kenya. A woman forever etched in his flesh.

He was married as well, his wife unreachable.

If not for my knowledge of Kenya, in our final moments, maybe I would have let Karl stay.

He'd dropped off discs containing all the erotic photos he had taken of me, everything from when we met at Stone Mountain to the orgasmic images he'd taken of me when I was inside his mini castle, had left it on my porch with a note saying that he was giving me all of that, as a gift, to destroy, or use as I saw fit. And he ended the note with three simple words: *I miss you.*

I.

Not *we*.

I.

From a man like Karl, *I miss you* was more powerful than hearing him say *I love you*. He was a heartbroken man, his seat of passion possessing a thousand fractures that only Kenya could fuse.

A heart fractured was always a broken heart, even when the damage was hidden behind smiles. Even when it was masked with sex. Some pains could never be fucked away.

The weakness I'd seen in his face, once when we were inside his home, and the last time I saw him, both times his face was filled with emotions, as if to say his feelings were deepening for me, that he wanted to break away from his pain, that he wanted to try to be more to me than he was at the moment.

I couldn't return to a place where I could only envision pain.

Karl. Mark. Jewell.

These homes no longer looked like mini castles. They were prisons. Desire chaining them to each other as if they were on a carnal chain gang. They lived in pain. Pain was their accepted rhythm.

I rejected monotony. I rejected sameness. But I also rejected pain.

This was their roundabout. A roundabout with no exits.

This was where they were the most comfortable.

It had to be, because this was where they remained.

It was impossible to get over someone when they remained in your presence. To let go there must be distance. There must be absence. Being in contact was perpetual renewal.

Kiki Sunshine, the woman forever enamored, forever haunted by Yasamin Kincade.

I stared at Kiki Sunshine's Yukon, felt a twinge of jealousy. Felt some envy.

She had earned a special place in my memory.

What I felt was natural. Tears. Fun. Resentment. Desire. Dreams. Fantasy. Reality. Orgasm.

They continued to engage me in my humanness, both the wanted and the unwanted emotions.

They had given me newness. Before the pain, they had given me what I needed.

I smiled a thankful smile.

Kiki Sunshine had arrived, and with her she brought Karl her own needs and expectations.

This was as it should be.

She had contacted him first. She had longed for him before I knew he existed.

Tonight she would see Harriet Tubman.

Tomorrow there would be delicious pancakes.

The absence of a lover would not move my hormones into a state of hibernation. The absence of a lover would not keep this body from needing to experience a sweet release.

Just as my absence didn't move my former lovers to celibacy.

Minutes later I was on I-285, heading back toward Cobb County, but a different desire touched me, a new curiosity, the kind that caused me to switch interstates at the last moment, take I-20 and head west. I exited at Fulton Industrial, turned left, and two lights later I made a left on Commerce, an area zoned for businesses. Motels and fast-food establishments lined Fulton Industrial. Many clubs were in the area, most employing beautiful women who earned their college tuition one dollar at a time.

I came upon a quiet business near the end of the block, a simple structure, its light bricks and dark brown awning and neon sign facing the other businesses in the community, the noise and commotion that was present on Fulton Industrial not present in this area.

I pulled over, parked with my engine running, sat watching people parking and heading toward the building across the street. Couples held hands, exchanged sultry glances designed as foreplay. Europeans. Spaniards. Canadians. Children of the islands. People of African descent. I watched the march of the libertine. Their strides were sexy and sensual, confident and anxious, filled with complete and open abandon, as if each step proclaimed they were not interested in being shackled by the values of others, that they lived by their own rules, their personal doctrine, their every breath filled with anticipation of having a fun evening. I smiled at the unafraid and stayed where I was, a spy in the house of love.

The neon sign read TRAPEZE.

Karl. I heard his voice. Heard what he had told me the first time I went to his home.

"Where women go to celebrate their sexuality. Where women are in charge. It's not always about having sex. Do as much or as little as you like."

I'd never been inside a den of pleasure, a haven of concurring spirits. I had never been in a place where desire was to be unashamed, where it was the religion of choice.

I moved my car to the parking lot, turned off my engine, but didn't get out.

I watched women with the faces of wives, mothers, politicians, and attorneys hurrying toward that neon sign. Men with the faces of fathers, judges, schoolteachers rushed with them. Voyeurs. Exhibitionists. The curious. Without disguise. Without costumes.

No one entered the building alone. They all traveled with a companion.

As did I.

I held Anaïs's tattered diary in my hand, smiled at her highlighted words, reread a few of the praises I had scribbled in the margins, felt affirmed and powerful, then put her journal inside my purse.

I eased out of my car, hair down and free, skinny jeans, heels clicking as I walked across asphalt.

I lived in mystery. I lived with my choices. I lived with my humanness. I lived with so many things. I lived afraid, yet unafraid. I lived with regret. I lived seeking experience.

I lived in the unknown. I lived knowing. I existed knowing I was growing. And in growth there was pain. Without shame I claimed that pain because that pain was my own.

I paused. Took deep breaths.

Once upon a time an imprudent man named Logan had asked me how many experiences it would take for me to be satisfied, asked me how many lovers would I have to take to end my journey. Back then I didn't know the answer. Now I did. I knew the answer.

I whispered, "As many as it takes."

I said that jokingly, sarcastically, knowing pleasure wasn't about the number of lovers.

Pleasure lived in quality, not quantity. It was just unfortunate quantity and pain had to be endured to achieve quality. I have kissed a lot of frogs. Beautiful frogs. But I have never been a whore.

A hypocrite, perhaps. Never a whore.

Pleasure was carnal love, spiritual love, peace, contentment, fantasy, its journey never-ending.

No man's words or actions would ever be allowed to cheapen my experience, because in cheapening the moments of my life, my life would be devalued, and no man or woman would ever be given the power to make me less than, not when his true fear, her true fear, when unmasked, was that I was greater than. I was resilient. I was sensitive. I was feminine. I was loving. I was sexual. I was giving. And I was stronger. I had weaknesses, but that did not make me weak. This was my life. This was me. My uniqueness. No one would be allowed to castrate my desires, they would not be allowed to diminish my needs. They would not be given power to revise my existence, whittle my spirits down, make me over, put me in their box of comfort. They would not lessen my humanness with their hypocrisies.

They would not pour beer on my caviar.

Warm air moved across my skin, gently removing thoughts of hurt and pain.

I held my head back and gazed up at the stars, many spots of light breaking through infinite darkness, light unseen in the day. So many constellations. Almost as many stars as I owned emotions.

I searched for the stars Castor and Pollux, the mythological twin brothers of Helen of Troy. Gemini. The sign of the twins. My astrological sign. My element air. My Indian sign Mithuna.

I searched for the heavenly representation of me.

One day I would meet a man as powerful and understanding as I. I would meet my mirror image, a hypocritical-idealist who understood that sometimes you had to lose yourself in order to find yourself. I prayed he would be a twin, and not of the astrological kind. I laughed at that selfish prayer.

But behind my soft and delicate laughter there was the echo of a fading pain. Memories of Ogden Circle, memories of the James River, memories of Twitchell Hall would always remain. The pain would fade. Hampton had been my rose, my first love my thorn.

With roses came thorns and with pleasure came pain.

Pain existed, the sting from those unwanted thorns always would exist, yet I remained powerful.

And so it goes. Life, may it go easy on me, most of the time.

I smiled as I took steps toward the neon sign, toward the unknown, toward living paradoxes, knowing the paradox of others would never be as challenging as the paradox that lived within.

I paused in front of the neon sign, deciding, perhaps resting.

I closed my eyes, went inside myself, ignoring the sound of anxious footsteps coming my way. Ignoring the scent of colognes and perfumes, ignoring the sound of intellectual laughter.

If my eyes had remained opened a few seconds longer, if I had kept my attention on the group that came from up the road, I would have seen her walking my way. I would've seen a petite woman, her hair pulled back, dark and modest, would've witnessed the Spanish, Cuban, and Dutch in her features, would have seen lips the color of my heart surrounding beautiful teeth. I would've have seen her and her traveling companions, her lovers, international luminaries, two of them men, both wearing wedding rings, and I would have seen the tall woman journeying with them as well, she too wearing a wedding ring.

I would've witnessed the petite woman pausing and smiling at me before entering the building.

Laughter between anxious lovers and the closing of the door pulled me away from my journey. I opened my eyes, again returning to the world, to the warmth of the night, to the stars.

Handsome men and beautiful women passed me as they entered, unable to take their eyes away from me. Smiling. Hoping I visited their world, entered into their fantasies.

A virgin-prostitute, the perverse angel, the two-faced sinister and saintly woman.

I stood there, unhidden, pulling my hair away from my ears, these ears tilted toward the heavens.

My dog-eared novel tight to the left side of my chest. Holding her words close to my heart.

Listening for Anaïs.

I am an excitable person who only understands life lyrically, musically, in whom feelings are much stronger than reason. I am so thirsty for the marvelous that only the marvelous has power over me. Anything I cannot transform into something marvelous, I let go. Reality doesn't impress me. I only believe in intoxication, in ecstasy, and when ordinary life shackles me, I escape, one way or another. No more walls.

—Anaïs Nin (February 21, 1903–January 14, 1977)

ACKNOWLEDGMENTS

Okay, once again, this is a work of fiction. That means I sat down and made it up.

☺

Today it's overcast and I'm sitting in my tiny bedroom looking at TiVo. I've been gone so long I have too many episodes of *Heroes, Cold Case, K-Ville, House, CSI: Miami, Shark, Without a Trace, Bionic Woman, Nip/Tuck, Women's Murder Club, CSI: NY, Dirty Sexy Money, Private Practice, Prison Break, Jail, Bones, Smallville, Desperate Housewives, Damages, Journeyman* . . . damn, when was the last time I was at home? Too long. I can tell because when I picked up the phone to make a call, I actually dialed the number 9 first, then waited for an outside line.

I guess that means I'll have to make my own twin-size bed . . . no room service . . . damn.

Too much hotel living rots the brain. The Courtleigh in Kingston ruined me.

Oh yeah. This book. *Pleasure.*

While I was in the UK working on *SWS/WWE*, the pleasure concept became part of its theme. Mrs. Jones, looking for pleasure. Gideon, looking for revenge and, in the end, redemption. Lola Mack looking for . . . a damn good time. I knew the next book (the one you're holding right now) wouldn't be rooted in crime. And since the last two had a male POV, I wanted to write a female character who was independent, in some ways in search of her sexual freedom, yet trapped by the rules and conventions of society. A character not so unlike the one I had seen years ago in the original

Red Shoe Diaries, or enjoyed reading about in Anaïs Nin's diaries, or had watched in so many European films it would be impossible to list them all. It amazes me that people are more comfortable and less critical about books with the details of horrific violence (Hannibal cracking open a victim's head and supping on his brain, the wonderful violence in many crime novels) than sex—the one act that, for the most part, every race or religion has in common—unless a man is the lead character. There was a lot more I wanted to do with Nia, so far as inner dialogue, and some very sexual scenes, scenes I wanted to include at the time, but didn't—I blame that on the twins, the way they showed up and never let her go. Characters have a way of becoming needy. So a lot of my other thoughts and ideas are on hold, remaining in the archives of this good old laptop, maybe never to be seen again.

Monique Pendleton, my UK homie, thanks for reading this as I worked on it, rewrites and all. You saw the first draft weighed in at about 180,000 words (damn! That was longer than the last two books combined!) and you stayed with it as it went through some sort of literary gastric bypass, much smaller, but still heavyweight. God, you read so many rewrites, word changes, scene rearranging, character changes . . . Nothing but love for you! You're the best.

John Paine, thanks for the wonderful input. The book has changed a lot (hopefully for the better) since those first pages and I hope you enjoy where I decided to take Nia on her journey.

Sara Camilli, my wonderful agent, how many more do I have to go? LOL. Getting closer to book 100. I hope this one keeps your attention as much as the others. Looking forward to the next one already! Time to get back to crime! Violence! Con men! Femmes fatales!

Brian Tart, thanks for believing in me. I've seen writers change teams many times over the last decade. I'm proud to say I've had the same home since day one. I love where I am.

Lisa Johnson and the crew in publicity at Dutton, thanks for keeping the faith and keeping me on the road. I might gripe and complain . . . wait . . . I don't gripe and complain. My bad.

Julie Doughty, the editor who has read so many versions of this manuscript that I'm surprised she still talks to me. LOL! Your suggestions were wonderful, as usual. Love ya!

Yvette Hayward and African American Literary Awards Show, thanks for the love. Yvette has been in my corner since the start. Go visit their site at www.literaryawardshow.com.

Rachel Neal, a thousand thanks. Your feedback was valuable.

Tiffany Pace, the über–copy editor. You rock! Hopefully this one will be error-free. LOL. Now go fix all the errors in the last two books, pro bono. I know, I know. Stop rubbing all the number of errors in. Geesh. The fans have spoken. You remain the best. I will write that on the blackboard one million times. Stop smiling. Dammit. I said stop gloating. Whatever.

To all the people who showed up during the Islands Tour, thanks for the love. It's hard trying to create characters whose existence is rooted in a different culture, so I hope I got most of it right. Hell, I hope I got it all right, at least enough for that portion of the characters to ring true. Nia Simone, Karl, Mark, The Jewell of the South are not meant to represent the islands, only to be people with roots in a different part of the world, and their actions are not representative, by any means, of people in the islands. (Fiction, remember?) The latter part of the *SWS/WWE* tour took me through the West Indies, subcultures that I wanted to include in my fictional characters.

Suzzanne and Collette, I had a great time in Kingston and doing the event at the Devon House. It was amazing. The house was packed! I look forward to coming back.

And I had a blast doing the events for Nigel Khan and Nigel Khan Bookseller in Trinidad. Cheryl Ali, thanks for taking me all over. Rhoda Ramkissoon, thanks for setting everything up. Send bake n' shark! *Subliminal message: I want to come to Carnival!* And of course, many blessings to Dr. Clifford at *The Morning Show*, thanks for having me on the air.

I met so many wonderful people at the Antigua & Barbuda Literary Festival. Had a chance to hang out with Victoria Christopher Murray and Donna Hill. Also had a chance to break bread with the local writers: Joanne Hillhouse, J. Nerissa Percival, and Floree Williams; it was wonderful meeting you and so many wonderful authors in Antigua. Same time next year. Until then, keep in touch.

And it was marvelous doing the island tour with the enthusiastic contest winners in Barbados, the land where the name Dickey means . . . well . . . Dickey. ROFL! I have never heard so many *Dickey* jokes in my life. Nor have I ever been in a place where women blushed when saying my name. Cracked me up when I did *Morning Barbados* with Belle Holder and she opened the interview with a Dickey joke . . . one that made the island blush at sunrise . . . now that was special. Love 104.1 and Hott 95.3 FM radio stations, thanks. Katrinah Best at the *Advocate* (my favorite English girl on the island) and Carlos Atwell at the *Nation*, thanks for the support. And to the crew who set everything up, I have to sing your praises. Angela Payne (Pages buyer), Andrea Stoute (marketing representative and my driver), Kim Tatem (events coordinator), Michael Maloney (Pages operations manager), Tracey Lloyd (regional marketing director), Kay Wiseman (local media and marketing manager), Rawle Culbard (photographer), Gillian Howard (Pages staff). And much love to the tour winners: Stacia Browne, Cecilia Walcott, Astrid Bovell, Terry Belgrave, Kathlyn Murray, Sasha Greenidge, and Carmen Grecia.

And I don't think any of the island tour could have been possible without Shanta Inshiqaq, my export sales manager in international sales who exported me to some wonderful places.

To all of my Caribbean fans, I look forward to coming back to see my new friends and extended family, hopefully more on holiday than for work, and I definitely look forward to visiting the other islands, each journey a learning experience, each trip taking me closer to my roots.

And the beaches weren't bad either.

Now somebody hook me up with a Visa and find me a place to sleep and write . . . hurry!

And, as usual, just in case I forgot anyone, which wasn't intentional, break out the pen and ink yourself into history. LOL. Just kidding. Grab a pen and join the crew.

I want to give thanks to _____ for _____, because without your help, insight, editing, professionalism, money, chicken soup, luggage, and/or _____, I'd be _____ at the _____ with a rash on my _____ wishing I was _____ with _____ at Carnival in _____ .

You're the best of the best!

Tuesday, November 20, 2007
1:30 P.M.
Latitude: 33.99 N, Longitude: 118.35 W
63°F / 17°C

www.ericjeromedickey.com
www.myspace.com/ericjeromedickey